W9-AZU-341

Horsemen from hell . . .

"My God! It's Quantrill!" Win heard one of the soldiers shout.

Having been seen, the Raiders gave a loud yell as they galloped down the hill toward the soldiers.

The Union soldiers raised their weapons and fired. Win heard and felt half a dozen bullets going by him. Two of the Raiders were hit and unseated, but the main group continued its charge down the hill toward the Yankee patrol.

The soldiers, having fired their one round, panicked at the sight of a body of men riding down upon them unchecked, firing their pistols as they came. Several of the soldiers leaped down from their horses and converted their rifles to clubs. They swung at the Raiders as they rode by, but their efforts were ineffectual and, to a man, they were shot down.

The remaining soldiers scattered to every direction like a covey of flushed quail. Win and the others galloped after them in hot pursuit.

"Go!" Quantrill screamed at his men. "Go, get them! Kill the Yankee bastards!"

DON'T MISS THESE
ALL-ACTION WESTERN SERIES
FROM THE BERKLEY PUBLISHING GROUP

THE GUNSMITH by J. R. Roberts
Clint Adams was a legend among lawmen, outlaws, and ladies. They called him . . . the Gunsmith.

LONGARM by Tabor Evans
The popular long-running series about U.S. Deputy Marshal Long—his life, his loves, his fight for justice.

SLOCUM by Jake Logan
Today's longest-running action Western. John Slocum rides a deadly trail of hot blood and cold steel.

BUSHWHACKERS by B. J. Lanagan
An all-new series by the creators of Longarm! The rousing adventures of the most brutal gang of cutthroats ever assembled—Quantrill's Raiders.

BUSHWHACKERS

B. J. Lanagan

JOVE BOOKS, NEW YORK

If you purchased this book without a cover, you should be aware that this book is stolen property. It was reported as "unsold and destroyed" to the publisher, and neither the author nor the publisher has received any payment for this "stripped book."

BUSHWHACKERS

A Jove Book / published by arrangement with
the author

PRINTING HISTORY
Jove edition / July 1997

All rights reserved.
Copyright © 1997 by Jove Publications, Inc.
This book may not be reproduced in whole
or in part, by mimeograph or any other means,
without permission. For information address:
The Berkley Publishing Group, 200 Madison Avenue,
New York, New York 10016.

The Putnam Berkley World Wide Web site address is
http://www.berkley.com

ISBN: 0-515-12102-9

A JOVE BOOK®
Jove Books are published by The Berkley Publishing Group,
200 Madison Avenue, New York, New York 10016.
JOVE and the "J" design are trademarks
belonging to Jove Publications, Inc.

PRINTED IN THE UNITED STATES OF AMERICA

10 9 8 7 6 5 4 3 2

BUSHWHACKERS

Jackson County, Missouri, 1862

AS SETH COULTER LAY HIS POCKET WATCH ON THE BED-side table and blew out the lantern, he thought he saw a light outside. Walking over to the window, he pulled the curtain aside to stare out into the darkness.

On the bed alongside him the mattress creaked, and his wife, Irma, raised herself on her elbows.

"What is it, Seth?" Irma asked. "What are you lookin' at?"

"Nothin', I reckon."

"Well, you're lookin' at somethin'."

"Thought I seen a light out there, is all."

Seth continued to look through the window for a moment longer. He saw only the moon-silvered West Missouri hills.

"A light? What on earth could that be at this time of night?" Irma asked.

"Ah, don't worry about it," Seth replied, still looking through the window. "It's prob'ly just lightning bugs."

"Lightning bugs? Never heard of lightning bugs this early in the year."

"Well, it's been a warm spring," Seth explained. Finally, he came away from the window, projecting to his wife an easiness he didn't feel. "I'm sure it's nothing," he said.

"I reckon you're right," the woman agreed. "Wisht the boys was here, though."

Seth climbed into bed. He thought of the shotgun over the fireplace mantel in the living room, and he wondered if he should go get it. He considered it for a moment, then decided against it. It would only cause Irma to ask questions, and just because he was feeling uneasy, was no reason to cause her any worry. He turned to her and smiled.

"What do you want the boys here for?" he asked. "If the boys was here, we couldn't be doin' this." Gently, he began pulling at her nightgown.

"Seth, you old fool, what do you think you're doin'?" Irma scolded. But there was a lilt of laughter in her voice, and it was husky, evidence that far from being put off by him, she welcomed his advances.

Now, any uneasiness Seth may have felt fell away as he tugged at her nightgown. Finally she sighed.

"You better let me do it," she said. "Clumsy as you are, you'll like-as-not tear it."

Irma pulled the nightgown over her head, then dropped it onto the floor beside her bed. She was forty-six years old, but a lifetime of hard work had kept her body trim, and she was proud of the fact that she was as firm now as she had been when she was twenty. She lay back on the bed and smiled up at her husband, her skin glowing silver in the splash of moonlight. Seth ran his hand down her nakedness, and she trembled under his touch. He marvelled that, after so many years of marriage, she could still be so easily aroused.

• • •

THREE HUNDRED YARDS AWAY FROM THE HOUSE, EMIL Slaughter, leader of a band of Jayhawkers, twisted around in his saddle to look back at the dozen or so riders with him. Their faces were fired orange in the flickering lights of the torches. Felt hats were pulled low, and they were all wearing long dusters, hanging open to provide access to the pistols which protruded from their belts. His band of followers looked, Slaughter thought, as if a fissure in the earth had suddenly opened to allow a legion of demons to escape from hell. There was about them a hint of sulphur.

A hint of sulphur. Slaughter smiled at the thought. He liked that idea. Such an illusion would strike fear into the hearts of his victims, and the more frightened they were, the easier it would be for him to do his job.

Quickly, Slaughter began assigning tasks to his men.

"You two hit the smokehouse, take ever' bit of meat they got a'curin'."

"Hope they got a couple slabs of bacon," someone said.

"I'd like a ham or two," another put in.

"You three, go into the house. Clean out the pantry: flour, cornmeal, sugar, anything they got in there. And if you see anything valuable in the house, take it too."

"What about the people inside?"

"Kill 'em," Slaughter said succinctly.

"Women, too?"

"Kill 'em all."

"What about their livestock?"

"If they got 'ny ridin' horses, we'll take 'em. The plowin' animals we'll let burn when we torch the barn. All right, let's go."

IN THE BEDROOM SETH AND IRMA WERE OBLIVIOUS TO what was going on outside. Seth was over her, driving himself into her moist triangle. Irma's breathing was coming faster and more shallow as Seth gripped her buttocks with his hands, pulling her up to meet him. He could feel her fingers digging into his shoulders, and see her jiggling, sweat-pearled breasts as her head flopped from side to side with the pleasure she was feeling.

Suddenly Seth was aware of a wavering, golden glow on the walls of the bedroom. A bright light was coming through the window.

"What the hell?" he asked, interrupting the rhythm and holding himself up from her on stiffened arms, one hand on each side of her head.

"No, no," Irma said through clenched teeth. "Don't stop now, don't . . ."

"Irma, my God! The barn's on fire!" Seth shouted, as he disengaged himself.

"What?" Irma asked, now also aware of the orange glow in the room.

Seth got out of bed and started quickly to pull on his trousers. Suddenly there was a crashing sound from the front of the house as the door was smashed open.

"Seth!" Irma screamed.

Drawing up his trousers, Seth started toward the living room and the shotgun he had over the fireplace.

"You lookin' for this, you Missouri bastard?" someone asked. He was holding Seth's shotgun.

"Who the hell are . . ." That was as far as Seth got. His question was cut off by the roar of the shotgun as a charge of double-aught buckshot slammed him back against the wall. He slid down to the floor, staining the wall behind him with blood and guts from the gaping exit wounds in his back.

"Seth! My God, no!" Irma shouted, running into the living room when she heard the shotgun blast. So concerned was she about her husband that she didn't bother to put on her nightgown.

"Well, now, lookie what we got here," a beady-eyed Jayhawker said, staring at Irma's nakedness. "Boys, I'm goin' to have me some fun."

"No," Irma said, shaking now, not only in fear of her own life, but in shock from seeing her husband's lifeless body leaning against the wall.

Beady Eyes reached for Irma.

"Please," Irma whimpered. She twisted away from him. "Please."

"Listen to her beggin' me for it, boys. Lookit them titties! Damn, she's not a bad-lookin' woman, you know that?" His dark beady eyes glistened, rat-like, as he opened his pants then reached down to grab himself. His erection projected forward like a club.

"No, please, don't do this," Irma pleaded.

"You wait 'til I stick this cock in you, honey," Beady Eyes said. "Hell, you goin' to like it so much you'll think you ain't never been screwed before."

Irma turned and ran into the bedroom. The others followed her, laughing, until she was forced against the bed.

"Lookit this, boys! She's brought me right to her bed! You think this bitch ain't a'wantin' it?"

"I beg of you, if you've any kindness in you . . ." Irma started, but her plea was interrupted when Beady Eyes backhanded her so savagely that she fell across the bed, her mouth filled with blood.

"Shut up!" he said, harshly. "I don't like my women talkin' while I'm diddlin' 'em!"

Beady Eyes came down onto the bed on top of her, then he spread her legs and forced himself roughly into her. Irma felt as if she were taking a hot poker inside her, and she cried out in pain.

"Listen to her squealin'. He's really givin' it to her," one of the observers said.

Beady Eyes wheezed and gasped as he thrust into her roughly.

"Don't wear it out none," one of the others giggled. "We'uns want our turn!"

At the beginning of his orgasm, Beady Eyes enhanced his pleasure by one extra move that was unobserved by the others. Immediately thereafter he felt the convulsive tremors of the woman beneath him, and that was all it took to trigger his final release. He surrendered himself to the sensation of fluid and energy rushing out of his body, while he groaned and twitched in orgiastic gratification.

"Look at that! He's comin' in the bitch right now!" one of the others said excitedly. "Damn! You wait 'til I get in there! I'm goin' to come in quarts!"

Beady Eyes lay still on top of her until he had spent his final twitch, then he got up. She was bleeding from a stab wound just below her left breast.

"My turn," one of the others said, already taking out his cock. He had just started toward her when he saw the wound in the woman's chest, and the flat look of her dead eyes. "What the hell?" he asked. "What happened to her?"

The second man looked over at Beady Eyes in confusion. Then he saw Beady Eyes wiping blood off the blade of his knife.

"You son of a bitch!" he screamed in anger. "You kilt her!"

"Slaughter told us to kill her," Beady Eyes replied easily.

"Well, you coulda waited 'til someone else got a chance to do her before you did it, you bastard!" He started toward

Beady Eyes when, suddenly, there was the thunder of a loud pistol shot.

"What the hell is going on in here?" Slaughter yelled. He was standing just inside the bedroom door, holding a smoking pistol in his hand, glaring angrily at them.

"This son of a bitch kilt the woman while he was doin' her!"

"We didn't come here to screw," Slaughter growled. "We come here to get supplies."

"But he kilt her *while* he was screwin' her! Who would do somethin' like that?"

"Before, during, after, what difference does it make?" Slaughter asked. "As long as she's dead. Now, you've got work to do, so get out there in the pantry, like I told you, and start gatherin' up what you can. You," he said to Beady Eyes, "go through the house, take anything you think we can sell. I want to be out of here in no more'n five minutes."

"Emil, what woulda been the harm in us havin' our turn?"

Slaughter cocked the pistol and pointed it at the one who was still complaining. "The harm is, I told you not to," he said. "Now, do you want to debate the issue?"

"No, no!" the man said quickly, holding his hands out toward Slaughter. "Didn't mean nothin' by it. I was just talkin', that's all."

"Good," Slaughter said. He looked over at Beady Eyes. "And you. If you ever pull your cock out again without me a'sayin' it's all right, I'll cut the goddamned thing off."

"It wasn't like you think, Emil," Beady Eyes said. "I was just tryin' to be easy on the woman, is all. I figured it would be better if she didn't know it was about to happen."

Slaughter shook his head. "You're one strange son of a bitch, you know that?" He stared at the three men for a minute, then he shook his head in disgust as he put his pistol back into his belt. "Get to work."

Beady Eyes was the last one out and as he started to leave he saw, lying on the chifforobe, a gold pocket watch. He glanced around to make sure no one was looking. Quickly, and unobserved, he slipped the gold watch into his own pocket.

This was a direct violation of Slaughter's standing orders. Anything of value found on any of their raids was to be divided equally among the whole. That meant that, by rights, he should give the watch to Slaughter, who would then sell it and divide whatever money it brought. But because it was loot, they would be limited as to where they could sell the watch. That meant it would bring much less than it was worth and by the time it was split up into twelve parts, each individual part would be minuscule. Better, by far, that he keep the watch for himself.

Feeling the weight of the watch riding comfortably in his pocket, he went into the pantry to start clearing it out.

"Lookie here!" the other man detailed for the pantry said. "This here family ate pretty damn good, I'll tell you. We've made us quite a haul: flour, coffee, sugar, onions, potatoes, beans, peas, dried peppers."

"Yeah, if they's as lucky in the smokehouse, we're goin' to feast tonight!"

The one gathering the loot came into the pantry then, holding a bulging sack. "I found some nice gold candlesticks here, too," he said. "We ought to get somethin' for them."

"You men inside! Let's go!" Slaughter's shout came to them.

The Jayhawkers in the house ran outside where Slaughter had brought everyone together. Here, they were illuminated by the flames of the already-burning barn. Two among the bunch were holding flaming torches, and they looked at Slaughter expectantly.

"All right, burn the rest of the buildings now," Slaughter said with a nod of his head.

One of the torch-bearers went to the smokehouse, the other went to the main house. They touched their torches to a few places here and there, and the dry wood caught as quickly as tinder. Within moments, every building on the place was completely enveloped in flames.

"All right, men," Slaughter ordered. "Mount up! Let's get out of here!"

The raiding party rode away as the house, barn, smokehouse, and even the outhouse burned furiously. Behind them, the bodies of Seth and Irma Coulter lay where they fell, the blazing house their crematorium.

2

THE ELITE HOUSE WAS ONE OF THE MOST POPULAR SA-
loons in Warrensburg, Missouri. The owner had brought in
a fine crystal chandelier to complement the bar of polished
mahogany. He had solid brass spittoons, a brass foot rail,
and, on the wall behind the bar, a three by six foot oil
painting of a nude woman reclining on a golden couch. She
appeared to be contemplating a letter she held in her hand,
while her young nubian servant poured water into a large
golden tub behind her.

Joe Coulter was at the bar, having a drink and studying
the whimsical expression on the face of the woman in the
painting. He wondered just what was in the note she was
reading. He wondered silently, however, for there was no
one nearby to talk to. At six feet, three inches tall, and with
shoulders the width of an axe handle, most people tended
to give Joe a lot of room.

Joe's brother, Win, was at one of the tables, playing
cards. Although older, Win was somewhat smaller in stat-
ure than Joe. Women considered Win very good-looking,
but there was a quality about him that frightened them, as
if they could see a flash of hellfire in his eyes.

Although Win wasn't having a phenomenal run of luck, he was winning more than he was losing, and now he had just been called on a rather modest bet. He spread his hand out on the table, face up.

"Three jacks. Looks like I win again," Win said, easily.

"The hell you say!"

The loud, hoarse curse exploded from the throat of one of the players in Win's game. His outburst was followed by the crashing sound of a chair tipping over as he stood abruptly. A woman's laughter halted in mid-trill, and the piano player pulled his hands away from the keyboard so that the last three notes hung raggedly, discordantly, in the air. All conversation ceased and everyone in the crowded saloon turned toward the cause of the disturbance.

A tall, lanky man with a drooping black moustache and cold fish-like eyes stood in front of the chair he had just overturned. He pointed a long accusing finger across the table at Win Coulter. The reason for his anger was Win's winning hand, and the money in the pot amounted to twelve dollars and eighty cents.

"You son of a bitch! Where'd you get that third jack?"

"Mister, all three of them came in the deal, fair and honest," Win said mildly. He had just been all but called a cheater, and he had to struggle to keep his voice calm.

"You expect us to believe that?"

"Take it easy, Billy," one of the other players said. "This is supposed to be a friendly game."

"And it has been until now," another said. "What you gettin' all worked up about? This here fella ain't won any more'n any of the rest of us has at one time or another."

"You two stay out of this unless you're fixin' to buy in to the trouble," Billy snarled. He looked at Win again. "Now, I'm askin' you a second time. Where'd you get that third jack!"

This time, Win didn't answer. The saloon suddenly grew deathly quiet, as everyone strained to hear every word spoken. The large clock standing against the wall by the coatrack, which normally marked the passage of the day unnoticed, now seemed to proclaim each syllable of passing time loudly. A customer came into the saloon then, and, sensing that something momentous was about to happen, checked his pocket watch against the clock, the better to fix the time in his mind so that every detail would be accurate for the later telling.

"I told you, I got it in the deal," Win said, still managing to keep control over his anger. Although he was the one being challenged, he was showing even less nervousness than Billy himself.

"Mister, if you try to rake in that pot, I'm just goin' to have to kill you," Billy said, his hands hovering menacingly over his pistol.

"What are you talkin' about, Billy? That wouldn't be no fair fight," someone in the saloon said. "You're standin' up, and this feller is sittin' down."

"I don't reckon it is fair," Billy agreed. "But that's the way of it sometimes. Life ain't always fair." His smile grew broader, and his hand hovered over his pistol. "Now, mister, if you're aimin' on defendin' yourself, this would be as good time as any for you to pull your gun."

Win made no move toward his own gun, nor did he attempt to improve his own position. Instead, he smiled up at the tall man, and his smile was even colder and more frightening than Billy's snarl.

"That won't be necessary," Win said.

Billy was obviously confused by the strange answer, and his face twisted into a scowl. "What do you mean?"

"Well, since you agreed that this wasn't a fair fight, then

maybe you ought to know that I already have a gun in my hand . . . under the table."

"Mister, who you trying to kid?" Billy asked. "Your gun is in your belt! I can see it."

"What I got in my hand is a hold-out gun," Win said. "A derringer, two barrels, forty-one caliber. From here, I could put a hole in your chest big enough to stick my fist into."

"You're bluffin'," Billy said.

Again Win smiled, a cold, unnerving smile that made Billy shiver.

"Then go for your gun," Win said. "Unless you would rather not try the experiment."

Billy stood for a moment longer, trying to decide whether or not he would call Win's bluff. His eyes narrowed, a muscle in his cheek twitched, and perspiration beads broke out on his forehead.

"All right," he finally said. "Only this ain't gonna stop here. Like as not, I'll run into you again sometime."

"Like as not," Win agreed.

Billy looked around at the others, then turned and left. Everyone in the saloon watched him leave, then they turned back toward Win, who was still holding his right hand under the table. Finally, he brought his hand up, and everyone saw that he wasn't holding a derringer as he had claimed, but a cigar. He put the cigar in his mouth, smiled broadly, lit it, and took a puff. He had just run a monumental bluff, and they had all seen it. When they realized what he'd done, they burst out laughing.

"Whoowee, mister, did you ever jerk a cinch in ol' Billy boy."

"Yeah, puttin' him down like that with nothin' but a cigar in your hand? You really took a chance."

"Oh, I don't know," Win quipped. He looked at the end

of his now burning cigar. ''What you gentlemen have to understand is that this is quite a remarkable cigar.''

Again, everyone in the saloon laughed.

''Hey, Win,'' Joe called. Joe had stepped over to the front of the saloon to follow Billy out onto the street. ''Looks like somethin' is goin' on out there.''

''Is he waiting for me outside?'' Win asked.

''Looks like that.''

Win walked over to look out through the window with Joe. The street, which had been busy with commerce just a moment earlier, had suddenly become deserted, except for Billy, who was standing in the middle of the street about one hundred feet away. Billy had his gun in his hand, pointing toward the saloon door. He was obviously prepared to fight.

In the meantime, men and women were scurrying down the sidewalks, stepping into buildings or behind them, to get out of the line of fire, while at the same time taking up observers' positions in the doors and windows so they wouldn't miss the action. Even the horses had been moved off the street, as nervous owners feared they might get hit by a stray bullet. Only Win and Joe's horses remained tied to the hitching post in front of the saloon. They whickered and stamped their feet nervously, as if sensing that something out of the ordinary was going on.

''Win, you don't have to do this, you know,'' Joe said. ''He's just a little hot under the collar right now. I could go out the back, sneak around, and come up behind him before he even knew what was going on.''

''No. I thank you, little brother,'' Win said. ''But this is my fight. I'm going to have to fight it my way.''

''The thing is, Win, 'your way' always gets someone killed.''

''Long as it ain't *me* gettin' killed,'' Win said. He

hitched up his gun belt then stepped through the front door outside. Billy was standing in the middle of the street, his gun already in his hand.

"Well, now, you did have guts enough to come out here, I see," Billy snarled.

"I don't plan to be here long," Win said. "Just long enough to take care of a little business."

Billy fired first, and his bullet fried the air just beside Win's ear, hit the dirt behind him, then skipped off down the street with a high-pitched whine. Win dropped and rolled to his left, drawing his gun as he did so, even as Billy got off a second shot.

Win, with the instinct of survival, had rolled to his right so that Billy's bullet crashed harmlessly into the wooden front stoop of the Warrensburg Cafe. A woman inside screamed with fear as she realized how close the bullet had come to what she had assumed would be a safe vantage point.

From his prone position on the ground, Win fired at Billy and hit him in the knee. Billy let out a howl and went down. He was still firing, and Win felt a bullet tear through the crown of his hat. Now Win took slow and deliberate aim and pulled the trigger. He hit Billy in the temple, and he saw a little pink mist of blood spray up from the impact of the bullet.

Billy was stopped instantly and, for a moment, the town was deadly quiet except for the dying echo of the shots.

"It's over!" someone yelled. "Everyone can come out now! The fight's over!"

"And the best man won!" another yelled, and, within a minute, the street was flooded with people, more people even than had been out before the fight began.

The street was alive with activity and noise as people

described the fight they had just witnessed, each one telling it from his own vantage point.

"Best shot I ever seen!" someone was saying. "Hell, that had to be fifty yards or more."

"I seen it from over there. I was that close, I was," said another.

With the excited babble still going on behind him, Win went back into the saloon. As he walked over toward the bar, he saw that his brother had already poured him a whiskey.

"Didn't want to do that," Win told his brother, as he tossed the drink down. "I gave him every chance to back out."

"Yeah, well, maybe you're ready to go home now. You know, we've been gone nigh on to a week. Ma and pa are goin' to start worryin' about us. Especially ma, the way she is."

"Yeah," Win said. He poured himself another drink, then smiled. "But when they see I won enough money to pay for all the seed we bought, don't figure they'll be too mad."

A dark-haired blue-eyed, well-dressed man stepped up to the bar then.

"Mr. Coulter?"

"Yes," Win and Joe replied simultaneously.

"Which one of us do you want?" Win asked.

"Both, actually," the man replied, smiling at the two. "My name is Frank James." He stuck out his hand, and first Win, then Joe, shook it.

"What can we do for you, Mr. James?"

"Mr. Coulter, I'm on a recruiting mission, you might say. You are aware that there is a war on?"

"We're aware of it," Win replied, then added, "but we ain't interested in it."

"Why not?"

" 'Cause it don't have anything to do with us."

"Patriotism doesn't have anything to do with you? The willingness to stand up and fight for the rights of a state to be free to do whatever it wants, without the Yankees telling us what to do?"

"Well, we don't have much truck with the Yankees," Joe said. "I'll give you that. And we don't much like other folks telling us what to do."

"That goes for the Yankees, or the state," Win added. "And we sure don't have anything in common with folks who own a lot of slaves. Me and Joe and pa work the farm our ownselves."

"Right," Joe said.

"The way I look at it, this is a war better fought in the east," Win said.

"It can't have escaped your notice, Mr. Coulter, that we Missourians have had quite a bit of our own war," Frank said. "Jayhawkers coming across to raid our towns, burn our farms, rape our women."

"And you're doing something about that, are you?" Win asked.

Frank James smiled. "I reckon we're putting a few things right, yes, sir," he said.

"Who, exactly, is *we*?" Win asked.

Frank James looked around the bar before he spoke again. "The men I ride with. Some folks call us Quantrill's Raiders," he said. "Maybe you've heard of us."

"I've heard of you," Win said.

"What have you heard?"

"Pretty much what you just said. That you've been givin' the Jayhawkers, what for."

"And what do you think about that?"

Win held his drink up. "I think you are probably a pretty

good man, and I'm willing to drink a toast to you. If me an' my brother was the joinin' kind, why, Quantrill would be the one we'd join. But for now, we're willin' to let you folks fight your battles, and we'll fight ours.''

The sheriff came through the door then, and Frank James, seeing him come in, spoke quickly.

''Looks like the sheriff's goin' to be askin' you a few questions,'' he said. ''And I don't need to be around while he's doing it. If you change your mind, Mr. Coulter, and decide you'd like to come ride with us, come to Blue Springs and look me up. I'll introduce you to the Chief.''

''I'll keep that in mind,'' Win said, as Frank turned and melted back into the room.

''You the fella that shot Billy Hargiss?'' the sheriff asked, coming over to Win.

''I reckon I am.''

''Sheriff, my brother didn't have no choice,'' Joe Coulter said. ''Soon as he stepped outside, that fella was gunnin' for him.''

''I know, I know,'' the sheriff said with a dismissive wave of his hand. ''Ever'one who saw it has done told me the same thing. I ain't plannin' on makin' no arrests or nothin'. I just need a statement, that's all. What's your name?''

''Coulter. Win Coulter.''

''Mr. Coulter, did you know Billy Hargiss?''

''Never met him before I sat down to play cards with him.''

The sheriff chuckled. ''I can believe that, or you probably wouldn't have played with him. Hargiss is about the sorest loser I ever knew. He was always gettin' into fights, but always before he's been able to bully people into seein' things his way. Reckon he just ran into someone he couldn't bully. All right, Mr. Coulter, that'll be all. There will be a coroner's inquest, but I don't figure you'll be called. It's just as well you killed the son of a bitch. Makes it cleaner all the way around. But do me a favor, will you?''

''What's that?''

''Next time you come into town, don't get into any card games.''

3

WIN AND JOE COULTER STOPPED AT THE GATE WHICH LED onto the Coulter farm and looked at the sign:

COULTER FARM
Established, 1835:

"The truth is, all might
be free if they valued
freedom and defended it as
they ought."
—SAMUEL ADAMS

A grasshopper was clinging to the faded lettering and a clump of weeds had grown up in front of the sign. Win dismounted and pulled the weeds so that the sign was clearly visible.

"I thought pa told you to repaint this sign," Win said.

"I thought he told you."

Win tossed the weed aside, then brushed the dirt off his hands. He tilted his head to one side and squinted. "It's not all that bad, is it? I mean, you can still read it."

"I can read it," Joe said. " 'Course, I could read it even if the words weren't there. Pa used to bring me out here and read it to me. It's the first thing I ever learned to read."

Win laughed as he remounted. "You weren't reading it, little brother, you were memorizing it."

Joe laughed as well, then he said, "I reckon you got me there. And when are you goin' to quit callin' me little brother? I'm near twice as big as you now."

"But you're still my little brother in spirit, Joe," Win said. "Come on, it's gettin' on time to eat. I want to make sure ma knows we're here in time to cook for us."

The two brothers rode through the gate and started up the long road. Although they were back on their own farm, they wouldn't be able to actually see the house until they topped the hill. Their horses frightened up a rabbit which bounded down the lane in front of them for several feet before darting off into the safety of the tall grass.

Joe sniffed the air. "Pa must've been burnin' some brush. I can smell it."

"Yeah," Win agreed. "I can smell it too." He laughed. "Seems to me like that was somethin' else we was supposed to do. I'm afraid pa is goin' to be some put out by us missin' all the work."

"Yeah," Joe agreed. "It's a good thing you were lucky in cards. When we tell pa that we've got a whole wagonload of supplies comin', all without it costin' him a penny, why he's goin' to be pretty forgivin' of our stayin' out a couple days longer, I think."

"He must've just burned the brush. I can still see a little wisp of smoke up there," Win said.

They reached the crest of the hill then and looked down toward where the house, barn, and other outbuildings should be. But there were no buildings there. Instead there were several blackened piles of burned-out rubble, all that remained of what had been the barn, smokehouse, out-house, and house. Two lonely brick chimneys marked each end of what had been the house and, from the charred skel-etal remains, wisps of smoke still curled up into the bright, blue sky.

"Joe!" Win shouted. He slapped his heels against the sides of his horse, and it broke quickly into a gallop. Joe did the same with his horse, and they covered the last hun-dred yards in just a few seconds.

"Ma! Pa!" Win yelled, leaping from his saddle and looking around. Joe was right behind him.

"How'd they let the place catch on fire?" Joe asked.

"It didn't catch on fire," Win answered. "This fire was set."

"How do you know?"

"Look around you, Joe. Every building on the place is burned down! There's no way something like this could happen in just a regular fire."

"Oh, my God, Win! Look!" Joe said, pointing into the jumbled heap of charcoaled boards and frames that was once the house.

What Joe was pointing to was the charred remains of a body. Win took a couple of steps forward, then stopped and spun around, unable to go any farther. "It's pa," he said in a tight voice.

"Where's ma?"

Win took several deep breaths in order to get control of himself.

"If pa's in there, ma is too," he finally said. "And if she is, we are going to have to go in there and find her."

"You mean find her like that!" Joe choked. "No, Win, I can't do that!"

Win put his hand on Joe's shoulder. "You have to get hold of yourself, Joe," he said, quietly. "Ma and pa deserve a decent buryin', and there ain't nobody but us goin' to do it."

Joe nodded as tears slid down his cheeks.

"Yeah," he finally said. "You're right. We have to do it."

WIN AND JOE WERE DRIVING IN THE TWO CRUDELY MADE crosses at the head of the fresh mounds of dirt.

"We need to do better by them than these homemade crosses," Joe said. "These markers won't last no time."

"They're just temporary," Win promised. "We'll go into town and have a couple of tombstones done. Real marble."

"With an angel carved on ma's," Joe said. "She would like that."

"And roses," Win added. "She was always partial to roses."

When both crosses were in place, the boys stood back and looked down for a long moment at the two fresh graves. Both had red-rimmed eyes and throats that were sore from holding back the sobs.

"Don't you think we ought to say somethin'?" Joe asked.

"Say what?"

"Hell, I don't know. You're the one that's read all the books. There ought to be somethin' you could say. We ought not just bury 'em without so much as a by your leave."

"I can only say what I believe," Win said. "The death of a good man, and a good woman, is not a matter of indifference to God. He will keep them in His hands."

At that moment, they heard the sound of hoofbeats, and they turned to look back up at the top of the hill.

"Who's that?" Joe asked.

Win shielded his eyes with his hand and looked toward the riders.

"It's Sheriff Paige."

Tossing aside the spades they were still holding, Win and Joe walked out to meet the sheriff as he and two men arrived. Though the others remained in their saddles, Paige dismounted.

"Sorry you had to find them this way," Paige said, nodding toward the new graves. "I brought a couple of men out with me. We were going to have your folks buried for you before you got back so's you wouldn't have to see them this way."

"Who did it, Sheriff?"

"Well, the fire . . ." the sheriff said, pointing toward the still-smoldering ruins of the house.

"Bullshit the fire!" Win exploded angrily. "In the first place, there's no way ma and pa would've just stayed in the house and burned up like that unless they had been shot first. And in the second place, this kind of fire doesn't just happen. It was set. I mean, look at it! Every building was burned! And I want to know who did it."

"As near as we can make out, a bunch of Jayhawkers came through here last night," the sheriff said. "This isn't the only farm they visited, but it is the only one they burned out. They killed a couple of folks over in Platte County too. They say it was Emil Slaughter and his bunch."

"So, what are you doing here? Why aren't you out chasing them down?"

"Come on, Win, you know how things are now. Things like this"—he took in the burned-out farm—"are no longer in my jurisdiction. There's a war going on. This is somethin' for the army."

"Which army? From what I've heard, Jayhawkers are

supportin' the Union. That means the Federal Army is on their side, doesn't it?''

Sheriff Page shook his head sadly. ''I'm sorry, boys, I truly am,'' he said. ''But you have to know that you aren't alone in this. You're just lucky you've been spared up 'til now. Things like this have been goin' on here along the Missouri-Kansas border since even before the war started. And I reckon it's going to keep on until the war is over. And who knows? Maybe even beyond.''

''What you're sayin' is, any bunch of murderin' bastards as might want to can just come over here from Kansas and do anything they want? And there's nothing we can do about it?''

''That's pretty much the way of it,'' Sheriff Paige agreed. ''But don't forget, for every gang of Jayhawkers, there's a gang of Bushwhackers. I suspect the decent folk over in Kansas are going through the same kind of thing.''

''There *are* no decent folk in Kansas,'' Win said bitterly. ''Not if they can spawn people who will do something like this.''

''Like I said, boys, I'm truly sorry,'' Sheriff Paige said, remounting his horse. He looked down at them. ''But under the circumstances, there is nothing that can be done about it. You understand that, I hope. Nothing.''

Paige clucked at his horse and pulled it around, then he and the men who had come with him rode off.

Win watched them ride away for a long moment, then he turned to Joe.

''What was that fella's name?'' he asked.

''What fella? You don't mean Sheriff Paige?''

''No. I mean the one who came up to speak to us in the saloon last night. What was his name? Jones?''

''Are you talkin' about the man who was tryin' to recruit us for Quantrill?'' Joe asked. Suddenly he smiled, and snapped his fingers. "Yes!" he said. "That's an idea! By God, Win, if we joined up with Quantrill, we'd get a crack at these bastards, there's no doubt in my mind."

"I don't think it was Jones," Win said, still trying to remember the recruiter's name.

"It was James! Frank James," Joe said.

Win smiled for the first time since the gruesome discovery.

"Yes," he said. "Frank James."

"How do we find them?" Joe asked.

"He said come to Blue Springs. I guess we'll do that and just start askin' questions. If we're lucky, he'll find us."

WITH NO HOUSE TO STAY IN, WIN AND JOE MOVED INTO a hotel room in Blue Springs. Word spread quickly as to what had happened to their parents out at the farm, and several people managed to stop by and express their sympathy. Some were very open in their support of the Union cause, but even they were quick to condemn the Jayhawkers. Others were openly sympathetic to the Confederate side and they hinted, darkly, that "what goes around comes around."

"What, exactly, do you mean by that?" Win asked Tom Poe when he passed that very remark in the saloon.

"Well, I mean that there are those who do more than just talk about what should be done. There are some people who are actually doing something."

"Such as?" Win asked.

Tom Poe was a lawyer, and he had a lawyer's way of obfuscating his remarks. He took a drink and studied Win for a long moment before he answered.

"Well, for example, there are those who join the Confederate Army," Poe said. "From what I've been told,

General Sterling Price is actively recruiting new men. I think something big is brewing down in Northern Mississippi, around Corinth. I understand that General Johnston is looking for men. Of course, since Missouri has been kept in the Union by martial law, you would have to be careful about letting your plans be known.''

"Suppose someone wanted to fight for the Southern cause, but he didn't want to go off to someplace like Mississippi to do it? Suppose he wanted to fight right here?'' Win asked.

Poe studied the liquor in his glass. "Yes, given the unique set of circumstances which have impacted upon you and your brother, I could see how the two of you might have more interest in fighting a Missouri-Kansas border war, rather than in Mississippi.''

"I've heard there is a group of men, Raiders, I think they call themselves, who are fighting just the kind of war we're talking about,'' Win said.

"I think you would be talking about Quantrill.''

"Yes. Do you know anything about Mr. Quantrill?''

"Suppose I did know? Mr. Coulter, you must understand that I am a lawyer,'' Poe said. "I cannot be perceived as an open advocate for the kind of guerrilla activity in which someone like Quantrill and his Raiders are engaged.''

"I understand,'' Win said. "And as far as I'm concerned, we are just having a conversation here. You are sharing what you know about certain elements of this war. You aren't suggesting that I join. But, in this same spirit of just sharing information, suppose a fella wanted to ride with Quantrill?'' Win asked. "Suppose a couple of men, brothers, say, who have a personal reason for wanting to keep their fighting here, wanted to ride with Quantrill?''

"I would say that depended upon whether or not Quantrill would be willing to have them ride with him," Poe replied.

"Would their cause be helped any if Quantrill had already tried to recruit them?"

Poe looked up quickly. "Quantrill tried to recruit you?"

"Not me, you understand. I'm talking about these fellas that I know," Win said. "Two brothers who had their parents killed and their farm burned by Emil Slaughter and his band of Jayhawkers."

"Just like you and Joe."

"Yes, just like my brother and me."

"Who contacted . . . uh . . . these two brothers you're talking about?" Poe asked.

"A man by the name of Frank James."

"Yes, he's . . . that is, I have been told, that he's one of them."

"Frank James said that if anyone ever wanted to contact him, they could do it here in Blue Springs. You got any idea how he might be contacted?" Win asked.

Poe laughed. "Mr. Coulter, believe me, an awful lot of people would like nothing better than to have that information. There's a sizeable reward out now for Quantrill, as well as several of the ones who ride with him. You can see, I hope, how information of that type isn't so readily shared."

"Yes," Win said.

Poe stood up then, and looked back down at Win and Joe.

"I'll tell you what," Poe said. "If I were giving information to these two brothers you are talking about, my information would be this. I would say to them, 'Just sit tight. The chances are very good that you'll be contacted again.' "

"I'll tell them you said that," Win said.

• • •

THE NEXT EVENING, WHILE JOE WAS OVER IN THE SALOON having a whiskey, Win told the hotel clerk he would like to take a bath. A large brass tub was moved into his room and the clerk's young son made several trips up to the room, carrying buckets of hot water. When the tub was sufficiently full, Win dismissed the boy with a dime, then took off his clothes and slipped down into the hot water. He picked up the bar of soap and began washing.

The door to the room opened, then closed.

"Hey, Joe, you're just in time," Win called back over his shoulder. "I'll finish here and you can have the water while it's still warm. You're getting seconds, but I paid for it."

"I'm not Joe, but that is an interesting idea," a woman's voice said.

Startled, Win turned so quickly that he splashed a good portion of the water onto the floor. His visitor was a strawberry blond with blue eyes and dimples. The dimples were deep when she smiled, and she was now smiling broadly.

"What the hell?" Win asked. "Who are you?"

"My name is Penny."

"What are you doing in here, Penny? Can't you see that I'm taking a bath?"

Penny came over to kneel down on the floor beside the tub. "Oh, yes," she said. "I can see that." She picked up a washcloth, wrung it out, then started scrubbing his back. "I just thought you might need someone to wash your back. It's part of the . . . service . . . you might say."

The warm water cascading down his back from the hands of this beautiful woman began to have its effect on him, and Win could feel himself "rising to the occasion."

"What else does the service provide?"

Penny leaned forward and kissed him. Her mouth

opened, and their tongues met. She put her hand down in the water, then moved it toward the hard shaft of his throbbing penis. That was when Win stood up.

Penny looked at him with confusion on her face, surprised by his sudden move.

"I'll be damned if I do this in a bathtub," Win said. "The bed is right over there."

Penny smiled, then handed him a towel. He wrapped it around himself for the walk over to the bed, then they kissed again. This time Penny pressed her body hard against his, and she opened her mouth hungrily to seek out his tongue. Win's arms wound around her tightly, and he felt the heat of her body transferring itself to his. Penny pulled the towel to one side, then ground her pelvis against his huge erection.

"Get out of your clothes," Win demanded, and Penny stepped back from him, then smiled as she removed her clothes, garment by garment, until she stood before him as naked as the day she was born.

"Do you like what you see?" she asked, turning and posturing before him.

"Too damned much talk," Win said, pulling her to him. He felt her naked breasts mash against his bare chest as they kissed again, then he picked her up and deposited her unceremoniously on his bed. He climbed on top, and she threw her arms around his neck, writhing and squirming beneath him. She spread her legs to receive him and when he entered her he felt her buck against him with the sudden rush of pleasure.

"Yes," she said, matching her rhythms to his in eager counterpoint.

Penny was soft and pliant beneath him, and her skin was as hot as if it were burning with a fever.

Finally, Win could hold it no longer, and he burst inside

her. Penny felt it, and she cried out with the pleasure of it and clasped him tightly to her as if unwilling to let him go.

Sated at last, Win collapsed atop her, staying there until his breathing returned to normal. He felt good, and he let out a sigh and rolled off her, then lay beside her, listening to the receding sound of her raspy breathing, touching her soft belly.

"Thank you, Mr. Coulter," Penny whispered.

Win raised up on one elbow and looked down at her. The breasts, which were small and hard when she was standing, were now gentle curves. Only the nipples, hard and erect, interrupted the smooth lines of her body. He reached down to touch one, and she shivered in pleasure.

"Who the hell are you?" Win asked. "A whore? Because if you are, I don't think I've ever run into one quite like you."

"Did I ask you for any money, Mr. Coulter?"

"No," Win said. "That's why I say I've never run into one like you."

"That's because I am not a whore," she said.

"But this," Win said. "I don't understand."

"Didn't you enjoy it?"

Win smiled. "Hell, yes, I enjoyed it!"

"Then I have done what I set out to do," Penny replied. "Let's just say that this is my contribution to the war. I give comfort and pleasure to those men I consider patriots."

Win chuckled. "How do you know which side I support?"

"Since you are looking for Quantrill, I would hope that you are a supporter of the Southern Cause," Penny said.

The smile left Win's face. "How do you know I'm looking for Quantrill?"

"It's my job to know." Penny got out of bed then, and began dressing.

"What do you mean, it's your job?"

"You and your brother meet me tomorrow morning behind the livery stable," Penny said. "At dawn. Oh, and take everything with you. You won't be coming back here."

"How do I know I can trust you?" Win asked.

Penny smiled. "That goes two ways, you know. I have to trust you as well. That's why we did what we just did. I don't know any better way to prove that a person is sincere, do you?"

"Now that I think about it," he said. "I don't guess I do."

Dressed now, Penny went over to the door. She turned and blew him a kiss. "Dawn, behind the livery," she said.

Win stared at the door after she left. "Well, if that's not the damndest . . ." he started, then he let the sentence hang and began laughing. It was the first good laugh he had enjoyed in several days, and it felt almost as good to him as what he and Penny had just done.

4

THE NEXT MORNING, JUST BEFORE DAWN, WIN AND JOE checked out of the hotel and, with their saddlebags tossed over their shoulders, walked down to the livery stable. They rustled the hostler from his slumber and, after paying him, retrieved their horses. Mounting, they rode out the back end of the livery just as the sun peeped over the copse to the east of town. A rider came toward them. The rider was dressed in a man's shirt and trousers, but as the distance closed, Win saw that it was Penny. He smiled.

"Right on time, I see," he said.

"I've been here for an hour," Penny replied. "I watched the two of you walk from the hotel." Her demeanor was much more businesslike this morning.

"You did say dawn, didn't you?"

"Yes. But I wanted to make certain that you weren't setting me up."

"I thought we settled that last night," Win said, and, for the first time this morning, Penny smiled as her cheeks were touched by a flash of pink.

"We have no time for small talk now," she said. "They'll be moving right after breakfast, and I won't know where they are."

Penny urged her horse into a canter and Win and Joe followed. They maintained that ground-eating pace for nearly an hour until, finally, Penny held up her hand as a signal for them to stop.

"Are we there?" Joe asked.

Penny didn't answer. Instead, she took a mirror from her pocket, caught the morning sun, then projected a flash of light on a rock just on the other side of a protruding ridge line. She moved the flash of light up and down. A moment later, another flash of light appeared on the rock, this one moving from left to right, so that the effect between the two mirror flashes was a cross of light.

Penny put the mirror away.

"All right," she said. "We can go in now."

Win and Joe followed Penny into Quantrill's hideout. A rider approached. He had long hair and a full beard. The brim of his felt hat was pinned to the crown and had a gold star. He wore a Confederate-gray jacket over an elaborately embroidered shirt. He rode up to Penny and kissed her, and Win wondered just how free Penny was with her "services."

"Bill, this is Win and Joe Coulter," Penny said. "This is my brother, Bill Anderson," she said to Win.

"Bloody Bill Anderson?" Joe asked.

Anderson said, "That's what the Yankees call me. I reckon I've given 'em enough cause. Come on in, I'll introduce you to some of the boys."

As they rode in, Win noticed something hanging from the halter of Bill Anderson's horse. At first he wasn't sure what it was, but when Bill saw him taking covert looks toward it, he smiled, then reached down and grabbed a single piece with his hand, holding it out so Win could get a better look.

"Yep," he said. "It's what you think it is. These are

scalps. I took this here'n off'n a red-haired Yankee captain.''

Win thought the notion was a little disquieting, but he forced himself to show no reaction to it.

"It's a little vain, I admit," Anderson said. "But the idea of maybe havin' one of their scalps wind up hangin' from my halter scares the shit out of the Yankees, and that sometimes gives me an advantage. When it comes to killin', or gettin' killed, you can't afford to be a little squeamish. You take ever' edge you can.''

"Yes," Win agreed. "I reckon so.''

They continued on into the meadow. When they reached the campsite, Win and Joe saw that there were fifty or sixty men, all in various stages of breaking camp. Most of the tents had already been taken down, though a few were still standing. There were at least a dozen fires, and the area was permeated by the aroma of frying bacon and boiling coffee.

"Have you folks eaten?" Anderson asked.

"No," Penny replied. "We left Blue Springs before breakfast.''

"You'd better eat fast," Anderson said. "We're moving out soon.''

"There's Frank James," Win pointed out.

"Who's the young girl with him?" Joe asked.

Bill Anderson laughed and Penny gasped. "That ain't no young girl. That's Frank's brother, Jesse. And you'd better not let him hear you say that.''

"What's a kid like that doing here?''

"That 'kid' as you call him," Anderson said, "is the best pistol shot I've ever seen, and as cool as they come. He can kill a man near as easy as I can.''

They dismounted and Frank James extended his hand.

He said, "I'm glad to see you have joined us, though I'm sorry to hear about your folks."

"But don't you worry," Jesse said, his voice not yet changed. "We'll pay 'em back, double."

Jesse's features were soft, his brown hair hung in a roll down his back, and his eyes were large and liquid blue. He looked like a choirboy, except for the brace of pistols stuck in his belt.

"Come on," Frank said. "Let me introduce you around to some of the boys." He pointed. "That fella over there is Little Archie Clement. Don't let his size fool you. He's killed many a six foot tall Yankee."

Archie Clement was barely five feet tall, and the low-crowned hat he wore seemed to accent his smallness.

A couple of men came over toward Win and Joe then, smiling broadly, and extending their hands.

"These are my cousins, Cole and Jim Younger," Frank started, but Cole interrupted him.

"Hell, Frank, no need to introduce us to these boys. Their farm is next to ours. We've known each other purt' near our whole lives," Cole said.

Jim Younger added, "In fact, Cole and Joe here wrestled at the Cass County fair for the county championship a couple of times."

"Who won?" Jesse asked, his boyish enthusiasm coming through, even in this situation.

"Near as I can recall, he won one, and I won one," Joe said, shaking hands with the Younger brothers. "It's good to see you boys."

"The only way I could beat him though, was to bite off part of his ear," Cole said, laughing. The smile left his face. "I was real sorry to hear about your ma and pa."

"I promise you, we'll get even for them," another man said, coming over to join them. "We may never find the actual ones who did it, but if you take my point of view, all those Yankee bastards are just alike anyway, so it doesn't make any difference which one of them you kill.''

The speaker was about five feet nine, slender of build, pale complexioned, and with a sweeping moustache. He was smiling a greeting at Win and Joe, but the smile didn't reach his cold, pale-blue eyes. Drooping eyelids gave the impression of a snake waiting to strike. He was wearing a Confederate officer's jacket, with the single gold star of a major embroidered on his collar.

"It makes a difference to me," Win said. "The son of a bitch I am looking for is Emil Slaughter."

"Ah, yes, Emil Slaughter. I know him. Mark my words, we'll meet him one of these days. My name is Quantrill. I'm glad to have you boys with us."

"Charley," someone called. "You want to look at this?"

"Excuse me," Quantrill said. "I'd better see what he has."

"Did that man call him Charley?" Win asked, as Quantrill stepped over to see what was wanted of him.

"He uses the name Charley Hart sometimes when he doesn't want to be known," Frank explained. "So he likes for people to call him that so he knows to answer to it."

Win studied Quantrill as he talked with the man who had summoned him over. Quantrill couldn't be more than twenty-four years old, yet he had already gained such a fearsome reputation that even the mention of his name made the people on the other side cringe in terror.

"Here, thought you might want this," Jesse said, and Win saw that the boy had brought him, Joe, and Penny biscuit-and-bacon sandwiches.

"Thanks," Win said.

Bill Anderson had to have been pulling his leg, he thought. There was no way this almost puppylike boy could be the cold-blooded killer Anderson described.

"Men!" Quantrill called out loud. "Gather 'round!"

From all over the little camp, men came to stand around and listen to Quantrill. Their leader climbed onto a tree stump to elevate himself above the crowd.

"George Todd has just come back from a little scout he took over into Kansas," Quantrill said. Quantrill was holding a little cloth bag. "It seems that the folks over in Shawnee Town are getting some really good bargains on such things as clocks, furniture, silverware, and china. They're getting bargains because *they* got a real good bargain from Emil Slaughter, if you know what I mean." He reached down into the little cloth bag and pulled out a gold candlestick. "Win and Joe Coulter, have you ever seen this before?"

"That's one of ma's candlesticks!" Joe said in surprise.

"Where did you get that?" Win asked.

"Like I told you," Quantrill replied. "It came from Shawnee Town, Kansas." He looked over at George Todd. "You want to tell them about it?"

Todd, who had been a stonemason before the war, ran his hand through his dark hair as he talked.

"I was in a saloon over there, trying to see what I could find out," Todd said, "when I heard a store clerk braggin' that he had some new stuff that he had just picked up from Slaughter. The way he was talking, I knew it had to be from that last raid the Jayhawkers pulled, and that meant when they burned the Coulter farm. So, I went there like I was really interested in getting a good bargain, and he showed me this candlestick."

"There are six of them," Win said.

"He only had this one candlestick, but you can bet that the other stuff is over there somewhere," Todd said. He looked at the others. "And not just from this one raid.

They've got a whole town that is full of bounty they've stolen from our people.''

"I say we take it back!'' Little Archie Clement shouted.

"Oh, we're going to do that,'' Quantrill said. He smiled broadly. "But we aren't going to stop there! We're going to take everything they got!''

The men let out a loud cheer.

"Now, finish breaking camp and get your horses saddled. We're riding out of here in half an hour!''

With another cheer, the men separated, then hurried to break the camp and saddle their mounts.

"What do you think about this?'' Joe asked his brother.

"What do you mean, what do I think?''

"I mean, raiding a town like this. It's not right, is it?''

"Was it right what they did to ma and pa?''

"No, but . . .''

"There are no buts about it, little brother,'' Win said. "The sons of bitches who did it must live in Shawnee Town.''

"But what if they don't? I mean, how will we ever know?'' Joe asked.

"It doesn't matter. The people in Shawnee Town who buy these good deals know where they came from. In my book, that makes them just as guilty as the ones who did do it.''

"Yeah,'' Joe said. "I guess you're right.''

QUANTRILL HALTED HIS BAND OF RAIDERS ABOUT THREE miles out of town. It was his belief that the best time to strike was at dawn, so he had the men make a cold camp and sleep on the ground without even pitching tents. The men didn't complain about eating hard tack and drinking water, but those who smoked were a little put out about not being able to light up.

"What would we accomplish by not having fires to cook food or make coffee," Quantrill asked, "if you're going to give away our position by smoking?"

If the men didn't like it, they at least understood the validity of it, so no one violated Quantrill's orders that night.

AT DAWN THE NEXT MORNING QUANTRILL DIVIDED HIS men into two groups. He sent one group around to come into town from the west end, while he kept one group back to enter from the east. Win and Joe, the Younger brothers, and the James brothers were with the group that circled the town.

"Win," Cole said. "If you or Joe get into more trouble than you can handle, look to Jesse."

Win snorted a laugh. "You expect me to have a boy pull my ass out of the fire if the going gets too rough?"

"Yeah, I do expect that," Cole said without further explanation.

It took half an hour for both groups to be in position, but they were there just as the sun peeked up over the eastern horizon. From the other end of the town, Win heard two shots fired.

"Let's go!" Frank James shouted and, drawing their pistols, the raiders rode at a gallop into town, firing into the air and through the front windows of the not-yet-opened stores.

Several people ran out into the street to see what was going on, then, seeing that it was a raid, they turned and ran back into the buildings. A few came out with rifles or shotguns in their hands. That was a mistake. They were cut down where they stood by half a dozen or more bullets.

The two groups of riders met in the middle of town, laughing, shouting, and still firing into the air.

"All right, you people!" Quantrill shouted out loud. "Turn out! Turn out into the street so we can see you!"

When no one showed up, Quantrill nodded at Bill Anderson and Anderson lit a torch, then tossed it onto the shake roof of an apothecary. The dry shakes caught fire quickly.

"You may as well come out!" Quantrill shouted. "Because we're going to burn every building in this town, whether anyone is inside or not!"

At that, several doors opened, and people started coming out into the street. As it was just dawn, most were still in their nightshirts and nightgowns.

Some frightened, some angry, and all confused, the townspeople gathered in a group in front of the Wells Fargo office.

"Ladies and gentlemen, I sincerely thank you for showing us such courtesy this morning," Quantrill said with a sweeping wave of his hat. "Now, I have a few requests to make. They are quite simple, really. I want the manager of this Wells Fargo office to open the bank and empty his vault and his money drawers into sacks. I want all the store-keepers to select their most valuable merchandise and put it into sacks, as well. In addition, I would like the restaurant owner to prepare breakfast for me and my men."

At that moment a shot rang out, startling in its loudness and in the fact that it was unexpected. Win looked around quickly and saw that Jesse James was holding a smoking revolver. The expression on his face was as calm as if he were sitting in a school classroom. But the result of his pistol shot was a man tumbling out of the second-story window of the nearby hotel. The rifle the man had been aiming slid across the porch roof and fell to the ground just one moment ahead of the man himself.

Win saw that the man didn't feel the fall, though. Jesse's

bullet had hit him right between the eyes, and he was dead before he even dropped his rifle.

"Well, now," Quantrill said, easily. "We can't have any more of that, can we?" He looked over at Bill Anderson. "Burn the hotel now," he ordered.

Nodding at the Younger brothers to help him, several flaming torches were tossed onto the roof and into the windows of the hotel. There were some loud shouts from inside the hotel, and three men came running out into the street, firing their pistols. Win was one of the earliest to react, and he shot down the first one. The other two went down under a hail of gunfire.

"I believe you see by now that resistance is futile," Quantrill said to the horrified townspeople. "Now, about my demands."

"Quantrill! Surely, you aren't going to burn the houses as well?" someone shouted.

"Well, now, let me see," Quantrill said, stroking his chin. "Were there ever any houses burned over in Missouri? Yes, I think there were. I guess that means we're going to burn the houses as well."

Win felt a little queasy about seeing the civilian houses go up in flames, but none of the women or children were harmed, and, so far, the only men shot were those who had offered resistance.

He thought of the charred bodies of his mother and father, lying underground back at the burned-out Coulter farm, and he was able to push the queasiness aside. So much so, that he grabbed a torch and set fire to a couple of the houses himself.

5

ALL SIX OF WIN AND JOE'S MOTHER'S CANDLESTICKS were recovered in the Shawnee raid, and Quantrill graciously presented them to the Coulter brothers. Win noticed, however, that no effort was made to find the rightful Missouri owners of the other stolen items. Instead, they were divided up among the band as bounty, to be disposed of in any way they wished.

"The distribution of such loot is the only way we have of paying our men," Frank James explained when Win commented upon it. "Besides, there's no way we could find the rightful owners. And the stuff is already stolen. We didn't steal it from the innocent, we just stole it from the guilty."

At first Win was appalled by Frank's rationalization. It wasn't too long, however, before he, too, began to see the logic of such a procedure and set aside any last vestige of conscience he may have had. After riding with Quantrill for three months, he was able to justify practically any act they committed, by blaming it on the war. By late fall, he was the consummate Raider. Justification was no longer needed.

• • •

ALTHOUGH QUANTRILL'S REPUTATION WAS THAT OF A murderer and plunderer of towns and innocent civilians, Win quickly learned that Quantrill's hatred for the Yankees included Union soldiers. To that end, Quantrill frequently engaged in battle with patrols, platoons, and companies of Union soldiers, even though there was no immediate payoff in terms of loot for him or his men.

"Look at it this way," he told his men when someone told him that they could see little advantage to attacking armed bodies of soldiers. "The more of them we kill, the less of them there will be out looking for us. And, if we attack them, we'll be fighting them on our own terms."

Fighting on their own terms was what they were doing this morning as Win and Joe, along with at least twenty more men, waited patiently for an armed Yankee patrol.

The Yankee patrol was platoon-sized in strength, meaning that there would be twice as many soldiers as there were guerrillas.

"You have to give the little son of a bitch credit for guts," Joe whispered as they waited. "He sure don't let numbers impress him."

Win said, "That's because he's smart enough to know that the odds are actually on our side."

"How do you figure that?"

"Well, think about it, Joe. Every one of us is armed with at least two pistols . . . that's twelve rounds apiece. The soldiers are all carrying muzzle-loading rifles. They'll get off one shot at best."

Joe said, "Yeah, now that you explain it that way, I see what you mean."

As Win sat in his saddle waiting for the Yankees to approach, he looked down the line at the other Raiders who would be taking part in the fight.

Frank James was sitting perfectly still, staring straight ahead. Of all Quantrill's Raiders, Frank seemed the most withdrawn. He was a brooder who would go for long periods of time without speaking to anyone.

Jesse was watching some squirrels cavorting in a nearby tree and seemed totally consumed by them. He was, by far, the most fascinating of all Quantrill's riders. He could shoot, without remorse, a man who was begging for his life. On the other hand he was extremely deferential to women and the elderly.

Cole Younger was, like Joe, a big man. He had a great sense of humor and kept the others laughing with his jokes. Jim Younger, who was four years younger than Cole, was fiercely loyal to his brother and to his cousins, Frank and Jesse.

Bloody Bill Anderson and Little Archie Clement were also on hand. Eighteen-year-old Archie Clement had begun decorating his own horse's harness with scalps, just as did his mentor, Bill Anderson. Archie seemed intent upon matching Bill Anderson, bloody incident for bloody incident, so that he was becoming as feared among his adversaries as was Bloody Bill himself. Recently, Archie had killed and scalped two soldiers, then left a taunting note which read: *"You come to hunt bushwhackers. Now you are skelpt. Little Archie Clement skelpt you."*

And then, of course, there was Quantrill himself. Quantrill had, by now, established himself as the most infamous of all guerrillas operating along the Missouri-Kansas border. Quantrill could fire both pistols with deadly accuracy from the back of a galloping horse. He was a natural leader and a man of daring and ingenuity. And though he was regarded by his foes as a brigand, outlaw, and murderer, Win was convinced that if he were in a regular army unit at the head of cavalry, he would distinguish himself as much as Jeb Stuart, Jeff Thompson, or any other Confederate leader.

Quantrill had just ridden to the top of the crest of the little hill behind which the mounted riders were waiting. Now he came riding back down.

"Get your guns out, boys," he said. "They're no more'n fifty yards over that rise. We can cut 'em down in about two sweeps."

Win, Joe, and the others pulled their pistols, then waited for the word.

Quantrill rode to a position in front of them, then stopped. Putting the reins of his horse in his teeth, he pulled two pistols, and without a word he slapped his heels against the sides of his horse.

The horse bolted forward, and the band of Raiders followed.

Win saw the Yankee soldiers as soon as they crested the hill. They were riding along at a plodding pace, obviously unaware that Quantrill was anywhere near, though, in fact, their mission was to look for him.

"My God! It's Quantrill!" Win heard one of the soldiers shout.

Having been seen, the Raiders gave a loud yell as they galloped down the hill toward the soldiers.

The Union soldiers raised their weapons and fired. Win heard and felt half a dozen bullets going by him. Two of the Raiders were hit and unseated, but the main group continued its charge down the hill toward the Yankee patrol.

The soldiers, having fired their one round, panicked at the sight of a body of men riding down upon them unchecked, firing their pistols as they came. Several of the soldiers leaped down from their horses and converted their rifles to clubs. They swung at the Raiders as they rode by, but their efforts were ineffectual and, to a man, they were shot down.

The remaining soldiers scattered to every direction like a covey of flushed quail. Win and the others galloped after them in hot pursuit.

"Go!" Quantrill screamed at his men. "Go, get them! Kill the Yankee bastards!"

Win looked to the riders all around him. The horses were magnificent, with their nostrils flared, their teeth bared, their manes flying, and their muscles working in powerful coordination. The Raiders were bending low over the animals' necks, the brims of their hats rolled back by the breeze, their eyes narrowed, their faces tautly set. It was a thrilling moment.

LATER, WHEN THE BATTLE WAS OVER, QUANTRILL learned from one of the dying soldiers that this was the garrison that occupied Independence, Missouri. That meant that, for the moment at least, Independence was unguarded. Quantrill made the decision then and there to go to Independence and "Recapture it for the Confederacy."

"Yeah," George Todd said. "We'll clean that town out!"

"We'll do no such thing," Quantrill insisted. "Independence is a Missouri town, and its citizens are loyal to the Confederacy. We will enter the town as liberators, not as conquerors."

WHEN QUANTRILL'S RAIDERS REACHED THE EDGE OF INdependence, Quantrill halted his men and had them form up in a column of twos. Then he broke out the Confederate flag and gave it to Joe to carry. Moving to the front of the column, Quantrill buttoned his gray tunic, then gave the order for his men to ride into town. They entered, not in an aggressive attack formation, but as an army on parade.

The sight of Quantrill riding boldly down the main street of Independence at first startled the town's citizens, then thrilled them. Most of Independence was composed of Southern sympathizers, so much so that many of the men were away fighting for the South. The Union occupation of the town, though it had been accomplished without incident, was nevertheless abhorrent to them, and now they cheered the Confederate flag being, once again, in their midst.

Quantrill halted the column in front of the town hall. There, he was met by Mayor Hawkings, Sheriff Paige, and a delegation of city officials and civic leaders.

"Major Quantrill, on behalf of the loyal Southern citizens of Independence, I welcome you," Mayor Hawkings said.

Chuckling, Quantrill leaned over to Win. "Well now, I've just been promoted from captain to major," he said. "What do you think of that?"

"Quantrill, Anderson, all of you men," Sheriff Paige said then, addressing the group. "There are federal warrants out on many of you. Obviously, I'm in no position to serve them, even if I wanted to. So, I'm going to ask you to strike a bargain with me. Don't break any of the laws of Jackson County, or the town of Independence, and I'll consider your stay here to be a time of truce. Can we have such a bargain between us?"

Quantrill looked to his riders. There were more than a hundred men with him, all armed, desperate men. Sheriff Paige had only one deputy.

"I'll give you this, Sheriff," Quantrill said, putting his hands on the pommel and leaning forward in his saddle. "You got grit. All right, any of my men that breaks one of your laws while he's here will have to answer to me, first, then I'll turn what's left of his miserable carcass over to you."

In appreciation for their liberation from Yankee oppression, Mayor Hawkings declared Independence an open town for Quantrill and his men. They were to be given free food at any of the town's restaurants, free drinks in all the bars, and the hotel would put them up, free. This was to continue, the mayor told them, for as long as they stayed in town.

Mayor Hawkings was generous because he knew that Quantrill could not possibly remain longer than overnight. And, as he explained it to the merchants who complained of the mayor's giveaway of their goods and services, this was much better than being sacked and burned.

"But he is fighting for the South," the saloon owner said. "He is on our side."

"Yes. And I propose that we keep him that way," the mayor suggested. The mayor's suggestion was accepted without further dissenting remarks.

To come into a town where they were welcomed, rather than shot at, and to have drinks and food thrust upon them, was a stark and welcome departure from their experiences of the last several months. Joe found it particularly pleasant because a great deal of the welcome mat that the little town was rolling out for them seemed to revolve around food, and good home-cooking was one of the things Joe missed most.

Thus it was that when Maggie Depro approached Joe to tell him, shyly, that she had just baked an apple pie, and asked if he would like some, he accepted the offer immediately.

Maggie was a big though well-proportioned woman. She was nearly six feet tall, therefore most men never got around to seeing that she was actually quite a pretty woman. They saw only her size, and as she was generally bigger than most of them were, they were intimidated by her. On the other hand, Joe was so big himself that he never even noticed Maggie's size. He did notice, however, that she was a very pretty woman.

"I can bring the pie to you," Maggie said. "Or," she smiled, seductively, "you could come down to my place and eat it there."

"Only if you'll eat a piece with me," Joe replied.

"Oh, well, I fully intended to do that," Maggie said.

WIN WATCHED HIS BROTHER LEAVE WITH MAGGIE, THEN he looked at the other men he rode with. Many were with women, their own, or those acquired for the occasion. Most had a bottle, and all were streaming toward one of the cafes to take advantage of the free food.

Win decided to take his pleasure in a somewhat more subdued way, so he went into a tobacco store. There, he filled his shirt pocket with at least six good cigars, then lit one of them and, puffing contentedly, sat on an upturned oaken bucket out in front of the leather-goods store, and watched the play of men who, but a few brief hours before, had been engaged in the deadly business of killing.

AT ABOUT THE MOMENT WIN WAS LIGHTING UP HIS FIRST cigar, Maggie was leading Joe into a house which was located at the far end of the street. It was a small frame house, consisting of a living room, kitchen, and bedroom.

"Sit there, at the table," Maggie invited. "I will cut the pie for you. Also, there is coffee if you want it."

"Thank you," Joe said. Looking around the room, he saw an oval-framed picture hanging from the wall. The subjects in the picture were Maggie, wearing a dress with puffed sleeves and a high collar, and a man who looked uncomfortable in the jacket and tight-collar shirt he was wearing.

"That was my husband," Maggie said, when she saw Joe looking at the picture.

"*Was* your husband?"

"He was killed at Shiloh, last spring," Maggie said.

"I am sorry to hear that."

"Yes, he was a good man," Maggie said, wistfully. She sighed. "But, as they say, it does no good to cry over spilt milk."

As she was talking, she put a big piece of pie in front of Joe, and he saw that the pie had been covered with a slice of cheese.

Joe smiled. "How did you know that I liked cheese on my pie?"

"Because you look like a man with a good appetite," Maggie said. "And men with good appetites enjoy cheese."

Joe helped himself to a big bite, then he closed his eyes and grunted in satisfaction.

"Uhmmm," he said. "I think I have died and gone to heaven."

Joe ate the first piece of pie very quickly, then accepted the offer of a second piece.

"Joe," Maggie said as she put the second piece of pie in front of him. "You will excuse me? I will only be a moment, I promise, and then I will return. Go ahead, enjoy your pie."

"Thank you," Joe said, forking another bite into his mouth. "I will."

Joe had just finished his last bite of pie when he sensed, more than heard, Maggie return. He looked up to tell her how much he had enjoyed the pie, then he gasped in surprise. Maggie was wearing a black camisole and nothing more. The nipples of her breasts protruded through the silk.

"Maggie?" Joe said.

"Joe, it has been so long," she said. "So long since I had a man." She walked over to him and, putting her arms around his neck, leaned forward so that her silk-encased breasts pressed against his face. "A real man," she added.

Joe reached up to touch her nipples and they grew harder. Maggie shuddered, then slipped the camisole over her shoulders and let it fall to the floor. Joe stood up and pulled her nude body against him.

Maggie reached down to touch the bulge in front of Joe's pants, then she began opening the buttons. A second later, Joe felt his organ spring free as she pulled it out.

"Please do not think, Mr. Coulter, that I meet everyone in this way," Maggie said. Her long cool fingers moved across his organ. She kissed him, and her tongue came out serpentlike to dart into his mouth. She raised one leg to the side of him and took him inside her.

Joe was taken completely by surprise and as his knees weakened, he had to move over to lean back against the wall. He put his hands on her hips, not to push her away, but to move her to him. As she hunched against him, his mouth moved down across her naked shoulders to her distended nipples. He bit them gently, and flicked his tongue against them.

Joe heard a couple of men laughing as they passed by in the street in front of Maggie's house and, because he was afraid their proximity might make her nervous, he tried, gently, to disengage from her.

"No!" she gasped urgently through clenched teeth. She continued to hump against him. "Don't you dare stop! Not for a minute . . . not even for a second!"

Joe started to explain why he nearly stopped, but the

sensations he was feeling were too strong. He smiled. To
hell with it. If it didn't bother her, it didn't bother him. He
stood there, letting her have her way with him until he
rocked back on his heels and shuddered, then put both his
hands on her ass and pulled her tightly against him. Finally,
long moments after the last tremors were gone, Maggie
dropped her leg and pulled away. With a contented sigh,
she smiled at him.

"Another piece?" she asked sweetly.

"What?"

"Of pie," she said, chuckling.

"Yes," Joe agreed. "I think that would be very nice."

6

DESPITE MAYOR HAWKINGS'S OFFER OF FREE FOOD, LI-
quor, and lodging, Quantrill allowed his men to eat free,
but he insisted that they pay for all the whiskey they consumed and any nonfood item they got from the merchants.
As a result, the next twenty-four hours turned out to be an
economic boom for the businesses of Independence, and
the merchants who had been anxious about Quantrill's presence in their small city became Quantrill's greatest sup-
porters.

At midmorning on the next day, a scout brought Quantrill word that an entire Yankee battalion was approaching
Independence, so Quantrill ordered an immediate evacua-
tion. As they left, the Raiders were given a warm and genuine send-off. The volunteer fire department band provided
them with music, and Quantrill's departure turned into a
street fair.

Many of men had lived in and around Independence before the war, and they had wives and children, parents and
siblings, and sweethearts and friends who were still here.
Others had made new liaisons just within the last twenty-
four hours, so that the street was lined with people who

were genuinely saddened to see them go. The women cried and waved handkerchiefs as the men rode away. Maggie Depro was in that number.

LESS THAN AN HOUR AFTER QUANTRILL LEFT TOWN, SHERiff Paige was making his rounds when he saw a body of men approaching. At first, seeing the undisciplined way they rode, and the number of riders who weren't in uniform, he thought Quantrill was coming back.

The prospect of Quantrill returning wasn't a welcome one for, although there had been no incidents while he was here before, Paige considered himself lucky, and he didn't want to press his luck. He also didn't want Quantrill in town when the Federal troops returned. That could bring about a battle right here in town, and Paige didn't want that.

He walked out to the edge of town and waited, hoping to be able to persuade Quantrill to change his mind about returning. As the body of riders drew closer, though, he realized that it wasn't Quantrill. At first he was puzzled as to who they might be, then he recognized them, and he stiffened.

"My God, it's Emil Slaughter," he said under his breath. He turned, and started running back up the street, shouting a warning.

"It's Slaughter! It's Emil Slaughter!" he yelled. "Get your guns! It's . . ." The sheriff's words were cut short by a sudden fusillade of shooting as a dozen or more of Slaughter's riders broke into a gallop and left the formation to run him down and shoot him.

When those first shots were fired, the rest of Slaughter's Jayhawkers began firing, shooting up the storefronts and into the fronts of houses, gunning down anyone they saw on the street regardless of age or sex. A woman, with a baby in her arms, was killed as she stood on the front porch of her own house. The blacksmith was killed when he ran out into the street carrying an old muzzle-loading rifle. An old man was run down and trampled, just because he couldn't get out of the way quickly enough.

Slaughter halted his riders in front of the general store.

"Go inside and take whatever he's got," Slaughter ordered. He saw a wagon parked out front, the bed of the wagon covered with a tarpaulin. "What's in the wagon?" he asked.

One of Slaughter's men climbed onto the wagon and pulled back the canvas. He laughed.

"What is it?"

"Ain't nothin' here but a bunch of hymnals," he said.

"Take 'em."

"Hymnals?"

"Maybe we can sell 'em somewhere," Slaughter suggested. "If we can't sell 'em, we'll use 'em as firewood."

Slaughter stood in the stirrups and looked up and down the now-deserted street of the town. "Whereat is the mayor of this town?" he shouted.

When no one answered, Slaughter pointed toward the nearby Methodist church. "Burn it," he ordered.

Laughing, a couple of men lit torches, then tossed them onto the church. Within a few moments the church began to blaze.

Slaughter cupped his hands around his mouth and yelled loudly: "Next place we're goin' to burn is the school building, 'lessen the mayor comes out to talk to us right now!"

A front door opened on a building just down the street from where Slaughter had halted his men, and Mayor Hawkings came out, moving nervously, haltingly.

"I am Mayor Hawkings," he announced. He licked his lips and looked into the faces of the second group of guerrillas to invade his town in less than two days.

"Well, Mayor Hawkings, my scouts tell me that for the last twenty-four hours the Confederate flag has flown over this town. Now, how can that be, what with Independence being the good, loyal Union town we know it to be?"

"We had no choice," Mayor Hawkings insisted.

"Is that a fact?" Slaughter asked in a tone of voice that indicated he didn't believe what the mayor was telling him.

"It's true. Quantrill was here, as I'm sure your scout also told you. As long as he was here, he was in charge."

"How is it that he was in charge? Didn't you just tell me you are the mayor?"

"Quantrill was at the head of a large body of armed men," the mayor said. He looked around at the men with Slaughter. "Surely, you can understand that."

Slaughter leaned forward in his saddle and looked down at the mayor. "Tell me, did Quantrill shoot any of your people?"

"No, he did not," the mayor replied.

"Then you relinquished command too easily," Slaughter replied.

By now, seeing the mayor engaged in what appeared to be a peaceful discussion, several of the townspeople had moved cautiously into the street.

Without another word, Slaughter suddenly turned his pistol on one of the more adventurous of these citizens, a man who had come close enough to see what was going on. Slaughter pulled the trigger, and the heavy lead slug buried itself deep in the man's chest. The man died with a quick expulsion of breath and a look of surprise on his face.

"My God!" Mayor Hawkings shouted in alarm. "What are you doing?"

With his pistol still smoking, Slaughter turned his attention back to the shocked mayor.

"Mr. Mayor, I believe you cooperated with Quantrill because you wanted to. But you are going to cooperate with me because you must. Otherwise your streets will be chocked with your dead. Do you understand me?''

"Yes," the mayor said, quietly. "I understand you."

"Good, I thought we might be able to come to some sort of agreement. Now, you tell your people to stay back out of our way. We'll tend to our business as quickly as we can, then we'll be out of here before the army arrives, and your lives can go back to normal."

"No one will resist you," the mayor promised.

Slaughter smiled, then put his gun in his holster. He twisted around in his saddle and looked at his men.

"All right, boys, you know what to do. Get busy."

A dozen men dismounted and, carrying large cloth bags, began to fan out through the town on a mission of looting. The other riders remained mounted, holding their weapons at the ready, their watchful eyes busily scanning every storefront, roof, and alley for anyone who might be foolish enough to threaten them.

SALLY PAIGE WAS ON THE FRONT PORCH OF HER HOUSE when she saw her husband shot down. She started to go to him, but gunfire from the thundering riders drove her back inside. As soon as it was safe to do so, she moved back to the window of her house and stared out into the street toward Ed's body which lay about fifty yards away. He had not moved a muscle since he fell and she knew, in her heart, that he was dead.

She was about to go to him when she saw one of the Jayhawkers coming up toward her house. He was a small man with a narrow nose and dark, beady eyes. In one hand the Jayhawker was carrying a sack that was already half full of treasure looted from her neighbors' houses. In the other hand he was carrying his pistol.

Quickly Sally looked around her house to see if there was anything she could hide from him. The first thing to come to her mind was the music box her mother had given her when she and Ed married. She grabbed it and stuck it in the back of the fireplace, hoping that, because a small fire was going, it wouldn't be seen. She was just straightening up when the Jayhawker kicked her door open and came in. The Jayhawker waved his gun around.

"Where's your man?" he asked.

"Dead," Sally answered in an accusatory voice. "He's lying out in the street. You killed him."

"Yeah? Well, the dumb son of a bitch should've had enough sense to stay out of our way." The Jayhawker's dark eyes darted around the house. "What have you got for me?"

"Nothing. My husband was the sheriff here. He didn't earn a lot of money."

"The sheriff? You mean that old man out there in the street was your husband?"

"Yes."

The Jayhawker examined Sally more closely. Uncomfortable under his gaze, she clutched at the neck of her dress.

"I don't hardly see how an old man like that could measure up to someone as young and as pretty as you. You ask me, someone like you needs a real man around, not someone old and half-dead. You know what I mean?"

"No, I do not know what you mean. My husband and I had a wonderful marriage," Sally said. Suddenly she realized, as if by hearing the word "had" spoken, that her marriage was a thing of the past. Her husband was dead. And with that realization, some of the numbness began to wear off so that tears formed in her eyes.

The Jayhawker put the sack down and started toward her.

"No need to cry, honey," he said. "You know what I'm goin' to do for you?" He began unbuttoning his pants. "I'm goin' to show you what you've been missing."

"No," Sally said, whimpering quietly. "No, don't do this."

"Oh, yeah, I'm goin' to do it. And you're goin' to like it," the Jayhawker said. "You're goin' to like it a lot."

NOT QUITE FIFTEEN MINUTES LATER, THE JAYHAWKER heard three shots fired, the signal for everyone to return. Getting up from the woman, he pulled his trousers up and began buttoning his pants. As he looked down at the woman, he could see his semen scattered in the dark tangle of hair at the junction of her legs.

The woman hadn't bled as much as he thought she would. But then his knife had made a quick, easy thrust into her heart, killing her almost instantly. She hadn't even cried out, she just shuddered, took a couple of labored gasps, then stopped breathing. Her eyes were open, but the fright he had seen in them earlier was gone now. Now they were dull and vacant.

The Jayhawker joined the others. With their sacks full of booty and more than a dozen stores and homes burning behind them, Emil Slaughter and his men rode out of town, leaving the weeping citizens to bury their dead.

THE COMMANDING OFFICER OF THE FEDERAL TROOPS cursed under his breath as he led his men into the burning town.

"Quantrill," he said as he looked around him. "Only Quantrill would do something like this."

ONE WEEK LATER, WITH THEIR HORSES SECURED AND THE guards posted, Win, Joe, and the others were gathered around a fire at their campsite. In addition to providing a fire for cooking and making coffee, the fire provided much-needed warmth, for by now the nights were becoming quite cold.

A little earlier that evening George Todd had joined them, bringing them news of Emil Slaughter's raid on Independence and of Sheriff Paige being shot down in the street.

Todd also brought a stack of mail for the men. Since Win and Joe had no one left at home, they had no one from whom to receive any mail. As a result, they sat beside the campfire drinking coffee and watching the firewood turn to glowing coals while the other men enjoyed their letters and exchanged the latest news and gossip.

"Here, listen to this," someone said, looking up from his letter. "Accordin' to my wife the damned Yankee army is sayin' it was us who come in and robbed and burned Independence. My wife says that ever'one in town has done told the Yankees it was Emil Slaughter who done the robbin', killin', and burnin', but the Yankees don't believe 'em. They think the townspeople are lyin' to protect us."

"They don't think any such thing," Quantrill said. "They're just sayin' that, 'cause they don't want folks to know what kind of a people the Jayhawkers really are."

"Oh, shit. They killed Sally," the man reading the letter said. He let the letter drop and pinched the bridge of his nose for a long, quiet moment.

Win looked at one of the men nearby, mouthing the question, "Who is Sally?"

"His sister," the man answered, quietly. "She was married to Sheriff Paige."

"Win, didn't Sheriff Paige say it was a fella named Slaughter who was the one who burned our place and killed ma and pa?" Joe asked a few minutes later.

"Yes, that's what he said," Win answered. Then to Quantrill. "Why don't we go after that bastard, Slaughter?"

"Don't be frettin' about it," Quantrill said. "We've got more important things to do, now, than worry about Mr. Emil Slaughter."

"What's more important than killin' that son of a bitch?" Win asked.

"We're goin' to catch up with him one of these days. And when we do, I'll let you kill him. You can count on that."

"I *am* counting on it, Charley," Win said. "If you recall, that's the whole reason my brother and I joined up with you in the first place."

"Oh, oh, look at this," Bill Anderson said, pulling a piece of paper from the letter sent to him by his sister. It was a printed poster.

"What is that?"

"It's trouble," Anderson replied.

"Read it, Bill," Quantrill ordered. "Read it aloud."

Bill Anderson cleared his throat, then began to read:

"The commandant of the Missouri-Kansas border district believes that order can never be established in the area until Quantrill and other raiders like him are brought under control," he read. *"And, as long as their women provide them with help and a safe-haven, that control can never be attained.*

"Therefore, from henceforth, any woman who gives aid and comfort to the enemy, in any form, even though she may be his wife, will be charged with treason against the United States Government. With the suspension of"—Anderson had trouble with the next two words, and he pronounced them very slowly—*"ha-be-as cor-pus . . . mere suspicion shall be considered enough for"*—again he had

to sound out the word—*"in-car-cer-ation. Those convicted of treason, be they male or female, will be executed."*

"The hell you say?" someone said angrily.

"You don't think they'd actually do that, do you?" Cole Younger asked.

"I think there's not much those Yankee bastards won't do," Frank James answered.

As the conversation about the Yankee threat to their women continued, Quantrill called Win over to talk to him and to George Todd. The three men stood just outside the bubble of light cast by the fire. There, Todd, who was the one who had brought the mail, was just getting around to having his supper. He was gnawing on a pork chop bone, and a piece of fat dangled from his chin.

"Win, Todd's been sniffing around to pick up some information for us, and I think he has come up with something that will be very useful to us."

"You know where Slaughter is?" Win asked, hopefully.

Quantrill waved his hands as if dismissing that subject. "No, and I told you, all that'll come about in due time. No, sir, the information Todd has is somethin' we can use right now. But we're goin' to need you to make it work. I want you to take the coach to Raytown next week," Quantrill suggested.

"All right," Win replied. "What do I do, once I get there?"

"Why, you take the coach right back," Quantrill said, with a laugh. "I think we are all going to find this very profitable."

7

WIN SHIFTED IN HIS SEAT, THE BETTER TO RESTORE THE circulation in his sore and cramped legs. He pulled the curtain back to peer through the stagecoach window at the blanket of white on the ground outside. The snow, which had started as a light powder when he boarded the coach in Raytown this morning, was now coming down in large, heavy flakes. It was falling so steadily that the line of woods to either side of the road was all but obscured.

The information Todd brought back to Quantrill was that this stagecoach would be carrying a payroll for the Yankee soldiers who were at Kansas City. Win's job was to find out if that was true, and if so, to leave the coach at a predesignated spot where his horse would be waiting, ride quickly to a place where Quantrill and the others would be waiting, and tell them.

"If it is, we'll hit the stage and take the money," Quantrill said when he was giving Win his instructions. "Nothing would be sweeter than for me to be able to pay our men with money that was meant for the Yankees."

At the present moment, Win was one of five passengers in the coach. Sitting directly across from him was a very pretty young woman who had, from the glint in her eyes and the hint of a smile on her lips, discovered him, as well.

"And what about you, sir?" someone asked.

As Win had not been listening to the conversation, he didn't even realize he was being spoken to until there was a tug on his sleeve. He looked around.

"I beg your pardon?" he asked.

The person who had solicited his opinion was a short, rotund drummer.

"I said this war is all but over now, only nobody else in here seems to agree with me," the salesman said. "I was just wondering what you thought about it, and if you would share your opinion with us."

"I haven't given it much thought," Win answered. "Therefore I don't have an opinion."

"But, surely you do, sir! How can you not have an opinion on such an important issue?"

"In a place like Missouri where you have folks on both sides of the issue, it is sometimes best not to have opinions on the war," Win answered. "Or at least, to keep one's opinion to oneself."

"That's where you are wrong, sir. We all have a constitutional right . . . no . . . make that an obligation, to make our opinions known. And, I'll tell you mine."

"I'm sure you will," a rugged-looking man in a sheepskin coat and fur collar said. Earlier, he had identified himself as Mason Sanders. The two other passengers, the pretty woman and the uniformed Union officer, laughed.

The drummer leaned forward, confidentially, as if sharing a war secret with the others. "You may joke about it if you wish, Mr. Sanders," the drummer said to the big man. "But I was in the St. Louis office last week and I saw dispatches that clearly showed that the Federal troops are now pushin' the Secesh all over the place. Why, at Antietam a couple of months ago, we killed Rebs by the thousands. And that's not even countin' what we did to them at Shiloh.''

"I was at Shiloh," the Union officer put in. "And I have to say, in all candor, that the Rebels did as much to us as we did to them. We lost a great many men there, and when it was all over, not a thing had been accomplished.''

"You'll excuse me for saying so, Lieutenant, but you were probably too close to everything to know the end result. You, no doubt, saw several of your friends killed and as a result you became . . . disheartened,'' the salesman said. "But believe me, Shiloh, like Antietam, was an overwhelming victory for the Union.''

"If you say so," the lieutenant said. By way of dismissing the drummer, the lieutenant looked out the window and, like Win, began contemplating the falling snow.

When the drummer realized that he would not be able to sustain a conversation on the war in general, or military tactics in particular, he fell into a sullen silence.

An hour later, the coach stopped at a way station to change teams and to afford the passengers an opportunity to stretch their legs. Win left the stage, then walked over to lean against the corral fence to watch as the old team was unhitched. As he stood there, the young Union lieutenant came over to speak to him.

"Too bad they don't have a railroad through here," the lieutenant said. "It would make our trip a lot easier.''

"Yes, I suppose it would," Win replied. He was glad the officer had opened the conversation, because his reason for being on the coach in the first place was to determine if the payroll was being shipped. If so, surely this officer would know.

"Metzger is the name. Lieutenant Lee Metzger.''

"John Parker," Win replied, using the alias he had chosen for himself.

"Mr. Parker, what brings you out on a day like this?" Lieutenant Metzger asked. "What I mean is, it's not exactly the best kind of weather to travel in."

"I reckon not," Win agreed, easily. "But my brother and I own a small farm near Kansas City. I went to Raytown to see if we could get a contract furnishing pork to the army."

"Yes," Metzger said. "Well, I suppose that while most of us are in uniform, a few have to continue doing business as usual."

"You have something against the army eating? Or just farmers making a profit?"

"No, nothing like that," the lieutenant apologized quickly. "I was making an observation, not an accusation. I meant no insult."

"No insult taken," Win said.

The new team was brought out at that moment. They were anxious to get going, and they tossed their heads and breathed clouds of vapor into the cold air. One man held the reins, while two others ran alongside to keep the team together.

"What about you, Lieutenant?" Win asked, as he watched the horses brought out. He feigned indifference to his question, though the answer was very important to him. "What are you doing riding a civilian stagecoach?"

"I am the payroll officer for the Fifteenth Missouri Infantry," the lieutenant said. "This coach is carrying the payroll, and it is my duty to accompany the money."

Win smiled at how freely the information had been provided. "Payroll, huh? Well, the army must have a lot of confidence in you to charge you with such a responsibility."

"Yes, I suppose they do," Metzger said, obviously pleased by Win's flattery.

"Henry, you want to check the right foreleg on that off-lead horse?" the driver suddenly called out to the hostler as the new team approached the coach. "Damn if it don't look like he has thrown a shoe."

Henry stopped the team, then squirted a steam of tobacco juice between his teeth, leaving a brown smear atop the snow. He nodded to one of his employees who had been running alongside the team, "Check it out, will you, Pete?" he asked.

Pete, who was near the off-lead horse stepped up to the animal, then lifted his right foreleg. He examined the horse's hoof, then he called back to Henry.

"The shoe's gone, all right," he said.

"Damn!" Henry swore. "When did that happen? We don't have another horse ready to go. I'm afraid we're going to have to re-shoe this one."

The driver sighed in frustration, then looked at his passengers, four of whom had already left the coach. "All right, folks, you may as well all go on inside and get yourselves out of the cold. Looks like we're goin' to be here for a while."

The woman had been the only passenger to remain in the coach, but now she, too, started to get out.

"Looks like no one is going to help the lady down," Win said. "Excuse me, Lieutenant Metzger, I'll go offer my services."

"You call her a lady?" the drummer said with a smirking laugh. "Hell, that's no lady, mister. Didn't you hear 'em talkin' back in Raytown? The only reason she's comin' to Kansas City in the first place is because the army run her out of Raytown. She's a whore."

Win glared at the drummer.

"I'm only sayin' what's true," the drummer defended. He looked quickly toward the Yankee lieutenant for confirmation.

"I'm afraid he is right," Metzger agreed. "I was told, myself, to keep an eye on her to make sure she didn't get off the stage before it reached Kansas City."

"That may be so, but right now she's a lady trying to get down from the coach in slippery snow," Win tossed back over his shoulder. "And I'm going to help her."

Win was at the side of the coach by the time the woman was ready to step down. He offered his hand and, with a charming smile, she accepted it.

"Why, thank you," she said, a little surprised by the offer.

"Let me walk you into the building. Otherwise, you might slip and fall in the snow."

"Aren't you the gentleman, though?" the woman declared, sticking her arm through Win's. She pulled a fur stole about her as they started toward the building.

"You can put a silk dress and fur stole on a whore, but she is still a whore," Sanders said, as they passed him by.

Win had his pistol out in a flash. He cocked it, then held it less than six inches from the big man's face.

"No, no!" the woman said, quickly. "Don't shoot him! He's . . . he's only telling the truth."

"Ma'am, there's a difference between fact and truth," Win said. "The fact is, you might be a whore. But the truth is, you're still a lady. And any lady who happens to be on my arm shall enjoy my protection."

The woman smiled broadly. "Well, then, it would be most ungracious of me to refuse your protection, wouldn't it? But, please don't shoot him."

Win turned his attention back to the big man. "The lady doesn't want me to shoot you, so maybe you would like to apologize to her before my thumb gets tired of holding the hammer back.''

''I . . . apologize,'' the big man said.

''I thought you might.'' Win eased the hammer down, then put the pistol back in his holster. There was a collective sigh of relief from the others who had stopped all activity to see how the moment was going to play.

Win escorted the woman into the way station and they walked over to warm themselves in front of the fireplace.

''By the way, my name is Belle Amberly,'' the woman said. Then she laughed. ''Well, I'll admit, it's not the name I was born with, but it is the name I use now because I wouldn't want to get back to the folks in Kentucky what I do for a living. I don't expect you to understand such a thing, Mr. Parker. I mean using a name other than the one you own.''

Win chuckled. ''Perhaps I understand better than you think,'' he said.

The other passengers came into the way station then, and Win noticed that they all stayed together on the opposite side of the room. Even the drummer, whose chatter had been barely tolerated in the coach, now seemed to be preferable company to the others, than that of Win or Belle.

''When I get . . . settled . . . in the Kansas City area,'' Belle said, ''you'll have to come see me.''

''I might just do that,'' Win agreed.

''All right, folks, we're all ready to go now,'' the driver said a few minutes later, coming into the room and stomping his feet to get rid of the snow. ''Should warn you, though. It's goin' to be some jarrin' once we get started. . . . I've got a little time to make up and I'm goin' to be pushin' the team pretty hard.''

• • •

THEY HAD BEEN UNDER WAY FOR THE BETTER PART OF AN hour when, from outside the coach, a pistol shot brought them to a sliding halt.

"What is it? What's going on?" the drummer asked in a frightened voice.

"I'm afraid it is a . . ." the lieutenant started, but the man in the sheepskin coat finished the sentence for him.

"A holdup," Sanders said. He smiled at the other passengers, and that was when Win noticed that he was holding a pistol. He pointed his pistol at Win. "Now, Mr. Parker was it? How does it feel to have a gun sticking in your face?" he asked.

Win looked outside the coach. He knew that Quantrill and the others were supposed to hold it up, but this wasn't where they had agreed to be. And, as he saw the men outside, he realized that he didn't know any of them. Ironically, someone else was robbing the coach before Quantrill could get to it.

"I'll trouble you for your pistol," the robber in the coach said, looking at Win. "You too, Lieutenant."

Win took his pistol out from beneath his coat and handed it over. Lieutenant Metzger pulled his pistol from his holster.

"You won't get away with this," Metzger said.

The big man smiled. "Hell, Lieutenant, I already have. Now, everyone outside."

When Win and the other passengers stepped down from the coach, they saw at least half a dozen riders, all of whom were holding pistols. None wore masks, though their faces were wreathed in the little clouds of vapor that issued from their mouths and noses.

"Driver, you want to throw down that there strongbox you're a'carryin'?" one of the riders called up.

Win noticed, then, that most of the riders were wearing the blue coats of the Union army.

"Here, wait a minute!" Lieutenant Metzger called to them. "You men are all wearing blue. I think you should know that this is a U.S. Army payroll! You're taking money away from your own fellow soldiers."

"Hell, they ain't our fellow soldiers no more, Lieutenant," the big man said sarcastically. He opened his sheepskin coat so his own blue uniform jacket could be seen. On each of his sleeves were the three stripes of a sergeant. "We've already given up on the army."

Metzger glared at them. "You, a noncommissioned officer, would join up with these deserters?" he asked in disbelief. "I am absolutely shocked."

"Don't be so shocked," Sanders said. He pointed toward the stripes. "Truth is, I got busted a few weeks ago, only I just ain't got aroun' to takin' off the stripes." He laughed. "So you see, in a way, this here money does belong to me and the others, after all."

The strongbox was on the ground now, and two of the riders dismounted to open it. One of them fired his pistol at the lock, but missed. The other fired and missed as well.

"You dumb shits couldn't hit a bull in the ass with a spade," Sanders said. He aimed and, with one shot, knocked the lock off.

The two men on the ground put their pistols away, and knelt by the box to examine the contents. The four other deserter-robbers, who were still mounted, were looking on in great interest, and even Sanders momentarily diverted his attention at the sight of the money.

Win knew that if he was going to save the payroll for Quantrill, now was his chance. What the big man didn't realize was that Win had surrendered only one of the two pistols he was carrying. Like all of Quantrill's riders, Win carried two pistols, and the second one was concealed by his coat. Without a moment's further delay or consideration, Win pulled his spare pistol and shot Sanders. The big man was Win's first target because he was on the ground, holding a pistol in his hand, and had already demonstrated his marksmanship.

"What the hell?" one of the riders shouted in quick surprise. He swung his pistol toward Win but Win had already turned his attention toward him, and Win shot first.

Lieutenant Metzger's own reaction had been surprisingly fast and, almost instantly, he bent over to grab the pistol the big man had been carrying. He turned it on the two men who had just opened the strongbox, and pulled the trigger. One of them went down, but the other fired back, just as Metzger was firing, and Metzger went down as well. Win dropped that robber with his next shot.

"Come on! Let's get the hell out of here!" one of the three remaining robbers shouted, slapping his legs against the sides of his horse. The other two went with him, and what had started out as a robbery, wound up as panic-stricken flight by the three who were still alive.

"You did it!" Belle shouted in excitement. "You ran them off!"

"How's the lieutenant?" Win asked.

"He's dead," the drummer replied. The salesman had knelt beside the young lieutenant and was now holding his hand over the lieutenant's heart.

"What are we going to do with him?" the driver asked, nodding toward the dead officer.

"I'll help you lift him. We'll put him up on top of the coach. When you get to Kansas City, give him to the army. They'll know what to do with him."

"Wait a minute!" the drummer protested. "You're going to put this man's body on top of the coach?"

"Yes."

"The same coach we are riding in?"

"Yes."

The drummer shook his head. "I'm not riding on any coach with a dead man."

"That's all right," Win replied easily. "You can wait here. I'm sure the driver will be willing to pick you up when he comes through the next time."

"Be glad to," the driver said with a chuckle, as he reached for the strongbox.

"No, no, I'll ride with you," the drummer said, quickly.

"Thought you might change your mind," the driver said.

"Maybe you'd better give that strongbox to me," Win suggested. "I'll carry it inside."

"All right. That's probably a good idea," the driver agreed without question.

A few minutes later, with the four dead would-be robbers lying in a row alongside the road, with a note explaining what happened to them, and with the dead lieutenant on top of the coach, the driver snapped his whip at the team and they got under way.

"Poor Lieutenant Metzger," Belle said. "To have fought in all the battles he has fought in, then be killed by robbers. And to think it was by his own soldiers."

"They weren't soldiers," the drummer said.

"They weren't?" Belle asked.

The drummer shook his head, confidently. "No. They just wanted us to think that they were soldiers. Union soldiers at that."

"Who were they?"

"Isn't it obvious to you? They were Quantrill's men, of course," the drummer said.

Win smiled. "Not much gets by you, does it?" he asked with a touch of sarcasm that the drummer didn't notice.

"Well, when you've travelled as much as I have, you get to where you know your people pretty well," the drummer bragged.

"I'll bet someone as smart as you even knows that I am a Pinkerton agent," Win said.

"I knew it!" the drummer said, excitedly. "The moment you got on the coach I said to myself, 'That man is a Pinkerton agent.' "

"Well, I'm glad you didn't give me away in front of the robber those men had planted on the stage," Win said.

"Oh, you needn't have worried. I figured you were here to protect the payroll."

"You knew about the payroll as well?"

"Of course," the drummer said. He pointed to his own eyes. "Not much gets by these eyes, I'll tell you. But I have learned to be pretty quiet."

Looking out the window of the coach Win saw that they were approaching the spot where he had arranged to have a horse waiting for him. By plan, he was supposed to do nothing but leave the coach right now. But circumstances had changed and Win, ever resourceful, took advantage of the newly presented opportunity. Now he reached down to the strongbox, and started putting the money in his pockets. When he had all the money extracted, he tossed the empty strongbox out the window. It hit in the road beside the stage, bounced once, then disappeared into a snowbank.

"Why, I'll just bet I don't even have to explain to you why I'm leaving the stage now, or why I'm taking the money with me."

"No, sir, not at all," the drummer said. "I agree, there has already been one attempt made to rob this stage. It is probably a very good idea to hide it on your person."

With the newly acquired money securely in his pockets,

Win tapped on the side of the coach and yelled up at the driver.

"Let me off here!" he shouted.

The driver called to his team and stood on the wheel brakes. The coach jerked and slid to a halt. When it was completely stopped, Win opened the door, then stepped outside.

From his position on the ground, he looked back inside the coach at Belle and saw, by the hint of a smile on her lips that she wasn't being fooled for a moment.

"And you, Miss Amberly," Win said. "I have a feeling you know all of my secrets as well."

"I . . . do have my suspicions," Belle said, smiling broadly.

"Perhaps I'll stop by and see you sometime," Win suggested. "I think we could do a little business together."

"Do stop by, Mr. Parker," Belle replied, her eyebrows raised provocatively. "But with you, it won't be business."

LESS THAN FIFTEEN MINUTES AFTER WIN LEFT THE STAGE, he met Quantrill and the others.

"So, what's the word?" Quantrill asked anxiously. "Are they carrying the payroll?"

"No," Win replied. "There is no money on the stage."

"Damn! I was certain my information was correct," Quantrill said in a frustrated voice.

"Oh, your information was correct, all right," Win said. "When we left Raytown the payroll was on the stage, just as Todd said it would be."

"Look here. Are you saying the money was on the stage when it left, but it's not there now? Where is it?"

Win smiled, then pulled out one of the packets of money. "It's right here," he said.

Quantrill laughed at the unexpected turn of events, and

he took one of the packets of money and examined it closely.

"Mr. Coulter," he said. "In case no one has ever told you this, you are becoming one fine guerrilla fighter."

"Why, thank you, Mr. Quantrill," Win replied.

8

TRUE TO HIS WORD, QUANTRILL HELD A "PAYDAY" USING the money Win took from the stage. After everyone was paid, he announced that he was suspending operations for the rest of the winter.

"I'm tired of the cold weather, so I'm goin' down into Texas," he said. "Any of you that wants to go with me are welcome. The rest of you are on your own 'til next spring, when I come back. You can go back to your families and get the crops in, or just lie around and get fat. It doesn't matter to me. Goodbye and good luck."

With no further announcement, Quantrill walked over to his horse, mounted, and rode off.

For several moments afterward, the men stood around just looking at each other, as if unsure of what had just happened. Then someone said, "I don't know 'bout the rest of you boys, but I'm goin' with 'im. I always had a hankerin' to see Texas."

"Not me. I'm goin' into the first town I can find and spend me some of this money."

"I'm goin' back to the farm," another said. Their movement energized the others so that, within less than five minutes, what had been an active camp of over one hundred Rebel guerrillas became an empty field, marked by horse droppings and blackened fire-rings.

IT WAS MID-AFTERNOON WHEN WIN AND JOE REACHED THE Coulter farm. They crested the hill on the road that led up to the place, then rode sadly down to where the house, barn, and outbuildings had been. There had been no effort made to clean up any of the rubble, so that burnt boards and charred bricks made ugly black scars in the snow.

"We're goin' to have to get us a plough and a team of good mules," Joe said.

"Then, come spring, we'll need to get some seed," Win added.

"What'll we put in? Corn? Wheat?" Joe asked.

"I reckon," Win said. He sighed, then ran his hand through his hair.

"How we goin' to get our crop out? We'll prob'ly be ridin' with Quantrill again."

"I don't know," Win admitted. They were silent for a moment.

"Joe," Win started, but whatever question he was going to ask died on his lips.

"What is it?"

"Do you really want to do this?"

"No, not really," Joe said. He took in the burned-out farm with a sweep of his hand. "It reminds me too much of ma and pa."

"Then, if you don't want to do it, and I don't want to do it, let's don't do it."

"If we don't do this, then what will we do?"

"Why don't we go to Texas?"

"Sounds like a good idea to me."

"I have another good idea," Win said. "Before we go,

let's take a day or so off to see some friends.''

"Friends?" Joe said. "Win, what friends do we have to see? We ain't got no friends."

"Oh?" Win asked with raised eyebrows. "You mean you don't consider Maggie Depro a friend?"

"Oh!" Joe said, now seeing the light. "You mean *that* kind of friend?"

"Yes," Win said. "That kind of friend."

"Well, then, what are we waiting around here for?" Joe asked.

To see Maggie, Joe had to go to Independence, while the woman Win wanted to see was in Kansas City. Making arrangements to meet at Blue Springs the following afternoon, the two split up to go their separate ways.

Win reached Kansas City just after dark. False-fronted shanties and a few substantial two-story buildings competed for space along both sides of the street. Subdued bubbles of soft light shined from the windows of houses that sat back off the street at the edge of town, while further down into town, half a dozen saloons spilled bright golden light onto the boardwalks. The street was alive with the cacophonous symphony of six pianos and two dozen lusty voices. Win could hear a man's hoarse guffaw and a woman's high-pitched cackle. Someone broke a glass somewhere and the crashing, tinkling sound was supreme for a moment.

There was also the sound of hollow hoofbeats on the street as Win rode between the buildings. He passed in and out of light and shadow so that his face was now glowing, now dark. Two Yankee soldiers came out of a saloon and, at the sound of his horse, looked up at him.

"Hey, you!" one of them shouted at Win.

Had he been recognized as a rider for Quantrill? Slowly, Win moved his hand to hover over his holster. He tensed his muscles, ready to shoot his way out of here if need be.

"If you plannin' on gettin' 'nything to drink in there, you can forget it," the soldier yelled. "Me an' Jimmy here has done drunk it all up!"

Both soldiers laughed at the declaration, then they started toward another saloon just a few buildings away, so drunk that they could barely stay on the boardwalk, their boots clumping loudly and awkwardly on the boards.

Win stopped in front of the saloon, got off his horse and tied it to the hitching rail, then went inside.

The Missouri House was one of the more substantial buildings on the street. A gilt-edged mirror hung on the wall above a long, handsomely carved bar. Several large jars of pickled eggs and sausages provided snacks for the customers, and towels, tied to rings every few feet on the customers' side of the bar, provided the patrons with a means of wiping their hands. Behind the bar was a big sign which read: "This is an honest gambling establishment. Please report any cheating to the management."

There were about two dozen people in the saloon. Most of them were alone, or in pairs, but one table had six soldiers playing poker. These soldiers, like the two who had left earlier, were all drunk on cheap whiskey. A cloud of noxious smoke hovered overhead.

One of the soldiers won a hand, and he let out a happy whoop, then got up and started doing a little dance. He got his feet tangled together and fell flat on his back. The others around the table laughed heartily, and Win chuckled with them, then turned back to the bar.

"What can I do for you, mister?" the man behind the bar asked.

"A shot of whiskey," Win said.

"Bartender, that whiskey's on me," someone called. When Win looked down toward the end of the bar to see who his benefactor was, he saw a man in the uniform of a U.S. Army sergeant.

The shot glass was put in front of Win and he picked it up, then held it out toward the sergeant in a salute before he tossed it down.

"Another one," Win said. "And this time, give the sergeant what he is having."

The sergeant moved down the bar toward Win. "I've seen you before, haven't I?" the sergeant asked.

"Could be," Win answered. "I've been around here all my life."

"Not me. I'm from Ohio," the sergeant said, killing his own shot of whiskey. "By God, I don't know how you people stand this place. As far as I'm concerned, the goddamned Rebels can have the goddamned state. Or you can give it back to the Indians, I don't care, one way or the other." He studied Win more closely. "You sure we ain't never met?"

"Like I said, we could have," Win said. "But I don't recall meeting you."

Win was beginning to get uncomfortable now. There was really only one place this sergeant could've seen him, and that was during one of the engagements between Quantrill and the army. And, if the sergeant ever put that together, it could spell trouble.

"You're not in the army, are you?"

"No."

"Militia?"

"No."

"Mister, how the hell can you be in a place like this, and not be in the army or the militia? Unless you're a Rebel?"

"Listen, Sergeant, it's been nice talking to you," Win

said. "And thanks for the drink." Win started toward the door, but the sergeant called to him.

"I will remember," he said. "It might take a while, but it'll come to me."

Win went to two more saloons before he found what he was looking for. Actually, he didn't find it at all. It found him.

"Your name John Parker?" a man asked.

For just a moment, Win was puzzled, then he remembered that John Parker was the name he used when he was riding the stage with the payroll.

"Yes," Win said. "I'm John Parker."

"Belle told me to give this to you," the man said, handing Win an envelope.

Win gave the man a quarter, then opened the envelope to read the letter:

Mr. Parker,

I saw you ride into town and took the liberty of writing you this note. I do hope you remember me. We recently shared quite an adventure during a stagecoach ride. If you are interested in seeing me, I have a very small house in the alley behind the hardware store.

Your friend,
Belle

Win finished his drink, then stepped outside and walked down to the alley opening. There were very few windows in the back of the buildings, and all but one of those that opened onto the alley were dark. There was a full moon out, however, and it reflected brightly off the few remaining snowdrifts from the last snow. That helped show Win the way. He moved toward a golden glow of light that shined from the little house behind the hardware store. When he stepped up onto the porch, the door opened at the first footfall.

"Good evening, Mr. John Parker," Belle greeted from just inside the house. She smiled, then stepped back away from the door. When she greeted him, her voice had the same low husky quality he remembered from their meeting on the coach. Even then there had been promise in the voice, but very little chance to deliver on that promise. Now, the opportunity was there.

This opportunity was not marked by preliminaries, courtship, or sexual teasing. Instead, the moment Win was inside, Belle met him with a kiss. She pressed her body hard against his, then opened her mouth hungrily to seek out his tongue. Win's arms wound around her tightly and he felt the heat of her body transferring itself to him. His blood felt as if it had changed to hot brandy as she ground her pelvis against his huge erection.

Belle stepped away from him for a moment. She was wearing a simple housedress which she quickly pulled over her head. Because she had on nothing beneath the dress, this action exposed her nudity to him. Her perfectly formed body was golden in the soft light of the dim lantern.

Belle got down on her knees in front of Win, then looked up at him. Her eyes glowed so brightly that Win could almost believe they were lighted by some inner fire. She put her fingers on the bulge in front of Win's pants, then began opening the buttons. A second later Win felt his organ free as she pulled it out.

Belle gasped, then chuckled as she looked at it. "My God," she said. "How can you carry something that size around?"

"I manage," Win replied.

"I want you to know," Belle said, as she reached up to wrap her hands around it, "that I don't do this for just anyone."

Belle was close to the head of it now, and as she spoke her warm breath moved across the skin like the most delicate silk. Her tongue slipped out from between her rose-red lips.

Win put his hands down to her head and gently moved her to him. Her lips opened to take him. As she worked on him with her mouth, his hands moved down to her distended nipples, causing her breasts to ignite fires of desire that swept through her body.

Win tried gently to push her away so he could get undressed, but she protested and reached for him again.

"No," she said. "Let me do this for you. I want it this way."

Win rocked back on his heels and shuddered, then he put his hands in her hair and held her as he exploded. Finally, long moments after the last tremors were gone, Belle stood up and started for the living room of her small house. She stopped and looked back over her naked shoulder.

"Oh," she said. "Where are my manners? Won't you please come in?"

WIN WAS FINISHING HIS GLASS OF CHAMPAGNE AND WAS a quarter of the way through his cigar.

"Those men who tried to rob the stagecoach, they weren't really Quantrill's men, were they?" Belle asked.

"Why ask me?" Win asked, examining the tip of his cigar.

Belle smiled at him. "Who better to ask than Win Coulter?"

Win looked at her in surprise, then he smiled. "I see that you know my real name."

"I also know that you ride with Quantrill," Belle said.

"What makes you think that?"

"I've heard that. Is it true?"

"You don't see me with him now, do you?"

"No, and you weren't with him when you robbed the stage," Belle said. She poured him another glass of champagne. "But I believe Quantrill got the money."

Win laughed. "He didn't get all of it. I got some," he said, sharing with her information that he had shared only with his brother. He had held back one thousand dollars.

"I knew it. Even before I knew your real name, I knew you were with him. But what are you doing here, in Kansas City? Are you about to make another raid?"

"No," Win said, shaking his head. "Quantrill and most of the others have gone to Texas for the winter. He won't be around for a while."

"You should've gone with him."

"You mean, you don't want me here?" Win asked.

"I do want you here. But it would be safer for you to go. I wouldn't want to see you hurt or killed."

"Maybe I am planning to go," Win said. "But I didn't want to leave until I told you goodbye."

"Oh, that's sweet."

"What I need now, though, is a safe place to spend the night. Do you have any suggestions?"

"Oh," Belle said, running her fingers through Win's hair. "I think you'll find that I have more suggestions than you'll ever be able to handle."

9

THE NEXT MORNING WIN WAS SITTING AT THE TABLE IN Belle's small apartment, enjoying a breakfast of fried potatoes and eggs, when he heard a series of gunshots. This wasn't one or two shots, this was a small war, and Win was on his feet in an instant with his revolver in his hand.

"What is it?" Belle asked anxiously.

"I don't know," Win replied as he started outside. "But I plan to find out."

Win ran down the alley, staying close to the side of the hardware store. When he reached the front of the building, he stopped and looked out toward a gathering crowd. What he saw, and what had gathered the crowd, was two men lying in a pool of their own blood in the middle of the street. On the far side of the street a soldier, in uniform, was lying facedown on the boardwalk. Farther up on the boardwalk, two more soldiers were dead, one sprawled on his back, the second sitting down, leaning against the wall of the apothecary, his gun still in his hand. These were the two drunk soldiers Win had seen come from the saloon the night before. A fourth soldier was a couple of buildings down the street, draped across a hitching rail.

Nearly a dozen people were crowded around the two men in the middle of the street so Win wasn't able to get a good look. He moved out for a closer examination. Because many were standing around with their guns drawn, Win felt no need to replace his own pistol. When he got close enough to them, he recognized them as being a couple of Quantrill's riders. Both were married, and had decided to winter in Missouri to put in crops next spring.

"I seen who they was the moment they come out of the farmers' supply store over there," a sergeant said, standing over the two dead Raiders. This was the same curious sergeant Win had encountered last night.

"That's Abner Calley and his brother," someone said. Win recognized the speaker as the same man who had given him the note from Belle. "They're a couple of farmers that live about five miles out of town."

"Maybe they was farmers before the war started," the sergeant said. "But what they been doin' is ridin' with Quantrill."

"If that's so, what was they doin' in town by themselves?"

"Probably gettin' ready to come in and sack the town," the sergeant said. "I seen another one last night in the saloon. Didn't come to me who he was 'til sometime later. If I see him today, he'll be just like these two."

"Or, you might wind up like your soldier boys over there," someone said. "Looks to me like Abner and his brother give a pretty good accounting for themselves."

Several of the others laughed.

"I know you Rebel bastards are probably happy to see a few boys in blue lyin' dead in the street," the sergeant said. "But just remember. We control Kansas City. And as long as we're in control around here, this is what's goin' to happen to ever' Rebel I see.'' He pointed to the two dead guerrillas.

Not wanting to take a chance on having the sergeant see him, Win moved cautiously through the crowd to the livery stable where his horse had been put up for the night. A few coins to the stablehand brought his horse out to him and, a minute later, he was saddled and ready to go. He rode out the back door, avoiding the crowded streets and another encounter with the curious sergeant.

JOE HAD HIS OWN STORY TO TELL. ONE OF QUANTRILL'S riders had been a native of Independence. When he went home to visit his family, he was recognized. Unlike the Calley brothers, however, he didn't get a chance to have a gun battle with the Yankees. Instead, he was taken to the edge of town and summarily hung from an elm tree.

"I'll be truthful with you, big brother,'' Joe admitted. "I'm just as glad I got out of there when I did.''

There were two men waiting for the ferry at the Osage River. Win and Joe approached them warily, then a broad smile broke out on Joe's face.

"Why, that's a couple of our boys,'' Joe said. "The tall one is Tate McGee, the one with the beard is Ethan Kelly.''

"So it is,'' Win said, "so it is.''

The four men had a friendly reunion.

"I thought you boys were goin' home,'' Tate McGee said.

"We changed our mind,'' Joe said. "What about you?''

"Well, we sorta got our minds changed for us,'' Tate explained.

"We was picked up an' put in jail,'' Ethan Kelly added. "We busted out last night, only we wasn't able to get our guns.''

Tate chuckled. "We ain't got nothin' but a pocketknife betwixt us."

"We was some glad you was friendly when you come up," Ethan said.

"I'll just bet you were," Joe said, laughing.

"So, tell me, you boys goin' down to Texas?" Tate asked.

"Thought we might," Win replied.

"Wonder if you'd mind if we rode along with you, so's we'd at least have your guns?"

"Sure, we don't mind," Win said. "But we'd all be better off if you had weapons too, don't you think?"

"I'll go along with that. You got 'ny idea where we might get some?" Tate asked.

"The best place to get a gun is to go where the guns are," Win answered. "What we need is to find us a Yankee militia outfit somewhere. Then we'll hit their armory."

WEST PLAINS, MISSOURI, FILLED THE BILL. IT HAD A COM-pany of militia that was loyal to the Union and a large armory located out on the edge of town. It was well after midnight when the boys arrived, and not one light shone from any of the buildings along the sides of West Plain's single street. A sign on the outside of the large white build-ing read: *140th Missouri Militia, U.S. Army.*

"Yankees," Win said. "All right, boys, this is what we want."

The armory doors were padlocked and the windows barred, but there were no guards standing by the doors. The boys tied their horses to a stand of poplar trees near the northwest corner of the armory.

Somewhere in surrounding woods, an owl hooted and it was answered by a dog in town. Atop the armory, a weather vane squeaked as it turned with a freshening breeze.

"Ethan, take a look all the way around the building to see if anyone is here," Win ordered, and neither Ethan, nor anyone else, questioned the fact that Win had just assumed command. It was as if it was expected of him.

Ethan started around the building, running swiftly in a low crouch, darting from shadow to shadow. In this way, he went all the way around the building, returning a couple of minutes later.

"I didn't see a soul," he reported.

Win smiled. "All right, boys, what do you say we help ourselves?"

Joe took an iron tent peg from his saddlebag, then put it through the hasp of the lock. With his great strength he was able to break it open with one jerk. After that, it was just a matter of opening the door and walking inside.

Win found a lantern and lit it, then let out a low whistle. The armory was full of all kinds of weapons, from pikes to artillery pieces. There were scores of rifles and pistols of every size and caliber.

"Look at this, boys, look at this!" Tate said. He began going through the pistols, hefting several different ones to test their balance and feel until he found one that suited him.

Ethan also found a pistol to strap on, then all four started looking around for additional weapons to give them an edge.

"Holy shit, look at all these guns! There's enough to fight a war!" Joe said.

Win laughed.

"What's so funny?"

"Goddamn, little brother," Win said. "What the hell do you think they're doin'?"

"Yeah, I guess you're right," Joe agreed sheepishly.

"Come on, boys, let's fill up a few bags with ammunition, then get the hell out of here,'' Win suggested.

''What about lookin' around for some food?'' Joe asked.

''I don't want to take the time. We've been here too long now. If anyone saw the lantern we lit, they'll be on us soon, like stink on shit.''

''Come on, Win, ain't nobody even awake,'' Joe pleaded.

Win looked all around the building, searching the shadows. ''All right,'' he agreed. ''We'll see what they've got. But, Joe, you get back outside and keep an eye open for us.''

''All right, Win. But, if they got 'ny canned peaches, be sure'n get some, all right?''

''If they got any,'' Win promised.

Win, Tate, and Ethan started filling up a burlap bag with tins of food while Joe waited with the horses outside. After a few moments, Win whispered harshly to the others.

''All right! We've got what we need! Let's go!''

Joe led the horses over to the door, and they were just throwing the bags across the saddles when someone called out from the darkness.

''All right, you Reb bastards, jus' throw your hands up, right where you stand!''

Win heard half a dozen metallic clicks as rifles were cocked in the shadows.

''Get ready, boys,'' Win whispered. He put his hands up, then called out loudly, ''Who's there?''

In the pale moonlight, shapes began materializing from the trees, and a moment later Win saw a Yankee sergeant with six soldiers. The sergeant was about six feet two, with a long brown beard, and he was holding a pistol pointed at the boys. The soldiers with him were holding rifles.

''I seen your lantern,'' the sergeant said. ''So I got me a squad together and come on down here to see what was goin' on.'' The sergeant squirted a brown stream of tobacco juice, then wiped his chin. "I reckon when my cap'n sees the bodies of you four Secesh in the mornin', me an' all the boys here'll be gettin' a little reward. On my order, boys,'' the sergeant said to his squad.

The soldiers started to raise their rifles.

"Now!'' Win shouted, and his pistol was in his hand as fast as his shout. He shot the sergeant first, hitting him right between the eyes. The sergeant died with the evil smile still on his face, never even realizing that he was in danger.

The soldiers fired, but just as Win had figured, they were surprised and frightened, and hurried their shots so that not one of the bullets struck flesh. The soldiers didn't get a chance for a second shot because Win and the others cut them down in a blaze of gunfire.

Thick gun smoke formed a billowing cloud, then drifted away from the scene as the echoes of the shots rolled back from a distant stand of trees. A nearby dog began to bark and a dozen others in the town took up the chorus.

"What was that?'' a voice shouted from the back of one of the houses.

"It came from the armory!'' someone answered.

"Let's get the hell out of here!'' Win growled, thrusting his smoking pistol into his holster.

The four men mounted, then Win yelled at them, "Pull your guns and shoot up the town as we ride through! We're goin' to make these folks think all the demons from hell are comin' through!''

"Demons from hell? Well, shit, that's what we are, ain't we?'' Joe asked with a laugh.

Not bothering to look back at the seven bodies their carnage had left dead, the four men slapped their legs against the sides of their animals. The horses bolted forward, then galloped down the main street of the town, followed by half a dozen barking dogs which ran and nipped at the pounding hooves of the running horses.

"Yahoo!" Win shouted, and he was joined by all the others as they gave the Rebel yell. Win fired at the windows and doors of the buildings to discourage anyone who might have an idea of ambushing. The exit was so terrifying that not one shot was fired in return.

They rode out of town at a full gallop, pushing their horses hard. When they had gone about a mile, they turned in their saddles and looked back.

Not one person was making an effort to follow them.

"Son of a bitch!" Tate shouted enthusiastically. "That was a hoot!"

"Did you see anyone stick their heads up?" Joe asked. " 'Cause I sure's hell didn't."

Ethan was strangely quiet.

"What is it, Ethan?" Win asked. "Were you hit?"

"No."

"Then what is it? What's wrong?"

"The soldiers back there? The ones we killed?"

"Yeah?"

Ethan ran his hand through his hair. "I been ridin' with you boys for a couple of months now," he said. "But, back there was the first time I ever kilt anyone. Leastwise, anyone that I actually saw. I have to tell you, I don't feel none too good about it."

"*We* killed them," Win said. "Not you."

"I kilt one of 'em myself," Ethan said. He stopped, then dismounted and stepped over beside a bush where he began to throw up.

Win, Joe, and Tate waited silently, and without censure.

Finally, Ethan finished retching, then he climbed back into his saddle.

"I'm sorry about that," he apologized to the others.

"Didn't mean to be such a baby about it. It's just that, well . . ." He couldn't finish his sentence.

"No need to apologize, Ethan," Win said easily. "I reckon we've all been through it."

"Does it ever get easier?"

The others were silent for a long moment, then Win answered for them.

"Yeah," he finally said. "I wish to God it wasn't so, but the more you kill, the easier it gets."

10

WELL-ARMED NOW, THE FOUR MEN PUSHED HARD ACROSS Arkansas and down into Texas. One week later they found themselves in Brushy Creek, a small Texas town that consisted of little more than a two block long main street with flyblown unpainted frame houses on either side. They stopped to stable the horses and to give them oats and a rubdown, then they walked across the street to the only saloon, where they had supper and a few drinks.

Supper was steak and beans, which were liberally seasoned with hot peppers and washed down with mugs of beer.

"Them beans'll flat set your mouth afire," Ethan said. "But, damn me, if they ain't about the tastiest things I've put in my mouth for a while."

Joe smiled at one of the bar girls, and she caught his smile and returned it. He pushed away from the table.

"Boys, I do believe I have a little business to take care of," he said, starting toward the girl.

The girl was a pretty redhead who, though she had been "on the line" for a while, had managed to retain her looks. Only in her eyes could one read the story of three years of going upstairs with men of all ages, sizes, and dispositions. Some treated her as if she were a queen, some were rude, and some were cruel. It was a risk every time she went up with a new man.

Joe smiled disarmingly at her. "You can trust me," his smile said, and the apprehension left the girl's eyes.

Shortly after Joe went upstairs with the bar girl, a man came into the saloon and stepped up to the bar. He stayed down at the far end where he could see the whole saloon, and he examined everyone through dark beady eyes. He was small and wiry, with a narrow nose and thin lips. He used his left hand to hold his glass while his right hand stayed down near the handle of his pistol.

Only Win had actually noticed the man, and he studied him quietly while he ate his supper. There was the look of sudden death about this man. He was a killer, as clearly as if he had been dressed in a black robe, carrying a headsman's axe, and wearing a death's mask.

The front door to the saloon opened a moment later, and two men came into the saloon. Both of them were wearing badges, and they stood just inside the entrance for a moment, looking around the room. One of them had eyes to match his gray hair and moustache. He was the sheriff. His deputy was much younger.

"Win," Kelly said uneasily. "It's the law."

"Easy, Ethan," Win said quietly. "Don't reckon they're after us."

Win watched the sheriff look around, then his gaze found the man at the bar. The lawman's muscles stiffened.

"Mister, was you at Dunnigan's General Store in Stedman yesterday?"

"I don't recall that I was."

"I got a telegram from the sheriff over there this mornin'. The man they described fits you pretty good," the sheriff said. "About your size, wearing clothes 'bout like them that you got on, and carryin' an Arkansas toothpick with a deer horn handle."

"Lots of men my size, lots of clothes like these, and lots of knives with deer horn handles."

"But you was there, wasn't you?" the sheriff asked. The sheriff looked over at his deputy, and the deputy took something out of his pocket and put it on a table. "I know you was, 'cause me 'n my deputy just took this sack of coffee outta your saddlebags. As you can see, it's marked right on the sack, 'Dunnigan's General Store, Stedman, Texas.' "

"Yeah, now that I recollect, I guess I did come through there yesterday afternoon," the man said. "I bought some coffee and some beans, too. Ain't no law against that, is there?"

"No law against that," the sheriff replied. "But there's a law against murderin' the storekeep and rapin' his wife."

There was a collective gasp from the others in the saloon.

"You got the wrong man. All I done was buy some coffee and beans."

"I might believe you, mister, if you woulda told me that in the first place. Now, I think I'd better hold you until we can get this straightened out."

"How you goin' to get it straightened out? If the storekeep and his wife are both dead, you got no witnesses."

"I didn't say anything about the wife bein' dead, did I?" the sheriff asked. "Oh, the fella that raped her, he stabbed her, but the blade missed all her vitals. The doc says she'll be all right, and she can identify the varmint who did it."

"I told you, it wasn't me."

"Then you won't have anything to worry about. Come on up to Stedman with us, let the woman have a look at you, and it'll all be over."

"I ain't goin' nowhere with you."

"Mister, you can come peaceable, or belly down across a saddle," the sheriff said. With those words, the others in the saloon began backing away, giving the belligerent room to operate.

The man put his drink on the bar, then turned toward the sheriff. The sheriff's deputy stepped several feet to one side then bent his knees, slightly, holding his hand in readiness over his own pistol.

"Well, now, I don't think you can force me to go where I don't want to go," the man at the bar said.

"You don't want this, mister," the sheriff said.

"Maybe I *do* want it."

Win watched the sheriff's eyes, the narrowing of the corners, the glint of the pupils, then the cold fear. Telegraphing his move, the sheriff made a desperate, awkward grab for his gun.

The man at the bar had his out first. By the time he had his pistol up, it was already spitting a six-inch finger of flame from the end of the barrel. It roared a second time, even over the shots fired by the sheriff and his deputy, and a large cloud of smoke billowed up to temporarily obscure the action. When the smoke drifted up to the ceiling a few seconds later, the sheriff and his deputy were both down, dead or dying on the floor.

Win heard footsteps running upstairs, and when he saw the gunman at the bar whip around, Win drew his own gun.

"Hold it!" Win called. He thumbed the hammer back and the deadly click of the sear on cylinders filled the room. He raised his pistol so that it was pointing at the man.

When the gunman looked over toward Win, he saw that Win had the drop on him.

"You plannin' to get in on this, mister?" the gunman asked.

"I had no such plans," Win replied. He nodded toward

the man at the top of the stairs. "But that fella standin' up there is my brother, and I can't say as I would take too kindly to you shooting him. So, why don't you just put your gun away?"

"And if I don't?"

"Then I'll just kill you where you stand," Win said easily.

The gunman slipped his gun back into its holster. "Look, it wasn't me who killed that storekeep. I just happened to stop there yesterday, that's all."

"Mister, it don't mean shit to me whether you did it or not," Win said. He nodded toward the stairs. "I'm just protectin' my brother, that's all."

"You got any objections to my leavin'?" the gunman asked.

"None at all, long as you keep your hands out where I can see them," Win replied.

"All right, all right, I'm going," the gunman said, holding his hands out as Win suggested. He glanced over toward the two dead law officers. "Probably wouldn't be too healthy for me to stay around here much longer now, anyway."

"No, I wouldn't think it would," Win agreed.

"On the other hand, we may run into each other again."

"Could be," Win answered.

"I'll be lookin' forward to it," the gunman said. Backing carefully across the floor, he put his hand behind him, and pushed open the doors. With one last look around, he stepped outside.

"Whew!" Tate said, letting out a long sigh. His sigh was followed by the collective expulsion of breath of everyone else in the room as all realized that the drama was now over. There was an explosion of disconnected dialogue.

"Let's have a drink!"

"Whoowhee, wouldn't you like to have seen them two boys go at one another?"

"Somebody better go get the mayor. What with the sheriff and his deputy dead, there ain't no one else to report this to."

Joe stood at the top of the stairs looking down toward his brother. He had only heard the shooting, he hadn't seen anything until he saw Win brace the shooter. The obvious question in his mind was, what should he do, now? He asked the question aloud.

"That all depends. You finished with your business up there, Joe?" Win answered.

Joe grinned sheepishly. "To tell the truth, big brother, we was just gettin' started."

The woman Joe had gone upstairs with now appeared beside him, wrapped in a robe. She stepped up to the rail and looked down toward Win. Then, seeing him, she smiled, broadly and unashamedly. Feeling her beside him, Joe draped his arm around her, letting his hand rest lightly over her breast.

"Then go on back and finish," Win said with a laugh. "We don't need you down here for a while."

"That is, if you're up to it!" Tate shouted with a guffaw.

"Honey, believe me, he is *up* to it," the woman called back down, and everyone who heard her laughed as well.

It was at that moment the mayor arrived, thus it made an incongruous scene with everyone laughing while the two peace officers lay dead.

The mayor buzzed around talking to several people to get the story on just what happened. Finally he came over to talk with Win.

"These folks are all sayin' you braced the fella who did this," the mayor said. "Is that true?"

"It must be true if they're all sayin' it," Win said easily.

"But before you get carried away, let me tell you that there was really nothin' to it. He was lookin' the other way at the time."

"Nevertheless, what you did took guts." The mayor watched some men as they were carrying out the bodies of the sheriff and deputy. He rubbed his chin, then looked back at Win. "How'd you like the job?"

"What? You mean you want me to be sheriff?" Win asked. He laughed, then shook his head. "No, I don't think so."

"It pays thirty dollars a month and found," the sheriff said.

"I appreciate the offer," Win replied. "But my brother and my friends and I need to be getting on our way."

"Too bad," the mayor said. "Brushy Creek could use someone like you."

TIRED OF SLEEPING ON THE GROUND, THE BOYS DECIDED to take hotel rooms after supper. Win and Joe took one room, while Tate and Ethan took the other. When the hotel rooms were taken care of, Tate and Ethan returned to the saloon to find a card game. Joe ordered himself a second supper. That left Win alone, so he decided to take a walk around to have a close look at Brushy Creek.

It was dark in town, and the street was lighted only by spills of yellow from the open doors and windows of the saloon. High overhead the stars winked brightly, while over a distant mesa the moon hung like a large silver wheel. Win could hear music, the thrum of guitars, and a lilting song in a language he couldn't understand. He knew that it had to be Spanish, for though he had never personally encountered any Mexicans, he knew that they were thick down in this part of the country.

"Well now," a voice said from the dark. "I was hopin' you'd come outside."

At the same time the words were spoken, a gun was cocked, and Win felt the hairs stand up on the back of his neck.

"Turn around, slow," the voice demanded.

Win turned. It was no surprise to him that it was the man from the bar.

For a long moment the two stared at each other over the end of the pistol. Then, inexplicably, the man put his pistol away and smiled.

"Sorry about that," he said. "But I wanted you to know what it feels like for someone to have the drop on you."

"I've felt it before," Win said. "I didn't like it then, either."

"You're one of Quantrill's riders, aren't you?" he asked.

"What makes you think so?"

"I saw you, back in Independence. The name is Hunter. Luke Hunter."

"Why the interest in Quantrill, Hunter?" Win asked.

"I want to join up with him," Hunter said. "I heard he'd come to Texas. I thought I'd come down here."

"They tell me Texas is a pretty big place," Win said.

"That's why I'm comin' to you. I want you to help me find him."

"What are you going to do if you find him?"

"I'm going to join up with him," Luke said. "As far as I'm concerned, he is the only one doing any real damage to the Yankees. Will you take me to him?"

"Why would I want to do that? Whether you killed that storekeep or not, they're going to be lookin' for you after the little fracas back there. We've got enough troubles of our own without bringing in another wanted man."

"Hell, mister, you think they're goin' to start lookin' any

harder for Quantrill, just because another wanted man joined up with him? Anyhow, I didn't think Quantrill was looking for Sunday school teachers. Now, what about it? Will you take me with you?''

''All right,'' Win agreed. ''I'll take you to Quantrill. Whether or not he lets you join up with us is up to him, but we'll take you along.''

'' 'Preciate it,'' Hunter said.

11

BACK IN KANSAS CITY, IN THE MIDDLE OF THAT SAME night that Hunter joined up with Win and the others, a couple of wagons stopped in front of a liquor store. The store was in an old, leaning, dilapidated three-story building, the brick walls of which glowed orange in the reflected light of half a dozen flickering, smoking torches.

The wagons were filled with women, the result of a sweeping raid made by General Ewing's Federal soldiers on the day before. Some of the women were brought in from adjoining farms and neighboring towns, others were taken from beds in their own homes, while still others were picked up from hotels, saloons, and whorehouses. Penny Anderson, Bloody Bill Anderson's sister, was one of the prisoners picked up from a farm. Maggie was in her own house over in Independence when the soldiers broke in on her. They didn't have to go far to capture Belle Amberly. Her "crib" was only two blocks from General Ewing's headquarters, and when the arresting party arrived, one of her customers, a Union officer, managed to slip out of her bed just before they came for her.

This disparate group of women, ranging in age from

fourteen to seventy-seven and consisting of housewives, sweethearts, sisters, mothers, and whores, were put into the back of wagons and brought to the liquor store without so much as one word of explanation as to what was happening to them. Now they were here; most whimpering in fear, some cursing in anger, the rest stoically quiet.

"All right, this is it," Captain Parnell shouted to the exhausted, confused, and frightened women. General Ewing had ordered that the women be delivered to Captain Parnell, so he found himself suddenly in charge of them. "Everybody out of the wagons!"

Prodded by the armed guards, the women started climbing down from the wagons. They found themselves standing between a double line of armed soldiers that led from the wagons to the building.

"Move it out!" Captain Parnell shouted. "We haven't got all night."

"Captain, have you no compassion?" Penny asked. "You are being very demanding, and some of the older ladies aren't very strong."

"Ladies?" the captain replied with a smirk. "What do you mean, ladies? I don't see any ladies here. All I see is Rebel trash."

"What is this place?" one of the older, and more confused, women asked. "Why are we here? I want to go home."

"Get in there and keep your mouth shut, you toothless old crone," Captain Parnell snarled. He pointed to the old building. "From now on, that *is* your home."

"You can't be serious," Maggie gasped when she looked at the old building. It was leaning so badly that there were actually timbers in place to hold it up. "You're putting us in a liquor store?"

"Upstairs, top floor," Captain Parnell said.

"But look at that building. It's about to fall down," Maggie complained.

"It's good enough for the likes of you. Now, either go through that side door there and climb up those stairs, or I'll have one of my men carry you."

"I'm afraid to go in there, it's so dark," the older woman said. "Please don't make me. I'm terribly frightened."

"I'll help you," Belle offered, extending her arm.

"You don't need to do that," Captain Parnell said. "She can go up on her own."

Belle glared at Parnell with such intensity that he wasn't able to meet her gaze. Parnell glanced away from her, then cleared his throat.

"Sergeant Berry, take them up," he ordered.

"You women follow me," Sergeant Berry said to them, holding up a lantern. Belle took the confused old woman by her arm and started toward the stairs with her.

Just as they stepped up onto the plank walk, Sergeant Berry spit a stream of tobacco, getting some of it on Penny's skirt.

"Please, sir, watch where you're spitting!" Penny complained.

Sergeant Berry smiled, his crooked teeth looking even more yellow than normal in the flickering light of the lantern.

"Miss, I always watch where I'm spitting," he said. To prove his point he spit again, this time hitting, dead center, a spittoon that was on the corner of the porch. "And I always hit what I'm aimin' for," he added.

The sergeant laughed at his joke, then he stepped through a door that opened onto the stairs leading up to the third floor, the lantern splashing a pale light before them.

The top floor of the building was illuminated by two more dimly glowing, smoking lanterns, which hung suspended from posts. The place where the women were being confined was a large open room, broken up only by several four-by-four timbers which, while obviously not a part of the original construction, had been called into service to help support the ceiling. It was from a couple of these posts that the additional lanterns were hanging.

"Here you are. Make yourselves comfortable," Sergeant Berry said, taking in the room with a sweep of his hand.

"Why have you brought us here?" Penny asked.

"General Ewing's orders," Berry explained. "He has decided that if we can't get the bushwhackers then we'll get their whores." Berry spit another stream of tobacco, this time on the floor. "That's you," he said. "All of you. You're Rebel whores."

"Sergeant, for some of us . . ." Belle paused for a moment, then pulled herself together. "For some of us the accusation is true. I am a . . . a woman who earns a living by selling herself to men. But not just to Rebels, I hasten to add. I am available to anyone who has the price, a fact to which I am sure many of your officers can testify."

At first there was a gasp of surprise from the other women. They weren't surprised that Belle was a prostitute, their own grapevine had already told them that. But they were surprised to hear someone actually admit to being a whore. Then, when she mentioned the Yankee officers, they all laughed in spite of themselves.

Belle continued. "But these other women are responsible citizens: wives, sweethearts, sisters, and mothers of men who happen to be fighting for the Confederacy. You have no right to accuse them of being prostitutes and no right to bring them to a place like this."

"I don't give the orders," Sergeant Berry said. "I just follow 'em. And you're goin' to follow 'em too."

"Sergeant Berry, would you please tell us just how you

expect us to stay here?'' Maggie asked. ''You've made no provisions for us. Why, look around this place. There aren't even any beds.''

''Beds? You don't need any beds. Go down there and get yourselves a blanket and make your bed on the floor. One blanket,'' he emphasized, holding up his finger. ''We'll prob'ly be bringin' in some more of your sisters pretty soon, an' we don't want you people of the gentler sex to start fightin' amongst yourselves over blankets.''

''I protest,'' Maggie said. ''These accommodations are totally inadequate. One blanket to be used for a bed? That's inhumane.''

''There's prob'ly good Union boys out fightin' somewhere right now that would love to have one of these blankets,'' Sergeant Berry replied. ''So quit your complainin'. One blanket is all you Rebel whores are goin' to get.''

''What about, uh, our, uh, needs of nature?'' a woman asked, too embarrassed to form the question.

''There's a couple of chamber pots over there,'' the sergeant answered, pointing toward them.

''But they're out in the *open*,'' Maggie protested. ''Surely you don't expect us to use those.''

''If you are all that modest, you can use one of the blankets to make yourself a privacy screen,'' Sergeant Berry consented.

''How very . . . decent . . . of you,'' Maggie said sarcastically.

''How can General Ewing hold us here like this? He has no right to hold us unless we have been charged with a specific crime,'' Belle said.

''Ha! You think whorin' ain't a crime?''

''But I haven't been charged with that. And you certainly can't make that claim about these other ladies.''

''As far as I'm concerned, any woman that has anything

at all to do with Rebel trash is a whore,'' the sergeant said.

"You don't actually think our men are just going to let you keep us here, do you?'' Penny asked angrily. ''They'll come get us out!''

Sergeant Berry smiled. ''Well, now, that's exactly what the general's a'wanting them to do, miss. Because when they come to get you, we'll get them. Oh, and, by the way, I wouldn't get any ideas about tryin' to escape if I was you. There will be guards posted around this place twenty-four hours a day and they have orders to shoot to kill, if they have to.''

When Sergeant Berry left, Belle heard him slip a heavy bar-lock across the door before he tramped back down the stairs.

"What do we do now?'' someone asked.

"I don't know about the rest of you,'' Maggie answered, "but I'm going to get myself a blanket and make myself as comfortable as possible.''

"Good idea,'' Penny said. ''I'm going to do the same.''

Belle joined the queue with the other ladies at the pile of blankets, then with blanket in hand, she found a spot near a window. As she spread the blanket out on the floor, she peered out through the window and saw several armed soldiers standing sentry duty in the dark street below. Sergeant Berry had not been bluffing about the security.

Across the street, standing near a lantern, Belle saw Captain Parnell staring up at the top floor. She had the feeling that he was looking right at her, though she knew that he wasn't, that there was no way he could be.

She wondered what was going through his mind right now. Had he willingly carried out General Ewing's orders? Or was there a tiny hidden spark of decency which screamed out at the injustice he was being asked to perform?

• • •

WIN AND THE OTHERS LOCATED QUANTRILL AT A PLACE called Snipe Creek, Texas. This was a strongly pro-Southern area whose men were away, fighting with General John Hood. There were no Union troops anywhere around nor were there any Union sympathizers. Unlike Missouri, where no place was safe, Snipe Creek was a haven, a long way from the war. It was for that reason, as much as for the warmer temperatures, that Quantrill had brought his men to Texas to wait out the rest of the winter.

Quantrill, George Todd, Bill Anderson, Archie Clement, and the other officers of Quantrill's Raiders had found a tailor to make fine uniforms for them. As a result they were now parading around town, resplendent in gray and gold, enjoying the accolades of the population.

In this part of Texas, Quantrill was not regarded as an outlaw, nor even as a bushwhacker. Here, he was regarded as the commanding officer of a cavalry troop, an irregular unit to be sure, but a band of men who fought against overwhelming odds, and yet scored victory after victory over the Yankees. Because of this perception, Quantrill and all of his men were treated as heroes by the citizens of the town.

George Todd was the first one Win saw. The big stonemason was sitting in a chair on the front porch of the town's only hotel. His uniform tunic hung open, and his chair was tipped back. He was eating from a large joint of meat, and a bottle of whiskey sat on the floor alongside him. Todd was watching the people move back and forth on the main street, and he saw Win before Win saw him.

"Win!" Todd called. "Joe!"

Upon being hailed, Win led the others over to the front of the hotel. They stopped, but didn't dismount.

"What are you boys doin' down here? I thought you two

was goin' to stay on your farm back in Missouri to get your spring crops in.''

"We changed our minds," Win said.

Looking at Tate and Ethan, Todd nodded. "McGee and Kelly, isn't it?" he asked.

"That's right," Tate said.

"Good to see you boys come down."

"Where is ever'one?" Joe asked.

"Same place they are ever' night, 'bout this time," Todd replied. He pointed. "They're all down there at the saloon, drinkin' whiskey and layin' up with the women," Todd replied. He picked the bottle up from the porch and took a long drink. When he pulled the bottle away from his lips, he wiped his mouth with the back of his hand. "Who are you?" Todd asked.

"The name is Hunter. Luke Hunter," Luke replied. "I've come to join you, if you'll have me." He dismounted and walked over to extend his hand.

Without taking his hand, Todd took another pull from his bottle as he studied Hunter. "You vouchin' for 'im, Win?" Todd asked.

"Nope," Win said. "He just tagged along with us."

Todd took another bite from his meat. "You don't say," he said. "Well, Hunter, it ain't my place to say you can join up with us. You're goin' to have to take that up with Charley."

THE SALOON WAS ALIVE WITH ACTIVITY AND BRIGHT WITH the light of two dozen or more lanterns. It was noisy with laughter and song, and except for a few older men, nearly everyone in the place was one of Quantrill's men. When they saw Win and his group come in, they greeted them warmly with much back-slapping and handshaking.

There didn't seem to be a shortage of women. They were

all over the place, leaning on the piano, sitting in on the card games, hanging onto the men. A couple of them came toward the new arrivals. One of them was clearly aiming her charm at Win, but he stepped aside and let Tate handle her.

Frank and Jesse James were sitting together, alone, at the back of the room. Win went over to join them.

"Take a load off," Frank invited, sliding a chair out with his foot.

"Where's Charley?" Win asked.

"I saw 'im go upstairs with a woman a while ago," Frank said. "Why? You got something for him?"

"Run into someone who wants to join up with us," Win said.

"What do you know about him?"

"Don't know anything at all," Win replied. "But if I was choosin' friends, don't think I'd choose him. I can't quite put my finger on it, but there's somethin' about him that I don't much care for."

"What'd you bring him along for?"

"He was planning on coming anyway," Win answered. "Figured I'd rather have him with us, so we could keep an eye on him, rather than following us."

"Sounds reasonable," Frank said.

Win looked back and saw that Hunter was leaning on the bar, watching what was going on. "Hunter," he called. He made a motion with his hand. "Come on over."

Hunter ambled over to the table.

"Luke Hunter, this is Frank and Jesse James."

Hunter laughed.

"Something funny?" Frank asked.

Hunter pointed toward Jesse. "That boy's still wet behind the ears. Don't tell me that Quantrill is so hard up for men that he lets pups like that'n ride with him?"

Jesse's smile turned to a frown, then his face grew cold and impassive. Slowly, and without fanfare, he stood.

"Mister, I'm going to kill you where you stand," he said in a flat dry voice.

Hunter laughed again. "*You* are going to kill me?" he asked.

"I reckon so."

Though Jesse said the words very quietly, they were powerful words. And, like a pebble cast into a pond, awareness of what was going on spread out in concentric circles through the rest of the saloon. Conversations halted, women's laughter stopped in mid-trill, the piano fell off in a ragged coda.

"Don't be a fool, boy. You don't want to fight me," Hunter said.

"I didn't say I was going to fight you," Jesse said calmly. "I said I was going to kill you."

"What if I kill you, instead?" Luke asked.

"I don't give a shit who kills who," Jesse said calmly. "As long as one of us is dead, and this is settled."

As Win watched the confrontation playing itself out in front of him, Luke Hunter underwent an amazing transformation. The man who had been so cold and deadly back in Brushy Creek when he faced down the sheriff and his deputy was now showing fear and indecision.

What was it? What did Hunter see in this boy that frightened him so? But even as Win studied Jesse's totally impassive face, he realized what it was. Jesse James was a rarity among men. He had a total disregard of death, whether it be his own or another. He had no more compunction about killing a man than he did about stepping on a bug . . . and if the bug who happened to be stepped on was himself . . . so be it.

On the other hand a man like Luke Hunter depended

upon engendering a fear of death in others to provide him with his edge. When he came face-to-face with a man who was as completely dispassionate on the subject of living or dying as was Jesse James, he lost that edge. Luke Hunter became the one who feared death, fearing it at the hands of a boy who was barely past puberty.

Realizing that the situation was reversed, that Jesse James had suddenly become the predator and he the prey, Luke Hunter began to sweat.

"Coulter," Hunter said in a desperate plea. "Coulter, stop this."

For a moment, Win thought to let it go on. But he realized that he was considering it only because of the dislike he had developed for Hunter. Finally he sighed and stepped in between Hunter and Jesse James.

"Dingus, wait. There's no need to do this. He's new. He doesn't understand."

"Listen, all I said was . . ." Hunter started, but his comment was interrupted when Win spun around and back-handed him sharply across his mouth.

"Keep your damn mouth shut," Win said.

"What the hell? Why did you do that?" Hunter asked, surprised by the sudden move.

"Hunter, if you open your mouth again, I'm going to kick your ass up between your ears," Joe said coldly, from close by. "In case you don't realize it, my brother just saved your life."

As if having suddenly lost interest in Hunter, the way a boy will tire of a game, Jesse sat down again. Hunter remained by the table for a moment longer, staring at his would-be adversary, whether trying to decide to test him or trying to save some face, it was difficult to tell. Win looked at Hunter with narrowed eyes, and sullenly Hunter slinked to the bar where he poured himself a drink.

Almost instantly, the conversations were reanimated, women found more things to laugh about, and the piano began, once again, cranking out a tune.

At the bar, Luke Hunter sulked over his drink, but Jesse James didn't show the slightest bit of emotion over what had just happened.

12

FOR THE NEXT SEVERAL WEEKS AFTER THE CONFRONTA-
tion between Luke Hunter and Jesse James, there was more
animus between Win and Hunter than there was between
Hunter and Jesse. As far as Jesse was concerned, the incident was no more annoying than a pesky mosquito, and he
let it drop. And Hunter, having learned his lesson, maintained a comfortable distance from Jesse, not wanting to
run afoul again of the dangerous youth. Instead, he transferred his rancor from Jesse James to Win Coulter.

"I was just funnin' with the boy," he told those who
would listen to him. "Win Coulter had no business buttin'
into it like he done. He coulda got either me or the boy
killed."

Although Hunter wasn't quiet around those who would
listen to him, he said nothing around Win or Joe, and Win,
taking a page from Jesse's book, tended to ignore Luke.

"Let him shoot off his mouth all he wants," Win told
Joe. "It gives him something to do."

Quantrill, in the meantime, was having his own problems
with both his top lieutenants, Bill Anderson and George
Todd. Once, during a card game, the disagreement grew so

hot that Quantrill and Todd actually drew on each other. Cooler heads prevailed, however, and the two men were separated without shots being fired.

Within the ranks the men began to allocate their loyalties. There were some who gravitated toward Todd, others toward Bill Anderson, while still others remained loyal to Quantrill. There were divisions within the divisions as arguments developed over card games, women, whiskey, even such minor things as to whether they preferred to call themselves "raiders," "bushwhackers," or "guerrillas."

"The boys are getting in a really ratty mood. We've got to get out of here and back up to Missouri," Win said.

"Yeah," Tate agreed. "I'd hate to run into any Yankees now. There's so much fightin' goin' on among ourselves that the Yankees could just stand by and laugh at us."

Not to be left out, Win, Joe, Tate and Ethan had formed their own little group, with Win as the natural leader. Frank and Jesse James and the Younger brothers, all related, had formed their little sub-group as well, and though they were not part of the Coulter group, both clans got along quite well with each other.

"Trouble is, we're getting fat and lazy down here," Cole Younger said.

"And we ain't doin' much to help the folks back home," Ethan added, "Unless you call struttin' around in a pretty uniform as bein' in the war."

"It's not just that," Win pointed out. "You see how we've become." He made an inclusive gesture with his hand. "We are friends, but we've reached the point to where we pretty much trust only each other. When we go into battle again, we're all going to have to depend on everyone . . . not just those who have formed close friendships. If we stay here too much longer, it's only going to get worse."

The conversation was suddenly interrupted by someone coming into the saloon, shouting in anger.

"They did it! The sons of bitches did it!" he yelled.

"Did what?"

"The goddamned Yankees have picked up all our women!"

"What women! What are you talking about?" someone asked.

"*Our* women, goddamnit!" the man shouted angrily. "Any woman that has anything to do with us . . . our wives, sisters . . . our mothers even, has all been picked up! The Yankees is holdin' 'em all in jail!"

This bit of news, bad though it was, acted as a tonic. Groups who had been moving apart now came together again, united in their outrage against what they were hearing.

Quantrill appeared at the landing on the top of the stairs. He was wearing his new gray trousers but no tunic, and his golden galluses hung down to intersect with the broad gold stripes on the pants. A woman, her nudity barely concealed by a sheet, stood just behind him.

"Where did you come by that news?" Quantrill called down.

"Over to the telegraph office," the messenger answered. "It just come in over the wire."

"Charley, what are we going to do about it?" someone asked.

Quantrill rubbed his chin for a moment as he studied the angry faces of the young men in his command. Finally he made a decision.

"Not a hell of a lot we can do right now," he said. "The Yankees have already got them. But when we go back, we'll make them pay dearly for treating our women like this."

"Well, goddamnit! When are we going back?"

"Soon, now," Quantrill answered.

"Soon? What does that mean?"

"It means soon," Quantrill said. When a rumble of discontent began to rise, Quantrill held out his hands. "Boys, don't you understand what this is? It isn't the women the Yankees are after. The only reason the Yankees did this in the first place was to get us all riled up."

"Well, by God, it worked. I'm plenty riled," someone said.

"Yeah, so am I. I want to go kill me a few of the Yankee bastards."

"We're goin' to," Quantrill said. "Trust me, boys, we're goin' to. All I'm askin' now is that you show a little patience."

"But they've got our women, goddamnit!"

"I know they do," Quantrill said. "But think about it. They'd be foolish to let any harm come to our women. They aren't in any real danger. The Yankees are usin' 'em for bait, and I don't plan to fall into their trap."

Win knew that Quantrill, personally, had no women close to him. His mother and sister were back in Ohio. He had no wife and no sweetheart, and so far all his liaisons with women had been temporary ones. He wondered if Quantrill would show such patience if he had someone of his own in the Yankee jail. He also knew, however, that Quantrill was right. The Raiders would not be well-served by heading back to Missouri, so hell-bent to rescue the women that they wound up riding into an ambush.

BACK IN MISSOURI, HOWEVER, GENERAL EWING FULLY EXpected Quantrill and his men to come riding in the very next day in an incautious attempt to rescue their women. And in order to set his ambush, he transferred two battalions of regular soldiers into the area where he kept them on around-the-clock readiness to meet Quantrill when he arrived.

Quantrill didn't come, so the immediate effect of General Ewing's transfer was to lessen some of the pressure on Confederate generals Price and Van Dorn in the southern part of the state. Frustrated because Quantrill didn't appear when he was expected, General Ewing kept additional units of the Union army in and around Kansas City for an indefinite period of time. The decreased pressure on Van Dorn and Sterling Price allowed them to utilize their own forces more efficiently.

"By staying away and avoiding General Ewing's obvious trap," one newspaper reported, "the guerrilla Quantrill has realized his first real strategic victory for the Confederacy. Because of him, so many Federal soldiers have been positioned to catch him that the Rebels in the southern part of the state are able to run rampant."

IT WAS LATE APRIL AND BY NOW THE REBEL WOMEN HAD been held prisoner for three months. Still, there was no sign of Quantrill nor of any other guerrillas coming to the rescue.

Belle knew, from conversations she had had with the other women, that Quantrill was in Texas. And while some of the women were convinced that he would come back for them as soon as he learned of their plight, others hoped that he wouldn't. Like Quantrill, they had already surmised that should he return, he and the loved ones that he had with him would be riding into a trap.

Because of Belle's background there were some women who didn't want to have anything to do with her. However, Belle was a good worker who not only did her own chores, but willingly did the chores of others who were ill, too old, or too weak to work. She began to win over some converts. Her two closest friends, Penny Anderson and Maggie De-pro, had declared their friendship in the earliest days of their confinement. Over the several weeks that the three women were together, they even became close enough to share their most treasured secrets with each other. It was in this way that both Belle and Penny learned they each had been bedded by Win Coulter. And, they both admitted with a ribald laugh, Win Coulter was "the best they'd ever been with."

Let in on the secret, Maggie confessed to the others that she had been with Win's brother, Joe.

"And I tell you now, ladies, there is no way Win Coulter could do more for a woman than his brother."

"Oooh, ladies," Belle said, fanning herself. "I swear, we're going to have to quit talking about this. It's pure-dee giving me the vapors." All three laughed.

Under normal circumstances, the three women would probably have never met. And even if they had met, such personal conversations as these would have never taken place. But here, in the artificial world created by their im-prisonment, all inhibitions against frank talk were removed.

One afternoon they were gathered near the window talk-ing. Belle was sitting on an upturned bucket, looking out toward the sky in the west, when she noticed that over the last several minutes the sky had changed from a bright blue to a rather strange greenish color. Curious about the trans-formation, she stopped the conversation to examine it.

"What is it?" Maggie asked, noticing the expression on Belle's face. "What do you see out there?"

"I don't know," Belle replied. "The sky . . ." She pointed to it.

On the western horizon great banks of clouds were be-ginning to build, then darken.

"Oh, my," Penny said gasping and bringing her hand to her mouth. "Oh my, that does look bad, doesn't it?"

By now, Maggie, too, was looking through the window. "Those clouds look awfully black," she said. "And, look at the way the light is coming through. I don't believe I've ever seen afternoon light quite like this."

Penny turned to call over her shoulder to an old woman who was sitting on one of the few chairs they had finally managed to acquire. "Miss Addie," Penny called. "Miss Addie, would you come over here and look at the sky?"

Miss Addie got up and walked over to the window, then peered through it, brushing a fall of gray hair back from her face.

"Uh huh," she said, calmly. "Looks like we're gettin' ready to have us a twister."

"A twister? My God! Do you mean a cyclone?" Belle asked.

"Looks like it to me," Miss Addie answered easily. Showing no sense of alarm, she returned to her chair.

"Surely we aren't going to have a cyclone," Maggie said. "The soldiers wouldn't keep us in here if we were going to have a really bad storm, would they?"

"I don't know about the soldiers, but Miss Addie knows storms," Penny said. "She's lived through a heap of cyclones over the last forty years, and if she says one is comin', then one is comin'."

"My God, we can't have a storm," Belle said. "Penny, this building can't stand up to a storm like that!"

"What we need is to get everyone into a cyclone cellar."

"So, how do we do that?"

Belle looked toward the door and saw a guard standing just on the other side.

''Let's go talk to the guard,'' she said. ''Maybe he'll let us talk to Captain Parnell.''

''Oh yes,'' Penny said sarcastically. ''Captain Felix Parnell. Now, there's a real compassionate man for you.''

''ONLY ONE OF YOU CAN GET OUT OF HERE TO SEE CAPtain Parnell,'' the guard said in answer to their request. He pointed to Belle. ''That'll be you. You other two, get on back inside.''

''Listen, why don't you let all three of us speak to him?'' Belle suggested. ''He is more likely to listen to three of us than one.''

''Look here, I'm stickin' my neck out as it is by lettin' even one of you go,'' the guard explained. ''Now, what about it? Do you want to see the cap'n, or don't you?''

''If only one of us can go, let it be one of the other ladies,'' Belle said. She looked at Penny. ''You go, Penny.''

''I'm Bill Anderson's sister,'' Penny said. ''Captain Parnell's not going to listen to me.''

''What about you, Maggie?''

''No, no,'' Maggie said. ''I'd be much too nervous. You are the best one.''

''Look, are you goin' to go or not?'' the guard asked impatiently. ''I'm not goin' to stand here all day.''

Belle sighed. ''All right,'' she said. ''I'll go.''

Waving goodbye to Penny and Maggie, Belle extended her hands so the guard could put on cuffs. Then, securely cuffed, she followed him down the narrow rickety stairs and out into the street.

Once she got outside, she saw that the sky was even more ominous looking. At the moment there was absolutely no wind and the air hung as heavy and oppressive as a wet blanket. Horses, tied to the hitching posts, stamped their feet nervously and tossed their heads, pulling against the reins. A few people were standing in the middle of the street, looking toward the west, while a few buildings down, in preparation for the impending storm, someone closed the shutters, then began nailing boards across the outside of them to protect the windows.

The guard led Belle up the steps to the front porch of Tom Poe's office. The lawyer's Southern sympathies had been discovered, and he had been run out of town. His office was now being used by Captain Parnell.

"Get inside there," the guard said roughly, pushing open the door.

Sergeant Berry was sitting at his desk working on the morning report when he was distracted by the loud entrance made by Belle and her guard.

"What is this?" he asked. "What is that prisoner doing here?"

"She insisted that I bring her over to talk to the captain," the guard said.

"Oh, *she* insisted, did she?" Berry said. "Has she been promoted to sergeant in our army? Maybe she got a commission and I didn't hear about it?"

"No, Sergeant, nothing like that," the guard insisted.

To the private's relief, Sergeant Berry turned his attention from the guard to Belle. "And you. You're getting pretty uppity, aren't you?" he asked. "Why do you think you have a right to be insisting on anything?"

"Sergeant, have you looked at the sky?" Belle asked anxiously.

"Yeah, I've seen it. So what?"

"Miss Addie says there's a cyclone coming."

"Could be. I hear-tell they do come through here from time to time. What's that got to do with you comin' over here?"

"Do you realize that there are forty-four women on the top floor of the ricketiest building in town? If a cyclone does come through here, that building will be blown down."

"It's an old building," the sergeant said. "I'm sure it's gone through cyclones before."

"Perhaps so, but that doesn't mean it can go through it again," Belle said. "Sergeant, you've got to get us out of there. We aren't asking that you let us go free, only that you move us to a safer place."

Sergeant Berry shook his head. "You're talkin' to the wrong person. I got no authority to move you ladies. It ain't my responsibility."

"Then, please, let me talk to Captain Parnell," Belle begged.

Outside a horse whinnied. It was a long eerie sound, as if the frightened horse were shouting a warning.

Sergeant Berry stroked his chin for a moment, then nodded his head.

"All right, wait here," he said. "I'll see if the cap'n will see you."

Belle waited while Sergeant Berry went into the inner office that was Captain Parnell's. A moment or two later, Berry stuck his head back out.

"You can come in and talk to him now," he said.

Belle looked down at the cuffs on her hands. "Do I have to wear these things?"

Berry turned to the guard. "Give me the key," he ordered.

The guard gave the key to Berry, and Belle held out her hands expectantly to allow the cuffs to be opened.

"No," Berry said. "I'll give the key to the cap'n. If he wants to uncuff you, he can do it himself."

In the distance, there was a long, deep-throated roll of

thunder. It was the first thunder of the impending storm.

Belle followed Berry into Captain Parnell's office. She saw Parnell standing at the window, looking outside. Over his shoulder, Belle could see that it had begun to rain, and the stillness was replaced by a sudden wind. In fact, the wind was blowing pretty hard, as evidenced by a hat that was rolling quickly down the street, chased after by a hat-less soldier.

It thundered again, this time a protracted peal which sounded like a long melodic roll of timpani.

"This here's the woman I told you about, Cap'n. The whore who wanted to see you," Sergeant Berry said. "I've got the key to her cuffs." He held it out in front of him.

"Put the key on the desk," Parnell said without turning around.

Berry set the key down with a little snap. "She wants to talk to you about . . ."

"Leave us, Sergeant," Parnell interrupted. He still had not turned around.

"Beggin' your pardon, Cap'n, but she's a prisoner and someone ought to be in here with her. Me or the guard, one."

"I said, leave us," Captain Parnell said again.

"Very good, sir," Sergeant Berry said. "I'll be just outside the door if you need me."

The sergeant withdrew and Belle was left standing in the room with the commandant of the makeshift prison.

Outside, the wind began to howl.

13

WITH HER WRISTS STILL CUFFED IN FRONT OF HER, BELLE stood in absolute silence, waiting for Captain Parnell to turn around, or at least to speak.

At the apothecary across the street, a sign blew down, crashing loudly onto the plank walk.

A woman carrying an umbrella started to cross the street from the general store to the millinery, but a sudden gust of wind grabbed the umbrella and turned it inside out. She fought it for a moment, trying to hold it and her dress together. Finally she let the umbrella go. It bounced and careened down the street as she retreated back to the general store.

Finally, Captain Parnell turned around to acknowledge Belle's presence.

"Have you told anyone?" he asked.

"I beg your pardon?" Belle asked, not knowing what he meant.

"About us, I mean."

"No."

"Why not?"

"I could see no purpose in telling everyone that you are

the one who ran from my bed on the night the soldiers came for me.''

Captain Parnell's eyes were hard and challenging.

''You are smart not to try and make trouble for me. Because if you did, I would only deny it, and believe me, there is no question but that my word would be accepted over yours.''

''Oh, I do believe you, Captain,'' Belle said. ''I'm sure that if I would say anything, my words would fall on deaf ears.''

''I'm glad you understand. That makes things easier all the way around. For both of us,'' he added. ''Now, why did you want to see me?''

There was another crash of thunder, this time much closer than before.

''I want to ask a favor,'' Belle said. ''Not for me,'' she added quickly. ''For all the ladies.''

''I see. And why did they choose you, a whore, to represent them? Is it because you convinced them that out of some sense of obligation and gratitude for your silence, that I would grant any request you might make?''

''No, it's not like that,'' Belle insisted. ''I told you, I've told no one about that night. Not even the other women who are being held in that awful place with me.''

A streak of lightning lit up the green sky. The thunder that followed was so close that it was there almost before the light receded. In addition, the roar of the wind was now nearly as loud as the almost constant crash of thunder.

''And what is this favor that you want?'' Captain Parnell asked.

Belle nodded toward the window. ''Have you seen what's going on outside?'' she asked.

''Of course I have. I am neither blind nor deaf,'' Parnell replied.

"There's a cyclone coming," Belle said.

"The storm isn't coming, it's already here," Parnell said.

"No, I don't mean just a storm. I mean a twister, a tornado."

"Why are you telling me this? I know you think I have a lot of power, Miss Amberly," Parnell said. "But I don't have the power to stop a cyclone. Not even General Ewing can do that," he added, laughing at his own joke.

Even as he spoke, he looked outside at the rain which was, because of the ferocity of the wind, being whipped by in horizontal sheets. "The storm seems to have taken hold now. And it could be that there is a twister in it."

"If there is, we are in great danger," Belle said.

"We?"

"The women and I," Belle explained. "We are on the top floor of a very old building. That's why I've come to you. Captain Parnell, you've got to get us down from there!"

"If you are frightened, you can stay down here until the storm has blown over."

"What? No, I couldn't do that."

"Why not? Isn't that why you are here? Because you think the building is unsafe?"

"Yes, it is very unsafe. But, Captain, I couldn't leave my friends exposed to danger while I am down here on the ground, safe from the storm."

Parnell laughed, a short bitter laugh. "Why not? Is it because you feel that it might be some kind of betrayal? Do you really think those women are your friends?" he asked.

"Some of them are, yes."

"I hate to disillusion you, Miss Amberly," Captain Parnell said. "But your friends signed a petition asking that you be removed from their midst. It seems they don't want a whore's presence screwing up their martyrdom.''

''I'm sure some of them would just as soon see me go,''
Belle said. ''After all, we didn't exactly move in the same
social circles.''

Parnell grinned evilly. ''Not some of them. *All* of them,''
he said. ''The petition was unanimous.''

''*All* of them?'' Belle asked in a small voice. She was a
little surprised by the news, and she took a sharp intake of
breath before she regained her composure. ''Miss Anderson
and Miss Depro as well?''

''Them too.''

''All right, so what if they did?'' she asked. ''The fact
remains that those women are in the path of a storm that
could destroy the building and kill them all. And I can't
stay down here safe, while they are in danger. I have to do
something for them.''

''And just what do you think that you, a handcuffed female prisoner completely in my power, can do?'' Parnell
asked. The harshness left his eyes, to be replaced by a look
that Belle had seen all her life. She could see tiny red lights,
deep in his eyes. It was the look of lust. The way was being
shown to her. All she had to do was take it.

''Surely,'' Belle said in a practiced reaction to that look,
her voice growing husky, ''I can do . . . something.'' She
let the word ''something'' slide out seductively, and she
shifted the weight on her feet so that her hip jutted out. Her
eyes became smoky, and her tongue slipped out to wet her
lips.

''How badly do you want your friends moved?''

''I beg of you to move them, Captain. If you do, you
will find me most appreciative.''

''Huh,'' Parnell said, shaking his head. ''You do first,
then I will move them.''

The roar of the wind grew even louder, and Sergeant

Berry, without knocking, stuck his head in through the door.

"Cap'n, we got to get out of here!" Sergeant Berry yelled, his voice barely audible above the roar of the wind.

"Then go!" Parnell yelled back at him. He pointed outside. "Be gone with you!"

Surprised at Captain Parnell's reaction to him, Sergeant Berry blinked once, then turned and left, closing the door behind him.

"Captain, please! Get the women out of that building now, before it is too late!" Belle begged after Sergeant Berry left.

Parnell picked up the key and unlocked one side of the cuffs which held Belle's hands together.

"Thank God!" Belle said, but to her shock and consternation, instead of releasing her, Parnell snapped the open cuff onto the leg of his desk, forcing her down to her knees.

"What? What are you doing?" Belle asked, looking up at him in fear and surprise.

"You want the women down from the building?" Parnell yelled.

"Yes!"

Parnell stepped in front of her, then opened his fly. He took out his penis.

"Then you know what to do," he said, thrusting his penis in front of her face.

"Captain, this is crazy! The storm . . ."

"Suck my cock, goddamn you! If you want those women out of there, there is only one way you can do it!"

"All right! All right!" Belle answered. Desperately, she reached for him, wrapping her hand around his already hard organ. She began moving her hand back and forth.

"No! Not like that, you bitch! Like this!" Parnell screamed. Putting his hand in her hair, he pulled her head to him, pushing himself angrily and fully into her mouth.

Belle's mouth was so filled with him that, at first, she nearly gagged. Then she managed to get control of her involuntary muscles, and began sucking.

The roar of wind sounded like a hundred freight trains passing at once, but Belle was hardly able to discern the difference between what she was hearing in her head and what she was hearing from outside.

"Make me come, bitch! Make me come!" Parnell was screaming at her.

Belle had been with many men, some of whom were so unpleasant that she could barely stand their presence long enough to service them. But there had been some, like Win Coulter, who had excited her, and with whom her "services" hadn't been business, but pleasure.

In order to make this moment pass, and in order to bring him off quickly enough to rescue the women, Belle resorted to an old trick she had learned when she first went into the business. Physically, the man she was with right now was Captain Felix Parnell. But in her mind, and in her fantasy, it was Win Coulter.

As a result of her fantasy, an amazing transformation took place. No longer was what she was doing unpleasant. With her eyes closed, she thought of the last time she had done this very thing for Win Coulter. And now, far from being an invasion, the feeling of her mouth being filled with a hot throbbing penis, the silken sensation of her tongue sliding along his skin and caressing his testicles became very enjoyable to her.

Parnell sensed the difference right away, though he didn't know what had brought it about. He knew only that her mouth felt like a perfumed cauldron of warm wax, and he was feeling pleasure like he had never felt before. His knees grew weak, there was a tingling in the small of his back, and a rolling in the pit of his stomach.

"What . . . are . . . you . . . doing?" he gasped. "No! No, it will be over too fast!"

Spurred on by his words, Belle increased her activity, sucking him in, then pushing him back out, sucking him in, then pushing him back out, flicking her tongue across the head, alternating the pressure along the entire length.

Suddenly Parnell put both his hands in her hair and pulled her head to him, thrusting his hips forward as hard as he could. He felt it beginning, starting in the souls of his feet, dropping down from his scalp, and meeting in the small of his back where every muscle and nerve ending in his body fired with pleasurable sensation.

"I'm . . . coming!!!" Parnell gasped, now pumping furiously as the muscle spasms gathered.

Belle took her mouth away and began a frenzied pumping of the skin.

Parnell ejaculated then, sending a white-hot stream of jism jetting forward for several inches, most of it falling on the floor, but a few white pearls landing on Belle's chin to gleam softly in the rain light.

Belle continued to whip the skin back and forth as two more squirts gushed out, then she slowed her motion as, gasping for breath, Parnell fell forward, and would have fallen entirely had he not saved himself by grabbing the corner of his desk.

"That was incredible," Parnell wheezed.

"Captain," Belle said. "Your promise?"

"All right," Parnell said, putting his penis back into his pants. "I am a man of my word. I said I would let them . . ." Parnell's words were suddenly interrupted by a terrible crashing sound. That was followed by the screams of women, screams so loud that their awful sound penetrated even through the roar of the tornado that was, at that very moment, cutting its destructive swath through the middle of Kansas City.

"What is that? What's happening?" Belle shouted, fearing the worst.

Parnell hurried over to look through the window. What he saw outside made him put his hand to his forehead.

"Oh, my God!" he said. "Oh my God, no, it can't be!"

"What is it?" Belle started jerking on the cuff that held her fastened to the desk.

Parnell came back to her then and released the cuff from her other wrist. Rubbing her wrist, Belle moved quickly to the window to see what was going on. She looked toward the three-story brick building where the women were being held.

There was no building. There was only a pile of rubble, twisted boards, and here and there a few incongruously bright patches of color, the dresses of the women who lay injured, dead, and dying in the wreckage.

WITHIN MINUTES AFTER THE STORM PASSED THROUGH Kansas City, the rain and the wind stopped. Now there was a breathless calm as soldiers and civilians alike emerged from their shelters, as if in a daze, to walk down the street and gaze upon the destruction wrought by the tornado.

Ivers' Saloon was gone. It was completely gone. Absolutely nothing, not one stick of lumber, remained on the empty lot where the saloon had once been.

The apothecary right next door was still standing, but it was without a roof.

The leather goods store had only two walls still upright.

The millinery was completely untouched.

The converted women's prison was totally destroyed, consisting only of a heap of broken brick and board from which issued a few piteous cries and whimpers.

"The women!" someone shouted. "The women were in there!"

Quickly, the citizens of the town gathered around the collapsed building. Despite their personal sentiments as to whether or not the women inside should have been held prisoner, they worked rapidly, tossing aside the remains of the building and searching for those who were still alive. Belle worked with the rescuers, for neither Parnell, nor anyone else, made any suggestion that she should be cuffed again or put once more into custody.

"What do we do with the ones who aren't bad hurt, Cap'n?" Sergeant Berry asked as he saw a handful of dazed, frightened, but otherwise uninjured women milling around. "Where do we put them now?"

"Put them nowhere," General Ewing said, arriving on horseback at that moment.

"General Ewing, sir, you didn't have to come down here," Parnell said. "We have everything under control now."

Ewing swung down from his horse and looked at the wreckage of the old liquor store building.

"Good Lord, Captain, why did you leave them in here during the storm?" Ewing asked. "Didn't you realize that this building would be unsafe during such a storm?"

"It . . . it all happened too fast, General," Parnell said. "We didn't have time to evacuate the women." Parnell looked over at Belle. She was working in the pile of rubble, and her arms, hands, and face were covered in mud, but she stopped long enough to glare at him.

"It's all right, Captain," Ewing said. He put his hand in his gray hair and shook his head as he watched the rescue operation. "It's all my fault. I never should have authorized their incarceration in the first place."

"What about the survivors, General? What are we going to do with them?" Parnell asked.

"Nothing," Ewing replied. "Let those who are uninjured go home. For the others, we'll do what we can. How many were killed?"

"We don't know yet," Parnell admitted. "We are still digging through the rubble."

IT WAS BELLE WHO FOUND PENNY ANDERSON AND MAGgie Depro. Both women were dead, crushed by falling debris. But Miss Addie, the woman who was lying under Penny and Maggie, survived. Frightened and dazed, though otherwise unharmed, she crawled out from under the two women when enough rubble was cleared away to allow her to do so.

The positions of Penny and Maggie's bodies told the story, later verified by Miss Addie when she was sufficiently recovered of her faculties.

"When things started tumbling down, they wrapped themselves around me," Miss Addie said. "Those two brave women saved my life. What a foolish thing for them to do."

"Foolish?" Belle asked.

"Yes, my child, very foolish," Miss Addie insisted. "They were young, with their entire lives ahead of them. Mine is nearly over. It wasn't a very good trade."

THE FINAL REPORT SHOWED FOUR WOMEN DEAD, INCLUDing Penny Anderson and Maggie Depro. There were sixteen inured: four gravely, eight seriously, and four not seriously. True to his word, General Ewing let the rest of the women return to their homes. They walked away, still dazed and

too thankful over surviving to allow the anger and hate to
show.

"Wait until Bloody Bill finds out his sister was killed,"
the people whispered among themselves. "Just you wait.
There will be hell to pay."

14

WHEN WIN HELD UP HIS HAND, THE TWO ADVANCE SCOUTS with him stopped. They were on top of a fairly prominent hill, but just below the crest so that they wouldn't be silhouetted against the background of a bright sky.

"What is it, Win?" Tate asked, noticing that something had caught Win's attention.

Win dismounted, then walked out onto a promontory and took out his binoculars to look down onto a road that wound through a cut about a quarter of a mile away.

"Yankees," he said. He stared for a long moment, then lowered the glasses. "I don't believe there is anything to worry about, though. There are just two of them, driving an empty wagon."

"You think I should go back and tell the others?"

Win put his binoculars back in the little case he carried around his neck. "I expect so," he answered.

"The Chief said he wanted to be told about anything we came across. You go ahead, Tate. Ethan and I will wait here."

Tate turned his horse and started back toward the main body of men. After spending the winter in Texas, Quantrill's Raiders, who were now fatter, better dressed, and in many cases, better mounted than they had been before they left, were returning to Missouri. They may have been better fed and better equipped, but the morale of the unit had been badly shattered by internal dissension.

Ethan got down from his horse, as well, and the two horses began to nibble on the grass while their riders stared down at the road below.

"Win, do you think Anderson is going to go off on his own?"

"I don't know. I know that things haven't been going very well between Bill and Charley. But why do you ask? Has he said that he might start his own group?"

"No, he ain't said nothin' like that," Ethan replied. He pulled up a long stem of grass and started sucking on the cool, sweet root. "But, like you said," he continued, "Bill and the Chief haven't been getting along. Anderson blames Quantrill for his sister and the other women gettin' killed."

"I know he does, but I don't think he has any cause to."

"Why not? It's true, ain't it? If Quantrill had come on back to Missouri when we first heard the women was took, why Anderson's sister and them others would be alive to-day."

"Ethan, you can't say that for sure. We don't know whether those women would be alive or not. But we do know that if we had come, some of *us* wouldn't be. The Yankees were laying a trap for us, you know that. And if Bill Anderson had had his way, we would have ridden right into it."

"We been in tight spots before. Seems to me like we coulda fought our way through it. Most especial' if we was lookin' for it, like we woulda been," Ethan suggested, not wanting to give up his conviction. "If we'd'a just come on then."

"Yes, and if a frog had wings, he wouldn't bump his ass every time he jumps."

Ethan laughed. "If a frog had wings, he wouldn't bump his ass. That's a good one. I'll have to 'member that one."

Shortly after that, the main body rode up with Quantrill in the lead. "What do you see?" Quantrill asked, swinging down from his horse and walking out onto the promontory with Win and Ethan.

"Nothing to worry about," Win answered easily. He pointed down to the road below. "Just a couple of soldiers driving a wagon is all. The only thing we have to do is wait here for a moment or two, and they'll be gone."

"Wait here, hell," Anderson snarled. Slapping his legs against the sides of his horse, he bolted ahead of the others and pushed his horse into a gallop down the long slope toward the road.

"Where's he going?" Win asked.

"I expect he's goin' to kill the soldiers," Quantrill said calmly.

"Why? They aren't any danger to us."

Quantrill spit out a stream of tobacco, then straightening back up, he wiped the back of his hand across his mouth.

"We've all got our devils to fight, Mr. Coulter," Quantrill explained. "You, of all people, should understand that, being as you want to go after Emil Slaughter."

Win thought of the man who was responsible for the death of his parents, and who was still out there, mocking him by just being alive. "Yes," he said. "I guess I do understand that."

They watched as Anderson, riding alone and bending forward in his saddle, galloped toward the soldiers. They saw Anderson draw his pistol, then point it forward.

For just a moment, the wagon continued on at its normal pace, the two soldiers in it blissfully unaware of the danger they faced. Then one of them, hearing something or perhaps just sensing it, turned around to look behind him. That was when he saw Anderson bearing down on them. Even from where he was, Win could see the quick expression of shock and fear register on the soldier's face.

Urgently, the soldier punched the driver on the shoulder and the driver looked around for just a moment as well, then turned back, quickly, to give his attention to the team. The driver slapped the reins against the horses, and the horses, reluctantly it seemed, broke into a gallop.

Anderson screamed out his rage at the two soldiers, his yell floating back up the hill to Win. From this distance it was thin and high-pitched, like the call of a distant hawk.

It quickly became obvious that the two Union soldiers had no weapons with them. Their only defense would be the speed of the team they were driving, and since the team was encumbered by the heavy freight wagon, there was pitifully little speed.

Win watched as Anderson closed inexorably on the wagon. From the gun in Anderson's hand, there was a flash of fire and a puff of smoke. The recoil of the pistol made Anderson's hand jerk up, and a moment later the dull, flat sound of a pistol shot rolled back up the hill to be heard by those who were waiting and watching, like the audience of a macabre play.

Anderson's first shot missed, but his second did not. Even before the sound of the second shot reached Win, the driver slumped forward, dropping the reins as he did so. Now the remaining soldier sat helplessly on the seat beside the driver, a prisoner of events he could not command, as the runaway team galloped in frenzy, no longer under control. The surviving soldier stood up, as if getting ready to leap from the wagon, just as Anderson fired again. This bullet, too, found its mark, and the soldier tumbled backwards across the seat to land belly-up in the wagon bed.

Anderson put his pistol away and continued the chase. It took but a few more seconds to catch up with the team and when he did so, he leaned down to grab their harnesses and pull them to a stop.

"What's he doin' now?" Tate asked.

Win turned away, because he knew what Anderson was about to do. The scalps of the two soldiers would soon join the scalps of the others that hung from Anderson's bridle.

Anderson collected his bloody scalps. Then, with another loud shout, he came galloping back toward the main body of men, holding the grisly trophies out before him.

"Here's two for my sister," Anderson said when he got back.

"Anderson, them two boys prob'ly didn't have nothin' a'tall to do with your sister gettin' kilt," Ethan said. "They wasn't nothin' but a couple of soldiers."

"A couple of *Yankee* soldiers," Anderson corrected as he held up the scalps. "And now they are dead, which makes them *good* Yankee soldiers," he added with a wild laugh.

IT WAS JUST BEFORE SUNSET WHEN QUANTRILL AND HIS band rode, unchallenged, into Blue Springs, Missouri. At Quantrill's orders, all had drawn their pistols and were prepared to fight, if challenged. All eyes were alert and all muscles tense as the riders entered the town. They were ready, but no one mounted a threat.

Then someone ran out to the edge of the street.

"Hey, ever'one, it's Quantrill!" the citizen shouted. "He's come back from Texas!"

Although Quantrill and several others swung their weapons in the direction of the citizen who yelled, it quickly became evident that the man represented no threat to them.

On the contrary, his shout was one of greeting, and it was picked up by another, and by another still, until soon much of the town had turned out to run and cheer alongside the men as they rode into town. Despite their readiness when they entered town, this was more in keeping with the reception Quantrill had expected for, like Independence, Blue Springs was strongly pro-Southern. And, unlike Independence, Blue Springs had no permanent Union garrison.

Win thought they made quite a spectacle as they rode in, smartly lined up in columns of fours, most wearing the glittering new uniforms they had picked up in Texas. Evidently the town did as well, for several young boys came out into the street to run alongside the body of riders. Then, as they moved farther into the town, young women also joined the welcoming throng by throwing flowers.

Quantrill stopped his riders in front of the post office. Here, the Stars and Stripes floated from the top of the flagpole, and glancing up at it, Quantrill ordered it hauled down.

Two of Quantrill's men jumped down from their horses and quickly pulled the flag down. One of them attached the Stars and Bars to the lanyard, and amidst cheers, rendered with equal enthusiasm by Raider and citizen alike, ran the new flag up the pole.

"Major Quantrill," a gray-haired, overweight man said stepping forward from the crowd. "On behalf of Blue Springs, sir, may I welcome you to our city."

"It is now *Lieutenant Colonel* Quantrill," Quantrill said, pointing to the two small stars on his collar. It was a self-appointed rank, attached to the collar by the seamstress who had made Quantrill's new uniform for him.

"I beg your pardon for my error, sir. And I offer you my most sincere congratulations on your promotion."

"Who are you?" Quantrill asked.

"My name is Botkin, sir. J.C. Botkin."

"Are you the mayor?"

"I am a businessman," Botkin explained. "Our mayor is in jail in Kansas City, placed there by the Yankees for refusing to sign a loyalty oath." Botkin smiled. "It is a token of our resistance to this unlawful order that we would rather continue our town without a mayor, than to select one who would give in to the Yankees' demands."

"Well, good for the town," Quantrill said. He swung down from his horse, then tied it to the nearest hitching rail. "And yet, the Union flag was flying when we arrived."

"It was," Botkin admitted. "But our resistance can only extend so far, and no farther. The Yankees have ordered the Stars and Stripes to be flown and thus it has. We are grateful to you for pulling it down."

"Wasn't hard to do," Quantrill said. He nodded toward the flagpole. "All we had to do was haul down the Yankee flag. There are no soldiers here, are there?"

"No," Botkin said. "That is, none who are billeted here. Although they do come through town frequently," he hastened to add. "And, uh"—he coughed to cover his self-consciousness—"they left me responsible to see to it that the Federal flag is treated with respect."

Quantrill stroked his chin as he studied Botkin. "Now, let me see if I understand this," he said. "They left *you* responsible for the flag?"

"Oh, yes. It is a most odious task, I agree. But they were most emphatic about what they would do to me if I disobeyed."

Quantrill smiled. "You aren't tryin' to tell me to put it back up, are you?"

"Oh, no, sir! No, sir, not at all!" Botkin replied quickly. "You see, with you bein' the one that took it down, why there's nothin' anyone could expect me to do. What you have done is to let me off the hook, so to speak.''

"Burn it,'' Quantrill ordered the two who had taken the flag down.

"You got it, Charley!'' one of them answered with a wild giggle and, a moment later, the flag was going up in flames.

"It's good to have you back in Missouri, Maj . . . uh, that is, Colonel Quantrill. We weren't sure when, or even if, you would be back. Some suggested that you had moved to Texas.''

"We were in Texas, but only temporarily,'' Quantrill confirmed. He paused for a moment, then continued. ''We were performing a needed service there by providing defense against any Yankees who might attempt to attack Texas during the absence of General Hood and his army.''

"And so now, your duty performed, you have returned to Missouri,'' Botkin said. ''We are most pleased to have you with us once again.''

"We're tired and hungry, so with your permission I intend to confiscate some grub and a few supplies,'' Quantrill said. He laughed. ''In fact, I intend to do it whether you give your permission or not.''

"But of course you have our permission, Colonel. We are here for you! All of us!'' Botkin shouted. ''Take anything you want!''

15

WITH CHEERS, THE RAIDERS DISMOUNTED AND BEGAN moving through the town, surrounded by genuine well-wishers.

"Me, for some whiskey," Joe said as he dismounted. "You comin' along, Win?"

"Not just now," Win replied. "The thirst I've got can't be slaked with whiskey."

Joe, Tate, and Ethan laughed.

"I know what you mean," Joe said. "All right, you go about your business . . . we'll go about ours."

Tying off his horse, Win started down the alley behind the blacksmith shop. According to Tate's cousin, Boykin McGee, Belle Amberly had moved to Blue Springs from Kansas City several weeks before.

"After the storm, she had a real hard time of it in Kansas City," Boykin told Win. Boykin was one of those who had remained in Missouri, rejoining them when they returned, and as a result was up on all the latest news and gossip. "There was talk about where she was while the storm was goin' on, and how she managed to get out of the buildin' while all the other women had to stay there," Boykin explained. "Some folks thought that was just real strange."

"What do you think about it?" Win had asked.

Boykin had already been told that Win had a special interest in Belle, so he couched his answer.

"Why, I don't think nothin' 'bout it, one way or the other," Boykin answered. "Like the Bible says, 'Judge not, lest ye be judged.' "

According to Boykin, when Belle arrived in Blue Springs, she moved into a house very similar to the one she had lived in back in Kansas City. That wasn't too unusual, for the tiny houses, called "cribs," were the most common quarters for prostitutes. And, because those who lived in cribs were not accepted in polite society, the cribs were invariably located either in an alley somewhere or at the outskirts of town. Here, her house was in the alley behind the blacksmith shop.

Win stepped up onto the porch and knocked on the door.

"Belle! Belle! Open up!"

Win waited for a moment, listening for any sound of life that might come from within. He knocked on the door again.

"Belle Amberly, it's me, Win Coulter!"

He waited for another long moment, listening without hearing anything. Finally, with a sigh of disappointment, he turned to step down from the porch. That was when he heard her. He turned back toward the door as it opened.

The apparition that greeted him from the other side of the door made him gasp.

"Win, it *is* you," a raspy voice said. "I thought you were gone. I thought all of you were gone."

It was Belle, the voice told him that. But the beautiful, robust woman he had known before he left for Texas was no longer there. The woman standing just inside the door of this tiny house was pale-skinned and as thin as a rail.

She also had on a nondescript dress, and her hair hung in a stringy mess, a condition in which the Belle that Win knew would never allow herself to be caught. As if aware of Win's silent condemnation, Belle put her hand weakly to her hair.

"I . . . I must look a mess," she said, understating the obvious.

"I've seen you look better," Win admitted.

Belle took a step back from her door. "Won't you come in?" she invited.

Win hesitated for a moment. His first inclination was to turn around and walk away, but he felt a sense of compassion for this woman who had once been so young, so vital, and so beautiful. "All right," he said. "Thanks."

Win followed Belle inside. When he had been in her little house in Kansas City, he had noticed that, though very tiny, it was kept spotlessly clean. She had also made her crib homey by little decorative touches here and there. But this house, like Belle, was a mess. The bed was unmade and flower vases either stood empty or displayed long-dead bouquets.

"Do you, uh, want to do anything?" Belle asked, making a casual wave toward the bed.

"No," Win answered quickly. "No, I just dropped by for a visit."

"Are you sure?" Belle tried to smile. "There wouldn't be a charge. Not for you."

"No, thanks," Win said. "We've ridden a long way today, I . . ." Win paused in midsentence. He had come to her exactly because he *did* want to do something. But seeing Belle like this deflated his ardor. "Belle, what the hell happened to you? Why are you"—he paused, then took a breath and went on—"this house and you . . ." He couldn't finish the question, but it wasn't necessary. Belle knew what he was talking about.

"I am sure, by now, that you have heard about what happened to the women the Yankees were holding prisoner. The 'Rebel women' as they were called."

"Yes. They were in a building that was destroyed by a storm."

"They didn't have to keep us in that building," Belle insisted. "They had every opportunity to move us."

"Us? You were with them?" He remembered that Boykin McGee had suggested that she wasn't with them.

"Yes," Belle answered quickly. Then she paused and took a deep breath. "No," she said.

Win looked confused. "Yes? No? Which is it?"

Belle made another futile attempt to brush her hair back before she answered.

"Just before the storm," she started in a hesitant, apologetic voice, "I went to see Captain Parnell, to plead with him to move the women out of the building where we were being confined. I begged him to let us go somewhere safe until the storm passed." She stopped and ran her hand through her hair again. "He . . . he put a price on my request. He said he would do it, only if I . . ." Again she paused, and Win could see how difficult it was for her to tell the story.

"You don't have to go on," he said, gently. "I think I can guess what the price was."

Belle sighed. "Yes, and so did the whole town. I was, uh, doing things for him, when the storm hit. The building collapsed, and four women were killed. Somehow, everyone in Kansas City learned that I was having sex with Captain Parnell during the storm. They knew what I was doing, but they didn't know why I was doing it. They all think I did it to save myself."

"But that isn't true," Win said. "You were trying to save the others."

"I know, but who do you think is going to believe that? Except for Penny Anderson and Maggie Depro, the women never wanted me anyway. The other prisoners, in fact, all the Southern sympathizers, were upset that no difference was drawn in the minds of the army between them as Southern patriots, and me, a whore. I had nothing to do with that distinction, of course, but they held it against me. Now, add to that the fact that I was spared while Penny and Maggie were killed by the cyclone, and I became the most hated person in Kansas City. I was even more hated than Captain Parnell or General Ewing, and it was their orders which caused the deaths in the first place."

"I see. They think you sold them out."

"Yes," Belle said. "The Southerners hated me because they believed I betrayed their women. And those who support the Union hate me because they know I didn't. And when you start from the fact that whores don't have that many friends anyway, it left my social calendar pretty bare." Belle laughed weakly at her own joke.

"I can see where it would be pretty bad for you," Win said sympathetically.

"It was so bad that I left Kansas City, and I moved here."

With a wave of her hand, Belle took in the little crib and the town. "It's funny. I thought that here I could escape the hate. But it hasn't worked out that way. The hate has followed me. Only it's even worse here, because there are no soldiers around. That means that not only do I have no friends, I don't even have any customers."

"You still have one friend," Win said, putting his arms around her.

"Oh, Win," Belle said, moving into his arms, then sobbing on his shoulder. "If only things could have been different. If there wasn't a war, if I weren't a whore, if we had met at a Sunday picnic . . ."

Win chuckled. "You're describing a storybook world," he said. He pulled away from her far enough to look into her eyes. "By the way, when is the last time you had a decent meal?"

"I ate something this morning."

"I don't mean just eating. I mean a real meal," Win said.

"I . . . I don't know. I don't pay much attention to that these days."

"Well, it's time you started. Brush your hair and get yourself into your prettiest dress. We're going out on the town."

"Oh, Win, are you sure you want to be seen with me? The people in this town . . ."

". . . can all go to hell," Win finished for her.

THE SIGN PAINTED ON THE WINDOW ADVERTISED LAMbert's Cafe as: "The finest eating establishment west of the Mississippi River." In fact, Win had eaten here before, and he had eaten in other restaurants west of the Mississippi. And, although Lambert's claim was a little exaggerated, as he recalled, the meal was pretty good.

Despite Lambert's grandiose advertisment, not one of Quantrill's men was present when Win and Belle stepped inside. That was because the various saloons in town also served food, in addition to drink and occasional female companionship. And, for the recently returned Raiders, drinks and women were enjoying a much higher priority than the quality of the food.

Despite the absence of any of the Raiders, or perhaps because of it, Lambert's was filled with diners from the town. And, by their mode of dress, Lambert's clientele represented the more affluent citizens of the community. Their smug sense of security was upset when Win arrived. The normal buzz of conversation stopped as Win and Belle entered, and the faces of the diners registered the chagrin at having their social haven invaded by such upstarts as Win Coulter and Belle Amberly.

A waiter hurried over to them, clearing his throat as he approached.

"Sir, I'm sure you have made a mistake by coming into here," he said. "I believe you want the Yellow Dog Saloon, which is next door."

"You serve food in here, don't you?"

"Yes, but . . ."

"Then we're in the right place."

"Waiter, ask them to leave," one well-dressed diner demanded. "I would prefer not to eat with a Raider and his whore."

"Hear, hear," someone else said, and there was a general, though more subdued, sense of agreement.

Win walked over to the table where the diner sat with the overdressed, overbejeweled, and overfed woman who was obviously his wife.

"I beg your pardon, did you say you would rather not eat with us?" Win asked.

"I did indeed, sir," the diner answered stiffly. "I find your presence, and the presence of that woman who is with you, to be an affront against all that is respectable."

"Then I suggest you leave," Win said coldly.

"I beg your pardon, sir," the diner said indignantly. "Our meal has just arrived."

"Take it with you, or leave it on the table," Win said. "But I want you out of here. Now."

The diner, who was a fat man with a walrus-type moustache, sputtered a couple of times, then he stood up. "Come, Cynthia," he said.

"You can't do that," one of the other diners complained to Win. "You can't just throw out a paying guest like that."

"I can, and I did," Win said. "You get out too." He looked at all the diners who had been following the sequence of events in shocked silence. "As a matter of fact I want all of you to get out. My friend and I want some privacy. Get out, now!"

For a moment the diners all looked at one another, as if unable to believe what they were being ordered to do. But one glance toward Win's hard eyes was all the convincing they needed. Quickly, and without one more dissenting voice, they began to get up from their tables and file out. But not before the fat man with the walrus moustache took all the fried chicken from his and his wife's plate and slipped it down into his jacket pocket.

16

LUKE HUNTER WAS STANDING AT THE BAR OF THE YELlow Dog Saloon when some of the men Win had run out of Lambert's Cafe came in. They were still angry over what had happened to them, and they were complaining loudly about it.

"Who the hell does that fella think he is, running us out of the cafe like that? And in our own town!" one of the men said. "I'll tell you this. I thought about not leaving. I had half a mind to call him down. It was only because I don't want to be a party to such boorish behavior that I didn't do it."

"Be glad you had only half a mind to do it. Win Coulter is a killer," the other answered. "And killers aren't people you want to challenge."

"Well, he had no right, coming in there like that with that whore on his arm, ordering everyone out."

"She's the one I'm going to have a reckoning with," the other answered. "The very idea of a whore being uppity enough to come into a decent place like Lambert's. Especially with a killer like that."

"She will get her comeuppance once Quantrill and his

men leave," the first said. "I can guarantee that."

The two men had been standing at the bar by Hunter while they were talking, but when a table opened up at the back of the room, they moved away from the bar to take it. Hunter watched them for a moment, then he slid his glass across the bar to signal to the bartender that he wanted another drink.

"You have any idea what them two are talking about?" Hunter asked.

"I believe so, yes, sir," the bartender answered as he poured the whiskey. "Another gentleman came in a few moments ago with the story. It seems that Win Coulter, one of your compatriots, I believe, went into the restaurant and ordered all the diners to leave."

"They said somethin' about a woman with him."

"Yes, that would be Belle Amberly, I believe. She is a . . ."

"I know who Belle Amberly is," Hunter interrupted.

The bartender studied Hunter for a moment. "Yes," he said. "I'm sure someone like you would know her."

Hunter started to have his glass refilled, but he decided to buy an entire bottle instead. Then, with the bottle in hand, he went outside, crossed the street, and sat on the porch of a darkened building to drink and to keep his eye on Lambert's Cafe.

The sounds of revelry floated up the dark street toward him as the others in Quantrill's band celebrated their return to Missouri.

He could hear a piano.

A woman's high-pitched laughter penetrated the night.

A man cursed loudly.

A horse and rider came down the middle of the street, the hoofbeats sounding unusually loud in the dark.

Luke continued to drink, feeling the warming and somewhat numbing effect of the whiskey as it spread through him.

Finally a man and woman came out of Lambert's and Hunter stepped back into the dark so that he could watch without himself being seen.

Win and Belle moved down the walk on their side of the street, passing now and then through the squares of light that splashed out onto the street from the buildings they passed, so that sometimes they were illuminated, sometimes they were not.

Hunter followed them, staying always in the shadows on his side of the street. He watched them go down the alley behind the blacksmith shop, then he moved quickly and silently across the street to get into position to see them.

Standing in the shadow of the eave of the blacksmith shop, he watched them go inside. Then, because he knew what was going to happen inside, he got an erection. He reached down to feel himself.

"WIN," BELLE SAID. "I CAN'T REMEMBER WHEN I HAVE ever had a better evening. Thank you for taking me to dinner."

"We could make the evening even more complete if you are interested," Win suggested.

"More complete?"

Win nodded toward the bed. "You made an offer earlier tonight. Does that offer still stand?"

"You know it does," she said. "But I thought you didn't . . . that is, when I offered earlier, you turned me down. I thought you didn't want me."

"Not true," Win answered. "I just didn't want to take advantage of you."

What Win didn't say was that cleaned up, with her hair done and with the awful look of hunger assuaged, Belle was much more attractive now than she had been earlier.

"I wouldn't consider it taking advantage of me. I would consider it succumbing to my seduction," Belle said, and the genuine smile she flashed him did wonders for her. She was almost the same woman he had met on the stagecoach the year before. "And it makes me happy to know that I still have some seductive powers remaining."

"Some? Honey, I've got a hard-on now that could drive nails," Win said.

"Well, then we will just have to see what we can do about that, won't we?" Belle replied. She lit a candle, then turned toward him to begin undressing, doing it slowly and teasingly. As she slipped out of her dress, Win saw that she had lost none of her appeal. Somehow, even the somewhat smaller breasts made her more attractive.

"Well?" she asked, holding her arms out invitingly. "Are you going to just stand there? Or are you going to get naked too?"

"Well, now, I reckon I just got caught up in the watching," Win replied. "I guess now I'd better get naked too."

There was no subtlety to Win's getting out of his clothes. A tug here and a yank there, and he was standing in the golden glow of the candlelight as naked as was Belle herself.

Belle stepped over to her bed, then knelt on it so that her small round breasts were at Win's eye level. She shivered as Win's fingers traced the rim of the globes, then she sighed as his lips touched first one then the other nipple with kisses. With each kiss he let his tongue circle the nipple as his hands kneaded the pliant breasts.

"It's just as I remembered it," Belle whispered, writhing and moaning. "I knew it would be like this with you again." She let herself fall backwards as his mouth continued to move from nipple to nipple, inducing each of them into stone hardness.

Win moved his tongue to the area between her breasts, then down across her stomach where it lingered for a moment to make patterns on her belly, before it was drawn to the musky aroma of her forest. It tickled, but he probed the bush with his tongue until it slid through the slickened nether lips to the little quivering button inside. He began to massage that sensitive piece of flesh with his tongue and lips, telegraphing jolts of pleasure throughout her body.

Win used his mouth and tongue as Belle writhed in pleasure, the palms of her hands circling her own nipples to keep them taut.

"You," she said, pulling on him. "I want you."

Win raised up to look at her. Her hair was fanned on the pillow, and her eyes were smoldering with the knowledge of what was to come.

"Put it in me," Belle said. "Let me feel it . . . all of it!"

Win felt himself slip into the moist box as her pelvic muscles tightened and relaxed and tightened again. Belle was practiced in the art of making love and, as he entered her, she squeezed herself down on inch after swollen inch to produce greater sensations.

"All of it!" she panted, clasping tightly on his butt cheeks. She cooed a rhythm into his ear and moved her body so that he would match it. If she was an artist, Win was her canvas as together they stoked the sexual inferno.

Belle nearly bit off his earlobe as she rose to a shuddering climax, then she kissed him passionately to bring him along with her. Her hands kneaded his shoulders and back until his lean form quivered in convulsive orgasm as he spent himself in her.

Win collapsed across her, breathing hard for a few moments before, finally, he rolled to one side.

"Oh," Belle said breathily. "If I died now, I would die a happy woman. That was wonderful!"

Laughing, Win sat up and began putting on his clothes.

"Well, let's don't be planning on dying anytime soon. But this would be a good time for me to go," he said. "That way, I can leave you happy."

"No," Belle said. "Don't leave me. Stay here."

"Belle, you know I can't do that."

"I don't mean stay with me forever. I mean, stay the night with me. Just tonight. You have to have some place to sleep, don't you?"

"I'm tempted," Win said smiling. "But I need to get back with the others. You never know what Quantrill is going to do. He could pull out in the middle of the night and leave me here."

"Would that be so bad?"

Win put his hand on Belle's cheek. "During ordinary times, no, it wouldn't be bad at all," he said. "But I am a Raider, Belle. The Yankees would like nothing better than to catch me alone."

"I understand," Belle said reluctantly. "Win, will you come see me again?"

"Sure," Win said.

"Promise?"

"I promise."

Belle slipped into a thin wrapper, then walked to the door with Win, where she kissed him goodbye.

"Thanks for coming to see me," she said as he stepped off the little porch and out into the night. "You'll never know how much I needed that."

"Good night, Belle," Win tossed back over his shoulder.

WIN FOUND JOE IN THE CATAWBA TAVERN, ONE OF THE saloons which graced the streets of Blue Springs. Joe and

Cole Younger were engaged in a arm-wrestling contest, and there was a crowd gathered around the table to watch.

Both Joe and Cole were big, powerful men and the veins in their forearms bulged and their muscles flexed as they pushed and strained against each other.

"Get 'im Joe, get 'im!" someone called.

"Come on, Cole, you can do it!" another exhorted.

The rooting wasn't based upon personal favorites, for both Joe and Cole had easy outgoing personalities that had won them many friends. They were, in fact, good friends of each other. The rooting was grounded upon more compelling reasons, that of greed. Several dollars had been wagered upon the outcome of this particular event, and the men held bills clasped in their fists as they urged their champion on.

"Hi, Win," Joe said, his voice straining from the effort. "You got here just in time to watch me teach Cole a lesson."

"Ha!" Cole responded, his voice showing as much strain as Joe's. "Wait until I tie your arm in a knot, then we'll see who is the teacher and who is the pupil."

"Yeah, well, it doesn't matter to me," Win said easily. "I'm going to have myself a beer."

"It should matter to you, Win," Joe said. His arm was beginning to give way, and he had to put on a super effort to hold it short of going all the way down.

"Why? Because you are my brother?" Win teased.

"No," Joe replied. "Because I bet one hundred dollars that I could beat Cole."

"Little brother, that sounds like your problem to me."

"Yours too," Joe wheezed. Now his arm was nearly horizontal. "Fifty dollars of it is your money."

"What?" Win asked. It was at that precise moment that Cole won the match, putting Joe's arm all the way to the table, followed by an outbreak of cheers from those who had bet on him.

"Got you!" Cole shouted triumphantly.

"Shit!" Win shouted. "There goes my fifty bucks!"

Joe rubbed his shoulder as he smiled across the table at Cole. "I have to give you credit," he said. "You beat me fair and square."

"It's about time I won one," Cole replied, raking in his money. "I've lost the last three to you."

"Yeah," Win said disgustedly. "Well, he fought harder then, because it was *his* money he was losing. This time it was my money."

"Only fifty dollars of it was yours," Joe said. "And I thought I would beat him."

17

WHEN BELLE HEARD SOMEONE STEP UP ONTO THE FRONT porch, she thought it must be Win coming back to spend the night with her after all. With a happy smile she jerked open the door. As soon as she saw who it was, however, the smile left her face.

"What are you doing here?"

"I came by for a little pleasure," her visitor said, laying a finger alongside his thin nose.

"I'm not in the business anymore," Belle said.

Her visitor snorted. "That's bullshit. Once you're in the business, you're always in the business. At least, as long as someone is willing to pay."

"As I recall from our last visit, you weren't all that willing to pay," Belle said.

The visitor held out a twenty dollar gold piece. "It's been a long dry spell for me. I'm willing to pay now."

"Twenty dollars?" Belle asked in disbelief. "You're willing to pay twenty dollars to go to bed with me?"

"Yes. That is, if you think you can show me twenty dollars worth of pleasure."

Belle smiled, a practiced, seductive smile, and she put

her hand down to the front of his pants to grab him.

"Honey," she said, pulling him into her little house. "I can show you pleasure like you've only dreamed of."

Once inside, Belle's visitor slammed the door behind him. Then he grabbed her shoulder and spun her around toward him.

"Honey, don't be so impatient," Belle said, trying to make a joke of it.

"Shut up, bitch!" the man said, slapping her so hard that she tasted blood in her mouth.

"No, what . . . ?" Belle started to scream, but it was cut off when he put his hand across her mouth.

"I know all about you, missy. I know how you screwed your way out of jail to save your own skin."

Belle shook her head no, and tried to speak, to tell him that it wasn't so. But his hand cut off not only her scream but any words she might say as well.

"Well, now you're going to screw me," he rasped, pushing her back against the bed. She felt the side of the bed against the back of her legs, then, instantly it seemed, she was on her back and he was on top of her.

Belle tried to speak, to reason with him, but his hand stayed so securely over her mouth that only a few squeaks could emerge. She looked into his cold beady eyes and had the mental image of a giant rat. She was being raped by a giant rat, and she nearly passed out in revulsion.

She wished she could pass out, for next, the rapist spread her legs, then thrust himself into her. And the action that had brought her pleasure only a short while earlier in the evening, now brought her pain. Calling upon all her powers, Belle forced herself to relax, to quit fighting against it so that the pain would subside.

The rat grunted over her, and his breath came in raspy wheezes as he thrust into her. Finally, she felt him stiffen, and she gave a sigh of relief that it would soon be over. Then she felt something else, a sharp, pricking sensation just beneath her left breast. The pricking sensation suddenly erupted into a white-hot pain, more intense than anything she had ever felt before. She felt an unfamiliar pressure inside her chest, then as he raised up from her, she saw him pull back a bloody knife. Her eyes grew wide in horror, and, as his hand was now removed from her mouth, she tried to scream. Despite her best efforts, the scream emerged only as a rattle.

"Ssshhh, hush, now," the rat said, laying his finger across his thin lips. "Be a good girl, and die quietly."

"IF YOU'RE UPSET WITH ME, BIG BROTHER, I'LL PAY YOU back soon as I get some more money," Joe promised.

Win laughed, then punched his brother on the shoulder. "Ahh, don't worry about it. I seem to recall losing a few dollars of yours once or twice in a poker game."

"Yeah. Yeah, that's right, you did, didn't you?" Joe said. "Damn! I still haven't forgiven you for that time over in Liberty. I had me a whore all lined up when you came to get my money."

Win, Cole, and several other laughed, as suddenly someone burst excitedly through the front door.

"Fire!" the intruder shouted, running into the saloon. "Hey, ever'body, they's a house a'fire!"

"Where?" Several started toward the door.

"Behind the blacksmith shop!"

"Behind the blacksmith shop? Is it Belle Amberly's house?" Win asked.

"Yes, it's the whore's house!"

"Joe, come on!" Win shouted, starting toward the door. "We've got to get over there!"

Not only Joe, but everyone in the saloon jumped into

action as they rushed outside then down the street where, behind the blacksmith shop, they could see sparks and billowing smoke climbing into the night sky. The walls of the blacksmith shop, as well as the building next to it, glowed orange in the reflection of the flames.

From the far end of the street a clanging bell signaled the approach of the fire wagon. A team of horses brought the apparatus at a gallop, while from all over town volunteer firemen were converging on the scene, carrying buckets and axes.

"Get some water on those two buildings!" someone shouted, pointing to the blacksmith shop and its neighbor. "Never mind about the house! It's too late!"

"Belle!" Win shouted. "Where's Belle?"

Win ran up the narrow alley between the two buildings, toward Belle's house. By now, however, the house was totally immersed in flames, and the heat was so intense that Win was forced to stop several feet away. He held his arms up in front of him, shielding his face from the intense radiated heat.

"Has anyone seen Belle?" he asked.

There was no answer.

"Belle!" Win shouted again. "Has anyone seen her?"

"I been watchin' that fire nearly since it started, and ain't nobody come out," someone said.

"Belle!" Win shouted at the top of his voice.

"Maybe she wasn't in there," Joe suggested.

Win shook his head sadly. "She was in there," he said. "I just left her. I shouldn't have. She begged me to stay the night with her. My God, if I had been here . . ."

Win's lament was interrupted by the collapse of the roof over the front porch. When it fell, flames shot up farther. Then, with a whoosh, the roof of the house itself fell in. That was followed by the walls tumbling in, until there was nothing left of Belle's little house but a fiercely blazing bonfire.

In the shadows, some distance away, Luke Hunter sat drinking his whiskey and watching, silently.

QUANTRILL AND HIS MEN LEFT BLUE SPRINGS THE NEXT morning. A subdued Win went with them.

"She begged me to stay with her," Win said to his brother, as the two men rode together. "She begged me, but I said no."

"That fire wasn't your fault," Joe said, trying to ease the guilt he knew his brother felt. "Folks are saying that a spark must've flown back there from the blacksmith's forge."

"Maybe I didn't start the fire," Win said. "But if I had stayed with her, it wouldn't have happened."

"Or, it might have happened just the way it did, and both of you would have been killed," Joe suggested.

"No. I would have been able to do something," Win said. "I know I would."

THAT NIGHT QUANTRILL CALLED HIS MEN TOGETHER. HIS band was larger now than it had been while he was down in Texas, larger even than it had been when he left Blue Springs this morning. That was because word had gone out that he was back, and he was rejoined by those who had not made the trip south.

Quantrill climbed up onto a rock and stood in the wavering orange glow of a campfire to address his troops. Sparks from the fire climbed high into the night sky, joining the little red stars with the blue ones that already peppered the vault above them.

"Men," Quantrill said. "I don't have to remind you of

what happened here, while we were gone. You know about General Ewing's orders and our women.''

"Yeah," someone said.

"And you know how he sent soldiers out, armed men to terrorize and round up innocent women, for no more reason than that they were our loved ones.''

"Yeah!'' the response was louder this time.

Quantrill's voice also grew louder. "And you know how those murderous bastards," he said, pointing in the general direction of Kansas City, "those sorry sons of bitches murdered our women, by leaving them in an unsafe building during a cyclone!''

"Yeah!'' Now the response was shouted by scores of Raiders.

Quantrill's voice dropped, as he played his audience.

"I know that there are some among you who questioned my decision not to come to their rescue, when we first learned of the situation.''

There was reaction to this statement as well, but it was a subdued mumbling, as opposed to the earlier shouts.

"Believe me," Quantrill went on. "There is nobody here . . .'' He looked directly at Bill Anderson before he went on. *"No one,''* he repeated emphatically, "who wanted to come back worse than I did.''

Quantrill paused for a moment, to let his words sink in.

"But," he continued, raising his index finger to the heavens. "I knew that the Yankees were lying in wait for us. They took our women for bait and they wanted us to take the bait, the way a mouse will try and snatch cheese from a trap. The mouse is always caught. And, if we had taken the bait the Yankees set for us, we would have been caught too. That means the women would have remained their prisoners, and they would have died in the storm, just as they did. The only difference is, some of you, many of you, would be dead as well.''

"It would've been worth the chance!'' someone yelled.

"No,'' Quantrill replied, holding up his hands to quiet them. "No, it would *not* have been worth the chance. If we had tried and failed, if we had allowed our band to be cut up in a futile attempt, then we would not be able to do what we are going to do now.''

"What are we going to do now?'' someone asked.

"We are going to pick us a town . . . in Kansas, where we know that everyone is a Yankee,'' Quantrill said. He paused for a moment, then he took a deep breath and literally shouted out the next line.

"And we are going to have our revenge!''

Quantrill's words were met with a deep-throated cheer from the men, so loud that it reverberated back from the nearby hills.

"As far as I am concerned,'' Quantrill went on with a snarl, "what those Yankee bastards did proves we are fighting against hypocrites. They raise hell about our outlaw ways, but have we ever harmed any of their women or children?''

"No!'' the men shouted.

"Did we ever round up all their women and put them in a deathtrap building, then collapse it on them?''

"No!''

"Well, by God, the Yankees did!'' Quantrill shouted. He pointed to Bloody Bill Anderson who was still grieving over the loss of his sister. "Ask Bill how he feels about the Yankees right now.''

"I'll tell you how I feel,'' Anderson shouted back. "I feel like riding into Kansas City right now and killing every goddamned one of them!''

"We can't kill ever'one in Kansas City, Bill,'' Cole

Younger said. "Some of us got kinfolk there. Not ever'one in Kansas City is a damn Yankee."

"Cole is right," Quantrill agreed. "Not everyone in Kansas City is a Yankee." He smiled. "But everyone in Lawrence is."

"Where is Lawrence?"

"It's in Kansas, about forty miles on the other side of the border," Quantrill answered. "It's got a nice fat bank, several rich stores, and it is all Yankee. And, get this," he added, looking over at Win and Joe. "Lawrence is where Emil Slaughter lives."

"Slaughter lives in Lawrence?" Win asked.

Quantrill nodded. "I just found out," he said. "What do you have to say about that?"

Win climbed up onto the rock beside Quantrill then looked out over the faces of the men who were gathered. "I say that anyone who finds him had better not harm a hair on his head. That son of a bitch belongs to me!" he shouted.

The men replied with a loud cheer.

"What do you say, men?" Quantrill shouted. "Do we go to Lawrence?"

"Hell!" Anderson shouted. "Let's do it!"

"Yahoo!" Jesse James shouted, and he took a shot at a nearby tree. That opened up a fusillade of shooting, and for the next few minutes it sounded as if a battle were under way as the Raiders, whooping and hollering, banged away at the tree, from which chips of bark began to fly.

18

THE LONG COLUMN OF HORSEMEN, RIDING IN ROWS OF fours, snaked its way across the Kansas plains under a star-filled but moonless night sky. Win and Joe were near the head of the column and when Win turned to look at the men following along behind them, it looked like a monstrous snake, creeping down upon its prey.

"Win," Joe said after they had ridden for several miles in silence. "You still thinkin' about Belle?"

Win sighed. "I reckon not," he replied. "You're right. I'm not the cause of it. But I sure am wondering why she didn't just run out of there when the fire started."

"Hell," Luke Hunter said, barging uninvited into the conversation. "They found her on the bed, didn't they? She was prob'ly asleep and never knew what was goin' on until it was too late. I mean, if them sparks fell on the roof and started burning up there, why the whole house would've been on fire by the time she woke up."

"But why was she still in bed?"

"What do you mean, why was she on the bed? Beds is where most folks sleep," Hunter replied.

"Even if she had been asleep when the fire started, she

must've awakened. And if she woke up, why didn't she get out of bed? I can understand that she might not make it out of the house, but I can't understand her just lying in bed, waiting to die.''

"You know what I've been wondering about?" Joe asked.

"What's that?"

"How did the sparks get out of the blacksmith's forge and onto the roof of Belle's house without setting the black-smith's shop on fire?"

"Yeah, I've been wondering about that too," Win said. "Besides which, the blacksmith swears that he left his forge cold.''

"He was just saying that to shift the blame away from himself,'' Hunter pointed out. "Don't forget, they found coals in his forge.''

"Yeah, but that's another thing. He says the coals weren't the way he normally laid his fire. And the man that works for him says the same thing.''

"What are you saying, Win? That someone just made it look like sparks from the blacksmith shop caused the fire?'' Joe asked.

Win nodded. "If someone deliberately set the fire, that would answer a few questions, wouldn't it?'' he said.

"Like what?'' Hunter asked.

"Like why she didn't get out of bed when the fire started,'' Win said.

"You mean you think she might've already been dead?'' Joe asked.

"That's what I'm thinkin',' Win said.

"But, who would do a thing like that? What reason would they have for killing her?'' Joe asked. "You said yourself she had fallen on hard times, that she didn't have a pot to piss in or a window to throw it out of.''

"That's where I'm stumped," Win replied. "She wasn't very popular, that's for sure. But she'd been there for several weeks without anything like that happening. Why now?"

"Maybe it's your fault," Hunter suggested.

"What do you mean?" Joe asked, bristling at the suggestion that his brother was at fault.

"She was a whore, remember? Only your brother took her into a restaurant and shoved her down ever'one's throat." He chuckled, insensitively. "That couldn't have set too well with the good people of the town."

"Watch what you're saying, you son of a bitch, or I'll . . ." Joe started, but Win stuck out his hand to interrupt him.

"No, Joe, hold it," Win said morosely. "I don't like to admit it, but Hunter may be right. Belle could very well be dead because of me."

"Yeah, well, even if that's true . . . which I don't believe, by the way . . . he doesn't have to shove it in your face," Joe said. He glared at Hunter with such intensity that Hunter shrugged, then moved on back along the column to get away from the Coulter brothers.

"You know something, Win?" Joe said. "You should have killed that son of a bitch when you threw down on him, back in Texas."

"Little brother, that thought has crossed my mind," Win admitted.

THE MEN RODE ALL THROUGH THE REST OF THE NIGHT. Then, just before dawn, Quantrill held up his hand, stopping the long column on the top of a hill about a quarter of a mile out of town. They sat quietly for a moment, studying their objective. Here and there in the little town before them, golden patches of light shined from the dark houses, indicating those who were early risers. The smell of frying bacon drifted up the hill toward the men.

Some roosters crowed.

They could hear the yap of a dog.

A door slammed, and they saw a man walking toward the outhouse, fitting his galluses over his shoulders as he hurried across the backyard.

A mule brayed.

"Look at that," Quantrill said. "They don't have the slightest idea that we are here."

"I don't know, Chief," Hunter said.

"What do you mean, you don't know?" Quantrill replied, without looking back at him. Quantrill had not taken his eyes off the town from the moment they had arrived.

"Don't forget, we been on the trail for two days now. Could be someone seen us and sent word back to these folks that we're comin'."

"Take a look. Does it look like they're waiting for us?" Quantrill asked.

"No," Hunter replied. "But, if it was a trap, if they was plannin' an ambush, they wouldn't be dumb enough to let us see 'em. Maybe you'd better let me ride in and have a look around first, just to make sure everything is all right."

"We have come this far to attack Lawrence," Quantrill said. "And, by God, that's exactly what we are going to do."

Without further discussion, Quantrill drew his revolver, spurred his horse into a gallop, and started down the hill.

"Charge!" he shouted at the top of his voice.

Quantrill's abrupt move galvanized the others into action, and as one, the entire column, including Luke Hunter, had no choice but to go with him. They thundered, four hundred riders strong, down the hill then onto the main street of Lawrence.

"Kill! Kill!" Quantrill was shouting as the horses pounded into town. "Lawrence must be cleansed, and the only way to cleanse it is to kill! Kill!"

At the house nearest the extreme edge of the town, a man was just sliding a bucket into place for the morning milking. He grabbed the cow's teats and started to pull when he was startled by the sudden appearance of a column of men. As Lawrence was too far from Missouri to have ever been involved in any of the frequent border clashes, Confederate guerrillas were the last thing on the man's mind. More in curiosity than fear, he stood up. One of the riders closest to him fired, and his bullet crashed into the milker's forehead, slamming him back, overturning the milk stool and splattering his blood on the freshly turned straw.

The hooves of four hundred galloping horses raised a thunder as Quantrill led his men on into the heart of Lawrence. The riders fired their guns indiscriminately and screeched like demons from hell, waking even the deepest sleepers. Several of the town's citizens, many still in their nightshirts, stepped into the front doors of their homes to see what was going on. It was a foolish move on their parts, for the moment they stuck their heads through their front doors, they were shot down, not by one bullet, but by fifteen or twenty bullets.

Lawrence was the home billet of a small detachment of Union soldiers, most of whom were awaiting orders to join the Army in the East, none of whom had ever seen battle. A makeshift army camp had been created right in the middle of the town, where, on Main Street, the soldiers had pitched their tents.

Seasoned soldiers would have reacted quickly to unexplained gunfire by perceiving it as a possible threat to them, and they would have had their weapons at the ready. But these weren't seasoned soldiers. They were green troops who had never been any closer to the war than the thrilling stories they read in the newspapers, and to them, gunshots at the edge of town were no more than a curiosity. They were still drowsy from sleep and just crawling out of their tents when Quantrill and his men suddenly appeared on top of them.

Thinking it might be a detachment of their own cavalry, the soldiers watched Quantrill and his galloping riders with excitement.

"Yankee soldiers!" one of Quantrill's riders shouted, noticing the young men in blue. "Kill them! Kill them!"

Several of the riders broke free of the column then started toward the just-waking soldiers. When the boys in blue realized that the wild-eyed riders coming toward them had hostile intent, they turned and tried to run. Some were clubbed down, some were killed by saber thrusts, some were shot, and others were trampled under the pounding hooves of the horses. Only a few managed to escape.

When they reached the front of the Lawrence Hotel, which was the most imposing building in town, Quantrill held up his hand, signalling a halt. Four hundred men, all brandishing guns, and mounted on steeds that were breathing hard and sweating foam from their morning gallop, filled the street. It was such a sight that, despite the danger, several townspeople were drawn to the scene to satisfy their curiosity.

One of the townspeople recognized one of the riders, and he called out to him. "Luke Hunter! Luke, is that you, riding with these men?"

Hearing his name called, Hunter, who was in the front rank, looked toward the man who was hailing him.

"I can't believe that you, of all people, are riding with

Rebels,'' the man said. ''Last time I heard about you, you was . . .''

A gunshot stopped the man in mid-sentence, and a spray of blood formed a halo of pink mist around the man's head as he tumbled back, dead, even before he hit the ground. Win saw the man go down, then he turned and saw that Hunter was pointing his pistol toward him. Smoke was curling up from the end of the barrel of Hunter's pistol.

''What the hell did you shoot him for?'' Win asked.

''Goddamnit, we're shooting everyone, aren't we?'' Hunter replied. ''And the son of a bitch was shouting my name out all over the place.''

''He seemed to know you. Makes a body wonder what he was going to say,'' Win said.

''Hell,'' Cole Younger said, laughing. ''Whatever it was, it wasn't going to be good. There ain't anyone who knows Luke Hunter can say somethin' good about him.''

Those who were close enough to hear what was being said, laughed, and even Hunter seemed to enjoy the joke told at his expense.

At that moment a frightened, dignified-looking man appeared at the front door of the hotel. He had taken the trouble to dress fully, and he was still fastening the buttons of his vest as he stepped out onto the hotel porch. He looked at Quantrill and those with him, then he glanced down the street where, already, several people were gathering around the half dozen or more bodies the Raiders had killed during their wild entrance.

''Sir, may I enquire as to who you are?'' the well-dressed man asked.

Quantrill smiled, and looked at those around him. ''He's a polite little son of a bitch, isn't he?'' he asked.

His riders laughed.

''I am William Clarke Quantrill, Lieutenant Colonel,

Confederate States Army,'' Quantrill said pointedly.

The man gasped and turned pale. "My God! Quantrill!''

"Well, it looks like he's heard of us,'' Quantrill said to his men. Then, turning back to the well-dressed man. "Who are you?''

"My name is Mr. Jones, sir, and I am the concierge of this hotel,'' the man answered.

"Concierge. Does that mean you are in charge?'' Quantrill asked.

"It does, sir,'' Jones answered.

"Well, Mr. Jones, I want you to bring breakfast,'' Quantrill ordered.

Jones looked around. "Good Lord, sir? To all of you?'' he asked.

"No, just to me,'' Quantrill said. "I'm sure the others can find breakfast for themselves.''

"Very good, sir,'' the concierge stammered. "What do you want for your breakfast?''

"Eggs, pancakes, bacon, sausage, ham, whatever you have. I want the best you have, and I want plenty of it!'' Quantrill ordered with an impatient wave of his hand.

"Yes, sir, I'll get on it right away.''

Quantrill stood in the stirrups and shouted out to his men.

"All right, you men, you are on your own for breakfast. Get it from the citizens of town. If anyone refuses, kill them. Then I want you to bring in everything of value: money, jewels, anything we can carry with us, to me, here in the hotel. After we've cleaned everyone out, burn the town. From now on, whenever someone says the name Quantrill, I want them to say it with fear.''

"You don't think the people of this town are just going to stand around and let you burn their town, do you?'' one of the nearby citizens shouted up at him.

Archie Clement was the closest to the challenging citizen, and he shot him down from nearly point-blank range. The others looked on in horror for just a moment, then even the bravest ran so that, very quickly, the street was cleared of all the townspeople.

"Bill, you want to come in and have breakfast with us? Or you want to take care of business out here?"

An evil grin spread across Bill Anderson's face. "I can eat anytime," he said. "I'd rather take care of business."

"All right," Quantrill replied. "You know what to do."

"You men," Anderson shouted. "Spread out into small groups and start riding up and down the streets of this town. Leave the women alone, but kill any man you see who is old enough to carry a gun."

"What if he ain't carryin' one?" someone asked. "You want him killed anyway?"

"Look around you," Anderson said. "Do you see anyone outside now? There ain't no one goin' to come out, 'lessen they're up to no good?" Anderson asked.

"I guess you have a point."

"Damn right I've got a point. Coulter, I want you and . . . !"

"Don't bother giving me any orders, Anderson," Win interrupted. "If Emil Slaughter is anywhere in this town, I'm going to find him and kill him. And I don't aim to be put off by you or anyone else."

Anderson glared at Win for a moment, then looked over at Quantrill, as if seeking support for his order.

"Leave the Coulter boys out of it, Bill," Quantrill said. "They'll be busy enough."

"Thanks, Charley," Win said. "Come on, little brother, let's get busy."

"Where do we start?" Joe asked. He waved his hand. "I mean, he could be anywhere in this town."

Win halted for a moment, pondering Joe's question.

Then he saw something that made him smile. "What if we started there?" he asked, pointing to the newspaper office.

Because it was still early in the morning, the newspaper office, like most of the other business establishments in town, was closed. Win opened it the same way the other Raiders were opening the other businesses. By kicking in the door.

Once inside, he stood for a moment, looking around to get his bearings. On the other side of a counter, in the back of the room, a Washington Hand press loomed large in the shadows, while along one wall there were boxes upon boxes of lead type.

"Damn," Joe said. "Look at all this stuff. I don't even know what I'm lookin' at, let alone what we are supposed to be lookin' for."

Suddenly Win smiled. "We're looking for that," he said, pointing to a ledger book. On the outside of the book was the word *Subscriptions*.

Win opened the book and started leafing through the pages until he came to the letter S. Then he ran his finger down the list of names.

"Here it is," he said. "Emil Slaughter, two-one-five Third Street." He slammed the ledger shut and started back toward the front door which was now hanging at a crooked angle by only one hinge.

Outside they could hear the bang of gunshots, sometimes singly, sometimes in clusters so that the rhythm of the shooting was somewhat like corn being popped in a pan. They could also smell smoke, and when Win and Joe went back into the street they could see that several buildings had already been set ablaze.

Just as they reached Third Street, someone with a rifle appeared on the roof of one of the houses. The rifleman fired and his bullet whined by Win's ear, kicked up dirt from the ground behind him, then skipped away erratically. Win returned fire. His bullet found its mark and the shooter dropped his rifle and grabbed his chest. The rifle bounced down the shake roof of the house, then fell to the ground, followed by the man who slid along behind it, facedown, before tumbling over the edge to land face-up on the ground below.

The smoke from all the burning buildings was getting thicker.

"Looks like we've set fire to a lot of houses here," Joe observed.

"We're just giving it back to them," Win said. "The way I plan to give it back to Slaughter."

"We going to burn his house?"

"Yes."

"What if he is married?"

"Ma and pa were married," Win said, bitterly. "That didn't stop him from burning our house."

"Yeah, but he did it, not his wife. And what if he has kids?" Joe asked.

"Any woman that would marry a son of a bitch like Emil Slaughter has to be as mean as he is. And any kids he might have will grow up to be just like him."

Joe looked at Win in shock. "Win, we aren't going to kill his wife and kids?"

Win stopped for a moment, then he pinched the bridge of his nose in contemplation.

"God in heaven," he said. "I'm getting as bad as Slaughter is." He sighed. "All right, if he's married, I'll give his family a chance to come out of the house before I set fire to it."

"What if he comes out too?" Joe asked.

"I intend to shoot the bastard," Win replied simply.

"Win, there's the house. See the number? Two-one-five,'' Joe said, pointing to a white frame house across the street.

There was a white picket fence around the house and a rather large elm tree just on the street side of the fence. The lawn was well-tended, there were flowers in window boxes, and the house was neatly kept.

''I don't know,'' Joe said. ''Win, are you sure this is the place?''

''Two-one-five,'' Win replied.

''But look at it. It looks like a storeowner's house or the house of a banker. It doesn't look like the house of a man like Slaughter.''

''Joe, you don't expect him to hang a sign out that says: 'I am a murderer,' do you?''

''No, I guess not.''

''This is the house,'' Win said. He pulled his pistol. ''I can feel it.''

Win and Joe moved quickly to the tree, using it to provide them with cover.

''Slaughter!'' he shouted.

When there was no answer, Win fired a shot through the front window.

''Emil Slaughter!''

''What do you want?'' a muffled voice called back.

''I want you, you son of a bitch!'' Win said.

''I'm not Emil Slaughter! You've got the wrong house!''

Joe looked at Win, as if questioning him again. Then, suddenly, Joe broke into a large smile and he nodded toward the fence. When Win looked in the direction Joe had indicated, he saw a brass nameplate on the gate. The nameplate read: ''Captain Emil Slaughter, Seventh Kansas Cavalry.''

''Sorry I questioned you, Win,'' Joe said.

''That's all right. I'm glad you found the sign,'' Win

replied. "I was beginning to question myself."

"Go away!" the voice called out to them. "I'm not the one you are looking for!"

"Come on out with your hands up. If you can prove you aren't Slaughter, I'll let you go."

"You go to hell!" the voice from the house called. Suddenly a shot rang out from the front window, and the bullet snapped off a branch just above Win's head.

Win and Joe returned fire, their bullets crashing through the glass windowpanes and causing the curtains to pop backwards.

There was another shot from the house from one of the other windows, and this, too, was answered by Win and Joe. Then there was a moment of silence, followed by a white flag tied to the end of a pole being poked out the window.

"Stop your firin'! Stop your firin'!" the voice shouted from inside. "I got my wife and kids in here with me."

Win and Joe held their fire.

"What do you want with me?" the voice asked.

"Are you Emil Slaughter?"

There was a moment of silence, then the question was answered. "Yeah, I'm Slaughter," the voice called back.

"Come on out, Slaughter. Come out with your hands in the air."

"Why should I come out? You're going to shoot me down as soon as I step outside."

"If you care anything about your family, come on out. Otherwise they're likely to be caught in the cross fire."

"All right, all right, I'm comin'."

Win and Joe kept their eyes on the front door. This was the man who had led the raid against their farm. On his orders their parents were killed, and their home was burned.

What did he look like? Win wondered. Did he have horns and a tail?

The door opened, and two young girls and an adult woman stepped out onto the front porch.

"All right, you people get off the porch and out of the way!" Win shouted. "I'm not after you."

The woman and children didn't move, so Win stood up and stepped out from behind the tree to make certain they could see as well as hear him.

"I told you, get out of the way!" he shouted, waving his hand.

Suddenly a shot came from the front porch and the bullet took out a chunk of Win's earlobe. He felt a burning pain, along with a sticky wetness. He put his hand up to cover his ear, then pulled it away, red with blood.

"What the hell!" Win shouted.

A second shot came from the porch, and that was when Win saw Slaughter, crouched down behind his family. He was using his wife and kids as a shield, while he was blasting away at Win and Joe from behind them.

Quickly Win bolted to get back behind the tree.

"Slaughter, you son of a bitch! What kind of man would hide behind his own family?" Win shouted. He raised his pistol, hoping to get a shot, but no opportunity presented itself.

Continuing to use his family for cover, Slaughter maneuvered to the side of the porch. When he reached the edge, he pushed them aside and jumped down to dash to the rear of the house, putting the side of the house between himself and Win and Joe.

"Win, he's gettin' away!" Joe shouted.

"The hell he is!" Win replied, stepping out into the open so he could see Slaughter. Standing sideways, Win raised his pistol and took a long, careful aim, sighting down the barrel. He touched the trigger and the gun boomed.

Just as Slaughter was reaching the outhouse, nearly seventy-five yards away, the bullet slammed into the back of his neck. He stumbled forward, lost his balance, then crashed through the outhouse door.

Holding his pistol at the ready, Win ran up to check on him. He stopped as he got close, then continuing to hold his gun on Slaughter's still form, advanced the last few feet very carefully, ready to react to any sudden moves on Slaughter's part. From here Win could smell the heavy stench of the outhouse, and he could hear the big green bottle-flies as they buzzed about noisily.

Slaughter was absolutely motionless, his head and shoulders through the door of the outhouse, the rest of his body outside. The gun Slaughter was carrying was lying on the ground alongside.

Win reached out to grab Slaughter by the back of his shirt. He pulled him out of the toilet, then let him fall onto his back, his arms flopping out to either side of him.

"Shit!" Joe arriving at that moment and seeing Slaughter's face.

The expletive was appropriate, for when Slaughter had fallen into the toilet, his head had gone down through the hole, burying itself in a foot of nightsoil. It was all over his face, in his eyes, nostrils, and mouth.

"All I can say is, I hope the son of a bitch was alive long enough to enjoy some of that," Win said. When Win looked back toward the front of the house he saw Slaughter's wife and kids standing at the corner, looking back at them, their faces contorted with terror.

"We going to burn the house, Win?" Joe asked.

Win looked at Slaughter's family for a moment longer, then he sighed and shook his head. "No," he said. "I'm satisfied."

• • •

WHEN WIN AND JOE RETURNED TO THE DINING ROOM OF
the hotel, Quantrill was just finishing his breakfast.

"Did you find him?" Quantrill asked, shoving a sausage
patty into one of the biscuits before taking a bite.

"Yes," Win answered.

"Kill him?"

"Yes."

"Good. If there was ever a son of a bitch that needed
killing, it was him. Did you boys get a chance to eat breakfast?"

"No," Joe said.

Quantrill picked up a couple of biscuits and tossed them
up to Win and Joe. "Here," he said. "No sense in letting
them go to waste."

"Thanks," Win said, taking a bite. "Damn, these are
good." He looked around. "Where's that fancy-dressed
man, I'd like to tell him."

"Don't worry none about him," Quantrill said. "He's
been taken care of."

"Charley, wait 'til you see it!" Bill Anderson shouted,
coming into the hotel then. "We've made quite a haul!
Bring it in here, boys!" he called.

At Anderson's order, men began bringing in money
boxes, jewelry cases, watches and rings, candlesticks, and
silver and gold goblets. Quantrill had finished eating by
now, and he made a place on the table for the booty by the
simple expedient of pushing everything, dishes, uneaten
food, and half-full coffee cups, onto the floor. Then, using
the table as a desk, Quantrill began taking inventory of the
spoils.

"Look at it, boys!" Quantrill said. He scooped his hands
through the pile of small jewelry and gold coins, then lifted
them, palms up, to let the gold, sparkling in the morning

light, spill through his fingers like water. "Did I tell you this was a good idea? Some of you didn't believe me."

George Todd came in with blood on his shirt and face and smelling of smoke. His eyes blazed wildly.

"Charley, we just got word that some Federal troops are on the way here."

"All right, get the boys together and let's get out of here," Quantrill said.

"What, we're leavin'?" Anderson asked, surprised by the order. "Hell, we've only got a little bit of the booty in this town. There's lots of places we haven't even been in yet."

Quantrill opened his watch and looked at it, then he snapped it shut. "It's half past eight," he said. "We've been here long enough, especially if there are troops coming. Now, have the boys load up as much food as they can carry, and let's get out of here."

"*Colonel* Quantrill," Anderson said, making a mockery of the rank, "would you mind tellin' me why the hell we are running? We've got nearly four hundred men here, now. That's the biggest our outfit's ever been. Why don't we just wait for the soldiers and ambush them?"

"Why would we want to do a damn fool thing like that? We've done what we set out to do," Quantrill answered. "We should leave while we are ahead."

"Charley, I have to agree with Bill on this," Win said. "If we could defeat a regular Union army unit here, in Kansas, it would legitimize our raid."

"*Legitimize? Legitimize?*" Quantrill said. He threw his arms out, then let them fall, disgustedly, to his sides. "God-damnit, am I the only one here who is not stupid? Don't you understand? We don't want to be legitimized. If we are legitimate, we have to follow all the rules of war. And if we were following the rules of war"—he ran his hand through a stack of gold coins, picking them up and letting them drop back on the table with a clink—"we wouldn't get to keep any of this."

"Yes, but think of the trouble we could cause for the Yankees by defeating some of their regulars here. *We* could force the Yankees to bring some of the war into Kansas, and that means they would have to bring in fresh troops from Missouri and Arkansas to handle it. That would relieve some of the pressure on our people in general, and on General Price and General Van Dorn in particular."

"To hell with Price and Van Dorn," Quantrill said, as he started stuffing money into his pockets. "Let them fight their own goddamn war. You know, they always figured they were a little better than us, anyway. Well, by God, they won't be getting any help from me. Now, come on, let's get out of here."

Without waiting for them to follow him, Quantrill stormed across the floor, then out the door.

When Win and Joe went back outside, they were faced with so much smoke and flying ash in the street that it was actually difficult to breathe. By now, more than three-fourths of the buildings, both commercial and private, were burning fiercely, including even Emil Slaughter's house, though neither Win nor Joe had set fire to it. Win didn't know if the Slaughter house had been set afire, or if it was ignited by flying firebrands, the cause of at least half a dozen fires in their own right.

In addition to the burning buildings, scores of bodies lay sprawled in the street, most of them shot more than once. One of the bodies, Win noticed, was the well-dressed corpse of Mr. Jones, the concierge of the hotel. Evidently, that was what Quantrill meant when he said that the concierge had been taken care of. It was, truly, a scene from hell.

Win left the front porch, and walked down into the street to move among the dead. He had seen this many dead before, especially after battles in which they had participated where armed men were locked in desperate struggle against other armed men. But the dead here had not been killed in battle. They had been murdered in cold blood; in some cases, hauled out of their beds while still in their nightshirts and hacked to pieces or shot down in front of their horrified families, while their wives and children pleaded for their lives.

Among the victims were some very young boys, no more than nine or ten, and some very old men, including a few who Win was sure were eighty or more.

And, standing in the street, crying bitter tears over their loved ones, were the women of the town. By Quantrill's orders, no woman had been molested or physically injured. But Win knew that the pain inflicted upon these women's souls would never diminish, and he could feel the heart-chilling loathing in their stares.

Win wanted to tell them that he was sorry. He wanted them to know that when he rode in here this morning, he had no idea that killing of this magnitude would happen. But he couldn't tell them because he knew it would be a lie. He had been with Quantrill for well over a year, and by now he understood, fully, what kind of man Quantrill was . . . what kind of men the Raiders were, and . . . he was forced to admit to himself . . . what kind of man *he* was. What did he expect would happen when four hundred armed men descended on a defenseless town?

"You leaving with us, Win?" Jesse asked. "Or are you going to stay and greet the Yankees when they get here?" Jesse laughed at his own joke.

It wasn't until that moment that Win realized he was the only one who had not yet mounted.

"I reckon I'd better go with you, boys," Win said, climbing into the saddle, then looking again at the weeping women. He looked at his brother, Joe, and saw that Joe was having as much difficulty handling the situation as he was.

Quantrill stood in the stirrups to address his men. "All right, men, we have accomplished our mission!" he shouted. "One hundred, maybe even two hundred years from now, men will speak in awe of what we did here today! Let's go!"

At Quantrill's order, the four hundred men left Lawrence the same way they had entered it . . . at a gallop. When they reached the top of a hill about a mile out of town, Win stopped. Twisting around in his saddle, he looked back toward the town. From here it looked as if the billowing black smoke from over a hundred burning buildings had collected into one huge column to roil and surge into the sky. And though there was no sound, in Win's mind he could still hear the wailing sobs of the grieving wives, mothers, and daughters of the slain.

"What was the name of that town, again, Win?" Joe asked, stopping beside him to have the same vantage point.

"Lawrence," Win answered. "Lawrence, Kansas."

"Lawrence," Joe repeated. He was silent for a moment. "I want to remember it."

"Why?"

"Because," Joe explained. "I want to remember where it was that I left my soul."

Win was glad to hear that his brother was fighting the same devils he was. That meant that he wasn't alone.

19

"YOU SENT FOR ME, GENERAL?" CAPTAIN PARNELL asked, reporting to General Ewing in his Kansas City head-quarters.

"Yes," Ewing answered. "Have you seen this?" He handed Parnell a newspaper. In dark print, at the top of the left hand column, the headlines leaped out at Parnell.

QUANTRILL RAIDS LAWRENCE, KANSAS
150 MEN AND BOYS BUTCHERED
MANY HOUSES AND BUSINESSES BURNED
BANK, STORES, AND HOMES LOOTED.
CAPTAIN EMIL SLAUGHTER MURDERED

"I haven't read the article in the newspaper yet," Parnell replied. "But I have seen the official report."

"What are you going to do about it?"

Parnell gulped. "What am *I* going to do about it, General?"

"Quantrill is making a mockery of us, Captain. The Federal army has become a laughingstock. Do you realize that? Not only that, when he murdered Captain Slaughter, he killed one of the most effective countermeasures we have against the bushwhackers.''

"If you ask me, General, we're just as well off to be rid of Mr. Slaughter," Parnell said. "He and Quantrill were cut from the same cloth.''

"That is precisely my point, you idiot," General Ewing snapped. "But now Slaughter is dead and making no trouble for anyone, while Quantrill is still alive, still a bone in our throat, and still at large.''

"Yes, sir, I know. He has been our number one mission around here for some time, now, but, as you know, we have been unable to catch him.''

Ewing sighed. "Captain Parnell, you must forgive me. I'm sorry for taking my anger and frustration out on you. In truth, I am more to blame than anyone else. I should not have let their women go when I had them in my hands," Ewing said. "Damn me for being so soft-hearted.''

"General, we really didn't have any choice; we had to let the women go," Parnell said. "We already had most of the people around here against us for that. And, after some of the women were killed in the storm, nearly everyone turned against us. Why, if we hadn't let the women go, we would've had a revolt on our hands.''

Ewing flashed a disgusted look at Parnell. "We've already *got* a revolt on our hands, Captain," he said. "It's called the Civil War. Or, don't you know what we have been doing these past few years?''

"Why, yes, sir, of course I know that we are fighting a Civil War," Parnell replied, stung by Ewing's criticism.

"Wait a minute," Ewing said. "You may have something there.''

"I beg your pardon?''

"A revolt," Ewing said. "If the people are in revolt, then the people, themselves, are our enemy. They are as much our enemy as Quantrill. So, if we can't get to Quantrill, we'll get to the people."

"I don't understand, General," Parnell said, shaking his head in confusion.

Ewing smiled and rubbed his hands together. "Captain, I am going to issue orders, effective immediately. I want you to remove every Missouri resident from the following counties: Platte, Clay, Jackson, and Cass."

"Remove, General?" Parnell replied, asking for clarification.

"Remove, as in force them to leave. And that means *every* resident, regardless of what loyalties they claim," Ewing insisted. "Then, once you have moved them out, I want you to render their property undesirable enough to discourage them attempting to re-enter."

"And, how am I to do that, General?"

"Easy enough," General Ewing said, offhandedly. "You just burn every farmhouse, barn, granary, tool-shed, hog-shed, chicken-coop and outhouse you can find. Close the wells, burn the fields, destroy the bridges, sink the ferries, blow up the trains and tear up the track. Once that's done you will have your soldiers conduct daily patrols of the area and, if you find anyone in there, man, woman, or child, you will hang that person to the nearest tree or telegraph pole."

"My God, General, if we do something like that, it will turn those four counties into little more than desert," Parnell said.

Ewing smiled. "Yes, it will, won't it?" he said. "That is exactly what I have in mind. Don't tarry, Captain. I want you to get started on that right away."

FROM THEIR POSITION ON THE HILL, WIN AND JOE COULD see as many as six columns of smoke, climbing like ropes into the sky. Each plume of smoke represented another farm family that had been burned out by Ewing's soldiers.

"Seems to me like instead of splitting up and going around to warn people, we'd do better to stick together and stop the Yankees," Joe suggested.

"Suppose we did stop them today," Win replied. "Then what would we do? We can't stay there and wait for them to come back. No, we're doing the best we can do, and that is just to warn them that the soldiers are coming. The Yankees aren't allowing them to take any wagons, carts, or pack-animals with them. They are being forced to flee with what they can carry on their backs. This way, at least, they can get some of their things out of there before the Yankees come."

"Win, have you ever stopped to wonder how it all came to this?" Joe asked.

"What?"

"The war," Joe said. "I mean, how can neighbors, sometimes even kinfolk, do somethin' like this to one another? I look at what the Jayhawkers did to our people, what we did to them in Lawrence, and what the Yankees are doin' here, and I wonder why God allows it. Seems to me like an awful lot of us are goin' to have some explainin' to do to ole St. Peter when we come up to those Pearly Gates."

"I reckon so," Win agreed. "But that's somethin' we'll just have to worry about when the time comes. For now, we've got more folks to warn."

LIKE WIN AND JOE, LUKE HUNTER WAS ALSO OUT VISITING the area families. Hunter was riding alone, in part because there were few who wanted to ride with him, and in part because he preferred to be alone.

When Luke came out of a little thicket of trees, he saw a small house, set back in the clearing. The smell of cooking food made his stomach growl, and he realized that he had eaten nothing since a piece of jerky earlier in the morning.

As he approached the house, he saw a woman drawing water from the well. She appeared to be in her late thirties, though the lines around her eyes showed signs of a lifetime of hard work. She met Hunter with an unflinching gaze as he rode into her yard.

"Who might you be?" she asked.

Hunter started to tell her his name, then he stopped.

"Coulter," he said. "My name is Win Coulter. And you would be?"

"I am Emma Rittenhouse. Is there somethin' I can do for you, Mr. Coulter?" Emma asked, totally unafraid.

"I came to warn you that the Yankee soldiers are comin' this way."

"Yankee soldiers, Rebel soldiers, don't either one of 'em mean nothin' to me, anymore," Emma said dryly. "Mr. Rittenhouse was kilt at Shiloh."

"Which side was your husband fightin' for?" Hunter asked.

Emma stared at him for a moment. "Seein' as how he's dead now, I don't reckon that's any of your business," she answered. "Anyhow, far as I'm concerned, the war's over."

"It may be over for you, Mrs. Rittenhouse, but not for General Ewing," Hunter said. "He's movin' ever'one out of Cass County. Ever'one, lock, stock, and barrel. When the Yankee soldiers come find you here, they're goin' to make you leave, and burn your house and barn behind you."

"Why would they want to do somethin' like that? Like I told you, I got no quarrel with the Yankees or anyone else."

"Yankees are Yankees," Luke said. "They don't need no reason to do what they do." Hunter sniffed, pointedly, then smiled. "Smells like I'm just in time for supper," he said.

"Don't recall invitin' you," Emma said. She sighed. "But I reckon it would be unChristian to send a body away hungry when you've the vittles to give him. Wait here, I'll see what I can rustle up for you."

"Much obliged to you."

Emma nodded toward a nearby tree stump. "Sit you down over there," she invited. "I'll send my girl out with a plate."

"Can I have some water for my horse?"

"Help yourself," Emma said. "There's the trough."

Emma went into the house where her seventy-five-year-old father and her fifteen-year-old daughter were sitting at the table.

"Who is it, Mama? Who are you talkin' to out in the yard?" the girl asked.

"Just some man," Emma replied. "He says the Yankee soldiers are goin' to come move us out of our house."

"The hell you say," Emma's father said. He stood up. "I'll get my gun."

"They ain't here now, Papa. This here fella just come to warn us, that's all," Emma said. "And even if they was, you couldn't fight 'em off with no one gun." She went to the stove and started filling a plate. "Laura, I want you to take some food out to him. I told the fella I'd feed 'im."

"All right, Mama," Laura answered obediently.

Suddenly the door opened behind her, and Hunter came in, uninvited.

"What are you doin' in here?" Emma asked, surprised to see him. "I seem to mind that I told you to wait outside."

"I decided to come in," Hunter said.

"If you are told to wait outside, you wait outside," Emma's father said angrily. "Who do you think you are?" Emma's father started toward the fireplace.

"Where you think you're goin' old man?"

"I'm goin' to get my gun and run your sorry ass out of here," the old man said defiantly.

Without another word, Hunter pulled his pistol and shot the old man. Emma's father was slammed up against the fireplace mantel before he fell. He lay for a moment on the hearth, his breathing coming in ragged gasps.

"Papa!" Emma screamed, running to him.

The young girl said nothing. She sat frozen to her chair in shock and fear, looking on as her grandfather's final breath was expended in a deep-throated death-rattle.

Hunter walked over to the table and grabbed a piece of meat from the platter. "This looks good," he said. He took a bite.

"You . . . you didn't have no call to come bustin' in here like this," Emma cried. "What'd you shoot him for? I told you I would send you out some food."

"Yeah, well, maybe I want me a little somethin' more than food," Luke said. He walked over to Emma and, in a sudden and unexpected action, ripped her dress down the front, exposing her breasts.

Emma emitted a short scream, then, quickly, she recovered. "Laura, get out of here," she ordered.

"Mama, I . . ."

"Get out. Now."

"Wait a minute," Hunter said, looking toward the daughter. "I might want to change my mind, here. Why have the cow, when I can have the calf?"

"No, please," Emma said, her defiance replaced now with fear and pleading. "Laura's just a fifteen-year-old girl.

You don't want nothin' to do with her. She don't even know what it's about."

"Ah, but you know, don't you, Emma? You said your man was kilt in Shiloh. Shiloh was what? Two, three years ago or better? Why, I'd be willin' to bet that you ain't had no man since then." Hunter giggled. "Truth be told, I expect you'd like me to screw you, wouldn't you? You're lookin' forward to it."

"Better me than my daughter."

"I don't know," Hunter replied. "Let me see what she's got."

Hunter grabbed the front of Laura's dress and jerked it down to her waist. Her just-forming breasts were topped by protruding little nipples.

"Well, now, ain't that pretty," Luke said.

Laura crossed her hands over her chest to cover her breasts.

"I'm sorry, Mama, but you lose," Luke said. Without so much as a blink, he brought his pistol down on Emma's head, and she went down, knocked cold.

"Mama!" Laura cried.

"Don't be worryin' none about your mama, girl," Hunter said. "All I did was knock her out for a spell. She'll have a knot on her head when she comes to, but that's all. If you do what I say, I won't hurt her any more. If you don't do what I say, I'll kill her now." Hunter pointed his pistol at Emma's prostrate form, and pulled back the hammer. "It's up to you, girl. Which will it be?"

"Please, don't shoot her!" Laura begged.

Hunter eased the hammer down on his pistol and smiled, evilly. "Are you going to be good to me?"

"I'll . . . do . . . whatever you want me to do," Laura promised.

*   *   *

A HARD RAIN BEGAN SHORTLY AFTER DARK, SLASHING down on the small weatherbeaten cabin in the middle of the clearing. Carrying a smoked ham and a side of bacon with him, Luke Hunter stepped outside and walked toward his horse which stood stoically in the rain, some thirty yards distant from the house.

Subconsciously, Luke reached down and felt himself. He was spent. The girl had lain absolutely still, accepting without protest his shoving, grunting, and slobbering over her. Since he had given a false name, he let both of them live. He couldn't help but think of how much more he would have enjoyed it if he had killed them.

IT WAS ALMOST SUNSET AND SEVERAL SCORE CAMPFIRES were cooking suppers in the camp of Quantrill's Raiders. The campsite was large and spread out, following along the edge of a meandering river, which provided them with an abundant supply of fresh water. Quantrill had chosen the place, not only for the river, but also because of a well-constructed and abandoned log cabin which he immediately took over as his own headquarters.

Quantrill didn't live in the cabin alone. Recently, he had acquired a girlfriend. The girl, named Kate, was only sixteen years old, and since coming into his life, she occupied so much of Quantrill's time that he lost all interest in the war. His inactivity brought all operations to a halt and Frank James wondered, only half-kiddingly, if she hadn't been sent here by the Yankees. "Let's face it," he said. "She has done what General Ewing and the whole Yankee army hasn't been able to do. She has stopped us in our tracks."

"Hey, Win," someone called from just upstream of Win and Joe's site. "The Chief wants to see you."

"You know why?" Win called back.

The messenger shook his head. "Don't have any idea. I'm just passin' the word down to you, is all," he said.

"What do you reckon he wants, Win?" Joe asked. "You think, maybe, he has somethin' in mind for us to do?"

Win, who had finished his supper, tossed out the rest of his coffee. "I guess there's only one way to find out, and that is to go see."

When he reached the log cabin, Win knocked on the door.

"Come in," Quantrill called.

Win stepped inside. "What's up, Colonel? Do you have another raid in mind?"

The cabin was dark, except for the burning kerosene lantern on a table. Quantrill was sitting behind the table and when he raised his hand up, Win saw that Quantrill was holding a pistol, and he was pointing that pistol directly at Win.

"What the hell is this?" Win asked, surprised by the unexpected move. "What's going on here?"

"Is this the man, Mrs. Rittenhouse?" Quantrill asked. His cold grey eyes didn't leave Win's face, and the gun didn't waver.

Win heard a sound to his right. Looking around he saw three women, standing so deep in the shadows that he couldn't make out their features. He did recognize Kate, however, by her general size and outline.

"I don't know if it's him or not," a woman's voice answered. "I'll need to take me a closer look."

"Pick up that lantern, Coulter, and hold it close to your face," Quantrill ordered.

"You want to tell me what this is all about?" Win asked.

Quantrill cocked his pistol. "I said pick up the god-damned lantern," he growled.

Win picked up the lantern, and the woman moved out

of the shadows. One of them stepped up closer to Win, then examined him, carefully. Finally, she shook her head.

"No, this ain't him," she said.

"Are you sure?" Quantrill asked.

"Yes, I'm positive," the woman answered. "This ain't him."

"What about you, girl?" Quantrill asked. "You ever seen this man before?"

A girl, who was just a little younger than Kate, stepped up close enough to study Win's face. Then she also shook her head no.

"Ma's right. This ain't the man what come by our place," she said.

"You are sure? Both of you? You don't have to be afraid of him now, you know. I'm not going to let him hurt you."

"I'm real sure. This ain't the man that, uh, done it," the girl insisted.

"You ladies said it was Win Coulter," Quantrill said. "Well, this, here is Win Coulter."

"This may be Win Coulter," the woman said. "But this ain't the man that murdered my father and raped my daughter."

"Raped?" Win shouted, hearing for the first time the charge he was suspected of. He looked back at Quantrill. "Colonel Quantrill, I have ridden with you for nearly three years now. Are you telling me you don't know me any better than to believe I could commit rape?"

"I don't know what I believe," Quantrill answered. "Accordin' to what this woman told me, her daughter was raped, and you was the one who done it."

"And you were willing to take her word for it."

"What are you so hot under the collar over?" Quantrill asked. "Soon as she saw you, she said you weren't the one."

"That's not the point," Win replied. "The point is, there should be enough trust between us that it wouldn't even have gotten this far."

Angrily, Win turned and walked out of the cabin.

WIN COULTER WALKED OUT OF QUANTRILL'S CABIN, BUT George Todd, Bloody Bill Anderson, and Little Archie Clement walked out of Quantrill's camp. The animosity that had been steadily building for the last two years between Quantrill and his top lieutenants finally erupted in a splitting of the band when Quantrill seemed to lose all interest in any further guerrilla activity.

Todd, Bloody Bill and Little Archie rode off to form their own groups, and when they left, a little over half of the men rode off with them. As a result, Quantrill's Raider Company enjoyed only a fraction of its former strength.

With men abandoning camp every day, Win, Joe, Ethan, Tate, and Boykin discussed the issue at some length. They were trying to decide whether they would stay with Quantrill or leave with one of Quantrill's dissatisfied lieutenants.

"You boys can do what you want," Win finally said. "But as for me, I joined up with Quantrill and I intend to stay with him."

"I thought you and Quantrill wasn't gettin' on any too good now, what with him accusin' you of rape and all," Ethan suggested.

"Yeah, well, whether you like someone or not doesn't have anything to do with loyalty. If you don't have loyalty, you don't have anything, and it seems to me that leaving Quantrill now would be disloyal. So, I'm goin' to stay."

"And I go where my brother goes," Joe said. "I reckon you boys are just going to have to make up your own minds."

Tate, Ethan, and Boykin talked it over among themselves

for a few minutes, then Tate came back to speak for all of them.

"We are going to stay with you, Win," Tate said.

"Tell 'im the rest of it, Tate," Boykin urged.

Win looked confused. "What rest of it?" he asked.

Tate smiled. "We ain't goin' to join up with Todd and we ain't goin' to join up with Anderson," he said. "But we've decided that if you ever want to start your own outfit, well, me 'n Ethan 'n Boykin would be proud to go with you."

Win was surprised, but pleased, to hear their vote of confidence. "I appreciate that," he said.

SEVERAL WEEKS LATER, AS WIN WAS TENDING TO HIS campfire, he looked up to see someone approaching the camp.

"Shit, look who's comin' back," he said, when he recognized the lone rider.

"Who is it?" Joe asked, sticking his head out of the tent.

"The bad penny," Win answered, nodding toward the rider.

"Damn, it's Luke Hunter," Joe said. "When he rode off with Todd, I thought we were rid of the son of a bitch for good."

Ethan, Tate, and Boykin also came out to meet Hunter. They weren't any fonder of him than Win and Joe, but they were curious to hear any information as to what was happening with some of their friends who left the group to go with Todd.

Hunter swung down from his horse, reached back to rub his ass for a moment, then accepted an offer of coffee.

"Thanks," he said. "I come through a cold rain this mornin' and I haven't been warm since. This will help."

"What are you doin' back here, Hunter?" Boykin asked. "We thought you was with Todd."

"You mean you fellas haven't heard about Todd?" Hunter asked. He took a swallow of hot coffee, sucking it in through extended lips to cool it.

Boykin and the others looked at each other. Finally Boykin responded for them all.

"No," he said. "We ain't heard nothin'."

"Todd is dead."

"Dead?"

"Shot through the neck outside Independence," Hunter said.

"I'll be damned."

"We got into a fight with a bunch of Jayhawkers," Hunter explained. "We got whipped pretty good and, when it was over, Todd was dead."

"I'm sorry to hear that," Win said. "Todd was a good man. I didn't like it that he and Anderson broke up our company, but I thought he was a pretty good man."

"Yeah, well, Anderson is dead too," Hunter said, nonchalantly.

"What? How do you know that?" Win asked.

"I was with him when it happened."

"You was with Anderson? I thought you was with Todd," Tate challenged.

"I was," Hunter said. "But after Todd got hisself kilt, I went off to be with Anderson. It was less than a week later when we run into a bunch of militiamen up north of Kansas City. They had us outnumbered pretty good, and I figured Anderson would run. But he didn't run. He put the reins of his horse in his teeth, pulled both guns, and charged anyway. He got shot right through the head."

"That would be the way Bloody Bill would do it, all right," Joe said. "He always did figure there was only one thing to do when he got into a battle, and that was charge ahead.''

"Hunter, do you mean to tell me you was with Todd when he was killed, then you was with Anderson when he was killed?'' Boykin asked. "Who are you? The angel of death?''

"Well, like I said,'' Hunter replied, defensively, "it was less than a week after Todd was kilt before Anderson got it too.''

"So you got Todd killed, you got Anderson killed, and now you are here with us?'' Win asked. "I think we would all feel better if you would just mount up and ride off before you get anyone else killed. Your kind of luck, we don't need.''

"You may be joking, but I don't think that is funny,'' Hunter said.

"Neither do I,'' Win replied.

20

Spring 1865

"SHIT," ETHAN SAID, USING A BURNING BRAND FROM THE fire to light his pipe. "I could understand stayin' here for the winter. But winter's over now, and it's time to get off our asses and do somethin'. I swear, if we don't do somethin' soon, I'm goin' to light out of here."

"You wouldn't be alone. There's quite a few men already done that," Joe said.

"Yeah, well, I can't say as I blame them," Tate replied. "I don't know what's got into Quantrill. He ain't like he was before Todd and Anderson left. Now he seems awful content to just stay holed up here and do nothin'."

"What do you mean, do nothin'?" Boykin asked. "Ole Quantrill's doin' plenty, I'll tell you. Ain't you ever heard that little ole sixteen-year-old gal of his squeal at night? Damn if she ain't got him so chained to that little pussy of hers that he don't get more'n ten feet away."

"Yeah, well, if I was chained to that little old pussy, I prob'ly wouldn't get more'n ten feet away neither," Ethan said. He laughed. "But I ain't. All I got to comfort me at night is Rosy Palm and you ugly bastards."

"Ugly? Why, Ethan, you never told me you thought I was ugly before," Tate teased. He picked up his skillet and began mugging at his own reflection.

"I'm serious, though," Ethan said, after he laughed with the others. "I'm tired of scratchin' my ass and pickin' my nose. I am ready to do something."

"I know where there's a bank to be robbed," Luke Hunter suggested. Hunter had been sitting by the fire listening to the conversation, but this was his first contribution to it.

"Are you talking about another Lawrence?" Win asked. "Because I'm not interested in doing anything like that again."

"No, it ain't nothin like that, believe me," Hunter said. "The place I got in mind is a real fat easy bank. It's just hangin' out there like a big old ripe plum, waitin' to be plucked."

Hunter got up and moved over to the coffeepot, where he poured himself a cup. He turned back toward the others, holding the cup with his hands wrapped around it to warm them against the cool April night.

"And this nice juicy bank you're talkin' about is just waitin' for us, huh?" Tate asked.

"That's right," Hunter insisted. "There's thousands of dollars sittin' in those vaults, just waitin' for us to come get it. That's more money than we ever got anyplace else."

"Damn," Ethan said. "That would be somethin', wouldn't it, Win?"

"I doubt that it's as easy as Hunter says," Win insisted. "If they have that much money in the town, then they probably have a couple of regiments of troops there to guard it."

"No," Hunter replied, shaking his head. "That's the beauty of it, don't you see? There ain't no soldiers there at all. Believe me, it will be real easy to rob. I've got it all worked out."

"What do you mean, you've got it all worked out?"

"I mean I've been there. I know the town. I know how to get in, rob the bank, and get out before anyone has time to react to our being there."

"Hunter, you've never been this helpful before," Win said. "Where the hell are you gettin' all this information?" Win asked.

"From around," Luke said.

"Around, where?"

Hunter shook his head. "Uh, uh," he said. "I don't give away all my secrets."

"What do you think, Win? You think the Chief will hit this bank?" Ethan asked.

"I don't know," Win answered. "You've seen him. Like you said a while ago, except for his woman, he doesn't seem interested in much of anything these days."

"He might be interested if you talked to him," Joe suggested. "Quantrill listens to you 'bout as much as he listens to anyone in the group."

"Not really. Not anymore," Win said. "It hasn't been the same since . . ." He started to say since his confrontation with Quantrill over having been accused of rape, but he held his tongue.

"Since Kate came, we know that," Boykin said. "But you could still talk to him," Boykin insisted.

Win didn't answer. Instead, he walked away from the others, down to the bank of the little stream where he stood looking at the water that was winking back at him in the moonlight.

He was alone for a few minutes, then Joe came to stand beside him.

"Win, maybe going after this bank isn't such a bad

idea," Joe said. "I mean, look around you. The men that are left are getting damned restless. If we don't do something soon . . ." He let the sentence hang.

"I know. You have a point," Win agreed. He sighed, and picked up a rock to toss into the water. "And a nice fat bank sounds awfully tempting. If it's really there," he added.

"You don't think it's there?"

"I don't know. I guess I would have more faith in the idea if it came from someone besides Luke Hunter."

"Yeah, I know what you mean. Well, Hunter is a son of a bitch, we all know that," Joe agreed. "But this doesn't really have anything to do with him."

"Except that it is his idea," Win said. "And I don't trust him."

"It may be his idea, but he's not going to be in charge of it," Joe said.

Win looked back toward Quantrill's cabin. Quantrill's girlfriend, Kate, stepped to the door then tossed out a pan of water.

"I don't think Quantrill has enough ambition left to be in charge of it either," he said.

"Well, what the hell? Even that might work out better for us," Joe said. "This way, you can lead us. And if you have Quantrill's permission, it won't be disloyal."

"If I have his permission."

"What? You think he's not going to give it to you, if we rob the bank and bring the money back here?" Joe asked.

"I guess you're right," Win said. "All right, let me think on it for a moment or two."

Win looked over toward Quantrill's cabin. The door was open, and Quantrill's hand reached out to pull Kate toward him. A moment later, the door was closed.

Win turned his attention back to the campsite. In the past the campsites had been orderly gatherings of the Raiders, with equipment clean and accessible, weapons loaded, and tents ready to strike in a moment's notice. But that wasn't the case now.

The problem, Win realized, was that this camp had been in existence since early fall. It was mid-spring now, and the camp was still here. The longer the men stayed, the more entrenched they became. And, the more entrenched they were, the less interest they had in moving at all.

Quantrill was living in a cabin to which Kate had added extras like curtains, tablecloths, and other such niceties. It was no longer a field headquarters, it was a comfortable home. Taking their cue from Quantrill, most of his men had brought about improvements in their own living conditions. More and more the campsite was beginning to resemble a village, with living quarters made of mud-chinked log walls, furnished with tables and chairs, the canvas tents became the roofs.

The men paid more attention to their quarters than they did to taking care of their equipment. As a result, weapons were dirty and rusting, powder was wet, and saddle and tack were mildewed.

"Look at this place, Joe," Win said, disgustedly. "Do you remember the first day we joined Quantrill? He gave the order to ride out right after we got there, and the entire campsite was struck and gone in less than fifteen minutes. Hell, this Sodom and Gomorrah couldn't be taken down in anything less than fifteen hours."

"If they would take it down at all," Joe said. "If you ask me, about half the people here have decided to homestead here. The more comfortable they are, the less likely they will leave, even if they were ordered."

Win stroked his chin for a moment. "All right, suppose

we do go after this bank? How many of these people do
you think we could get to give up the good life and go
with us?''

"We could round up enough to pull it off, I know," Joe
said, showing his enthusiasm over the fact that Win was
beginning to lean in favor of it. "Tate, Ethan, and Boykin
will go, that's for sure. And probably half a dozen or so
more. Not everyone is content to just lay around on their
ass day in and day out. The problem is, this was Hunter's
idea, and he will want to go."

"Hunter's going is not a problem, it's a necessity," Win
replied. "I'd rather have the son of a bitch with us than
behind us. I want to keep my eye on him."

Joe smiled. "So, does that mean you'll do it?"

"Yeah," Win answered. "I'll do it. I need to talk to
Quantrill about it, but I'll take care of that. In the meantime,
you round up the men."

"How many do we want?"

"No more than ten," Win replied. "And that includes
Hunter, you, and me."

"I'll get them together," Joe promised.

THE BANK THEY WERE GOING AFTER WAS LOCATED IN
Springhill, Kansas, and they were about five miles out when
they stopped to go over their final plans. Win found a little
stream-cut gully that offered his band of riders concealment
from anyone who might be coming down the road, and he
called for a halt. While they were resting the horses and
men, Win had Hunter draw a map of the town in the dirt.

"This here is the main street," Hunter said, pointing out
the features of the town with the stick he had used for
drawing the map. "It comes into town this way, and leaves
that way."

"Does it run east and west, or north and south?"

"Sort of north and south," Hunter explained. "This here is the north end."

"Any other way in and out of the town?"

"No, not really," Hunter answered. "This here is the only road."

"All right, fine. Tate, you take half the men and go around so you can come in from the south," Win ordered. "I'll bring the other half in from the north. If all ten of us rode in together that would like as not arouse suspicion. But five can ride together without getting anyone too curious. Now, show me what buildings there are on either side of the street."

"Well, uh, this here is the bank," Hunter said, drawing a square. "It's on the west side of the street. I think this here's a saloon, or maybe a general store. There's a livery stable here, somewhere, and maybe a hotel, but I don't recollect all that well."

"I thought you knew the town. You said you had it all worked out," Win challenged. "Now you say you aren't sure."

"Well, I didn't have no idea you'd be gettin' so particular about such little things," Hunter replied.

"Paying attention to the little things is what takes care of the big things," Win said. "Now, what about army? Any troops there?"

"No, I don't think so," Hunter said.

"You don't think so?" Win repeated. "First you were sure there was no army, now you say you don't think so."

"I'm pretty sure there is no army," Hunter said.

"What about the law? The town marshal's office?" Joe asked. "Where is it located?"

"I don't rightly recall," Hunter said.

"How many deputies does he have with 'im?"

"Don't know."

"Shit, Hunter, what the hell *do* you know?" Win asked in disgust. He stood up from the drawing on the ground and walked away, heading toward the stream.

"I know that the bank is full of money," Hunter called after him. "That much I do know."

Joe followed his brother to stand at the edge of the stream with him.

"You all right, Win?" Joe asked.

"Joe, I got a awful bad feeling about this," Win said. "If you ask me, I think we ought to turn around and go back."

"We've come this far. Seems to me like we ought to go through with it," Joe said.

Win looked at his brother. "Are you telling me you aren't the least bit nervous about it?"

"No, why should I be nervous? That's not my job," Joe answered. Then he chuckled. "You're in charge here, it's *your* job to be nervous. Besides, I figure if we get into any kind of trouble, you'll take care of it."

"Yeah, well, thanks for the vote of confidence," Win answered dryly.

"Listen, why don't we ask the others what they think about it?" Joe suggested. "If they want to go through with it, we go. If they want to back out, we back out. What do you say?"

Win nodded. "All right, fair enough," he answered. He and Joe walked back up to where the others were, and got their attention.

"My brother's got somethin' he wants to say to you," Joe announced, and all turned their attention to Win.

"Boys, we are here on Hunter's word," Win said. "He says there's money in the bank, and he says that the bank isn't that well-guarded. He may know what he's talking about, or he may be as full of shit as a Christmas goose.

But we've come this far, so I'm going to leave it up to you whether we go on or not.''

"I say we go on," Hunter said.

"You stay out of this, Hunter. You've got no say," Win said, sharply. "This is for the others to decide."

"If we decide to go on, you'll still lead us, won't you, Win?" Ethan asked.

Win nodded. "Yes," he said. "If we vote to go, I'll go, and I'll still lead you."

"Then I say we go."

"Me too," Tate pitched in.

To a man, everyone else voted in the affirmative. Win looked at them for a moment, then he nodded his head.

"All right, we go," he told them. "All I can say is, you fellas are going to have to be on the alert at all times. This won't be like any of the raids we've ever been on before. This time we're going to be badly outnumbered, and we are going to be in a place where we have no friends but each other. So, look out for each other, and if we have to scatter when it's over, then make your way back to the main camp best you can. Good luck to you."

"Good luck," they all replied in one voice.

SPRINGHILL, KANSAS, WAS A BUSY LITTLE TOWN, BUILT around a square. When Win and his group rode in from the north they saw half a dozen wagons parked along both sides of the street.

With Win and Joe were three men, named Phil, Ed, and Curly. Coming into town from the south, Tate had Ethan, Boykin, Hunter, and a rider named Johnny with him.

"What the hell are all these wagons doin' here?" Win asked.

"You still some worried?" Joe asked.

"Too late to be worrying now," Win replied. "Now's

the time for doing. You boys see Tate anywhere?''

"Ain't seen 'im yet,'' Phil answered.

"There he is down there, just comin' in,'' Joe pointed out.

"Yeah, I see him,'' Win replied. He squinted his eyes. "Damn! Where's Hunter?''

"What?''

"Hunter.'' Win repeated. "The son of a bitch is not with them.''

"Maybe his horse threw a shoe or something,'' Joe said. He snorted. "Hell, as far as I'm concerned, it's good riddance.''

The two groups of riders met in front of the bank. "Where's Hunter?'' Win asked.

"Hunter?'' Tate seemed surprised by the question, and he looked around. "Hell, I don't know,'' he answered. "He was with us just a moment ago, when we come into town. Any of you fellas see what happened to him?'' he asked the others with him.

No one had seen him leave.

"We're down to the nut-cutting now. Maybe the son of a bitch just showed the white feather,'' Phil suggested.

"That would be about like him,'' Boykin agreed.

"Yeah, well, it's too late to worry about him now,'' Win said. "Phil, you and Johnny mind the horses. Joe, you and Boykin post yourselves just outside the door and keep your eyes on the street. The rest of you boys, inside with me. All right, let's go.''

All but Phil and Johnny dismounted. Joe and Boykin took up their position just outside the door, while Win and the others went inside.

As soon as they were in the bank, Win took a quick look around, making a mental note, not only of the layout, but also of how many were inside. Along the left-hand side of the bank was a counter, behind which were two teller cages. There were two men on the teller's side and four men on the customer side of the counter.

On the wall opposite the counter there was a chest-high table, around which stood three more men. There were no women in the bank.

A half wall formed an office at the rear of the bank, and when Win looked in that direction, he saw Luke Hunter. For just a second, he thought Hunter had sneaked around and come in the back way in order to help them. Then he realized that Luke Hunter's presence there had to mean something else.

"That's them, boys!" Hunter yelled "Quantrill's men!"

"Shit!" Win shouted to the others. "Hunter's betrayed us! It's a trap!"

"We're U.S. Marshals!" one of the men standing outside the teller's cage shouted. "You bushwhackers throw down your guns!"

Win swung his pistol toward the man who had yelled at him. The marshal fired first and his bullet went wide, hitting an inkwell on the table, and sending up a spray of ink. Win returned fire and his bullet found its mark. The marshal went down with a wind-sucking hole in his chest.

Curly, who was carrying a sawed-off shotgun, let go with a blast that shattered the shaded glass around the teller cages, driving the men behind the counter to the floor.

Win turned his gun toward Hunter, fired, and missed just as Hunter jumped through the back door.

One of the men at the table fired and Curly went down. Another bullet cut a hole in Win's jacket.

"Let's get the hell out of here!" Win shouted, pulling Ethan with him, and firing back into the bank as they ran out front.

When they got outside they encountered four more marshals on the roof of the building opposite the bank. One of the marshals opened up with a shotgun but he was too far out of range to do any real damage, so the blast merely sprayed a pattern of pellets that barely penetrated the skin. A shot from one of the others on the roof caused the front window of the bank to come crashing down. A third shot killed Joe's horse just as he got to it. Phil, who was minding the horses, realized that Curly wasn't coming out of the bank, so he offered that horse to Joe.

Win saw a man kneeling behind a water trough, taking slow and deliberate aim with a rifle. Win fired, and the man fell forward, his unfired rifle sinking in the water.

As Ed was swinging into his saddle, he raised up at just the right time to catch a bullet between his eyes. He went down.

With Ed and Curly dead behind them, Win led his men at a gallop toward the end of the street. Before they got there, two loaded wagons were pushed out into the street to be used as barricades, and half a dozen men started firing from behind them. This time, Phil went down.

Despite the fact that he was fighting for his life, Win couldn't push back the dispassionate thought that arose over the quality of his leadership. This was his first test and in a little less than a minute he had managed to get three of his men killed. Not a very auspicious beginning.

When Win turned away from the roadblock, he saw that the road behind them had been blocked as well. Now, both ways out of town were closed.

"We've got 'em!" someone shouted. "We've got 'em trapped in the street like fish in a barrel! Kill 'em, boys, kill 'em!"

"What'll we do, Win?" Boykin shouted in fear and confusion. "What'll we do?"

Looking around in desperation, Win saw a large window fronting a dress-making shop.

"This way!" he shouted, and he rode straight toward the window, urging his horse to leap through it. The window, which consisted of dozens of small squares held in place by thin strips of wood, collapsed inward under the weight of the leaping horse. There was a tremendous crash of glass as the horse leaped from the walk outside onto the wooden floor inside.

The other riders, with the window taken out of the way, urged their horses through the open space behind him, though Johnny, who was the last to make the leap, took a hit in his shoulder.

Win and those who were still with him clattered across the wooden floor, past three women who were crouching in fear at the rear of the store, then out the back door and into an open field. It was a brilliant move. None of the townspeople were mounted, and by the time the marshals did reach their horses and came around the edge of town, Win and his men had completely disappeared.

The boys rode hard for nearly half an hour before they came to a road. Behind a little hill just to the side of the road, they stopped to let the horses recover their wind.

"Who's hurt?" Win asked.

"I've got a few shotgun pellets in my ass," Tate said. "Nothing serious."

"Yeah, me too," Boykin said. "Ain't none of 'em deep, though."

"I've got a ball in my shoulder," Johnny said, his voice more strained than the others. "Hurts like hell, but it didn't hit none of my vitals."

"We'll get you taken care of soon as we get back," Win promised. "Might take a few days, though. We can't go back the same way we came 'cause they'll be lookin' for us. Think you can make it? All you have to do is hang on to your saddle. We'll lead your horse.''

''Don't you fellas worry about me,'' Johnny said. ''I'll make it.''

''Win, what the hell happened in there?'' Joe asked. ''You boys weren't in for more'n a second or two when all hell broke loose.''

''Luke Hunter happened,'' Win said.

''Hunter?''

''The son of a bitch was in there, Joe. He turned on us.''

''What do you say we go back and get the son of a bitch?'' Ethan suggested.

Win shook his head. ''No, that's just what they are wanting us to do. If we go back now, they'll be waiting for us. We're going to have to let it go for now.''

''Let it go? You mean, we're going to let Luke Hunter get away with this?'' Joe asked.

''I didn't say that. Don't you worry about Luke Hunter getting away with anything, little brother. I promise you, one way or another, I'll catch up with that son of a bitch. And when I do, he is dead meat.''

21

LUKE HUNTER KNEW THE ROUTE THEY HAD USED TO COME to Springhill, and he knew the way they had planned to return. That meant that he would be able to tell the Yankees where to set up ambushes for Win and his men. In order to prevent that, Win took his men back by a very circuitous route, avoiding any possible encounter with marshals or soldiers. Going back that way, however, meant that it took several more days than it would normally.

SOME DRAMATIC CHANGES HAD TAKEN PLACE AT THE campsite during the few days Win and his group were gone. The most noticeable thing was the decrease in the size of the campsite. There had been nearly a hundred men there when they left, now there were fewer than twenty. They looked as if they were getting ready to leave.

"Ben," Win called out to one of the remaining men. Ben ambled over to him. "What is it?" Win asked, taking in the nearly deserted campsite with a wave of his hand. "Where is everyone?"

"They've all gone for the amnesty," Ben answered.

"Amnesty? You mean from the Federals? Why would they do that?"

"Hell," Ben said. "Ain't you heard? We're *all* Federals, now. The war's over."

"When did that happen?"

"A couple of days ago. Lee surrendered to Grant at some place down in Virginia."

Behind Win, Johnny moaned, and Win remembered his wound. "Is there anyone still around who can take care of Johnny?"

"What happened to him?" Ben asked.

"He's got a ball in his shoulder."

"Hank's still here," Ben said. " 'Course he's better with horses than he is with people, but I reckon he can get a bullet out."

"Boykin, you and Tate take him over to Hank, will you?"

"Sure thing, Win," Boykin replied. "Come along, Johnny."

"How'd it go with you fellas?" Ben asked.

"Not good," Win said. "Not good at all. We lost three men. Charley's not going to like it that the whole thing was a failure, but it was a trap, and Luke Hunter led us right into it."

"Hell, it won't matter none to Quantrill," Ben said. "He ain't here."

Win looked up toward the log cabin that had been Quantrill's headquarters and saw that it was deserted.

"I'm surprised that the Yankees offered amnesty to Quantrill."

"Ha," Ben laughed. "They didn't. They got reward posters out for him, dead or alive."

"Where'd he go?"

"Nobody knows for sure. But the word is that he went to Kentucky. He took the girl with him."

"Tell us about this amnesty, Ben," Joe asked. "What is it?"

Ben ran his hand through his hair. "It seems simple enough, I reckon. All you gotta do is go into Kansas City and turn in your guns, then swear that you will be loyal to the United States government."

"And then what?"

"And then they let you go, like nothin' ever happened. You can go back to farmin', or clerkin', or whatever it was you was doin' before the war."

"Are you going to do it, Ben?" Win asked.

"I tell you the truth, it galls me havin' to take the oath . . . havin' to say I'm sorry for all that I done while those Yankee sons of bitches gloat. But, I reckon I'm goin' to do it. I still got me some land I can work. Got no house, the Yankees burned that, but I ain't lived in no house for the last four years anyhow. What about you boys? You goin' to take it?"

"I don't know," Win said. He sighed. "I never gave this day much thought. I just sort of figured I would go on fighting until . . ." He let the words trail off, leaving the sentence incomplete.

"Until you got yourself kilt?" Ben asked.

"Yeah," Win answered. "Something like that, I suppose."

"I know what you mean. I reckon we was all thinkin' the same way. But now, with the war over maybe we can stop thinkin' about killin' and dyin' and start thinkin' about livin'."

"You know, Win, we still have our land too," Joe said.

"Is that what you want to do, Joe? You want to take amnesty and farm the land?"

Joe nodded. "Yeah, I think so."

Win looked at the others in the camp and saw that they, too, were getting ready to leave. "You think we can do that, Joe?" he asked. "Be farmers again, I mean? Seems to me like we've come a long way from that over the last few years."

"I don't know if we can be farmers again or not," Joe admitted. "But I think we owe it to ma and pa to at least try."

"All right," Win said. "As soon as we see how Johnny's getting along, me an' you'll ride into Kansas City and take the oath."

KANSAS CITY WAS A CITY TRANSFORMED. THE STREETS were full of wagons, buckboards, and horses. Hotels and restaurants were bustling, including the new restaurant which had been built on the lot left vacant when the storm destroyed the women's prison.

Wearing long dusters and black hats pulled low over their eyes, Win and Joe rode into Kansas City with the same sense of caution they had entered every town for the last four years. They automatically checked roof lines, open windows, and alleys for potential danger.

Glancing up one of the alleys, Win saw that the little crib Belle had occupied during the time she was in Kansas City was now gone. Whether it had been destroyed when the storm had hit the town, or whether it had been torn down by reformers since that time, he didn't know. What he did know was that he felt a twinge of grief thinking about her.

"That must be the place, there," Joe said, bringing Win's attention back to the street. "Look, up ahead."

Stretched across a building at the far end of the street was a large painted banner that read: AMNESTY HEADQUARTERS.

"Yeah, I reckon so," Win said. "Joe, you sure you want to do this?"

"It's our only chance to start over," Joe replied.

"All right," Win said. "Let's give the Yankee bastards their pound of flesh and get it over with."

As they rode toward the amnesty building, Win began to

notice the reaction they were getting from the people on
the street. Men stopped to stare at them, and women whispered to each other as they passed by. Joe evidently saw it
as well, because he commented on it.

"Win, does it seem to you that we are getting an undue
amount of attention here?" Joe asked.

"Yeah," Win said. "But they probably do that to
ever'one who comes in for amnesty."

"How do they know we're comin' for amnesty?" Joe
asked.

Win chuckled, then caught their reflection in the front
window of a millinery shop. He nodded toward it.

"Look at us in the window there, little brother," he said.
"Do we look like we're comin' in to sell eggs?"

THEY TIED THEIR HORSES OFF AT THE HITCHING RAIL IN
front of the amnesty building, then went inside, where they
were met by a sergeant who was standing behind a counter.

"I'm Sergeant Berry," the sergeant said. "What can I
do for you boys?" he asked.

"We've come to get amnesty," Win said.

"All right, let me just fill out a paper here," Sergeant
Berry said, reaching for a form and a pen. "Now," he said,
dipping the pin in an inkwell. "Now, who were you boys
with? General Price? General Van Dorn?"

"No," Win answered. "We were with Quantrill."

Sergeant Berry looked up in interest. "You were with
Quantrill?"

"Yes."

"Uh, would you two boys wait here for a moment?"
Berry asked.

"What for? Is there something wrong?"

"No," Berry replied. "It's just that I can only do amnesty for men that was in the regular army. The irregulars have to get their amnesty from Cap'n Parnell. Just wait here a moment. I'll be right back.''

Sergeant Berry stepped through a door that led into a room in the back of the building. That left Win and Joe alone.

''I don't like this,'' Win said nervously. ''There's something wrong.''

''Maybe it's like he said, Win,'' Joe said. ''I mean, we have to at least give it a chance, don't you think?''

Win stroked his chin and looked around nervously. That was when he saw several wanted posters on the wall.

''Joe,'' he said. ''Look over there.''

''What are those?''

''Wanted posters,'' Win said, stepping over to look at them. ''Here's one for Quantrill, and one for Archie Clement,'' he said, looking at them. ''Oh, shit.''

''What?''

Win jerked the poster off and brought it back to show Joe.

REWARD
$500
In Gold Coin
Will be paid by the U.S. Government
for the apprehension
DEAD OR ALIVE
of
Win and Joe Coulter
Wanted for Robbery, Murder, Treason
and other acts against the peace
and dignity of the U.S.

Thomas Ewing
General, United States Army

"Son of bitch!" Win said. "They aren't going to give us amnesty. Let's get out of here!"

At that very moment, Sergeant Berry returned with a captain. Both were holding pistols in their hands.

"Hold it right there!" the captain ordered. "Put your hands up."

Two more soldiers came in through the front door at the same time.

Win and Joe had no option but to comply. They stuck their hands up.

The captain called through the open door to someone in the back room.

"You want to come out here and see if you can identify these men?" he shouted.

Win waited for whoever it was the marshal was speaking to in the back room.

The man who emerged was Luke Hunter. Hunter smiled broadly when he saw them.

"Congratulations, Captain Parnell," Hunter said. "You've caught yourself the Coulter brothers. That would be Win Coulter, and that is Joe."

"Thank you, Mr. Hunter. All right, men," Parnell said to the two privates. "Get their guns and shackle them."

"Yes, sir," one of the soldiers answered, putting down his rifle to tend to the task at hand.

"I'll just bet you boys thought you would never see me again," Hunter said to the two brothers as they were being divested of their weapons and put in handcuffs.

Win shook his head. "Oh, no, I figured I would see you again," he said.

"Really?" Hunter replied. "Now, how is that?"

"Because, I'd have to see you again in order to kill you," Win said.

Hunter laughed. "Oh, you were going to kill me, were

you?'' he said. ''Well, too bad for you it's not going to
work out quite the way you had it planned.''

''That's all right. Maybe we won't get you, but someone
will, you traitorous bastard,'' Joe insisted.

''Funny that you would call *me* a traitor, when *you* are
going to be hanged for treason,'' Hunter said. ''The truth
is, I was a part of the Kansas Militia, all along. I was spying
on you boys, for the whole time I was with you, providing
information on where you were and what you were doing.
Todd? Anderson? They were killed because I set them up.
Just like I set you up with the bank robbery.''

''That's enough, Hunter,'' Parnell said. ''We'll take it
from here.''

''What about my money?'' Hunter asked.

''I'll give you a voucher.''

''Money?'' Win asked.

Hunter smiled. ''I get one hundred dollars for ever' one
of you Quantrill bastards I identify. I figure about the time
that hangman's noose is snapping your neck, I'll be somewhere enjoying myself with a couple of whores. Goodbye,
boys. I'll see you in hell.''

Hunter laughed fiendishly as he left through the back
door.

The soldiers piled Win and Joe's weapons on the table.
There were a total of four pistols and two knives.

''Sergeant Berry, check their horses out front,'' Parnell
ordered. ''Look for a saddle scabbard in their saddlebags
and their bedroll.''

''Yes, sir.''

''You two men have anything to say?'' Captain Parnell
asked.

''What happened to amnesty?'' Win asked.

Parnell chortled. ''You didn't really think we would give
people like you amnesty, did you?''

"Why not? We were soldiers."

"You were criminals and butchers," Parnell snarled. "Did you men really think you could sack Lawrence and get away with it?"

Neither Win nor Joe answered, for they knew they couldn't defend Lawrence, even to themselves, let alone to anyone else.

"You know, men, there is a way to save your necks," Captain Parnell said.

"How is that?" Win asked.

"You can tell us where Quantrill is."

"I don't know where he is," Win answered. "But even if I did know, I wouldn't tell you."

"Oh? Well, we'll see if your tongue gets any looser when you climb those thirteen steps to eternity."

22

CAPTAIN PARNELL WAITED AT THE KANSAS CITY RAIL-
road depot for his prisoners to be delivered to him. General
Ewing had personally selected Parnell to escort Win and
Joe Coulter to St. Louis.

"ONCE WE GET THEIR SORRY HIDES THERE," EWING HAD
told him when he gave Parnell his orders, "we'll have a
big trial, covered by all the newspapers. Then we'll build
a gallows on the banks of the Mississippi and invite the
whole country to witness their hanging. That will loosen
their lips. They'll be begging to tell us where Quantrill is,
before all that is over."

"General, we aren't going to let them off the hook, just
because they cooperate with us, are we?" Parnell had
asked.

Ewing had smiled and replied, "Hell no. We're going to
convict them for more than one murder. If we let them off
the hook for one, they'll still hang for the others."

Parnell had laughed. "I'm going to enjoy seeing the expression on their faces when they learn that."

AS IT HAD BEEN FOR SEVERAL DAYS NOW, THE DEPOT WAS
crowded with men in blue and men in gray, for soldiers

from both armies were going home. It was easy to tell the difference, even if the men had shed all or part of their uniforms, for the Union soldiers moved with a bouncy step and jaunty airs, whereas the Confederates were much more melancholy.

Three veterans of the failed Confederacy, in dirty gray uniforms, sat on an unused baggage cart, watching the activity. One of the soldiers had an empty sleeve, another an empty trouser leg, and all three had empty spirits.

A couple of black men, freed by the war, were earning a few pennies by carrying baggage or loading cargo onto the train. A wagon carrying three kegs of gunpowder stopped at the platform.

"Here, you, nig'ra. You want to make some money?"

One of the blacks looked toward the man who had called them, a red-faced well-dressed, heavyset civilian.

"Yes, sir."

"Load these here three kegs of gunpowder onto that last car there."

"Hold on there!" Parnell called, overhearing the transaction. "You can't load powder in that car. That's where my men and I will be riding."

"Sorry, Cap'n," the civilian said, showing the captain some papers. "But that's the rules of the Frisco Railroad. They won't carry gunpowder in the baggage car."

"But it's only three kegs."

"That don't make no difference. They won't carry no amount a'tall."

"All right," Parnell said after reading the papers. He handed them back to the civilian. "But they'll be hearing from General Ewing, soon as I get back from St. Louis."

The civilian chuckled. "You tell your general. You tell him to write 'em a good letter." The civilian signalled to the black man, who started loading the kegs of powder onto the front end of the passenger car that was attached to the end of the train.

"I seen 'em," a young boy shouted, running up to the platform. "I seen 'em comin'."

"You see who, boy?"

"Why, Win and Joe Coulter," the boy said excitedly. "They got 'em in chains in a wagon. They're comin' this way."

"Win and Joe Coulter? Who are they?" one of the nearby civilians asked.

"Who are they? Why, where was you durin' the war? They was just two of Quantrill's most ferocious guerrillas, that's all. You heard of Bloody Bill Anderson and Little Archie Clement?"

"Yeah."

"Well, these here boys made them seem like Sunday school teachers."

"They prisoners of war?"

"No such a thing. These boys is goin' to St. Louis where they're goin' to be hung."

Parnell smiled at the interest already generated by the Coulters. He planned to stay on in the army, and his part in capturing the Coulters would have to bode well for his career.

The wagon arrived at the edge of the platform and Sergeant Berry and two soldiers jumped down. Holding their rifles at port arms, the soldiers watched as Win and Joe, bound together by a heavy iron chain, climbed down from the wagon.

"Sergeant Berry, get them into that last car," Parnell ordered.

"Yes, sir. This way, men," the sergeant said. "Oh, Captain Parnell, will you be riding in the car with us?"

"Absolutely," Parnell replied. "I've chased these boys

for the entire war. I don't intend to let them out of my sight from now, until the moment the rope is put around their necks. Now, get 'em on board. We don't have all day.''

"Yes, sir."

On board the train Win and Joe were seated in two facing wooden benches. An iron bar ran across the floor between them. Their chain was unlocked, passed through the bar, then locked again.

"You two boys get real comfortable," Berry said, jerking on the chain so that the leg irons dug deep into their legs. Joe grunted in pain. "But not too comfortable," he added, laughing as he moved to the front of the car to join the soldiers.

Parnell got on board then and, with a sidelong glance at Win and Joe, he, too, went to the front of the car where he took a seat across the aisle from Berry and the other two soldiers. Shortly after that the train rolled out of the station in a series of jerks and squeaks.

Once they were under way, Parnell found a newspaper to read, while Sergeant Berry and the two privates began playing cards. No one was paying any attention to Win and Joe.

"Joe," Win whispered.

"Yes?"

"Look, there. You think you can do anything about that?"

Win was pointing to one of the bolts that held the iron bar retaining plate. The bolt was loose.

"I'll see what I can do," Joe said. "You keep a lookout."

The way they were sitting put Joe's back to the front of the car. Win, who was sitting just across from Joe was facing the front, so he could see their guards. With Berry and the two privates playing cards, and Parnell engrossed in his newspaper, no one was paying any attention to what Joe was doing.

By the time the train was twenty miles east of Kansas City, Joe had worked the bolt loose. After that it was easy to slip the chain out from under the bar.

"Captain Parnell?" Win called.

"What do you want?"

"Could you spare a cigar?"

"A cigar? Now what makes you think I would want to give a cigar to Confederate trash like you?"

"I can pay for it."

"How are you going to do that, Coulter?" Parnell asked. "We already took everything you had."

"I got some money hidden."

Parnell laughed. "So, you're going to tell me where it's hidden, so that, someday, I'll be able to find it. Is that it?"

"You can get it today, on the way to St. Louis," Win said.

Parnell put down his paper.

"Keep talking."

"How about the cigar?"

"What if you're lying?"

"I guess you've got to trust me," Win said, smiling.

"Do you think I really believe you would tell me where all your money is hidden, just for one cigar?"

"Oh, I'm not telling you where all of it is. Just a little, like a few hundred dollars from a job we did at Sedalia a couple of months ago. When we stop for water you could jump off the train, get the money, and get right back on the train. If I'm lying, you can settle with me when you get back on."

"All right," Parnell said. "Tell me and I'll look for it. If I find it, I'll give you a cigar."

"No, I won't do it like that. Suppose I tell you, and you

don't give me the cigar? I'd be out the money then, and no cigar.''

"What difference does it make? You're going to hang anyway.''

"Hell, Cap'n Parnell, if you ain't goin' to give him a cigar, I will," Berry said. "Then he can tell me.''

"No you aren't, Sergeant. It's my deal.''

"Don't you other boys worry about it," Win said. "I think Captain Parnell is a sharing man. Otherwise I'm sure you would tell the general how Parnell made a deal with his prisoners.''

"Damn you," Parnell said, angrily. "Keep your damned mouth shut!''

"Cap'n, he didn't tell us nothin' we ain't already been thinkin' about," Berry said.

"All right, all right," Parnell agreed. "We'll share the money. I'll give you your damn cigar, Coulter. But you only get one between the two of you.''

"One's enough," Win said.

Captain Parnell walked back and put the cigar in Win's mouth, then lit it. Win took several puffs, letting each puff out in a loud, satisfied sigh. Finally, when a substantial cloud of blue smoke had been raised, he reached up with his manacled hands and pulled the cigar out of his mouth to pass it over to Joe.

"Now, where's that money?" Parnell asked.

"You were with her, weren't you?" Win asked.

"What?''

"Belle Amberly.''

"What are you talking about?''

"She begged you to let the women go, but you wouldn't do it unless she . . . did . . . things for you. She wasn't buy-ing her freedom, she was trying to get you to move the other women to safety. She told me all about it. That's true, isn't it?''

"So what if it is?" Parnell asked. "Were you sweet on her, or something?"

Win didn't answer, and Parnell grinned, evilly. "Son of a bitch! That's it, isn't it? You were sweet on that whore." He laughed. "Well, Mr. Bushwhacker, I'm not only taking you to St. Louis to hang, I also screwed your woman. I screwed her because she begged me to screw her. Do you like thinking about that?"

"Cap'n Parnell, he's just trying to get out of tellin' us where the money is," the sergeant said.

"Sergeant Berry is right," Parnell said. "I gave you the cigar, now you tell us where the goddamned money is."

"When you stop for water, go to the northeast leg of the water tank," Win said. "Look up under the bottom of the tank, and you'll see a shelf. The money's in a burlap bag on that shelf."

"How much is there?" Berry asked eagerly.

"Well, Sergeant, this may just be the most expensive cigar I ever smoked," Win said. "As near as I can recall, there's a little over eight hundred dollars in that bag."

"Son of a bitch!" the sergeant said, smiling broadly. "Think of that, boys. That's two hundred dollars apiece!"

Parnell went back to his newspaper, not happy that he was getting two hundred dollars, but upset that he was losing six hundred. Sergeant Berry and the two privates got into an animated discussion as to how they would spend their money.

"Win, there's no money there," Joe whispered.

"Doesn't matter," Win answered. "We'll be gone long before the train gets there."

"You got a plan?"

"Pass me the cigar."

Win took several puffs on the cigar until the end was glowing cherry red. He looked toward the front of the car, and seeing that no one was paying any attention to him, flipped the cigar toward the three kegs of gunpowder. The cigar landed on the cracked top of the nearest keg.

For a minute, nothing happened.

"It caught," Win finally said. "I can see smoke. We'll give it ten seconds, then we have to duck behind these seats."

"Win, that's three kegs of powder. We might get blown all to hell," Joe suggested.

"So what? It's better than hanging," Win answered.

"Yeah, I guess you're right at that," Joe agreed.

Slowly and quietly Win counted. When he reached ten, he yelled, "Now!"

They stood up quickly, then jumped around behind Win's wooden bench.

"What the hell?" Berry shouted, rising to his feet and pulling his pistol. "They're gettin' away!"

Berry fired at them, and the bullet crashed through the back of the seat, then fried the air just between Win and Joe.

"Goddamn!" Joe shouted. "When's that son of a bitch going to blow?"

Suddenly one of the Yankee soldiers saw the smoke curling up from the gunpowder.

"Cap'n Parnell, look!"

"Shit!" Parnell shouted, and he started toward the window.

It was too late. At that moment the powder went off with a blinding flash and a deafening roar. The front half of the car, where the solders were, was completely blown away, separating the back half, and leaving it slanting down toward the track bed from the rear wheels. The back of the car was filled with smoke from the charge. The train had been running at better than thirty miles per hour when the gunpowder exploded, so the severed car continued under its own momentum for a while before coming to a rough stop. The main body of the train went on for several hundred feet before the engineer realized what had happened. When he saw that he had lost the rear-most car, he applied the brakes, bringing the train to a screeching dead stop.

Win and Joe were coughing furiously, trying to clear their throats, nostrils, and eyes of the acrid cordite. When the smoke cleared, Win looked around the car. It was as if some giant had cut it in two with an axe. The front half was completely gone, and so were Captain Parnell, Sergeant Berry, and the two privates.

"You all right?" Win asked.

"Yeah."

"Come on," Win said. "We've got to get out of here before the train backs up."

"We won't be movin' very fast like this," Joe grumbled, rattling the chain that joined them.

"We'll take care of that later. Now we've got to get out of here."

Win and Joe jumped out of the open end of the car, then ran down the coal-and-cobble-covered berm to hide in some brush by the track. They watched as the train backed up. Several people got off the train and ran up to the wreckage to look around.

"I said all along, we ain't got no business carryin' gunpowder on the same train as passengers," the conductor said.

"What d'you think caused it?" someone asked.

"Hell, it coulda been anything," the conductor said. "Maybe one of 'em was smokin'. Maybe a spark flew in from the engine. Who knows? All I know is, six men are dead.''

"Six?" Joe whispered.

Win held a finger to his lips.

"Hell, for them poor Coulter boys, it's prob'ly just as well they went this way, 'stead of hangin'. Leastwise, this way, they never knew what hit 'em. Come on, folks, we have to get back on the train. We've got to get to Sedalia and send a telegraph so they can get the track cleared.''

The train crew and curious passengers reboarded. Then, with several chugging puffs of steam, the train began rolling again. Win and Joe waited for several moments until the sound of the train had faded in the distance. Now there was only the whisper of the wind and the flutter of grasshoppers.

"They think we're dead," Joe said.

"Yeah," Win said. "And if we stay in Missouri and someone who knows us, sees us, it's only a matter of time until we are.''

"So, what do you think we should do?''

Win held out his arms. "Well, the first thing to do is to get out of these chains.''

"You have any ideas on how?" Joe asked.

Win smiled. "Nope. You're more resourceful than I am when it comes to things like this. I'm going to let you handle that part of it.''

"All right," Joe said. "I'll get us out of the chains. Then what?''

"Then, little brother, we're going to get the hell out of Missouri.''

23

Western Kansas, one year later

WIN AND JOE HAD NEVER BEEN IN THE LITTLE TOWN BE-
fore, but they had seen several just like it since the war.
They dismounted in front of the livery, and a gnarled old
man came shuffling outside. He waved his hand at the flies
which were buzzing around his head.

"You boys wantin' to board your horses?" he asked.
"Fifty cents a night. That includes the feedin'."

"No, we won't be staying," Win answered. "Just give
'em some water and oats, then tie 'em off over in front of
the saloon." Win gave the old man a couple of coins.

"I'll take care of 'em. You boys come into town to see
the sight, did you?" the old man asked.

"The sight?"

"Over in the saloon," the old man explained. "Folks
been comin' in from all over to see it for two, three days
now. I keep tellin' ever'one, them boys is goin' to get ripe
pretty soon, never mind that they pack 'em in ice ever'
night."

"Mister, I don't know what the hell you are talking
about."

"Hmm. Don't know where you been the last couple days that you didn't hear about it," the old man said. "But it seems that last Monday mornin' three boys come ridin' into town, plannin' to rob the bank. Only thing is, our marshal got word they was comin' in, an' near 'bout the whole town was waitin' for 'em. They was shot down 'fore they ever got off their horses."

"Wait a minute," Joe said. "Are you telling me they were shot down *before* they went into the bank?"

"Hell, they wasn't even halfway to the bank when the shootin' commenced," the old man replied. "I told you, the marshal got word. He had the whole town waitin' for 'em."

"But if they hadn't done anything yet, how did you know they were going to rob the bank? Hell, they might've changed their minds and decided to just ride on through," Joe said.

"Coulda done that, I s'pose, but the marshal never give 'em no chance to change their minds. He know'd about their plans, and he took care of 'em. Now them three boys is over to the saloon, strapped to boards, standin' up against the wall. Marshal Hunter says that if they don't get too ripe, he's goin' to keep 'em there for two whole weeks as a warning to any other outlaws as might think our town is fair pickin'."

Both Win and Joe reacted to the name.

"Did you say Hunter?" Win asked. "Your marshal is named Hunter?"

"Yep. Luke Hunter," the old man replied. "He rode with Jim Lane and Captain Emil Slaughter durin' the war. Reckon you heard of Emil Slaughter."

"I reckon we did," Win said.

"That's what makes it so ironic about them three boys that rode in on Monday," the old man explained. He chuckled. "You know what the word 'ironic' means? I had to ask the newspaper fella what it meant when he put it in his story. It means a joke that's not really funny."

"What about the three boys do you find ironic?" Win asked.

"Well, accordin' to Marshal Hunter, they was once riders for Quantrill. What do you think about that?"

"I think I'd like to have a look at them," Win said.

"Figured you'd want to," the old man said. "Like I said, it's a mighty interestin' sight. You go on over there and take a look. I'll have your horses fed and in front of the saloon in no more'n five minutes."

"Thanks," Win called back over his shoulder as he and Joe started across the street.

THE SALOON WAS SO CROWDED THAT THEY HAD TO TURN sideways to pick their way through the crowd to the bar. There was a particularly large gathering in the rear, near the piano.

"You want to go back there?" Joe asked.

"Not yet," Win said. "I think I need a drink first."

"Yeah, me too."

They found an opening at the end of the bar.

"What'll it be for you gents?" the bartender asked, sliding down to greet them.

"Two whiskeys," Win said.

The bartender nodded, and started to turn away when Joe said: "And I'll have the same."

The bartender brought out four shot glasses and filled them. "You boys strangers in town?" he asked. "Don't think I've seen you before."

"We're just passing through."

The bartender nodded toward the back wall. "Well, you don't want to miss the sight," he said.

"It looks a little crowded over there right now," Joe suggested.

"It ain't goin' to get any less crowded," the bartender said. "It's drawin' people from all over."

"How long does the marshal plan to keep them there?"

"Oh, they'll stay 'til they're so ripe that folks won't come in and see them anymore. They've been great for business, and I'm givin' the marshal a percentage of ever' drink I sell. I reckon he's in no more of a hurry to bury 'em than I am." The bartender laughed, and looked toward the ceiling. " 'Course, I'm gettin' that all back too, since he spends so much time with the girls that work here."

"He's up there now, is he?" Win asked.

"Went up with the new girl about five minutes ago," the bartender said.

"Bartender, how about a couple drinks down here!" someone called.

"You boys excuse me, I got to get back to work," the bartender said. He nodded toward the back wall. "Now, don't you forget to go over there and take a look. It's somethin' worth seein'."

Win and Joe downed their second whiskies, then with a nod to indicate that they were ready, moved through the crowd to the back of the room. They were halfway there when they recognized the dead men.

"Win!" Joe said with a quick intake of breath.

"I know," Win replied quietly. "Don't say anything."

The bodies were those of Ethan, Tate, and Boykin. Tied to boards, they were standing up against the back wall, pistols clutched in their stiffened hands, mouths set in a snarl, and their eyes open and sightless. There were half a dozen or more bullet holes in each of them: little black punctures in their chests and heads, arms and legs. Three or four of the men closest to the bodies were drinking heavily, laughing and "toasting" the dead men, bragging as to whose bullets made which holes.

"Yes, sir, I'll just bet them boys was mighty sorry they chose our bank to rob," one of the men said.

"Joe," Win said under his breath. "Get the horses. Bring them to the alley around back."

Joe nodded, then left without questioning Win's order.

Moving slowly, so as not to call any attention to himself, Win slipped back through the crowd, then up the stairs. When he reached the landing at the top of the stairs, he looked down. Not one eye was on him.

Win moved down the hall, stopping outside each room to listen. Then he heard Luke's voice.

"Do it, bitch! You know what I like!"

Win opened the door very quietly, then looked inside. Luke was standing by the bed with his back to the door. A woman was kneeling in front of him. Her eyes were closed and her mouth was full. Her hands were holding onto Luke's naked butt.

"Ah, that's it," Luke cooed. "Suck it, baby, suck it."

Still unnoticed, Win moved up behind Luke. Pulling his pistol, he stuck the end of the barrel just barely into the rim of Luke's butt-hole.

"Oh, yeah, baby, that's good!" Luke said.

Win jammed it in, hard, about an inch.

"Ouch, what the hell?" Luke shouted in sudden pain. It wasn't until that moment that the woman opened her eyes. They grew wide when she saw what Win was doing.

"You want to take his cock out of your mouth and step away, ma'am?" Win asked quietly. "Oh, and don't make a sound. I wouldn't want you to get hurt."

Luke started to move but Win shoved the pistol in a little deeper. "Not you, you son of a bitch. You stay where you are," he said.

Quickly, the woman moved over to sit, naked, on the side of the bed. She looked at Win with frightened eyes.

"Take your gun out of my ass, you bastard," Luke ordered. "You know you can't shoot me. This is my town. You shoot me and the folks downstairs will tear you from asshole to teakettle."

"The folks downstairs are all drunk," Win said. "They are celebrating killing Ethan, Tate, and Boykin."

"Yes, and they'll kill you too if you try anything," Luke insisted.

"Maybe I'll just take my chances."

"What do you want to kill me for, anyway, Coulter? Because of what we did durin' the war? Hell, we was on opposite sides," Luke said. "And when you get right down to it, I don't figure either one of us can be proud of what we done. You shot Slaughter down in front of his wife an' kids. Did that make you feel proud?"

"What happened downstairs didn't have anything to do with the war," Win said.

"Yeah, well, I didn't kill those boys by myself," Luke answered. "Half the town was in on it. After you shoot me, what are you going to do? Take them on?"

"Maybe."

"Listen, maybe we can work something out. You got any money? I'll bet you're broke, aren't you?"

"What are you going to do, Luke, pay me not to shoot you?"

"Why not?" Luke said. "I've got twenty dollars in my pocket."

Win laughed. "Twenty dollars? Yeah, that's probably a pretty good price, considering that's about all you're worth. But it's not enough."

"Wait, wait, I've got somethin' you might be interested in," Luke said. "I've got me a gold watch that I carried through the whole war. It's real gold. Hell, the gold alone is worth a hundred dollars or more. It's all yours, if you'll put that gun away and walk on out of here.''

''Where is the watch?''

''It's in my pants pocket.''

Win looked over at the woman who was still sitting, naked and frightened, on the bed. ''Get it,'' he told her.

''You want to take that gun out of my ass now?'' Luke asked.

Win jammed it in a little harder.

''Ouch!''

''Not yet,'' Win said.

The woman emptied Luke's pants pocket, pulling out a knife, a few coins, and a pocket watch.

''Take a good look at that watch,'' Luke bragged. ''I took it off some dumb dirt farmer, right after the war started. Can you imagine a dirt farmer having a watch like that? There's no tellin' what that watch is worth, and it's yours, if you let me go.''

Win held out his hand and the woman gave him the watch. Even before he touched it, he knew that it was his father's watch.

''What happened to the farmer?'' Win asked in a choked voice.

''Are you kidding? We killed the son of a bitch,'' Luke replied. ''Him and the scrawny-assed woman too. You don't have to worry about anyone comin' aroun' tryin' to claim this watch.''

At that precise moment the grief Win felt over his mother's and father's deaths was as intense as it had been on the day he and Joe discovered the burned farm and the charred bodies. He almost gave in to the grief, then he felt the white-heat of anger. He let that anger build until it washed throughout his entire body. The anger had the effect of pushing the grief away.

"Look, Coulter, are you going to take the deal or not?" Luke growled. "I ain't got all day. Either shit, or get off the pot."

"Shit, or get off the pot," Win replied. "Yeah, that's a good idea."

He pulled the trigger.

First in an all-new series from the creators of Longarm!

BUSHWHACKERS

They were the most brutal gang of cutthroats ever
assembled. And during the Civil War, they sought justice
outside of the law—paying back every Yankee raid with one
of their own. They rode hard, shot straight, and had their
way with every willin' woman west of the Mississippi. No
man could stop them. No woman could resist them. And no
Yankee stood a chance of living when Quantrill's Raiders
rode into town...

Win and Joe Coulter become the two most wanted men in
the West. And they learn just how sweet—and deadly—
revenge could be...

BUSHWHACKERS by B. J. Lanagan
0-515-12102-9/$4.99

BUSHWHACKERS #2: REBEL COUNTY
0-515-12142-8/$4.99

Coming in November 1997: BUSHWHACKERS #3:
THE KILLING EDGE 0-515-12177-0/$4.99

VISIT THE PUTNAM BERKLEY BOOKSTORE CAFÉ ON THE INTERNET:
http://www.berkley.com

Payable in U.S. funds. No cash accepted. Postage & handling: $1.75 for one book, 75¢ for each
additional. Maximum postage $5.50. Prices, postage and handling charges may change without
notice. Visa, Amex, MasterCard call 1-800-788-6262, ext. 1, or fax 1-201-933-2316; refer to ad #705

Or, check above books   Bill my: ☐ Visa   ☐ MasterCard   ☐ Amex _____ (expires)
and send this order form to:
The Berkley Publishing Group   Card#_____
P.O. Box 12289, Dept. B   Daytime Phone #_____ ($10 minimum)
Newark, NJ 07101-5289   Signature_____
Please allow 4-6 weeks for delivery.   Or enclosed is my: ☐ check ☐ money order
Foreign and Canadian delivery 8-12 weeks.

Ship to:
Name_____   Book Total $_____
Address_____   Applicable Sales Tax $_____
                                        (NY, NJ, PA, CA, GST Can.)
City_____   Postage & Handling $_____
State/ZIP_____   Total Amount Due $_____

Bill to: Name_____
Address_____City_____
State/ZIP_____

JAKE LOGAN
TODAY'S HOTTEST ACTION WESTERN!

__SLOCUM AT DOG LEG CREEK #199	0-515-11701-3/$3.99
__SLOCUM'S SILVER #200	0-515-11729-3/$3.99
__SLOCUM #201: RENEGADE TRAIL	0-515-11739-0/$4.50
__SLOCUM AND THE DIRTY GAME #202	0-515-11764-1/$4.50
__SLOCUM AND THE BEAR LAKE MONSTER #204	0-515-11806-0/$4.50
__SLOCUM AND THE APACHE RANSOM #209	0-515-11894-X/$4.99
__SLOCUM AT DEAD DOG #215	0-515-12015-4/$4.99
__SLOCUM AND THE TOWN BOSS #216	0-515-12030-8/$4.99
__SLOCUM AND THE LADY IN BLUE #217	0-515-12049-9/$4.99
__SLOCUM AND THE POWDER RIVER GAMBLE #218	0-515-12070-7/$4.99
__SLOCUM AND THE COLORADO RIVERBOAT #219	0-515-12081-2/$4.99
__SLOCUM #220: SLOCUM'S INHERITANCE	0-515-12103-7/$4.99
__SLOCUM AND DOC HOLLIDAY #221	0-515-12131-2/$4.99
__SLOCUM AND THE AZTEC PRIESTESS #222	0-515-12143-6/$4.99
__SLOCUM AND THE IRISH LASS (GIANT)	0-515-12155-X/$5.99
__SLOCUM AND THE COMANCHE RESCUE #223	0-515-12161-4/$4.99
__SLOCUM #224: LOUISIANA LOVELY (11/97)	0-515-12176-2/$4.99

Payable in U.S. funds. No cash accepted. Postage & handling: $1.75 for one book, 75¢ for each additional. Maximum postage $5.50. Prices, postage and handling charges may change without notice. Visa, Amex, MasterCard call 1-800-788-6262, ext. 1, or fax 1-201-933-2316; refer to ad #202d

Or, check above books   Bill my: ☐ Visa ☐ MasterCard ☐ Amex _____ (expires)
and send this order form to:
The Berkley Publishing Group   Card#_____
P.O. Box 12289, Dept. B   Daytime Phone #_____ ($10 minimum)
Newark, NJ 07101-5289   Signature_____
Please allow 4-6 weeks for delivery.   Or enclosed is my: ☐ check ☐ money order
Foreign and Canadian delivery 8-12 weeks.

Ship to:

Name_____	Book Total	$_____
Address_____	Applicable Sales Tax (NY, NJ, PA, CA, GST Can.)	$_____
City_____	Postage & Handling	$_____
State/ZIP_____	Total Amount Due	$_____

Bill to: Name_____
Address_____City_____
State/ZIP_____

Explore the exciting Old West with one of the men who made it wild!

__LONGARM AND THE LUSTY LADY (GIANT #16)   0-515-11923-7/$5.50

__LONGARM AND THE MINUTE MEN #213   0-515-11942-3/$4.99

__LONGARM AND THE RACY LADIES #214   0-515-11956-3/$4.99

__LONGARM AND THE WHISKEY WOMAN #217   0-515-11998-9/$4.99

__LONGARM AND THE BOARDINGHOUSE
    WIDOW #218   0-515-12016-2/$4.99

__LONGARM AND THE INDIAN WAR #220   0-515-12050-2/$4.99

__LONGARM AND THE BACKWOODS
    BARONESS #222   0-515-12080-4/$4.99

__LONGARM AND THE DOUBLE-BARREL
    BLOWOUT #223   0-515-12104-5/$4.99

__LONGARM AND THE MAIDEN
    MEDUSA #224   0-515-12132-0/$4.99

__LONGARM AND THE DEAD MAN'S PLAY
    #225   0-515-12144-4/$4.99

__LONGARM AND THE LADY FAIRE #226   0-515-12162-2/$4.99

__LONGARM AND THE REBEL
    EXECUTIONER #227 (11/97)   0-515-12178-9/$4.99

Payable in U.S. funds. No cash accepted. Postage & handling: $1.75 for one book, 75¢ for each additional. Maximum postage $5.50. Prices, postage and handling charges may change without notice. Visa, Amex, MasterCard call 1-800-788-6262, ext. 1, or fax 1-201-933-2316; refer to ad #201g

Or, check above books   Bill my: ☐ Visa ☐ MasterCard ☐ Amex _____ (expires)
and send this order form to:
The Berkley Publishing Group   Card#_____
P.O. Box 12289, Dept. B   Daytime Phone #_____   ($10 minimum)
Newark, NJ 07101-5289   Signature_____
Please allow 4-6 weeks for delivery.   Or enclosed is my: ☐ check ☐ money order
Foreign and Canadian delivery 8-12 weeks.

Ship to:

Name_____   Book Total $_____
Address_____   Applicable Sales Tax $_____
                                 (NY, NJ, PA, CA, GST Can.)
City_____   Postage & Handling $_____
State/ZIP_____   Total Amount Due $_____

Bill to: Name_____

Address_____   City_____
State/ZIP_____

J. R. ROBERTS

THE GUNSMITH

__THE GUNSMITH #165:	THE DENVER RIPPER	0-515-11703-X/$3.99
__THE GUNSMITH #170:	THE ELLIOTT BAY MURDERS	0-515-11918-0/$4.50
__THE GUNSMITH #174:	GUNQUICK	0-515-11880-X/$4.99
__THE GUNSMITH #181:	THE CHALLENGE	0-515-11999-7/$4.99
__THE GUNSMITH #182:	WINNING STREAK	0-515-12017-0/$4.99
__THE GUNSMITH #183:	THE FLYING MACHINE	0-515-12032-4/$4.99
__THE GUNSMITH #184:	HOMESTEAD LAW	0-515-12051-0/$4.99
__THE GUNSMITH #185:	THE BILOXI QUEEN	0-515-12071-5/$4.99
__THE GUNSMITH #186:	SIX FOR THE MONEY	0-515-12082-0/$4.99
__THE GUNSMITH #187:	LEGBREAKERS AND HEARTBREAKERS	0-515-12105-3/$4.99
__THE GUNSMITH #188:	THE ORIENT EXPRESS	0-515-12133-9/$4.99
__THE GUNSMITH #189:	THE POSSE FROM ELSINORE	0-515-12145-2/$4.99
__THE GUNSMITH #190:	LADY ON THE RUN	0-515-12163-0/$4.99
__THE GUNSMITH #191:	OUTBREAK (11/97)	0-515-12179-7/$4.99

Payable in U.S. funds. No cash accepted. Postage & handling: $1.75 for one book, 75¢ for each additional. Maximum postage $5.50. Prices, postage and handling charges may change without notice. Visa, Amex, MasterCard call 1-800-788-6262, ext. 1, or fax 1-201-933-2316; refer to ad #206g

Or, check above books	Bill my: ☐ Visa ☐ MasterCard ☐ Amex _____ (expires)
and send this order form to:	
The Berkley Publishing Group	Card#_____
P.O. Box 12289, Dept. B	Daytime Phone #_____ ($10 minimum)
Newark, NJ 07101-5289	Signature_____

Please allow 4-6 weeks for delivery.   Or enclosed is my: ☐ check ☐ money order
Foreign and Canadian delivery 8-12 weeks.

Ship to:

Name_____	Book Total $_____
Address_____	Applicable Sales Tax $_____ (NY, NJ, PA, CA, GST Can.)
City_____	Postage & Handling $_____
State/ZIP_____	Total Amount Due $_____

Bill to: Name_____

Address_____ City_____
State/ZIP_____

W9-BBX-277

How I Changed
— My Life —

How I Changed My Life

— My Life —

BY TODD STRASSER

Aladdin Paperbacks

you purchased this book without a cover you should be aware that this book is stolen property. It was reported as "unsold and destroyed" to the publisher and neither the author nor the publisher has received any payment for this "stripped book."

First Aladdin Paperbacks edition August 1996

Copyright © 1995 by Todd Strasser

Aladdin Paperbacks
An imprint of Simon & Schuster
Children's Publishing Division
1230 Avenue of the Americas
New York, NY 10020

All rights reserved, including the right of
reproduction in whole or in part in any form

Also available in a Simon & Schuster Books for
Young Readers edition

Printed and bound in the United States of America
10 9 8 7 6 5 4

The Library of Congress has cataloged the Simon & Schuster
Books for Young Readers edition as follows:

Strasser, Tom.
How I changed my life / Todd Strasser
p. cm.
Summary: Overweight high school senior Bo decides to change
her image while working on the school play with a former star
football player who is also strggling to find a new identity for
himself.
ISBN 0-671-88415-8
[1. Identity—Fiction. 2. Weight control—Fiction. 3. High
schools—Fiction. 4. Schools—Fiction. 5. Plays—Fiction.]
I. Title.
PZ7.S899Hp 1995 [Fic]—dc20 94-13065
ISBN 0-689-80895-X (Aladdin pbk.)

To my wife, Pamela,
with great love and appreciation

How I Changed
— My Life —

KYLE

Today I stood up in the front of Pinhead science class and gave an oral report.

"Depending on what sex you are, you either have seven or eight openings in your body," I began.

"All right, Kyle!" Karl Lukowsky stuck his fingers in his mouth and whistled from the back of the room where he'd tilted his chair up against the wall. Karl is thin and gawky with a case of acne that makes his face look like the dark side of the moon. His entire wardrobe consists of four Bart Simpson T-shirts, a couple of pairs of black and white checked pants, and a humongous key ring hanging from his belt.

"That's enough, Karl," said Mr. Orillio, our science teacher.

"The opening I'm going to talk about is the ear," I said.

"Booo!"

"That's enough, Karl."

"It's not one opening, it's two!" yelled Peter Ferrat.

"Hey, Kyle," Jeff Branco shouted. "Didn't Chloe go over your report with you first?"

"Go over it?" Ferrat said. "She usually writes them for him!"

Mr. Orillio told them to shut up, but the Pinheads were on a roll. Mr. Orillio can't be more than five and a half feet tall. His head is so bald it shines. Teachers at my school don't have to wear ties, but he wears one every day. And he always rolls up the sleeves of his shirt to show off his hairy forearms and let everyone know that he may be small, but he's one tough mother of a science teacher.

Crack! Mr. Orillio smacked his yardstick against his desk.

"Either calm down or get sent to the office," he threatened. Then he turned to me. "Continue, Kyle."

"Actually, what I want to talk about is earwax," I said. "Have you ever thought about earwax?"

"No!" several Pinheads shouted and then started to laugh.

Crack! went the yardstick.

"Well, I did," I continued. "I asked myself, where does it come from? What is it for? I mean, the idea that our ears make this stuff is pretty bizarre."

In the back of the room a couple of the Pinheads made snoring sounds.

"Earwax is called cerumen," I said. "It's produced by tiny glands in the ear canal and its job is to keep dust, insects, and other small particles from injuring the inside of the ear."

Lukowsky stuck his finger in his ear and scraped out a glob of brownish-yellow wax.

"Gross!" shouted the Pinheads.

Crack! went the yardstick.

"When we move our jaws to talk or eat, the motion forces the wax upward and out of the ear canal," I said. "When too much wax gathers in the canal, it should be removed by a doctor. Otherwise it can block the canal and impair hearing."

"What'd you say?" Peter Ferrat shouted, and a bunch of Pinheads laughed.

The yardstick went *Crack!*

I spend most of my time on the catwalk in the auditorium. The catwalk is a narrow piece of metal grating about two feet wide that runs about thirty feet above the stage. There are ladders at either end. The techies use the catwalk to hang lights and mikes for stage productions. I use it to hide.

Today Mr. Goodrich stepped onto the stage. Mr. Goodrich is the head of the school drama society. He also teaches honors English, a class I have been known to attend when more attractive alternatives are unavailable. Tall and stooped, with sandy hair that's turning gray, he wears the same yellow cardigan sweater with leather elbow patches every day.

"Bo?" he said, peering up at me.

"Herself," I replied.

"The fall play will be *The Diary of Anne Frank*. We can use some of the props from last spring's production of *Little Women*. I think if you and Bobby do some murals—"

"I can't," I said.

Mr. Goodrich's jaw went slack. "Of course you can, Bo. You've always done it. We'd be lost without you."

I could have suggested that he purchase a compass, or possibly even a sextant. A good road atlas at the very least. But these words I could not utter, for it is not in my nature to be snide.

"I'm sorry," I said.

"I don't understand." Mr. Goodrich looked slightly baffled.

"Chloe Frost."

"So?" Mr. Goodrich pretended to be puzzled, but he understood perfectly. I rested my chin on the catwalk rail and wondered if high school was the same everywhere in the universe—a massive, but unavoidable waste of golden youth.

Mr. Goodrich glanced at the empty auditorium spreading out before us like a huge mouth with 854 upholstered maroon teeth. I think he wanted to make sure Chloe wasn't out there hiding behind a seat and listening.

"Maybe she won't try out," he said in a low voice. "She's already the class treasurer and on the prom planning committee. She might be too busy for the play."

The bell rang. As much as I dreaded mingling

5

with my fellow detainees, I knew it was time to climb down and attend AP History. Mr. Goodrich waited at the base of the ladder.

"Bo?" Mr. Goodrich went from his desperate look to his helpless look. When I didn't respond, he tried looking like a basset hound puppy that had lost its mother. "Seriously, Bo, I need your help. I believe this will be one of the most important productions I've ever done."

Just between you and me, that wasn't saying much.

KYLE

At the end of the class, Mr. Orillio stood near the door picking his teeth with a toothpick. "Hold up a minute, Kyle."

"Say what?"

"We need to talk."

"Sorry, gotta go," I said.

"Where?"

"Uh, study hall."

Mr. Orillio gave me a "get real" look.

"It's a very important study hall," I said.

"Yeah, right." He smirked. Then he took a pen out of his pocket and turned to a white sheet of paper pinned to the wall next to his collection of "The Far Side" cartoons:

THE FOLLOWING STUDENTS ARE BEING CONSIDERED AS SERIOUS CANDIDATES FOR MR. ORILLIO'S SUMMER SCHOOL SCIENCE SESSION:

Jeff Branco
Peter Ferrat

Under Peter he wrote my name, Kyle Winthrop.

Summer school?

"But I did my report," I protested.

"You had three weeks to do this report," Mr. Orillio said, clicking his pen and putting it back in his pocket. "You didn't want to write it out so I gave you special permission to do it orally. So you copied two paragraphs out of the encyclopedia and read them out loud. They do that in third grade, Kyle."

Out in the hall, groups of kids were pushing toward their next class. I wanted to be out there, lost in the crowd.

"You're not captain of the football team anymore," he said. "It's a new world, pal."

I needed *him* to tell me that?

BO

It isn't easy to compete in a universe populated by the likes of Chloe Frost, who is gorgeous and perpetually tan because she spends every vacation in far-off places where the temperature is always 85 degrees and the ozone layer is virtually nonexistent. She has sand-colored, sun-streaked hair and a model's face with high cheekbones, big brown eyes, a slim nose, and a petite mouth. Her teeth are straight and white, and she has such a perfect body that girls ogle her just as much as boys do.

Chloe and I have been doing school plays since junior high. We never talk. She never attends the cast parties after the shows, probably because she thinks she's above all that. To me, Chloe symbolizes everything that's wrong with our society, everything that's self-centered, hypercompetitive, materialistic, superficial, insincere, and shallow.

Do I sound jealous?

KYLE

Senior lounge is this open space outside the cafeteria with wooden benches along the walls and the sweet sticky smell of lunch in the air. Jeff Branco was stretched out on one of the benches, asleep with his mouth open and the black bandanna he wears on his head pulled down over his eyes. He was wearing a sleeveless black leather motorcycle vest with a hooded gray sweatshirt under it. Timothy Zonin High's very own James Dean.

Chloe was sitting by herself in a corner, bent over a notebook, writing.

I sat down next to her.

"Just a minute," she said, and kept writing. I caught a whiff of perfume and looked at the notebook. Her handwriting is perfect, every letter smooth and flawless as though it was carved by an Olympic figure skater.

"There." She got to the end of the page,

closed the notebook, and put it into the white and blue canvas sailing bag she carries around. It has her initials embroidered in blue: CHF— Chloe Hollow Frost.

"How are you today?" she asked.

"Orillio says I may have to do summer school."

Little creases appeared on her forehead. She hooked her blond hair behind her ear. Three small diamond earrings glinted in her earlobe.

"It was just a warning," I added.

Chloe nodded and reached into her bag and rummaged through all the books she had crammed in there. She picked up a few and put them on my lap. "Hold these a second, Kyle."

On top of the pile was a thin light gray book. *"The Dairy of Anne Frank,"* I read.

"It's *Diary*, silly."

"So it's not about a farmer named Anne, huh?"

"No," Chloe said, taking the books back and putting them in her bag again. "It's the fall play."

"Think you'll be the star?"

Chloe fixed me with her clear brown eyes. "Why do I always have to be the star?"

"I don't know, but you always are."

She pulled a black ledger out of her bag, opened it to a page with a long column of names and numbers on it, and began to add, her slender fingers racing over the keys of the calculator like she was an accountant.

"I just don't know how I'm going to get it all done," she said, more to herself than to me. "Between being the class treasurer, president of SafeRides, head cheerleader, and on the prom planning committee, when am I going to have time to do the play?"

That's what she always says.

BO

Chloe hurt her ankle playing volleyball this afternoon. Nobody actually cares about winning in gym except Chloe, who always must be the best in everything. So while most of the girls were merely pushing the ball back and forth over the net, and praying they wouldn't break a fingernail, Chloe was Ms. Gung Ho. "Come on, you guys, try!" she shouted at us when we started to fall behind the other team. Imagine, if you will, a gaggle of girls wearing baggy maroon shorts and oversized T-shirts who would prefer to be anywhere but gym. And standing in our midst was Chloe, whose T-shirt was practically skin-tight and whose gym shorts were tailored to fit snugly around her perfect tan thighs. She was the only one on our team wearing knee and elbow pads, but then she's the only one who'd ever think of diving for a dig.

"Chill out," snarled Sandra O'Donnell, who's

early six feet tall and towers over Chloe. "It's only a game."

"Does that mean you can't try?" Chloe's face was red from exertion. No one else had even broken a sweat.

"It's not important," Sandra said.

"If this isn't important, what is?" Chloe demanded with her hands on her hips.

Sandra rolled her eyes. "Life."

"And this isn't life?" Chloe asked.

"No, it's gym," I said. A couple of girls chuckled, but Chloe pursed her ultraglossy lips and glared at me. I felt myself start to wilt; I'm such a chicken.

"It's so easy to make fun, Bo," she said. "It's so easy to laugh. But I think you're just afraid of what will happen if you try and still lose. Because that would really put a dent in your fragile self-image."

I wished I'd had some clever retort. Maybe something about how I didn't know that Chloe had added psychology to her already prodigious list of abilities. But nothing came to mind, and besides, it didn't matter. Nothing I could say would have fazed her.

"Why don't you all just try for once," she exhorted. "Maybe something truly amazing will happen. Like we might actually win."

Everyone grumbled and groaned and got back into position.

The remarkable thing is, Chloe can be so obnoxious that she actually does get her team to try hard—just so they can get her off their backs. Pretty soon the game was tied, and that was when Chloe leaped up to block Ellen Michner's spike. When she came down, you could hear the "Pop!" as her ankle went out and she crashed to the floor.

The next thing we knew, she was writhing on the ground clutching her ankle and groaning through clenched teeth. Ms. Acevedo, the gym teacher, ran into the office to get an ice pack and the rest of us stood around and watched. Sandra O'Donnell and I glanced at each other and I sensed that she wanted to smile because Chloe had finally gotten what she deserved. But the poor girl really was in pain, and even though we all hated her we were touched by her misery. Ms. Acevedo and two girls helped her to the nurse's office.

I heard she went to the hospital from there.

Perhaps she won't try out for the part of Anne Frank after all.

KYLE

There's a lot of talk about BMs in my house lately. IT's BMs to be precise. IT is my father's one-and-a-half-year-old son. My mother died when I was ten. About four years later my father married this woman named Jackie. She's forty and my father's fifty-two. A year and a half ago, Jackie had IT.

If IT goes three days without a BM, Jackie gets worried. If IT has three bowel movements in one day, Jackie gets nervous. If IT's BMs smell bad, Jackie wants to know why. Likewise if they smell good.

Tonight IT had a BM that didn't smell at all. I was sitting in the den watching college ball on TV. My father was in the kitchen. From the stairs I heard Jackie say, "Brian, could you come here?" in that nervous tone of voice that always gets my father's attention. He went upstairs to the nursery.

"What's the problem?" I heard him ask.

"Smell this," Jackie said.

"That?" I bet my father was thrilled.

"Please, Brian."

I can just see my father bending over and taking a whiff.

"So?" I heard my father say.

"It doesn't smell," Jackie said.

"Well, that's great."

"It's not normal," Jackie insisted. "A baby's BMs should smell."

"Maybe it depends on what he eats," my father said.

"Do you think I should call Dr. Huber?" Jackie probably calls the pediatrician five times a day.

"Let's wait a day and see what happens," my father said. That's his standard reply. On the way back downstairs he stopped in the den.

"A BM that didn't smell." I winked.

"Yeah." He smiled slightly. "Be nice if we could patent it. So who's playing?"

"Syracuse and Georgetown. Third quarter. The Hoyas are up by six."

"Homework all done?"

The Hoyas' quarterback stepped into the pocket and hit the tight end for a fourteen-yard gain. My father stood in the doorway and waited for my answer. When it didn't come, he said,

17

"Come on, Kyle, it's senior year. Just get through it. You're going to need that diploma."

I stared at the TV, and my father stared at me. It was like he wanted to say something more, but it had all been said before.

BO

I know it's wrong to delight in other people's misfortunes, but Chloe's the kind of person who makes you want to break that rule. It's not just that she's so obnoxious. What truly galls me is that she doesn't seem to care whether we like her or not. And she's so . . . *perfect*. (Her father is a plastic surgeon. Maybe he created her in his laboratory.) If I looked like her, I really think I'd be content . . . just to be me.

KYLE

I wheeled Chloe to the audition for that play today. Half a dozen people were sitting in the auditorium when we got there. Everyone started to whisper as I pushed Chloe down the aisle.

Mr. Goodrich was up on the stage, holding a clipboard. He teaches Pinhead English and we always give him a hard time.

"Why, Chloe." He looked surprised. "What are you doing here?"

"I'm going to audition," Chloe said as I helped her onto the stage.

"In your condition?" Mr. Goodrich frowned. I got the feeling he wasn't too thrilled.

"I'll be walking in a few days," Chloe said.

"Well, er, I see." Mr. Goodrich wasn't doing a great job of hiding his disappointment. "I suppose you want to be Anne."

Chloe responded by reciting by heart about five minutes worth of lines from the play.

Everyone in the auditorium became silent.

"Uh, that was very impressive, Chloe," Mr. Goodrich said when she was finished. He turned and looked out at the kids sitting in the audience. "Does anyone else want to try out for the part of Anne Frank?"

No one said a word.

"Now come on," Mr. Goodrich said. "I know several of you said you were going to."

"That was before Chloe," this voice said from above us.

I looked up and saw two girls and a guy with long blond dreadlocks sitting on the catwalk above the stage.

"I assure you I'll be absolutely fair in my decision, Bo," Mr. Goodrich said.

"That's what they're afraid of," the girl said. She was wearing black jeans and a blue plaid shirt. Her long, thick brown hair was pulled back in a ponytail. I knew her because she sometimes baby-sat for IT.

Mr. Goodrich sighed and looked down at his clipboard. "All right. That ends the audition for Anne. Next we need an able-bodied male for the part of Peter Van Daan. Any volunteers?"

No one volunteered. I noticed that there weren't many guys in the audience. Mr. Goodrich turned and looked at me. "How about you, Kyle?"

"Me?" Act in a school play?

"No," said Chloe.

I was surprised she'd answered for me. Mr. Goodrich looked surprised, too.

"I, uh, just don't think it's a good idea," Chloe sort of stammered.

"Shouldn't that be Kyle's decision?" Mr. Goodrich asked.

"Kyle . . . " Chloe had this pained look on her face. It was pretty obvious she didn't want me to do it.

"Guess not, Mr. G," I said.

BO

I was sitting on the catwalk with my dear friends Alice Hacket and Bobby Shriner. Alice is five feet four inches, has short black hair and the palest skin imaginable, which she accents by wearing thick black mascara and deep red lipstick. Someday she's either going to be a vampire or a great character actress. Bobby is six feet tall and must weigh ninety pounds. He has deep blue eyes and long blond dreadlocks that are the envy of every girl in school. He's a fabulous artist and someday he's going to be a world-renowned set designer.

It's wonderful to have friends who are going to be famous.

We were waiting for the audition to begin when Chloe made a grand entrance in her wheelchair, propelled by her ever-present attendant/paramour—the former captain of the football team and a hunk of major crush proportions named Kyle Winthrop.

"I thought you said she wasn't trying out," Alice whispered as if it was my fault Chloe had chosen to tread in the holy sanctuary of the auditorium.

"I didn't think she would," I whispered back. "But don't worry. You're a much better actress."

"According to whom?"

"Everyone."

Alice rolled her mascaraed eyes toward the ceiling, which was only a few feet away. Then she crossed her arms unhappily. We watched Kyle lift Chloe out of the wheelchair and place her ever so gently on the stage.

"Didn't he hurt his knee last year?" Alice whispered.

"I heard they had to completely reconstruct it," whispered Bobby. "They say he can never play sports again."

Kyle picked up the wheelchair and put it on the stage. Then he climbed up and helped Chloe back into it.

"Such a gent," I said with a wistful sigh. "The head cheerleader and the captain of the football team. . . . It's as American as capital punishment."

"I always wondered what those two saw in each other," Alice whispered. "I mean, Chloe's practically the class valedictorian. Isn't Kyle sort of dumb?"

"No," Bobby said. "He and I used to be in the resource room together, like when we were in elementary school."

"*You* were in the resource room?" Alice asked, surprised.

"Forever," Bobby said. "And I had a reading tutor twice a week."

"But you love to read," I said.

"Now," said Bobby. "I had no choice. I *had* to learn to read to survive."

"What about Kyle?" Alice asked.

"Kyle had sports."

KYLE

Skipped math and went down to the senior lounge. Eddie Lampel was there, decked out in prepster khakis and a blue oxford shirt. Eddie's the first string quarterback and probably my best bud at school.

"Yo, bro." We slapped high fives and I slid down next to him on the bench.

"How's the knee?" he asked.

"Still attached."

"Swelling?"

"Not bad. Had it drained last week."

"Bummer." Eddie shook his head. "But, hey, no sense in being crippled for the rest of your life, right?"

"Right." It was bull and Eddie and I both knew it. It killed me not to be on the team anymore.

"How's the scholarship scene?" I asked.

"Lookin' good, bro. Couple of scouts comin'

to the game Saturday. Schools callin' the house. I …" Eddie caught himself. "Aw, maybe I shouldn't talk about it."

"Naw, it's okay."

"What a pisser, man. It was gonna be you and me. We were gonna bite the big enchilada, right? Get those four-year rides, meet in the Rose Bowl someday."

For a second we were both lost in the vision of 100,000 screaming fans cheering us on that warm New Year's day in Arizona that would never be. Then Eddie started to chew the skin on the side of his thumb. I could tell there was something else on his mind.

"What's up?"

"Coach Cicippio wants me to ask you about something. I told him you'd never go for it, but he made me promise I'd ask anyway."

"Sorry, Eddie, I've already got a date for the prom."

Eddie grinned for a second. "I just want you to know this was his idea, not mine."

"Okay, okay. The suspense is killing me."

"He wants to know if you want to be the equipment manager."

I stared at him in total disbelief. *The dweeb?*

"I told him you'd never do it."

I didn't know what to say. The dweeb is always some loser too small or uncoordinated to play ball. So he gets the job of keeping track of the team's equipment and hauling it around to games.

"I think Cicippio was just trying to figure out a way you could be with the team," Eddie said. "So you could still be part of it."

"Yeah."

We sat there for a few moments without saying anything more. Then Eddie got up. "Gotta skate, bro."

So I sat there alone, in a state of semishock. The dweeb, I kept thinking. Was that all I was good for anymore?

BO

I read *The Diary of Anne Frank* tonight. It's so sad. You almost wish it wasn't a true story, and that she really didn't have to hide in an attic to escape the Nazis during World War II. At a time when she should have been outside playing and having fun with her friends, she had to spend day and night cooped up in a small room with her parents and assorted other peculiar people, almost none of whom she got along with.

The one thing I found truly difficult to understand was how she managed to remain cheerful and hopeful in such a miserable situation. Even at the end, after the Nazis found her and she was about to be sent to a concentration camp, she wrote, "In spite of everything, I still believe that people are really good at heart."

I think if she'd gone to the same elementary school I attended, her outlook would have been different.

KYLE

They had a career fair in the gym today. Chloe said you could walk around and talk to people about careers in the health profession and accounting and sales and so forth. She said there's going to be a couple of career days this fall. Like Time Zone High has finally figured out that they better prepare us for something before it's too late.

Of course, being Persons In Need of Supervison, the PINS got sent to the library instead. It's not that the Pinheads are dummies. It's just that most of us have "demonstrated an inability to behave responsibly in an unstructured environment." In other words, we tend to screw up. In the library we usually just sit around and look at magazines, but today I went over to the desk where Ms. Shepard, the librarian, works.

"Can I help you, Kyle?" she asked.

"I'm looking for a book," I said.

"Then you've come to the right place." Ms. Shepard winked. She's okay. I mean, at least she doesn't act afraid of us the way some teachers do.

So she found the book of Anne Frank's diary. Then we figured out that what I really wanted was the play. She found that, too. Then she had us get in a circle and talk about careers. Like on the off chance one of us actually has a goal in life.

"Do any of you think about a career?" she asked.

Lukowsky raised his hand, so you knew the answer was going to be perverted. "I wanna own an adult video store," he said, and displayed his dumb toothy grin.

"So what else is new?" Ms. Shepard asked, and everyone laughed.

Then Jeff Branco raised his hand.

"What kind of career are you interested in, Jeff?" Ms. Shepard asked.

"A career in crime," said Jeff. That cracked everyone up.

"I'm serious," said Ms. Shepard.

"So am I," Jeff said. "If you just do burglaries and stuff, you can do okay."

"You'll go to jail," said Ms. Shepard.

"Naw, the first couple of times you get caught they just slap your wrist and let you go," Jeff said. "Then when they figure out you're a repeat offender, you'll do a few months in the slammer, but you always get out early 'cause they need the cells for the really violent criminals."

"How do you know that?" Ms. Shepard asked.

"My Uncle Benny," said Jeff.

"How does he know?"

"He's a crook."

Way to go, Jeff.

BO

My full Christian name is Bolita Helena Chatsworth Vine. Is that a name or a curse? Still, I'd rather have people address me by my full first name than what most of them do call me, which is Bo. Bo Vine. That's right, as in cows.

In ninth grade the school psychologist told me I had poor communication skills. If that's true, I must've inherited them from my mother. Instead of speaking to me, she leaves articles from newspapers and magazines in my room. I would estimate that close to 90 percent of the articles concern weight loss and/or having a positive self-image.

Every week nearly six thousand children around the world die of disease and malnutrition. We are poisoning our environment, and millions of people are homeless. All my mother can think about is cellulite. Then again, what would you expect from a woman who named her only child Bolita?

A lot of my self-image has to do with the school theater. If it wasn't for the theater, I'd probably be a bag woman. All I live for is the next production. When you're working on a play, you're in a different world. The only thing that matters is putting on the most fabulous performance possible. I admit it's an escape. But have you ever noticed that escape always involves going from something undesirable to something desirable? We escape from fires, or jail, or go on a vacation escape.

What's so bad about that? Nothing as far as I can see. Except that how can I escape if I'm not going to do *The Diary of Anne Frank*?

KYLE

I came out of the lunch line and headed toward the football table, where all the guys from the team sit. To get there, you have to walk past the Pinhead table. I guess I've walked past it for years.

"Hey, Kyle!" Peter Ferrat waved at me. Peter's a little guy with dark hair and a big pointy nose. Everyone calls him the Rat. He was sitting with the other PINS, and they were all looking at me.

"What?"

"How come you never sit with us?" Peter asked.

"I sit with the team," I told him.

"Yeah, but you're not on the team anymore."

I just stared at him for a second, then headed over to the guys and sat down next to Eddie. Alex Gidden and Jason Rooney, the two defensive ends, were there.

"What'd the Rat want?" Jason asked.

"Wanted to know why I never sit with them."

"Sit with those dirtbags?" Alex sneered. "Get real."

"They're not so bad," I said.

"Lukowsky's a pervert," Jason muttered smugly.

That kind of pissed me off. Not that it isn't true, but Jason doesn't even *know* the guy.

BO

Bobby and I talked today while we made the rounds with the recycling wagon. Picking up recyclable paper in the classrooms is one of the few activities for which I will voluntarily leave the catwalk. Bobby's so gorgeous. But at ninety pounds, there just isn't enough of him. He's not only an incredible artist and set designer. He's also one of the most perceptive people I know.

"You can't not do *Anne Frank*, you know," he said, gazing at me through his beautiful blond dreadlocks.

"How can you say that?" I said.

"I know you. Without the theater you're lost. Like a virgin without a sacrifice."

"Aren't we getting a little personal?" I asked as we emptied the blue recycling crate in Mrs. Porter's room.

Bobby just smiled, revealing his brilliant white teeth. I've never talked about sex with him.

He just *knows* things like that.

"You can't go through life letting people like Chloe stop you from doing what you really want to do."

"But she's so obnoxious."

"I don't find her obnoxious," Bobby said.

"You don't have to play volleyball with her."

"You think she's obnoxious just because she wants to win all the time?" Bobby asked. "She's a perfectionist, Bo."

"Since when does *she* get to dictate what our collective vision of perfection should be?" I asked.

"She doesn't," Bobby replied. "She's just one of many people who contribute to that vision."

"Well, if you ask me, she contributes a lot more than her share," I said.

"If you give up the theater because of Chloe, you're just cutting off your nose to spite your face."

"Who's going to stage-manage?" I asked.

Bobby straightened up and brushed the blond hair out of his blue eyes. "Is that what this is about? Making everyone realize how valuable you are? Are you waiting for us all to come crawling on our knees begging?"

"Not you and Alice." I grinned. "But everyone else would be nice."

KYLE

TV sports gets a little dicey on weekday after-noons. Volleyball's pretty cool. It's fast and they make some amazing digs, but it's not on the tube that often.

Today I watched Hovercraft racing from England, but it was completely bogus. They float around a grass track like bumper cars, except every once in a while one of them flips over. After a while I got bored. Then I remembered I'd brought home that *Anne Frank* play.

I've always had a hard time concentrating when I read. When I was younger, I had to have a lot of help at school, like in the resource room and stuff like that. Then I got into sports and people would say things like, "Thank God Kyle's got football."

Today it was doubly difficult to read because IT is teething. That means he staggers around the house screaming and drooling while Jackie runs after him trying to rub pink junk into his gums.

I was staring at the cover of the play when the door to my room opened and IT waddled in pulling a wooden train on a string.

"Wha dis?" he asked, holding up the train.

"A boat," I said.

"Bo, bo." IT waddled back out. Of course I had to get up and close the door again.

I kind of skimmed through the play. Surprise, surprise: Peter is sort of Anne's boyfriend. Now why do you think Chloe wouldn't want me to have that part?

BO

Every so often I baby-sit for Jake Winthrop, the child of Jackie and Brian Winthrop. Brian is also the father, by his first marriage, of Kyle Winthrop, who is the Kyle in Kyle and Chloe. Jake is an adorable little boy, except he gets the names of things mixed up. The other night he kept pointing at a box of Ritz crackers and saying "Soap, soap." He also calls trains boats and soda milk.

When I baby-sit for the Winthrops on Saturday nights, Kyle is usually gone before I arrive and I assume he returns after I've left. When I do run into him, he will most likely nod and say hello. I will most often nod and say hello back. I believe he knows who I am, but I'm not certain he knows I exist.

There was a time when I was intimidated by people like Kyle Winthrop and Chloe Frost. They seemed so popular and special that I questioned why they would want to talk to me. But recently (and perhaps because of all those articles my mother leaves on my dresser) I've begun to wonder why I should have such a poor self-image. I'm a nice person, a good person, a smart person. Besides, we're all just human beings, granted equal rights under the constitution and in the eyes of the law, etc. It has occurred to me of late that if a Chloe Frost or a Kyle Winthrop were ever to refuse to talk to me, I could make a strong case arguing that they were the jerks, not me.

Anyway, I baby-sat for Jake last Saturday and when I arrived, Kyle was just going out. We met at the front closet where I was taking off my jacket. Kyle's shirt and slacks looked pressed and neat, so it was obvious he was going out with Chloe.

Kyle is tall and broad-shouldered and very handsome in an all-American, square-jawed kind of way. Despite everything I just said about improving my self-image, my immediate reaction was to be completely overcome by an acute case of tingly girlish nervousness, and to grow totally silent for fear of saying anything that might cause him to think I was a complete bozo. Of course, nothing would make him think I was a complete bozo faster than if I just stood there and didn't say anything.

So I said, "Hi."

"Hi," he said and stood there in the hallway

waiting for me to hang up my jacket.

Normally, I would have quickly hung up my jacket and then hurried down the hall pretending that Jackie was in desperate need of help with Jake. At best, while hanging up my jacket, I might have tried to think of something intelligent to say and of course rejected every idea I came up with, and then hurried down the hall. Finally, I would have spent the rest of the night in self-flagellation for being such a chicken and not saying anything to Kyle.

But something different happened last Saturday.

I hung up my jacket.

I turned to hurry down the hall.

But then I stopped and looked up. Kyle's eyes met mine. His were deep blue and mesmerizing. I felt like I was in a trance, but I knew if I didn't say something I'd look like an idiot just staring at him like that.

So I said, "How's your knee?"

He blinked and said, "Not so great, I guess."

"Will you ever be able to play football again?"

"It's probably not a good idea."

"You must be really disappointed," I said. Inside, I felt like I was on a bobsled hurtling down the side of a mountain, barely able to steer and completely unable to stop. It felt both terrifying and thrilling. *I was talking to Kyle Winthrop!*

And he wasn't acting like I was a total boob. In fact, Kyle was studying my face with astonishment, as if I'd just made some wildly brilliant deduction. "Yeah, actually I am."

"That's too bad," I said. "I'm sorry."

I could tell by the way Kyle looked at me that this may have been the first time he ever registered me as a human being. So then I did the oddest thing. I reached into the closet and said, "Denim or leather?"

Kyle gave me a blank look for a moment. Then he said, "Uh, what's it like out?"

"It's not bad," I said. "May I suggest denim?"

"Sure."

I handed him his denim jacket.

"Bo?" Jackie called from Jake's room. "Can you come here?"

"Okay," I called back and then turned to Kyle. "Guess I have to go to work. See ya."

"Yeah," said Kyle.

I went down the hall without looking back. It took every ounce of will power not to break into a joyous skip or burst out in triumphant, hysterical laughter. I even giddily imagined him standing there, staring at my back, thinking, *Who was that incredibly intelligent and sensitive young woman?* and *How have I lived this long without getting to know her better?*

Well, *that* may have been stretching things.

As soon as everyone was out of the house, I called Alice.

"You won't believe this," I said. "You know Kyle Winthrop, Chloe's boyfriend?"

"Never heard of him," Alice deadpanned.

"The funniest thing just happened," I said. Then I told her about Kyle and me and the closet. "And what I found so amazing was that while I was nervous, it wasn't that awful I-really-hate-this-and-wish-I-would-die kind of nervousness! It was a wonderful this-is-fabulous-and-really-exciting kind of nervousness!"

"Amazing," Alice said unenthusiastically.

"Well, I think it is," I said.

"That you talked to Kyle Winthrop?"

"That we communicated. That we related. That I got him his jacket."

Alice was quiet for a moment. Then she said, "Want to know what I think?"

"Yes."

"I think you're coming unglued, Bo," Alice said.

KYLE

We were sitting on the couch in Chloe's house watching MTV on her father's giant screen TV. Her foot was still bandaged and she had it propped up under a couple of pillows.

"I took that play, *Anne Frank*, out of the library," I said.

Chloe's head turned slowly until she was facing me. It was like she didn't want to rush it because she was collecting her thoughts and wanted to know exactly what she was going to say when we were face to face.

"Why?"

"Just curious."

"You've never read one of our plays before."

"I wanted to see the part this guy Peter has," I explained.

Like a high punt, the words hung in the air between us for two, three, four seconds. . . .

"I don't understand," Chloe finally said.

"Well, now that I'm off the team, I've got all this free time."

Chloe is not a relaxed person. She almost *never* relaxes. But after I told her this, I swear she grew twice as tense as normal. Instead of saying anything more, she turned back to the TV.

"So guess what?" I said.

"What, Kyle?"

"Turns out this guy Peter is Anne's boyfriend."

"Barely."

"How come you didn't want me to play that part?" I asked.

Chloe didn't answer. She wouldn't even look at me. I could see it wouldn't do any good to upset her, so I changed the subject.

"Why don't we get out of here for a while?" I asked, sliding a little closer to her on the couch.

Chloe didn't budge. "Dr. Honigman said the more I'm off my ankle, the faster it will heal."

"You'll just be in the car."

"Cruising?" Chloe made a face like she was sucking on a lemon.

"We could park."

"You know how I hate that." Chloe crossed her arms in front of her.

"Well, we could fool around here."

"I'll never do that again."

Right. One night last year, Chloe and I were

messing around on the couch and her parents came in *with another couple*. We weren't even doing anything serious, but it was still incredibly embarrassing, especially for Chloe, who really hates to be caught off-guard doing anything.

Of course there was my house, but even though my father and Jackie were out, the baby-sitter was still there with IT.

So that meant we were stuck at Chloe's watching the tube all night. Somehow, I wasn't surprised.

BO

"Don't try to be who you're not." You've probably heard that saying. But the question is, who are we? And who decides who we are? A good actor becomes the character he's playing. Why stop when the performance is over?

❖   ❖   ❖

I was hiding on the catwalk, minding my own business, when I heard footsteps on the stage below. Looking down I saw Mr. Goodrich.

"You're looking well, Bo."

"Thanks, but flattery will get you nowhere."

"I mean it. You've lost weight, haven't you?"

I was secretly delighted that someone had noticed, but I wasn't about to succumb to sweet nothings. "Let's cut to the chase, Mr. G."

Mr. Goodrich slid his hands into his pockets. "Chloe is going to be Anne."

"How can the lead be played by someone in a

wheelchair with a cast from her hip to her ankle?"
I asked.

"Don't exaggerate. She's only wearing an Ace bandage and walking with a cane."

"I thought she was still supposed to be on crutches this week," I said.

"She's made an unusually fast recovery."

"Figures."

"You have to stage-manage this production," Mr. Goodrich said.

"Isn't it time you found someone new?" I asked. "What are you going to do next year when I'm gone?"

"I'll . . ." Mr. Goodrich hesitated. "I'll worry about it then."

"Tsk, tsk." I wagged a finger at him. "Short term planning."

"Just say yes, Bo."

I took a dramatic pause. "I can't, Mr. G. I can't take her prima donna attitude, and I can't stand the way she manipulates you and everyone else in the cast."

"Chloe doesn't manipulate me."

"Then why has she had the lead role in every play for the past three years?" I asked.

"Because she's a fine young actress and she deserves it."

"Alice Hacket can act circles around Chloe, and you know it."

"If the right play came along, I'm sure Alice would have the lead," Mr. Goodrich said.

"If the right play came along?" I repeated in disbelief. "It's not like these things are left up to chance, Mr. G. You choose the plays."

Mr. Goodrich got stern. "Now listen to me, Bo, you are the best stage manager I have."

Mr. Goodrich is so cute when he tries to be firm. But he'd probably make more of an impression if his lower lip didn't quiver so much.

"No," I said.

And then it happened. Another person stepped onto the stage. I looked down and saw the top of Kyle Winthrop's head.

Kyle stopped about ten feet from Mr. Goodrich. He glanced up at me on the catwalk.

"Didn't mean to interrupt," he said.

"Not at all, Kyle," Mr. Goodrich said. "What's up?"

Kyle cleared his throat. "Uh, I was just wondering about the part of Peter in *The Diary of Anne Frank.*"

"What about it?" Mr. Goodrich asked.

"Is it still available?" Kyle asked.

Mr. Goodrich looked up at me. The expression on his face said, "Is this a joke?"

"Forgive me for asking, Kyle," Mr. Goodrich said, "but have you ever acted before?"

"Is it a problem if I haven't?" Kyle asked.

I knew what Mr. Goodrich was thinking: The role of Peter could basically be played by a cardboard cutout. In fact, it probably would be if he didn't find a willing male soon.

"You've got the part," Mr. Goodrich said.

Kyle looked surprised. "Uh, well, I uh . . . I'm not really sure I want it. I mean, I was just wondering. I really have to think about it, okay?"

"Fine, Kyle," Mr. Goodrich said. "But try to let me know soon or I may have to give the part to someone else."

"Okay, sure," Kyle said. Then he waved at me. For some reason, nearly everyone waves at me when I'm thirty feet above them. "Uh, see ya." He left the stage.

I gave Mr. Goodrich an incredulous look. "Give the part to someone else?"

He responded with a wink. "I was just trying to sell him on it, Bo."

KYLE

In the student lounge today Chloe poked her finger into my stomach. "What's this?"

"Uh, last night's pizza with mushrooms and sausage?"

"I'm serious," she said.

"So am I."

"You're not going to get fat, are you?" she asked.

"Wasn't planning on it."

"Nobody plans to get fat," she said.

The conversation sort of ground to a halt. That seems to happen a lot lately. Used to be she and I could talk for hours about the team, the games, what parties we were going to . . . I mean, it wasn't earth-shattering stuff, but it was what we had in common. Now, I don't know. It feels like something's missing.

Chloe reached down into her bag and took out her gray copy of *Anne Frank*. I watched over her shoulder. She'd highlighted all of her lines in yellow and she moved her lips as she read and made little gestures with her head and shoulders, as if acting out the words. Naw, I thought, I couldn't do it. I couldn't memorize all those lines. I couldn't get up on the stage in front of everyone and act. It was a dumb idea.

BO

Two or three times a week I swim. Except for me, hardly anyone under the age of twenty-five uses the junior high pool at night. I can go there with a reasonable amount of certainty that I won't be seen.

Last night I was leaving the house when my mother came in carrying two plastic shopping bags filled with groceries.

"Swimming again?" she asked, setting the bags on the kitchen table.

"No, I'm just taking my towel for a walk."

My mother gave me a weary look. "Why do you always have to be this way?"

"It's the age," I said.

"This is the fourth night in a row you've gone swimming," she said as she started to put away the groceries. "Usually you're gone for forty-five minutes. Lately you've been going for an hour and a half."

I was surprised that she'd been keeping track. Then she pulled a familiar looking ice-cream container out of one of the shopping bags.

"Not Ben & Jerry's Monster Mash!" I gasped.

"I thought you liked it," she said.

"I love it," I said. "That's the problem."

"What's the problem?"

"Mom. Look at me for God's sake."

She squinted at me. "You don't look well."

"What are you talking about? I've lost five pounds."

"Why?"

"I don't know. I just felt like it."

"Are you sure you're not sick?"

"Mom, I feel great. I swear, I've never felt better."

"You've never wanted to lose weight before," my mother said.

"People change," I said.

My mother studied me with a somewhat bewildered look on her face. I've always wished someone would think of me as exotic and mysterious. I just wish it wasn't my mother.

◇ ◇ ◇

I wear goggles to keep the chlorine out of my eyes when I swim. They always fog up so badly that I can hardly see anything except the heavy black lane lines painted on the bottom of the pool. Until recently I swam at a leisurely pace and never pushed myself. The water was my friend. It was there to soothe and give temporary relief from the harsh realities of the world at large. Lately I've been swimming harder and longer. The water has become my ally in the war against liposomes.

At some point in my swim I noticed that someone was doing laps in the lane next to mine, but I didn't think much about it. Lots of people swim at night, but I rarely look at them.

Later, after I finished my last lap in a blinding burst of Olympic-record speed, I hung onto the edge of the pool and caught my breath. That's when I noticed that the swimmer in the lane next to mine had also stopped. Of course, with my swimming goggles still on he was just a big foggy blur.

"I'm impressed," he said.

"Why?" I asked without my usual girlish nervousness. After all, I didn't feel like I was talking to a guy. I felt like I was talking to a blur.

He said something, but I couldn't hear clearly because my ears were full of water. I asked him to repeat it.

"You swam a lot of laps," he said.

"I wasn't counting."

"You come here a lot?" he asked.

That's when I noticed something familiar about his voice. I pulled off my goggles and gasped. "Oh, my God!"

"What's wrong?" Kyle asked. He was bobbing in the lane next to me with his black hair plastered down on his head.

"It's you."

"So?"

"Well, I . . ." I stammered. "I had these goggles on and my ears are filled with water."

"You thought I was someone else?" Kyle asked.

"I just didn't know," I said. My heart had started beating so hard I expected to see little waves rippling away from my body. "When did you start swimming here?"

"My first time."

The pool drains made gurgling sounds. I felt like my heart was starting to slow down. I had to get calm. I had to stop acting like a total bozo.

"You just felt like swimming?" I asked.

"Doctor says this puts the least strain on my knee."

I could think of no appropriate response. Normally, my nervousness would have made me get out of the water, pronto, but I was reluctant to let Kyle see me wet and fat. So I tried to think of something to say. And that's when I remembered the play.

"Did you make up your mind?" I asked.

"Huh?"

"About the play."

"Oh, yeah, I don't think so," he said.

I was surprised by the enormity of the disappointment I suddenly felt. Why did I care? But as I floated in the chilly water, clearly in danger of succumbing to hypothermia, I realized I did care.

"Can I ask why not?"

"Guess I just realized it wasn't a good idea."

"You probably imagined what it must feel like to stand up in front of four hundred people and blow your lines."

"Well, that doesn't bother me," Kyle said.

"It doesn't?" I was surprised.

"You know how many times I've stood up in front of eight hundred people and dropped an easy interception?" he asked.

"No."

"Plenty. You get used to it."

"Then what's the difference?"

"I may have blown the catch, but at least I knew what I was doing."

"This is a high school play," I said. "You don't have to know what you're doing."

Kyle grinned. I would have grinned back, but then Kyle would have noticed that my teeth were chattering. He still appeared to be in no rush to go. Meanwhile, I'd been in the water for so long I felt like I was going to turn into a blue prune.

"Anyway, Mr. G has probably given the part to someone else by now," Kyle said.

"There is no one else," I said. "He was just trying to stampede you into a decision."

"Serious?"

"Uh-huh."

Kyle studied me for a moment. "Do you think I should do it?"

I pictured Chloe bossing everyone around and being her usual prima donna self . . . and Kyle being there to see it all.

"Well, if you really want my opinion," I said, "I think you should."

Kyle didn't really react. I couldn't tell if my answer meant anything to him or not, and I couldn't wait around any longer to find out.

"I'd love to stay and talk to you, but I'm starting to freeze to death," I said.

"You mean that isn't blue lipstick?" Kyle asked playfully.

"Very funny." I gave him a cute smile and climbed out of the pool, quickly pulling a towel around me. When I turned, Kyle gave me a slight wave.

At least he wasn't throwing up.

❖   ❖   ❖

Later I had a burst of inspiration and called Alice. Last year she started subscribing to a computer bulletin board, and she tends to fall in and out of love with other hackers at an alarming rate.

When she answered, she was crying. "It's over, Bo."

"Excuse me?"

"A college student I met on-line," she explained.

"You didn't tell me about him."

"I didn't have time," Alice said. "It happened so quickly."

"Maybe you should try having a relationship with someone in person."

"Easier said than done, Bo. So what's up?"

"Can you use this fabulous computer service of yours to find out how many former football players went on to become actors?"

"Easy," Alice said. I heard the plastic tapping of computer keys. "There's a sports RTC almost every night."

"A what?"

"Real time conference," Alice said. "Get a piece of paper."

I grabbed a paper bag from the garbage and a brand-new eyebrow pencil while Alice typed in the question and started getting answers.

"Joe Namath, Brian Bosworth, Jim Brown, John Matuzak, Ed Marinaro, Alex Karras, and Bubba Smith. What's this for, anyway?"

"Hold it," I gasped, scribbling furiously on the bag. "Okay, got 'em. That's amazing."

"Just a pit stop on the information super-highway."

"Well, thanks," I said. "Gotta go."

I hung up and called the Winthrops' house. Jackie answered and I asked to speak to Kyle.

"Hello?"

"Hi, it's Bolita Vine."

"Huh . . . ?"

"From the pool tonight."

"Oh, Bo. What's up?"

"What do Brian Bosworth, Jim Brown, Joe Namath, Ed Marinaro, Bubba Smith, Alex Karras, and John Matushuk all have in common?"

"It's Matu*zak*," Kyle corrected me.

"Okay, okay."

"Let's see. Matuzak was a defensive tackle and Bosworth was a middle linebacker. Namath was a QB. Brown was a running back. Namath had the knee. I don't think Bosworth was ever on a Super Bowl winning team . . ."

"They were all football players who became actors," I said.

"Hey, that's right."

"So if you decide to play Peter, you won't be alone."

Kyle was quiet for a moment. Then he said, "You *really* think I should do it?"

I felt a thrill rush through me. Kyle Winthrop

was asking my opinion about something, and he sounded sincere!

"Yes," I said. "I really think you should."

KYLE

Welcome to Pinhead English. Today Mr. Goodrich wanted to talk about this book called *The Outsiders* we were supposed to read over the summer.

"Did anybody read it?" he asked.

I looked around the room. The only kid who raised his hand was the Rat. But he was probably lying. Mr. Goodrich took off his glasses and rubbed his forehead. He does that when he's ticked off.

"This was the only assignment you had all summer," he said. "Why couldn't you do it?"

"Cause there were no sex scenes," Lukowsky said.

"Thank you for that insightful reply," Mr. Goodrich said.

"I'm serious," said Lukowsky. "You want us to read, right? How about giving us something we'll like."

"I think the school's position is that if you want to read pornography, you can find it on your own," Mr. Goodrich said.

"He's not talking about porn, you dork," Jeff Branco said.

"Watch your mouth or you'll be paying a visit to Mr. Rope," Mr. Goodrich warned.

"Wimp," Branco muttered.

"What?" Mr. Goodrich said.

"Nothing." It was obvious that Jeff was peeved about something.

"I'm not talking about porn," Lukowsky said.

"Then what *are* you talking about?" Mr. Goodrich snapped impatiently.

"Uh-oh, watch it," someone whispered. "He's getting pissed."

"I'm talking about *books* with sex scenes," Lukowsky said. "I mean, books are supposed to be about life, right? Well, sex is part of life."

"Not part of *your* life, Zitface," Jeff Branco said.

"Eat it, Branco," Lukowsky shot back.

"One more uncalled for remark and you're out of here," Mr. Goodrich pointed a finger at Branco.

"Ooh, I'm terrified," Branco said in a high girlish voice that got the class tittering.

Mr. Goodrich walked over to the wall, picked up the phone, and called the office. "Please tell

Mr. Rope to expect a visit from Jeff Branco. I'm sending him down right now, and if he's not there in three minutes he'll be in even more trouble."

Mr. Goodrich held open the door. Jeff Branco got up slowly and sauntered across the room. As he passed Mr. Goodrich, he made a sudden move at him. Mr. Goodrich winced and scrunched up as if he was going to get hit, but Branco was just faking. He waved to us.

"Later, dudes." He went out.

Mr. Goodrich returned to his desk and sat down. He took some kind of inhaler out of the desk and breathed in with it. Then he patted his forehead with a handkerchief.

"Okay, where were we?" he asked.

"Sex scenes," Lukowsky said with a big grin.

Mr. Goodrich buried his head in his hands and groaned. Then the bell rang and everyone cleared out. When Mr. Goodrich looked up, I was the only one left in the room.

"Why haven't you loped out with the rest of the herd?" he asked.

"I think I made up my mind, Mr. G," I said. "I want to do the play."

"You do?" He looked surprised.

"Yeah."

Mr. Goodrich folded his handkerchief neatly and slid it back into his pocket. "This will require a serious commitment, Kyle. You'll have to learn your lines and come to rehearsals. The rest of the cast will be depending on you. If you can't take it more seriously than, uh . . ."

He trailed off like he didn't want to say what was coming next.

"More seriously than I take *school*, Mr. G?"

"I'm sorry, Kyle. I shouldn't have put it that way."

"It's okay," I said. "I'll give it my best shot."

"That's all I can ask for, Kyle." Mr. Goodrich stood up and offered his hand.

I shook it. It was sort of like shaking a dead fish.

BO

Today I told Mr. Goodrich I'd stage-manage *Anne Frank* after all. I changed my mind because I felt bad for him. Between Chloe and Kyle and all his other headaches, he doesn't need a stage manager who doesn't know what he or she is doing.

Of course, this is going to put a damper on my incredibly busy social life, but I'll just have to cope.

KYLE

Angie Sunberg's parties are kind of renowned because her parents have a big house and they usually make themselves scarce.

Chloe always likes to give the impression that she's got six social engagements a night, so even though Angie's party started at eight P.M. she told me not to pick her up until ten. I'll bet you anything she spent the time watching TV.

"Maybe we should do something else," I said after she got in the car.

Chloe gave me this look of disbelief. "Like what?"

"I don't know. Go to a movie or something."

"What about the party?"

I shrugged. "It's always the same thing. Same kids, same dumb stuff."

"But I thought you liked that."

"Guess I've changed."

"Everyone's expecting us."

So we went. We got to Angie's and it was the same old thing. A lot of people and noise and music and everyone acting crazy. Chloe was right. I used to love scenes like that. Now I almost dread them.

Chloe went off to chat with the girls and I hung out with my buds. Then Lukowsky must've said something crude to Angie because she slapped him pretty hard, and someone got the idea of tying Lukowsky up, so they raided the linen closet and got a bunch of sheets. They gagged him and wrapped him up like a mummy, then locked him in the downstairs powder room.

Later I was in the kitchen with Eddie and some of the guys. Pizza Hut had just delivered a Big Foot and we were chowing down. I have to admit that I was enjoying myself. I mean, if you can't play sports anymore, eating pizza and talking sports with the guys is probably the next best thing. I almost felt like I was on the team again.

Then Chloe came into the kitchen wearing her jacket and whispered in my ear, "I want to talk to you."

"What?" This caught me totally by surprise.

"Let's go outside."

"Why?"

Chloe obviously didn't want to say why in front of the guys. She just turned and left.

I grabbed my jacket and started to head out.

"Hey, bro," Eddie said.

"Yeah?" I stopped in the doorway.

"Married life's a drag, huh?" He winked.

I gave him the finger.

Outside Chloe was leaning on the car with her arms crossed. It was a clear, cool night and the stars were out. Cars lined both sides of the street—the universal sign of a party.

"I can't believe you didn't tell me you were going to be Peter," she said. "I had to find out from Beth Villeta. Do you know how embarrassing that is?"

"I was going to tell you," I said.

"When? At the first read-through?"

"No, I probably would have told you tonight."

Chloe glared at me. "Why?"

"Why what?"

"Why do you suddenly have to be in this play?"

"Why is it such a big deal?" I asked back.

Chloe let out a big sigh and stared up at the stars. "There are a million other things you could have done besides be in my play."

"*Your* play? Wow, Chloe, I didn't know you owned it."

Chloe gave me a withering look.

"I want to go home, Kyle."

Now I felt bad. Like maybe I should have

told her sooner. "Come on, Chloe. This is dumb." I stepped close and stroked her hair, but she turned away.

"I'm tired, Kyle. And my ankle hurts."

She didn't say a word on the way home. We got back to her house and she hopped out of the car and ran up the walk to the front door. It sure didn't look to me like her ankle was hurting.

BO

I was in such a good mood today. Rumor has it that Kyle and Chloe had a fight outside Angie Sunberg's house Saturday night. Then reality set in. Alice and Bobby were waiting for me on the catwalk.

"Ah, the welcoming committee," I said as I started to climb up the ladder.

"Look who decided to stage-manage *Anne Frank*," Bobby said.

"It's a free country," I said.

"Isn't she looking thinner?" Alice asked.

"I'm graduating this spring, and I don't want people to remember me as the understudy for the Goodyear blimp."

"Is that makeup you're wearing?" Bobby asked.

"Yes!" I cried. "I'm guilty. I've lost weight, put on makeup, and decided to be stage manager again. Bring on the gladiators! Throw me to the wolves!"

"This wouldn't have anything to do with a certain former football captain who's suddenly turned thespian, would it?" Bobby asked.

I stopped halfway up the ladder. He'd caught me completely off guard. "What? Of course not."

Bobby gave me that look. *He knew!* I couldn't believe it.

"There's no sense denying," Alice said.

I felt my shoulders sag. "It was the phone calls, right? Being so excited about talking to him, and asking about those football players who became actors. I knew I should have kept it to myself."

"That and the sudden change of mind concerning stage-managing," Bobby said. "Especially coming so soon after Kyle committed to doing Peter."

"So sue me."

"That's not the point," Alice said.

"Then what *is* the point?" I asked.

Alice and Bobby glanced at each other. I could see they'd prepared for this. They wanted to tell me THE TRUTH!

"Bo, we're talking about Kyle Winthrop," Bobby said.

"Please," I begged. "Don't do this to me. Don't foam the runway. Even if I'm flying blind, let me crash and burn on my own."

"It's for your own good," Alice said.

"I've heard that before. From every pediatrician who ever gave me a booster. From every orthodontist who ever tightened my braces."

"Stop being so dramatic." Alice sounded annoyed. "You only had one orthodontist and you know it."

"Excuse me for taking poetic license," I apologized.

"We don't want to see you get hurt," Bobby said.

"Thank you for that extreme vote of confidence," I said. "Thank you for thinking so highly of me."

"I hate it when you get maudlin," Alice said. "Be realistic."

"No," I said, and started to climb back down. "I won't be realistic and I won't take any more of this abuse. If I want to be insulted and ridiculed, I'll go home and let my mother do it."

"Wait," Bobby said. "You can stay. I have to go talk to Mr. G about the set budget anyway."

He started to climb down the other ladder. I headed back up toward Alice. I crossed the catwalk and sat down next to her. The air was stuffy and warmer than down below, but I didn't care.

"Did you hear what happened to Karl Lukowsky?" she asked.

"What now?"

"They tied him up at the party and left him

in the downstairs bathroom. Except Angie forgot he was there. They didn't find him till the next afternoon."

"Too bad," I said.

"That they forgot?"

"No, that they found him."

Alice pulled her knees up under her chin and gazed down at the stage below. I could see that she was depressed. Alice is a little awkward and she tends to wear baggy clothes and be quiet and unassuming. She looks a little depressed even when she's happy, so when she is depressed, she looks very depressed.

"Mr. G posted the cast list this morning," she said. "Why do these things always happen to me?"

"You can't be upset about being Mrs. Van Daan," I said. "Because you *knew* that's who you'd be."

"I know," said Alice. "Why do I always get the most unlikable parts?"

"Because you're the best actress in school," I said.

"If I'm the best actress, why does Chloe get the leads?" asked Alice.

"Because she's a star," I said.

"Just for once I'd like to be a star," Alice said wistfully.

Wouldn't we all.

KYLE

Tonight I was listening to this tape Eddie lent me. It's by this singer named Meatloaf. The whole tape is pretty good, but it has one totally outstanding number called "Paradise by the Dashboard Light." Knowing me and Chloe, Eddie thought I'd appreciate it. He was right.

So I was in my room listening to it, and all of a sudden I looked up and there was Jackie standing in my doorway with this goofy smile on her face and IT drooling in her arms.

"I love that song," she said.

I looked at her for a moment, and then looked away. What was I supposed to say? Meanwhile, Jackie stood there waiting for me to say something. Out of the corner of my eye I saw the smile slowly evaporate from her face, sort of like someone who thinks a joke is being played on them. Finally she just turned and left.

I guess she was upset. Maybe she thought that because we both liked that song it finally gave us something in common. Us and about fifteen million other people.

BO

At the end of a play the actors take their bows. Sometimes they'll bring out the director to take a bow and then gesture to the orchestra conductor and the musicians and they'll all take bows. Occasionally, if the playwright is present, he or she will even take a bow.

You will never see the stage manager take a bow. I toil in anonymity at a difficult, thankless task in which I act as a marriage counselor, divorce lawyer, mother, and foreman to the rest of the cast and crew. It is my role to coordinate the entire production, to make sure all the pieces of the puzzle—cast, crew, sets, props, and costumes—fit together. It is my job to nag and badger and soothe and commiserate. I will be blamed for everything that goes wrong and never appreciated for all the things that go right. And in the end, when the curtain falls for the last time, I won't be out there basking in the warm glow of applause like the rest of them.

Worst of all, I will have to deal with Karl "The Letch" Lukowsky, who runs AV.

Step inside the AV room and you enter a time warp. Where else do you find guys (it's very rare to find a female AV person) who still wear bell bottoms and have shaggy haircuts? Where else do they still listen to the Grateful Dead and Led Zeppelin? Where else do they still read *Mad Magazine*?

But from somewhere in the dank dark depths of that room will come the "techie" I'll depend on to handle the lights, curtain, and sound cues for the show. If I'm lucky, he won't skin his knuckles when he walks.

"Hey, lookin' good, babe." Inside the AV room The Letch leered at me through the industrial shelving holding film projectors and VCRs. The Letch has a shaggy haircut, buck teeth, and a case of acne that makes his face resemble a relief map of the Alps. Subscribing to the (misguided) theory that he who has the most keys is the most important, he wears a key ring with enough keys to open the doors of a small city.

"I hear you've been spending a lot of time in bathrooms lately," I said.

The Letch just laughed. "Har, har, har."

"I need a techie for the play."

"No problemo, babe." The Letch must be

twenty years old. I think he keeps getting left back because the only place he feels at home in is the AV room. Or because there's no such thing as janitor's college.

"We're going to need lights, curtains, and some sound cues."

"No problemo, babe."

"It would be nice if you pick someone who can be available for all the run-throughs and dress rehearsals."

"No problemo, babe."

"I'd appreciate it if you stopped calling me babe."

"Har, har, no problemo . . . er, honey."

KYLE

In the boys' room today, instead of the usual cigarette smoke and bathroom odors, it smelled like pizza. I was in there minding my own business when two freshmen came in and went down to the third toilet stall and knocked.

"Yeah?" answered someone inside the stall.

"Joey sent us," one of the kids said.

"How many?" asked the person inside the stall.

"Two."

"Okay. Four bucks."

The next thing I knew, one of the freshmen kneeled down and slid four bills under the door. A second later two slices of pizza on paper plates came sliding out. The freshmen took them and left.

I went down to the stall and knocked.

"Yeah?" the voice answered.

"Arnie sent me."

"Arnie? I don't know no Arnie."

"How about Ralph?" I asked.

"Get lost."

"Hey, Jeff, it's me, Kyle."

The stall door opened. Inside, Jeff Branco had four pizza boxes stacked on the toilet seat. "Yo, Kyle," he said, slapping me five.

"When did you get into the pizza business?" I asked.

"I got a friend who delivers for Sal's Pizza in town," Jeff said, handing me a slice. "Whenever Sal ain't around, my friend cops a few pies, brings 'em over here and slides 'em through the bathroom window to me. We split the profits. Tell me this ain't superior to that junk the cafeteria sells."

A couple of sophomores came in and bought four slices. Jeff pocketed the money.

"I never knew you were such an entrepreneur," I said, only half-kidding. I always thought he was just a hood. Who could have guessed he had the brains to think up something like this?

"I gotta score some heavy dollars," Jeff said. "Special occasion coming up."

I finished the slice he gave me. "Well, thanks."

"Sure," Jeff said. "Hey, Kyle, you want in?"

"Huh?"

"I'm thinking of franchising. They got six boys' rooms in the school. That's six pizza franchises. I'll even cut you a deal 'cause you're one of us."

One of them?

"Uh, thanks for the offer, Jeff. Let me think about it."

I got out in the hall and started walking. *One of them? Me?* I never thought I was one of them.

BO

This afternoon I ventured to The Gap and invested in a new wardrobe. Nothing fancy, just some jeans and tops. But the tops were mediums and the jeans were size ten. It's amazing how much difference eight pounds can make. Then I went home and packed some of my old clothes in a box and left it by the front door.

A little while ago my mother came in.

"What are those things doing in that box by the front door?" she asked.

"The Salvation Army is going to pick them up tomorrow," I said.

"Those are perfectly good clothes," she said.

"Except they're too big," I said.

"I am not going to buy you a whole new wardrobe when you gain the weight back," she said.

"Thanks for the encouragement," I grumbled.

My mother blinked at the shock of realization. "You're right. I'm sorry."

"I'm losing weight gradually. I really think it's going to work."

My mother stared at me. "What's gotten into you?"

Not that I'd ever tell her.

KYLE

Here are the first ten lines Peter speaks in the play:

> 1. "Please, Mother."
> 2. "Yes, Mrs. Frank."
> 3. "Mouschi." (the cat)
> 4. "He's a tom. He doesn't like strangers."
> 5. "Huh?"
> 6. "No."
> 7. "Jewish Secondary."
> 8. "I used to see you . . . sometimes."
> 9. "In the schoolyard. You were always in the middle of a bunch of kids."
> 10. "I'm sort of a lone wolf."

More like a lone wimp. Do I really want to be this guy?

BO

Tonight after swimming I was coming out of the girls' locker room when someone came in through the pool doors. I didn't really get a good look at the person because I was busy pulling my fingers through my wet stringy hair, having forgotten to bring a brush. Suddenly the person stopped in my path, and I looked up. It was Kyle.

"Oh, it's you!" I said.

"How come you're always so surprised to see me?" he asked.

I waited for that nervous inadequate sensation to take hold and wrap me in its straitjacket of fear. But for some reason it didn't.

"I'm not sure it's so much surprise as embarrassment," I said, grabbing the wet ends of my hair in my fists and tugging at them. "I mean, look at me."

"You look like you have wet hair," Kyle said. "I think it would be really tough to swim and then have dry hair."

"Some people bring a hair dryer," I said.

"That doesn't seem like something you'd do."

I guess I gave him a startled look. "How would you know that?"

Kyle smiled rather sheepishly. "I don't know. Just a feeling, I guess."

Suddenly I remembered something. I opened my bag and took out a playbook. "This is for you."

"Thanks, but Mr. G already gave me a copy," Kyle said.

"Not like this."

Kyle opened the book and thumbed through it. Then he looked up at me with surprise on his face. "You highlighted my lines."

"You really don't have to learn the other parts," I said, "as long as you know when you're supposed to speak."

"That's really nice of you."

"One of my jobs is to make it easier for the greenhorns," I explained. Although, the truth was, I'd never done anything like that before.

Kyle slipped the playbook into his jacket pocket. "Maybe I should talk to you about that."

"About what?"

"This play. It's uh . . ." Kyle glanced past me at the pool and changed the topic. "What's the water like tonight?"

"Just slightly warmer than glacial," I said.

He winced. I could see he wasn't keen about throwing himself into the chilly, chlorinated depths. Then I did the most outrageous thing. I mean, I still can't believe I said, "Want to go to the diner?"

(Before I go any further, let me state clearly that I have never in my life tried to steal another girl's boyfriend. Moreover, had I honestly believed that there was even the remotest possibility that Kyle had a romantic interest in me, I would never have suggested going to the diner. I would have suggested a much more romantic setting, such as the dock at the Post Point Yacht Club.)

Meanwhile Kyle only scowled. I suddenly froze in terror over what I'd done. Look out! Foam the runway! Crash landing! He's going to say no. He's going to reject me. He's going to tell all his friends. I'll be the laughing stock of the entire school! Oh, why didn't I listen to Bobby and Alice? Kyle started to open his mouth, but there was still time to avert disaster.

"On second thought, it was dumb of me to suggest that," I quickly said. "I mean, you came here to swim. The last thing you probably want to do is eat. I really don't know why I suggested it. Let's just forget it."

"You're right," he said. "It's bad enough that I'm not gonna swim, but going to the diner's only gonna make it worse."

Hold it! Had I heard him correctly? Did he say he *wasn't* going swimming? Maybe I'd misunderstood. But Kyle turned and held the door for me. The next thing I knew, we were walking out in the cold air toward the darkened cars in the parking lot.

"So where do you want to go?" he asked.

"Uh, I don't know." I was still in shock.

"Well, want to take one car or two?"

"Unless you're into grand felony auto theft, we better take one."

Kyle gave me a funny look, then smiled. "I get it. You didn't drive here."

"Not here, not anywhere."

"Don't you have your license?" he asked.

"I believe the world is a safer place without me behind the wheel," I said.

Being all but oblivious to the universe of automobiles, I can only tell you that Kyle's car was small and possibly of Asian origin. We wound up at the Post Point Yacht Club. Believe me, I wouldn't have suggested it, except that Kyle clearly didn't want to do anything that involved increasing his daily caloric intake.

"Isn't this trespassing?" he asked as we climbed over a low metal gate and walked around the dark porch of the club.

"Only if we get caught."

We walked out to the end of the dock. It was

cold and breezy. Small waves were splashing against the pilings. The moon was three-quarters full and a pair of sea gulls hovered almost perfectly still in the night sky, riding the wind.

"Come here a lot?" Kyle asked.

"No."

"No?"

"Just on nights when the moon is almost full and it's a little too cold and I'm with someone who doesn't want to eat," I said. I could feel the cold breeze sting my face and a single thought floated in my mind: *What in the world am I doing here with him?*

Kyle turned and looked down the shoreline.

"What are you looking at?" I asked.

"Chloe's house."

"Where?" I knew Chloe's father was a doctor and they were well-off, but I'd always thought the people who could afford homes on the water were in the socio-economic stratosphere.

"Over there." Kyle pointed. It was hard to see in the dark. Several very large houses stood beside the harbor, windows lit, their tall, dim silhouettes just visible against the night sky, their lawns sloping down to stone sea walls and private docks. I couldn't tell exactly which house Kyle meant. Maybe it didn't matter.

"What's she doing tonight?" I asked.

"Got me."

What did *that* mean? Did he wish he was with her and not me? Were they having problems? Maybe they didn't like each other anymore. Kyle turned back to me and slid his hands into the pockets of his pants. "I'm kind of glad I ran into you."

"Because I saved you from swimming?"

"No, it's about the play."

"That's right. You said something was bothering you."

"Peter's sort of a geek," Kyle said. "His father's a jerk. And in a way, it's Peter's fault that Anne and everybody gets caught and sent to concentration camps."

"It's only a role," I said. "It's not something that reflects on you personally."

"I just wish he wasn't such a wimp," Kyle said.

"I promise no one is going to think of you as a wimp-by-association."

Kyle smiled a little and muttered something about going from athletic to pathetic.

"What?" I asked.

"Nothing."

The dock rocked slightly as the waves rolled under it. It was a little like trying to stand up in a boat. I looked up and noticed the sea gulls had vanished. Kyle was glancing at his watch. I was starting to shiver.

"We can go," I said, not wanting him to feel

like he was stuck with me.

"I could probably catch the last quarter of Tulane and SMU," he said.

He drove me home. Did it mean that given the choice between watching football and being with me, Kyle would choose football?

Don't answer that.

KYLE

There's this girl at school whose name (you won't believe this) is Bo Vine. Bo is short for something, but it doesn't matter because everyone calls her Bovine. Like a cow. To make it worse, she's always been on the chunky side. I remember in grade school and junior high she really got kidded a lot, like to the point of tears a couple of times.

When Jake was about a year old, Bovine started to baby-sit for him every once in a while. I saw her at the house a couple of times, but I never said more than hello because I didn't know her or anything. Well, that's not the total truth. I didn't talk to her much because she seemed kind of strange. Maybe it was because she got picked on so much when she was younger. Or maybe because now she just sort of keeps to herself at school and never talks to anyone except a couple of her friends in the theater group.

The other thing is, except for her classes, she spends almost all her time on this catwalk above the stage. Like she's a pigeon or something.

Anyway, now I see her almost every day because she's the stage manager for the play. I've seen her at the pool a couple of times, too. It actually looks like she's lost some weight, which is more than I can say for myself.

So tonight we ran into each other at the pool and wound up at this yacht club standing on the dock. She's got a kind of quiet, sarcastic sense of humor, and I sort of enjoyed talking to her.

Especially since Chloe and I don't have much to say to each other these days.

BO

On Saturday afternoon Alice wasn't around so I begged Bobby to drive me to the mall.

"There's a bus, you know," he said.

"I need moral support."

"You need moral support to go to the mall?" He raised a blond eyebrow. "That's a new one."

"You'll see," I said.

When we got there, I dragged him to Hair Affair, a unisex salon. Inside, three hair stylists instantly crowded around him, just dying to get their hands on his long, beautiful blond dreadlocks.

"Sorry, girls, I'm not the one," he said, and pointed at me.

You never saw such looks of disappointment.

An hour and a half later my hair was done.

And I mean *done*.

Where it used to be straight, dull, and brown, it was now a glorious shade of auburn and flowed onto my shoulders in waves.

"You look great! We have to celebrate!" Bobby led me by the hand to The Slice of Life pizzeria. Inside we sat on bent wire chairs around a little red plastic table. The walls were lined with mirrors and that's where I saw myself, not in the make-believe world of Hair Affair, but in the real world of discarded pizza crusts, twelve-year-olds smoking cigarettes, and young women with too much eye makeup, red stiletto nails, and big hair.

The effect was devastating. I suddenly realized I was doomed.

"Why the long face?" Bobby asked as he sprinkled garlic and oregano on his pizza.

"You'd have a long face, too, if you'd just signed your own death warrant."

Bobby scowled. "What are you talking about?"

"Do you have any idea what I'm going to face in school on Monday morning? I can just hear them. 'Did you see Bovine?' 'Who does she think she is?' 'Maybe she can change what's on the outside, but she'll never change what's on the inside.'"

Bobby scowled at me. "What's wrong with your insides?"

I was plummeting so fast into new hair despair that I hardly heard him. "Why did I do this?" I moaned. "Who am I kidding? Why did I have to be so stupidly obvious? Did I really think I could go from Jabba the Hut to Princess Leia overnight?"

"Bo . . ." Bobby looked alarmed.

"That's right, I'm Bo. Bovine. The cow. Did you ever see that Amazon movie where they throw the cow in the river and the piranhas get it? Three minutes later all that's left is a skeleton. That's going to be me Monday morning. It's going to be a feeding frenzy . . . a massacre."

I was seized by a dread so great I began to hyperventilate. The thought of walking into school on Monday filled me with a terror a hundred times worse than a visit to The Dentist From Hell. I was a sitting duck, a sacrificial lamb, a big round jack-o'-lantern on Halloween night. . . .

I jumped up.

"Where are you going?" Bobby asked.

"Back to Hair Affair!" I gasped. "I have to get rid of this hair. I have to get back to mousy old unattractive me before someone notices!"

"Stop!" Bobby shouted.

I froze, suddenly aware that everyone in The Slice of Life was staring at me. The swarthy countermen with dark stubble on their chins and tomato sauce stains on their white T-shirts, the twelve-year-olds smoking their first Marlboros, the big-hair girls with their raccoon eyelids and garden-stake fingernails, the overweight grandmothers with their shopping bags—every single one of them was staring.

Bobby stood up and pointed at me.

"Will you look at her hair?" he said to everyone.

"Please don't, Bobby . . ." I whimpered. My face was burning. I was dying of embarrassment.

"Doesn't she look great?" Bobby asked.

Around The Slice of Life heads bobbed.

"Bobby, please . . ." I begged.

"Would you believe she's terrified that the kids at school are going to laugh at her?" Bobby asked.

"No way. She looks gorgeous," said one of the countermen.

"What do you care what other people think?" asked one of the big-hair girls.

"They're just jealous, honey," said one of the overweight grandmothers.

"Uh, thanks, everyone," I said to them all. "You see I just got it done and it's really a big change for me and, well, you know . . ."

"If anyone laughs at you, smash 'em in the face," said one of the twelve-year-old Marlboro smokers.

Bobby gave me a triumphant smile. "See? You have nothing to worry about."

"Can we get out of here?" I whispered.

Bobby grabbed his slice. We waved at my

impromptu support group and left.

"Smash 'em in the face!" Bobby and I were laughing so hard we practically tumbled down the handicapped ramp as we staggered past Foot Locker and Bed Bath & Beyond. I gave him a gentle shove. "I can't believe you did that!"

"What makes you think you're so unique?" Bobby asked. "I mean, aren't you being a little egocentric?"

"Of course," I said. "But you still can't deny that people are going to talk when they notice something different Monday morning."

"And you think you're the only one who looks different? You don't think that people notice I have shoulder-length blond dreadlocks?"

"But they're used to you," I said. "And besides, you're gorgeous."

"Do you think it's easy to be a gorgeous boy?" Bobby asked. "I mean, God, Bo, all you have to do is go to school on Monday looking pretty."

I'd never thought of it that way.

KYLE

About ten minutes ago, Jackie called my father into the nursery.

"He's got diarrhea," I heard her say.

"Remember what the doctor said," my father replied calmly. "It's not the consistency, it's how often they go. It's not diarrhea unless he goes four or more times in one day."

My father, the diarrhea expert.

"I'm just worried," Jackie said.

"Didn't the doctor say it was common in babies while they're teething?" my father asked.

"What if this is something else?" Jackie asked.

"Let's wait a day and see what happens."

While they're having this conversation, guess who waddled into the den with pink drool dripping off his chin?

"Wha dat?" he pointed at the magazine I was reading.

"A movie," I said.

"Mooey, mooey," he said, and waddled off toward the nursery.

BO

I asked Alice to meet me in the parking lot before school started. I stood between some cars. It was a cold, gray day. The last few yellowed leaves were falling from the trees.

A voice cried out from behind me, "Bo, is that you?"

I turned. Alice stood there with her mouth agape.

"What do you think?" I asked.

"Halloween was three weeks ago," she said. But then she smiled. "Just kidding."

"It's not funny!"

"No, I like it, really," Alice said. "It's just so different. I mean, if you did this as a before and after in *Vogue* no one would believe it was the same person."

❖   ❖   ❖

In terms of my emergence in a new form, the inhabitants of Time Zone High can be divided into four groups:

1. Those who didn't notice. (Most)

2. Those who noticed and thought it was someone new. (Some)

3. Those who noticed and realized it was me but didn't say anything. (Several)

4. Those who noticed and realized it was me and said something. (A few)

The Few Who Spoke:

Mr. Goodrich: (Eyes wide, startled expression) "Bo! Is that you?"

Bobby: "Now, is this so bad?"

The Letch: "Woof!"

At lunch I waited until after the bell and then went into the girls' room to check my makeup. I thought I had the bathroom to myself, but then the door swung open and Chloe dashed in, as if she was trying to avoid someone. I watched her catch her breath. Then she went straight to the mirror and started primping.

I froze. She glanced at me, then back at herself, then did a double take.

"Bo?" she said.

"Oh, hi, Chloe." I'm so subtle.

"You . . . you look . . ."

I'm not sure I'd ever seen Chloe tongue-tied before. I braced myself for some clever, cutting remark.

Finally, Chloe got it out. "You look great."

I wanted to kill her.

KYLE

Some people have built-in radar. Take Chloe. Usually I'll pass her a couple of times a day in the hall and see her at least once in the senior lounge. But I haven't seen her since the party. That's what I mean by radar. She must sense me in the hall and hide long before I have a chance to notice her.

I usually don't go over to her house during the week because she's too busy studying, but tonight I did. Mrs. Frost peeked through the little window in the door and saw me outside. I caught a glimpse of the surprised look on her face, but then she made a superfast recovery and smiled warmly.

"Kyle, what a surprise," she said, pulling the door open. "Come in. I'll get Chloe."

Chloe's mom disappeared down the hall. She's always been kind of warm, but distant with me. I get the feeling she thinks of me as a "phase" in Chloe's life. Like someday she'll get out the family album and show some visitor Chloe's baby pictures. And then maybe a picture of Chloe with her Barbie dolls during her "Barbie phase" and a photo of Chloe on her horse during her "horse phase" and then a photo of Chloe with me during her "Kyle phase."

I stood in the entryway and waited. Near the door was a security keypad with half a dozen tiny red and green lights. Chloe once told me they even had sensors under the lawn so that if someone stepped on it at night the alarm would go off. I guess you can never be too safe.

After about ten minutes—which meant Chloe was putting on her makeup and fixing her hair—she came to the top of the stairs, dressed like she was ready to go out. Except it was ten thirty on a weekday night and she wasn't going anywhere.

"Surprise, surprise," she said.

"I was in the neighborhood and thought I'd stop by. Haven't seen you around school much."

"I've been hard to find," Chloe said.

I wasn't sure what she meant by that. "I thought maybe we should talk."

Chloe didn't look thrilled, but she said, "Come up."

Chloe's bedroom is like an office. She's got a bed and dressers and posters on the walls like everyone else, but the thing you notice most is this big black lacquer desk with a PowerBook and a printer, an ink blotter, a telephone, and a fax machine. On the wall beside the desk are shelves filled with books and paper and supplies.

Chloe sat down at the desk. "Why didn't you just call?"

"Because I wanted to talk."

Chloe frowned a little.

"Sometimes when we talk on the phone," I said, "I feel like you're doing three other things at the same time."

Chloe didn't deny it. She looked down at some papers on her desk, then back at me. "What did you want to talk about?"

"Us."

Her eyes narrowed slightly.

"Look," I said, "maybe I should try to explain to you why I decided to—"

"Because you were a star, Kyle." Chloe decided to explain for me. "You were a hero. You were the captain of the football team and basked in everyone's adoration. Even teachers were afraid to offend you. It must be terrible not to have that anymore, so you're trying to find it somewhere else."

I guess deep down I knew there was some truth to that. "You're not jealous, are you?"

Chloe has this way of reacting by not

reacting. It's almost like, the bigger the impact of the question, the less she shows it.

"It's more like a feeling of being violated."

"Huh?"

Chloe looked back at the papers and toyed with a loose paper clip for a moment.

"You mean, it's like I don't belong in the play?"

"Do you?"

"Look, I'm not going to make acting a career," I said. "It's just something I feel like trying."

"All the world's a stage, and all the men and women merely players," she said as if reciting a poem.

"What's that?"

"Shakespeare."

"You really wish I wasn't in the play?" I asked.

"It doesn't matter."

"It doesn't matter because I'm already in it, or it doesn't matter because you don't care?"

"It's too hard to explain."

I got up and pulled on my jacket. I guess I'd had enough of her mysterious attitude for one night. "Maybe it is too hard to explain," I said. "Or maybe, for once, you just don't have an answer."

BO

Bobby and I were sitting on the catwalk at lunch today. The school band was practicing on the stage below us.

"God, they're awful," Bobby whispered.

"They're not awful," I replied. "They're high school."

"Why does everything in high school have to be so unprofessional?" Bobby asked. "Can't we raise our standards?"

I stared at him. "You're starting to sound like Chloe."

Bobby locked his eyes on mine. "Have you noticed that we can't have a conversation without you bringing up Chloe? No matter what we talk about, it always winds up being about her."

"Not true," I said.

"It is, Bo. You're obsessed."

I didn't answer. But inside I suspected he was right. Only I wasn't sure if it was Chloe I was obsessed with . . . or her boyfriend.

KYLE

We read through the play today. Mr. Goodrich said we were just supposed to read our lines, not act, but you should have seen Chloe. At the point where Mrs. Frank wants to kick the Van Daans out because Mr. Van Daan was stealing bread, I really thought Chloe was going to throw herself on the stage floor. I won't be surprised if she does it during the performance.

After the read-through, Mr. Goodrich told everyone to go home. Chloe and I had sort of made up after what happened the other night, but she still took off like a shot. She's driving again so she doesn't need me to chauffeur her around.

I waited until I thought everyone had left. But when I went back out to the stage, Mr. Goodrich was there talking to Bo. I almost didn't recognize her. Looks like she changed her hair and decided to really bone up on her makeup skills. Anyway, both she and Mr. Goodrich looked surprised to see me.

"Seems like I'm always interrupting you two," I said.

"That's okay, Kyle," Mr. Goodrich said. "What's up?"

I didn't want to talk in front of Bo. She got the hint pretty quick and went backstage.

"Is something wrong, Kyle?" Mr. Goodrich asked.

"I hate to say this, Mr. G," I said, "but I'm having doubts about the play."

Mr. Goodrich nodded. "Right now it must look overwhelming. The lines, the stage directions, working with actors and actresses you don't know. That's why we'll rehearse for so long. By the time we open, a month and a half from now, you'll know your lines, blocking, and the other actors better than you know your own family."

He patted me on the shoulder. "The only difference between you and the rest of the cast is that they've all been through this before. Believe me, there have been plenty of times when they wanted to quit, too."

I believed him, but I wasn't sure it made it any better.

"Is there something else, Kyle?" Mr. Goodrich asked.

There was. It was something that had been

bothering me ever since I read the play, but until that moment I'd never been able to put it into words.

"It's a true story, isn't it? I mean, what happened to the Franks and Van Daans."

Mr. Goodrich looked a little surprised. "Why yes, of course."

"I don't get it. They were just ordinary people. They weren't in the army. They had nothing to do with the war. They didn't do anything wrong."

"That's the tragedy of the story," Mr. Goodrich said. "Anne was a sweet impetuous young girl. Stifled and confined at a time of her life when she should have been growing and free."

"Then she dies for no reason," I said.

"Millions died for no reason," Mr. Goodrich said. "Children, mothers . . . The greatest horror of modern history. That's what makes this such a powerful play, Kyle. Anne Frank was an everyday person like you and me, and yet this is what happened to her."

"Isn't there another play we could do?" I asked.

Mr. Goodrich seemed sort of surprised. "Well, yes, I suppose, but few have the kind of impact this play has. It's such an important lesson about good and evil and hope. Think of the service you'll be doing by performing it."

"Well, that's just it," I said.

"What's just it?" Mr. Goodrich looked puzzled.

"I guess the thing that really gets me is that this is such a serious play," I said. "I've never acted in a play before and I'd feel really bad if I blew this."

"I assure you, Kyle, you won't," said Mr. Goodrich.

It was nice of him to say that, but let's get real, folks. How does he know?

BO

I followed Kyle into the parking lot. It was dark and cold and the moon was going in and out of the clouds. "Wait!"

He turned around. I could barely make out the features of his face in the shadows. He looked surprised. "Oh, hi."

"This time you're the one who looks surprised," I said. My heart was beating fast. I didn't know whether it was from running, or just being near him again. "I heard what you said to Mr. G."

"You listened?"

I nodded. "Do you hate me?"

Kyle bent his head and ran his fingers through his hair. "I guess it doesn't matter."

"I just wanted to tell you not to worry so much about making a mistake," I said. "That's what rehearsals are for."

"Even after a hundred rehearsals you can still go out and drop the ball."

"Everyone flubs a line now and then," I said. "A good actor just keeps right on going and carries the audience with him."

"And a bad actor?"

"Does the same thing, just not as well."

Kyle smiled slightly in the dark.

"Guess I'm on a new team," he said. "Only instead of being a linebacker, I'll probably be a line-hacker. Anyway, need a ride?"

"Uh, okay."

We got in his car. I fought the temptation to ask why Chloe had left so quickly before. Instead, I just basked in the thought that he was driving me home and not her.

"I noticed you changed your hair," he said as we pulled out of the parking lot.

"You like it?" I asked.

Kyle glanced over at me. I smiled back. Perhaps this is one of the great differences between the sexes. Females notice something looks different and decide right away whether they like it or not. Males simply notice that something is different. Deciding whether they like it is a whole separate thought process.

"Yeah, I do."

I'm in love! I thought.

KYLE

I was heading for the football table with my lunch tray.

"Yo, Kyle!" Lukowsky waved at me from the Pinhead table where he was sitting with Branco, the Rat, and the others.

"What's up?" I asked.

"Heard you're in the play."

"Yeah."

Suddenly they all pulled out pens and pieces of paper. "Can we have your autograph?"

"You guys are such jerks," I said with a smile.

"No, man, we want to say we knew you when," said the Rat.

This cracked the rest of the Pinheads up. One thing you can say for these guys, they may be misfits, but they have a sense of humor.

The laughter died down and an awkward moment followed. Like I could go to class with them, I could joke with them, but somehow, I wasn't one of them.

"Later, guys," I said, and headed over to the football table.

"Hey, bro, what's this about you bein' in a play?" Eddie asked as I sat down. "How come you didn't tell us?"

"I don't know. Guess I wasn't sure I was gonna stay with it."

"So is this your new career?" Alex Gidden asked.

"Nah, it's just something to do."

"Chloe must've talked him into it," Jason said sort of snidely.

"Actually, she's really against it."

The guys gave me these looks like they were amazed to hear this. It's like everyone assumes Chloe directs my life. Like I need her permission to do things. Maybe they thought I was her robot or something.

"Isn't she in the play, too?" Eddie asked.

"Yeah."

The guys scowled at each other. Like this didn't make *any* sense to them at all.

BO

This morning I left a note in the AV room for The Letch to send my techie to the auditorium during lunch.

Later I was sitting on the stage with Bobby trying to estimate how much paint we'd need when The Letch himself strolled down the aisle.

"Here I am, babe," he said.

Bobby and I glanced at each other. "You're the techie?" I asked.

"Yup."

"Don't you usually send one of your gremlins to do it?"

"No one's available," said The Letch. I could feel him undressing me with his eyes. No one had ever done that before. . . . I might've enjoyed it if it wasn't The Letch.

"So when do we start?" he asked.

"I'll let you know," I said, turning back to Bobby.

The Letch wouldn't know a hint if Jimi Hendrix walked in and played it for him. Instead of leaving, he said he wanted to check the lights. He climbed up on stage and proceeded to test every light in the house. It was so distracting that Bobby and I finally went to the lunch room.

I'm not a mean person. Believe me, I can't afford to be. But if The Letch were the last man on Earth, I would become a lesbian.

KYLE

Nobody ever asked if I wanted to be a Pinhead. The decision was made for me. After my mother died, I began to get into trouble. They started calling my father in for conferences. Then I was sent to the school shrink who gave me a bunch of tests. And the next thing I knew, I was in the PINS.

I think deep down most of the Pinheads would rather be with the "normal" kids, but they cover it up by acting goofy and pretending they don't care. I never really cared, mostly because I had football.

I'm the only athlete in the PINS. The Rat was on the cross-country team for a while, but they could never get him to run in the right direction.

Anyway, I was hanging out in the senior lounge after school today, waiting for rehearsal to start, when Mr. Orillio walked by.

"Hey, Mr. O." I gave him a wave.

"Hey, Kyle." He waved back. Then he must have thought of something because he stopped. "Say, you got a minute?"

I glanced across the hall at the auditorium. Ben McGillis and Beth Villeta were already on the stage, but most of the others hadn't arrived yet.

"Uh, sure. What's up?"

"Come out to my car with me," he said.

I gave him a questioning look.

"Hey, only my wife gets to look at me that way." He winked.

We went out to this old beat-up yellow Volvo, and he opened the trunk. Inside, was the typical trunk stuff like a spare tire and some rags and jugs of windshield washer fluid. There was also a ragged cardboard box filled with old record albums.

"Let's see now." Mr. Orillio thumbed through the albums. He pulled one out and handed it to me. On the cover were five guys with long hair, white bell-bottoms, and granny glasses. The group was called The Bongs and the album featured the hit single "Gettin' By on Love."

"This is from the sixties, right?" I asked.

"Very good, Kyle. It was made in 1968." Mr. Orillio got into the car and motioned me to join him.

"We going somewhere?" I asked as I got in.

"Back in time," Mr. Orillio said as he slid a tape into his dashboard cassette player. This tinny rock music started to play. Mr. Orillio turned the volume up.

When you see me comin' down the street
I look like someone you would like to meet.
I got this feelin' fits me like a glove
Cause baby, I'm gettin' by on love . . .

"I've heard that," I said.

"Oh, yeah, they still play it on the oldies stations," Mr. Orillio said. "We were number one for three weeks that summer."

"What do you mean, *we*?"

"Take a look." He tapped the album cover.

I looked closer at the cover and noticed that one of The Bongs was short and had frizzed-out hair like Jimi Hendrix. His shirt sleeves were rolled up and his arms were crossed. They were hairy arms.

I looked back at Mr. Orillio and felt my jaw drop. "No way . . ."

"Yes, way," Mr. Orillio said. "We opened for The Strawberry Alarm Clock, Traffic, The Kinks, Big Brother, The Jefferson Airplane, The Blues Project, Paul Butterfield, The Yardbirds . . ."

"Who?" I asked.

"You've never heard of the Yardbirds?"

"I've never heard of any of them."

Mr. Orillio looked disappointed. "I must be getting old. They were big groups, Kyle. The only ones bigger were the Beatles, the Stones, and Led Zep."

"That's incredible, Mr. O. What did you play?"

"Rhythm guitar," Mr. Orillio said. "We were on TV, Kyle. *American Bandstand*, *The Smothers Brothers Show*. We played the west coast, Europe—"

"Woodstock?"

Mr. Orillio shook his head. "We were done by then."

"Done?"

"Our second album bombed. The record company dropped us like a hot potato. We went from playing five-thousand-seat halls in San Francisco and New York to two-hundred-seat clubs in Toledo, Ohio. After five months of that the band broke up."

"Bummer, Mr. O."

"You're telling me," he said. "One week we were met at the airport by a limo. The next week we were driving around in a beat-up van with our amps tied to the roof."

"So what'd you do?"

"Went back to college and got a teaching degree." Mr. Orillio hit the eject button and the tape popped out.

"Anyone at school know about this?" I asked.

"A few."

"How come you told me?"

Mr. Orillio just gazed at me for a moment. "Because I wanted to show you that life goes on, Kyle. You don't give up just because they turn off the spotlight."

I stared down at the frizzy-haired musician on the cover of the album. "You weren't a Pinhead."

"No, I wasn't, Kyle. And I wasn't a big good-looking guy like you either. We all get dealt a hand. Whether we like it or not, those are the cards we have to play with."

I knew what he was saying was probably true, but I also felt like I'd heard enough. Maybe there's a limit to how much wisdom you can absorb at any given time.

"Yeah, thanks," I said. "Gotta get back to rehearsal." I started to get out of the car, but Mr. Orillio grabbed my arm.

"Just one last thing, Kyle."

"What?"

"It's better to be a has-been than a never-was."

"Huh?"

"Think about it."

BO

Today at lunch Alice drove me to the county clerk's office. Alice is terrified of driving and travels everywhere at speeds five to ten miles an hour under the legal limit. She leans forward so that her face is only inches from the windshield and grips the wheel so tightly that her knuckles turn white. She's about the most unrelaxed driver I've ever seen.

"Would you please stop humming?" she snapped.

"Huh? I didn't realize I was," I said.

"You've been humming for days. I've never seen you in such a good mood. It's scary."

"Sorry."

"Did something happen with Kyle?"

"No." Nothing that I'd want to talk about, anyway.

"You know, Mr. G isn't very happy about him," Alice said.

"He'll loosen up."

"Bo, if he were any more wooden he'd be a cigar-store Indian."

◇   ◇   ◇

Alice stayed in the car while I went into town hall. About half an hour later I returned.

"You took so long!" Alice gasped, pointing at the digital clock in her dashboard. "We're going to be late."

"It was worth it," I said.

"What did you find out?" She inched her car out of the parking lot.

"It was very intelligent of me not to get a driver's license, credit cards, or open any bank accounts," I said.

"Why?" asked Alice, since we were both aware that at least two of those items were things most people our age can't wait to get.

"Because it will make it easier for me to change my name," I said.

KYLE

I was sitting in the den watching monster trucks crush piles of junked cars. I don't know what it has to do with sports, but it's fun to watch. It was dinner time, and I was eating a giant peanut butter and jelly sandwich on French bread. The front door opened and my father came in. His collar was pulled open and his tie was loose. Looked like he'd had a bad day.

"Where's Jackie?" he asked, pulling off his coat.

"Don't know."

"Anything for dinner?"

"Choose-your-own-adventure."

"Great," he grumbled.

The front door opened again and Jackie came in carrying a sleeping IT swaddled in a light blue blanket.

"Where were you?" my father asked.

"I took Jake to see Dr. Huber."

"Again? That's the third time this month. What's wrong now?"

"He wasn't acting right." Jackie started down the hall toward the nursery.

"Wasn't acting right?" my father called after her. "What does that mean?"

"Would you keep your voice down? You'll wake him."

My father turned to me. "He wasn't acting right so she took him to the doctor."

I didn't say anything. This whole thing of IT going to the doctor too much had been brewing for a couple of months. A moment later Jackie came out of the nursery and started to take off her coat. My father was standing behind her with his hands on his hips, looking mad.

"Would you please tell me what not acting right means?"

"He just didn't seem right," Jackie said, sounding pretty upset herself. "I can't explain it. It's just something a mother knows."

"Does a mother happen to know what it costs each time she takes Jake to the doctor?" my father fumed.

Jackie glared at him. "I thought it was covered by insurance."

"Some of it is. But when you're going four or five times a month, the part that isn't covered starts to add up."

"Well, maybe I wouldn't have to go as often if I had some help around here," Jackie snapped. "Between taking care of Jake and the house and cooking for you and Kyle, it's just too much. Nobody helps me. You don't even care!"

The next thing we knew she started to sob and ran out of the living room. A second later the bedroom door slammed. My father turned and looked at me wondrously.

"How did we go from taking Jake to the doctor to cleaning the house?" he asked, totally mystified.

What could I say? My father let out a big sigh and started down the hall to the bedroom.

I guess it's like Mr. Orillio said: We all get dealt a hand.

BO

The strangest thing happened Saturday night. I was baby-sitting for Jake Winthrop. It wasn't fun. He's teething and he cries most of the time. Around 9 P.M. a car pulled into the driveway and doors slammed. It was too early for the Winthrops to come home, so I assumed correctly that it was Kyle and Chloe.

They came into the den and we did the awkward hellos. I told them Jake was asleep, and asked if I should go. Kyle started to nod, but Chloe said, "You think he might wake up?"

"It's possible. He's teething."

"She better stay," Chloe said.

The next thing I knew, they went upstairs. I sat there telling myself, *No, this can't be what I think.*

Footsteps upstairs. A door slammed. The argument began. I can only assume neither Kyle nor Chloe realized how thin the walls are.

"This is no good." (Kyle)

"Why?" (Chloe)

"She's here." (Kyle)

"So?" (Chloe)

"So . . . I don't know. It's just weird." (Kyle)

"If it bothers you that much, tell her to go." (Guess who?)

"And what about it?" (I think he meant Jake.)

"What will happen if he wakes up?" (Chloe)

"He'll scream." (Kyle)

They went on like that for a while. Then the door creaked. Two sets of footsteps came down the stairs. Chloe passed without even looking at me. Kyle gave me a little wave. Outside, car doors slammed and the engine started. A screech of rubber in the driveway and the star-crossed couple disappeared into the night.

❖   ❖   ❖

The Winthrops came back from the movies around 11:30. I live about six blocks away so I usually walk home, but it had started to rain so Mr. Winthrop said he'd drive me.

"How's school this year?" he asked in the car as the windshield wipers swished back and forth.

"Fine, Mr. Winthrop. Did Kyle tell you about the play?"

"Play?"

"He didn't tell you he was in the school play?"

Mr. Winthrop glanced at me. "My son Kyle?"

"Uh-oh." I'd spilled the beans.

KYLE

My father and I were watching football. It was Sunday afternoon and Jackie had taken IT to visit her parents. During halftime my father turned to me and said, "You're in a play."

"How'd you find out?"

"Bo, the girl who baby-sits."

"Oh."

"I think it's interesting," he said.

"It's all right."

My father gave me his all-knowing fatherly smile. "It's a step toward something new, Kyle."

"Don't get your hopes up, Dad. I don't think I'm gonna be an actor."

"I wasn't expecting you to," he said. "I'm simply glad that you're finally starting to come out of your shell."

"I was in a shell?" I pretended to be surprised.

"Don't joke. Between me getting married again and your knee, you've been so withdrawn I was worried you'd never come back."

"I'm not so sure I have."

"The acting's a start."

"I was talking about you getting married again," I said.

My father was quiet for a moment. Then his chest heaved. "What happened with your mother was . . ." He shook his head. I'd never really heard him talk about it. It's something neither of us can discuss. "It doesn't mean we stop living, Kyle, even if there are times when we feel like we want to."

I looked back at the halftime show. Mom died. He had a right to marry Jackie. I can't explain what bothered me about it. Something just did.

"You don't have to talk to me about it," my father said. "But it's important that you talk to someone."

"I'm not seeing a shrink," I told him for the billionth time.

"Someone, Kyle."

Sure. Maybe one of the lunch ladies.

BO

Kyle kept giving me looks during rehearsal today. Of course I knew what it had to be about, so when we got to a part where Peter is offstage I went over and said I was sorry.

"Don't tell him anything about me, okay?" he said.

"Your wish is my command," I said.

I thought he'd walk away, but he stayed. We were standing alone in the wing, only a foot apart. His eyes were on me and I felt goose bumps.

"Your face looks thinner," he said.

"So does the rest of me."

"And I'm getting fatter." He pinched a fold of his stomach.

"It doesn't show," I said. Well, maybe it showed just an eensy weensy bit, but who was looking?

"I still eat like I'm in practice six days a

week," he said.

"It must be hard to stop."

"You still swimming?"

"Yes. I haven't seen you there lately."

"It's not my thing," he said.

"Kyle?" Chloe was standing a dozen feet away. I saw surprise in her eyes. As if she was seeing something she hadn't noticed before.

She stepped closer to him. "Can I practice my air raid speech on you?"

"Okay." She and Kyle started to walk away, but as she did, she looked back over her shoulder at me with a curious expression on her face. As if she were thinking, *Is it possible?*

Oddly, I was thinking the same thing.

KYLE

Chloe asked me to come to her house to practice the play today. We've been rehearsing *Anne Frank* for a couple of weeks, working mostly on characterization and blocking. After my knee operation I never thought I'd do any blocking again. Except this kind of blocking means learning where to move onstage.

I got to Chloe's house and she let me in, turning away before I could kiss her, and leading me into the living room.

"Where're your parents?" I asked.

"They went to the city," she said. "I've set things up so that it's like the stage. You can use this as the cat carrier"—she handed me a shoe box, then pointed to a chair—"and we can pretend that's the stove."

I guess she wanted to make it clear that it was all business today.

"Okay." I took off my jacket and got out the playbook.

"We'll start where you take Mouschi out of the carrier."

"Right."

"Go ahead," she said.

I pointed at the playbook. "You're supposed to ask me the cat's name."

"You haven't taken Mouschi out of the carrier," she said.

"Mouschi isn't here."

"Pretend, Kyle. We're rehearsing."

"Okay." So I pretended to take the cat out of the carrier.

"That's not the way you do it," Chloe said.

"Huh?"

"It's your cat, Kyle. You have to treat it like a living thing. If it was a real cat, you wouldn't just take it out of the box and drop it to the floor. You'd gently put it down."

"Well, that's what I'll do."

"Then do it now."

"Here?"

"Yes."

"What's the point?"

"The point is we're rehearsing for a show. You don't rehearse one way and then do it differently when you're onstage."

So I pretended to take invisible Mouschi out of his carrier, gently placed him on the floor, and patted his invisible head. "Nice kitty."

"No," Chloe said.

"Now what?" I asked.

"Don't say 'nice kitty.'"

"What's wrong with *that*?"

"For one thing, it's not in the play. For another, it conveys the wrong mood."

"Mood?"

Chloe gave me this look, like she couldn't believe what a dummy I was. Boy, that pissed me off.

I reached for my jacket. "Look, let's just forget it, okay? I'm already rehearsing this stupid play three hours a day, five days a week. I don't need your help."

"You do, Kyle."

"Says who?"

"Mr. Goodrich."

I stopped and stared at her. "What are you talking about?"

"He asked me to work with you," Chloe said.

"You mean, this was *his* idea?"

"Yes."

"I don't get it."

"He says you need extra help."

"Well, why didn't *he* tell me?" I asked.

"He didn't want to upset you. He's afraid you'll quit."

I stood by the floor-to-ceiling windows and looked out at the water. It was a cold gray day.

The waves had white caps. "Am I that bad?"

"You're inexperienced, Kyle."

"It's just a high school play. I didn't think experience was necessary."

Chloe frowned. "Think of Ben McGillis walking into the middle of a football game."

"He'd get killed."

"Why should a play be any different?"

BO

Today I went to the second career fair in the gym. As I walked past the booths, I sensed a presence following me. It was The Letch. Finally I stopped and confronted him. "I thought you weren't supposed to come to events like this."

"I'm ditching, babe," he said.

I turned around but he continued to follow me, so I stopped at the legal professions booth. The woman there wasn't a lawyer, she was a paralegal. While I talked to her, The Letch stood at the waste management booth next door—rather apt, I thought.

"Is there any way to prevent someone from following you around?" I asked loudly.

"You can have a court order of protection sworn out," the woman said. "But you have to prove that the person is a continuing nuisance."

I turned to The Letch. "Hear that?"

The Letch shrank back into the crowd.

Someone next to me laughed. I turned and found Chloe.

"Is he bothering you?" she asked in a confidential whisper.

"I don't think he can help himself," I whispered back.

Chloe grinned. "It's when he *doesn't* stare at me that I worry."

We started to walk together. Just like that.

"I was in our basement yesterday and found a set of old glasses and a fringed tablecloth," Chloe said. "They must have belonged to my grandparents. Can you use them?"

"Yes!" I exclaimed. "You can't believe how hard it's been to find props like that."

"We have some old chairs, too," she said. "But I'll have to ask my parents."

"Would you? Everything in the prop closet is either un-speakably grungy or broken. We'll take anything you've got."

Chloe stopped. "I know. My basement is full of things I bet you could use. Why don't you come over tonight and we'll go through it together?"

"Uh, okay." Was I hearing her correctly?

"I'm at 4 Bay Street. Know where that is?"

"I have a rough idea," I said.

"It's a dead end and we're the last house. Around eight?"

"Okay."

The bell rang. I could see Chloe's mind skip to her next responsibility. "Great," she said, moving toward the exit. "See you then."

"Chloe?"

She stopped and turned. "Yes?"

"Thanks," I said.

She gave me that winning smile. "Anything for the play, huh?"

In shock, I watched her hurry from the gym. Chloe had just invited me to her *home*?

KYLE

Chloe said everything you say and do onstage sends a message. It's body language. It's the tone of your voice. It really is the way you act. She said the scene with Peter and Anne and the cat isn't about Anne meeting the cat. It's about Peter being shy and withdrawn. My job is to get that message across to the audience.

Acting is a lot harder than I imagined. I really see how I could blow it and look like a fool. So I should quit, right? I mean, there's got to be *someone* at school who can play the role of Peter better than me.

Damn that Chloe. She was right when she said it was hard not to be a hero anymore. Mr. Orillio says it's better to be a has-been than a never-was, but let me tell you, learning to be a has-been ain't easy.

BO

I'm not going to tell you how big Chloe's house is, or how they have this incredible view of the water and a heated pool in their backyard. I'm not going to tell you about all the original art that's hanging on their walls, or how rich I think her parents must be.

But I do wonder how and why she's kept it a secret for so long. I mean we all knew she was well off, but not *that* well off. It's a side of Chloe we've never seen.

Anyway, Chloe and I went through her basement, which is probably larger than my entire house. We pulled sheets off stored furniture and opened dusty cardboard boxes. Just as she'd said, we found sets of plates and glasses and tablecloths and chairs. We picked out what we needed and carried it out to the driveway and packed it into her parents' station wagon.

"I'll drive it to school in the morning and get

Kyle to help me unload it," she said.

"Do you really think you should?" I quickly asked.

"Why not?"

"Doesn't he have a bad knee? Maybe it would be better if I helped you."

"Well, okay."

There was an awkward moment when neither of us was certain what to do next. Chloe looked around and frowned.

"Where's your car?" she asked.

"I don't have one."

"How did you get here?"

"I walked. Anything for the play, remember?"

Chloe smiled. "Come on, I'll give you a ride home."

We got in her car. I don't know what kind it was, but it was a small red convertible and smelled like leather. I gave her directions to my house.

"I'm really glad you changed your mind about stage-managing this production," Chloe said as she drove. "Could you imagine having to deal with someone who didn't know what they were doing?"

"Yes."

Chloe nodded. "Of course. That must be half the people you deal with."

"It *is* a high school production," I said.

Chloe looked at me out of the corner of her eye. "Doesn't that kill you? Why does everyone have this attitude that it has to be unprofessional just because it's high school? Why can't we try to make it the best thing we've ever done?"

"We do," I said. "But there are limits on how much money we have, how much time, and, to be really blunt, how much talent is available."

"I know that, but sometimes I think those limits are used as an excuse not to try."

"I know you feel that way," I said.

Chloe turned into my driveway and stopped. Instead of reaching for the door handle, I just sat there. I felt like she and I had reached a crucial juncture—the central difference in our philosophies toward life in high school.

"I know you don't like me," Chloe said, staring straight ahead as if she couldn't face me.

"I used to not like you," I said. "Now I'm not sure."

She smiled a little. Even in the shadows of the car she had a perfect profile.

"I haven't changed," she said.

"I know."

She hooked her hair behind her ear and looked at me. "You've changed. You've lost weight and bought new clothes. You've done really nice things with your hair."

Yes! I felt like shouting. *Don't you know I'm*

madly in love with your boyfriend?

"I think it's really great," Chloe said.

"Thanks," I said, hating to admit that she sounded sincere.

"Why don't we make this a really great production, Bo?" she said. "This is the last serious play we'll ever do in high school. Why don't we go out with a bang? You and me together."

How could I say no? Nobody *wants* to do a mediocre job, and frankly, I don't think I ever have. But I knew what Chloe meant. I could do a good, competent job, or I could do a *great* job. And why not? Together Chloe and I could make it the best thing we'd ever done.

Chloe and I?

KYLE

Couldn't sleep last night. It's been a long time since that happened to me. For some weird reason I didn't feel like watching TV, so I picked up this book called *North Dallas Forty*. It and *Ball Four* are the only two books I've ever read.

The hero of *North Dallas Forty* is this guy named Phil Elliot, who reveals all this "inside" stuff about professional football. I guess in 1973 when the book came out it must've been a real shock to the football fans of America that these great pro players took drugs off the field to get high and took them on the field to kill the pain so they could play. And I guess it was also shocking that the coach and team management would approve of playing injured and using painkillers. Maybe it was even a shock that players on the same team could hate each other so much and curse each other out.

The thing about *Ball Four* is that it's also

shocking. It's about all the crazy, goofy things a bunch of baseball players did back in the 1960s. But it's also funny and no matter what those guys did, you still get the feeling they loved playing ball and loved being on the team. *North Dallas Forty* makes you feel like Phil Elliot hated the team, hated everything about football except playing the game. He makes the coach and the team owners out to be a bunch of evil cretins who only cared about winning and making money.

I wonder what Phil Elliot would say today, with players earning more than $5 million a year. Everything in sports these days is money. A baseball star making $5 mill a year will sit out the first four or five games of the season and pray his team loses. Why? Because then the owners will give in to his contract demands just to get him back in the lineup. These guys charge $20 for an autograph, and $2,000 an hour to stand around and shake hands at the grand openings of appliance stores.

Team spirit isn't dead. When some guy weeps after losing in the play-offs, it's not just because he won't get a World Series bonus. But the fact that there is a World Series bonus really makes you wonder. It's like nothing's pure anymore. Everything has the taint of money. It used to be the team came first. Now the team may be important, but everyone's looking out for number one, too.

Maybe being in high school is about dreams. About making it big. Almost every guy I know on the football team thinks he's going to the pros. Everyone in the play dreams she or he is headed for Hollywood. Jeff Branco probably hopes he's headed for the FBI's Most Wanted list.

Anne Frank had a dream. She didn't want to be on a professional team, she didn't want a billion-dollar contract. She just wanted to go outside. She just wanted to walk in the street and look at the sky. How many Anne Franks were there, hiding in attics and basements? Six million Jews died in concentration camps. The Nazis also killed people with mental and physical handicaps. They all came under the heading of Undesirables.

They all had dreams.

BO

The phone rang tonight. It was Alice. We've both been so busy the last few days that we haven't had time to talk.

"Remember me?" she asked.

"Sorry, I've been distracted. So, how are things on-line?"

"It's over," Alice said. "I've disconnected."

"What? Why?"

"Self-preservation. I was out of control, giving my love away to anyone who could type more than fifteen words a minute. I think I was in love with the idea of being in love."

"What's wrong with that?"

"I was in danger of making romance the central concern of my life," she said. "I almost forgot that I have a life of my own. There's something you must never forget about guys, Bo."

"What's that?"

"They're just guys. They don't make the sun

come up, and they shouldn't change your life."

"I'll remember that," I said.

"So anyway, how are you?"

"Uh, in love."

The phone line grew quiet. I could hear the faint strains of another conversation taking place somewhere in the distance on the information superhighway.

"Hello?" I said.

"I . . . I don't know what to say."

"Join the crowd."

"Does Kyle know?" Alice asked.

"I don't think so."

"Are you feeling okay, Bo?"

"Yes! I'm feeling great! In fact, I can't remember feeling this good."

"All because you're in love with a completely unattainable male who's been going with the same woman for three years and is *still* going with her? I mean, doesn't it seem a little hopeless to you?"

"I'm not thinking about the future," I said.

"That's obvious."

"Why can't you be happy for me?" I asked.

"Because I'm worried," Alice said. "Bobby's worried, too. We think you've either gone completely psycho or you're going to get really hurt."

"What if it's neither?" I asked. "What if it just so happens that Kyle and I enjoy talking and like each other's company?"

"How much time have you spent together?" Alice asked.

"We've talked a few times."

"Oh, Bo . . ." Alice sounded thoroughly disheartened.

"You sound just like my mother before we stopped communicating," I said, getting aggravated. "'Oh, Bo, don't you see what you're getting yourself into?' 'Oh, Bo, how can you do this to yourself?' Oh, Bo, nothing. All my life people have been telling me to take chances. Everyone's always telling me how I never take risks and how I'm too busy trying to protect myself. Now here I'm finally doing something wildly adventurous and everyone I know is trying to protect me."

"Bo, taking risks means learning to skydive or changing the color of your hair."

"Which I did."

"That's the kind of risk you should take."

"But not falling in love with Kyle Winthrop?"

"Be realistic, Bo."

"No."

KYLE

When I got home after rehearsals tonight my father and Jackie were waiting for me in the living room. IT was sitting on the floor chewing on an old red-checked dishrag. Jackie's bought about a hundred different teething toys—rubber pretzels, rings, even something that looks like a dog bone—but IT prefers the rag.

"Have a seat, Kyle," my father said. He looked serious. Jackie looked serious. I felt like I was in court.

"What's up?" I asked.

"Did you tell Jake that Ritz crackers were called soap?" my father asked.

I looked at Jackie. Her eyes were glistening with tears.

"You told him a train was a boat?" my father asked. "And a book was a movie?"

I looked at IT. He had the whole rag in his mouth. His cheeks were bulging and little red and white threads hung out from between his lips.

"Today he kept asking for his boat," Jackie said with a sniff. "Every time I gave it to him he had a tantrum."

"It wasn't a bright idea, Kyle," my father said.

"You might have affected his development," Jackie said.

"It probably won't," my father added. "But you're playing with a small child's mind."

"It's not like I did it on purpose," I said.

"You call it a joke?" Jackie asked, her eyes growing wide.

"I was just fooling around."

My father sighed. "I wish I understood you, Kyle."

BO

Chloe and I went backstage at lunch today. Bobby was there alone, sketching the large panels of canvas that will be the backdrops for the stage. He gave us a wary look, then forced a smile onto his face.

"Hi, Bo, Chloe."

"Hard at work?" I asked.

Bobby's eyes darted around apprehensively. I knew he was wondering what Chloe and I were doing there together.

"Bobby," Chloe said, "we were wondering if we could talk to you about the set."

"What about it?"

"Is there a way that we could make it look more realistic?" I asked.

Bobby put down his pencil and gave us a nervous look. "Like how?"

Chloe and I glanced at each other. We'd talked it over that morning while we unloaded the new props from Chloe's parents' station wagon.

"Suppose instead of drawing windows covered with blackout curtains, we actually had real windows with curtains on them?" I asked.

Bobby winced slightly. "Real *glass* windows?"

"Or just a window frame with the curtains," Chloe quickly added.

"Well, I guess . . ." Bobby said hesitantly.

"And is there any way we could actually use a real bookcase for the secret door?" I asked.

"Instead of a door with a bookshelf painted on it," added Chloe.

"With *real* books?" Bobby's eyebrows rose in horror.

"Maybe you could make some shallow shelves out of wood and draw rows of fake book jackets inside them," Chloe said.

"Well, I guess I could do that," Bobby said. "I mean, I'll have to see what kind of wood we have."

"Maybe some of the guys in the cast could make a bookshelf in wood shop," I said.

"I guess I could ask," Bobby said.

I went over and kissed him on the cheek.

"What's this all about?" Bobby asked.

"It's about going out with a bang," I said.

KYLE

Look, I'm not a sadist. I was just fooling around, okay? There's no way IT is going to turn twelve and still be calling a car a boat or whatever. Lots of kids call things by the wrong names. Then they learn the right names. I'll bet anything if Jackie had already raised a couple of kids this wouldn't have bothered her half as much.

On the other hand, I think Jeff Branco's parents probably have a lot to be worried about. I got into class this morning and all the Pinheads were huddled around the Rat, who was holding a newspaper.

"You gotta see this, Kyle," Lukowsky said. "It's about Jeff. Read it, Peter."

"'A seventeen-year-old man was arrested yesterday for attempting to break into the Fairview Home for Girls,'" the Rat read.

"Wait a minute," I said. "Isn't that the girls' detention home?"

"Yeah."

"'Jeffery Branco, of 243 Oak Avenue, was apprehended inside the facility, which houses young female criminals.'"

"I never heard of anyone trying to break *into* a detention home," said Lukowsky.

The Rat read: "'Police marveled that Branco was able to scale a fifteen-foot chain-link fence topped with razor wire, and pry open a heavily secured door before being discovered in the hallway outside the room of a young woman he claimed was his girlfriend.'"

"Did anybody know he even had a girlfriend?" I asked.

The other Pinheads shook their heads.

"I guess he got really horny," Lukowsky said.

BO

At rehearsal today everyone was talking about Jeff Branco, who might just be the most romantic psychopath since Jack the Ripper. Even Mr. Goodrich was in a good mood.

"Well, it's obvious we should have done Romeo and Juliet this year," he said with a smile.

But his good mood didn't last very long. "All right, everyone," he said, clapping his hands, "let's start from the top of scene three. Peter and Anne, you're sitting at the center table, doing your lessons. It's late in the afternoon and Mr. Frank gives you the signal that you can finally make noise after a long day of silence. Anne playfully takes Peter's shoes, and Peter tries to catch her. Okay? Let's try it."

The scene went all right until the point where Peter shouts, "You're going to be sorry!" and starts to chase Anne. Kyle went after Chloe like a bull through a china shop, knocking over a chair and banging into a table so hard that a glass crashed to the floor. Chloe was supposed to hide behind Cathy Reiner, who plays Mrs. Frank. But Kyle knocked Cathy over and practically tackled Chloe.

"Kyle!" Chloe gasped.

"Ow!" Cathy Reiner sat up, holding her elbow and sobbing.

"Uh, sorry." Kyle offered Cathy a hand, but she looked up at him in terror and backed away. Mr. Goodrich rubbed his face with his hands and shook his head like he was seeing things. "Let's try to remember that we're not on the football field, Kyle."

"Sorry, Mr. G." Kyle looked down and scuffed his shoe against the stage floor. You could see how frustrated and humiliated he was.

"Next time, just *pretend* you're chasing Anne."

"But then it's not going to look real," Kyle said.

Ben McGillis snickered.

"Your job is to make it look real," Mr. Goodrich said. "That's what acting is."

"You'd think he had plenty of experience chasing Chloe," Ben pretended to whisper, but he said it just loud enough for everyone to hear.

Kyle's hands balled into fists and he stormed across the stage toward Ben shouting, "What's *that* supposed to mean?"

Ben backed against a wall and cowered. His eyes darted around in fear as he looked for a way to escape. It looked like Kyle was going to beat him up.

"Kyle, don't!" Chloe and I shouted at the same time and stepped between him and Ben.

Kyle stopped and gave us both a startled look.

Chloe scowled at me.

I realized I'd made a boo-boo.

"Oh, uh, after you," I said.

KYLE

I drove Chloe home after rehearsal tonight. Her car's in the shop and her mom went to the city to meet her father for a show. She hardly said a word.

"Something wrong?" I asked.

She glanced at me. Her eyes said something was wrong, but her mouth said nothing.

"You think I'm wrecking the play?" I asked.

"I really don't want to talk about it."

"Why not?"

No answer. I pulled into her driveway and she started to reach for the door handle. Suddenly she stopped.

"What is it?" I asked.

"The front door."

The house was dark and the front door was wide open.

"We'd better call the police," she said.

"Wait, Chloe, maybe your mom left it open. There're no cars around."

"But someone could be inside."

"If anyone was going to rob your house, I doubt they'd leave the door open."

"You think?" Chloe seemed uncertain.

"Let's check it out." I started to get out of the car.

We walked up the path and peeked inside. Chloe reached in and turned on the hall and living room lights. Nothing looked disturbed.

"This is weird," she said, pointing at the keypad on the wall that ran the alarm system. "It's not even on."

"Your mom was probably in a rush," I said.

"It's not like her. She's usually super careful."

At Chloe's insistence, we searched every room and every closet, plus the attic, basement, and garage. By the time we finished, every light in the house was burning.

"I think it's okay," I said as we stood in the front hall.

Chloe bit her lower lip and hugged herself. "I don't feel safe, Kyle."

"Want me to stay until your parents come home?"

I could almost see the gears in Chloe's mind spinning. Who would've thought it would be such a big deal for me to stay a couple of hours?

"Okay, Kyle."

It was late and we hadn't eaten so Chloe ordered in a pizza for me and a salad for herself. We sat in the kitchen. Chloe picked at her salad.

She seemed tense, like she didn't know what I would do or say. I knew she felt trapped and I didn't want her to feel uncomfortable, so I just said the first thing that came into my mind. "What do you like about acting?"

Chloe gave me this look, like why would I ask *that*?

"I'm serious," I said.

"I . . . I think I like pretending I'm someone else."

"Why?"

"It's an escape," she said. "A relief from being me."

"Huh?" I'd never heard her say anything like that before.

"There's another part of it," Chloe added quickly, as if she regretted what she'd just said and wanted to get past it fast. "I like the idea that everybody's watching me, and that if I'm doing it well I can move them emotionally. I can make them laugh or cry. And sometimes, if I'm really good, I can make them love me."

"That's what you want? For everyone to love you?"

Chloe picked a sliver of onion out of her salad and bit it. "I never thought about it that way, but yes, I probably do." She paused. "I mean, isn't that what everybody wants?"

"I'd settle for just one person," I said.

BO

It's amazing how fast time passes. Dress rehearsals are suddenly two weeks away.

I was in the prop closet behind the stage today. Chloe and I want to find the most authentic-looking suits and dresses possible. Mr. Goodrich said there might be some old things in the closet so I went to take a look. The prop closet is big, dusty, and dark with lots of old props and backdrops leaning against the walls. I couldn't find the light switch so I left the door open to let the light in.

I was digging through old sofas, papier-mâché trees, and assorted junk when the room suddenly grew dimmer. I spun around and saw a silhouette standing in the doorway.

"Who is it?" I asked, gripped by a sudden nervousness.

"Lookin' good, babe." It was The Letch.

"What are you doing here?" I felt my breath

grow short as a number of truly unpleasant scenarios raced through my mind.

"Just lookin' for some lights."

"Wouldn't they be in the electrical closet?" I asked.

"I figured I'd check here, too," he said.

"You know they're not here. Can't you think of anything better to do than follow me around?"

"Sure, I can think of something better to do. Interested?" He started to close the door behind him.

I felt my heart start to pound. "Have you ever heard me scream? It's really quite an experience."

"Hey, lighten up." The Letch let go of the door. "I was only foolin' around."

"Go fool around in someone else's closet," I told him.

Then The Letch did the most shocking thing. His shoulders sagged and he said, "How come you're always so mean to me?"

I was utterly dumbfounded. Could it be that under that dumb lecherous exterior lurked a dumb but sensitive human being? Suddenly I felt terrible.

"I really don't mean to be such a crab," I told him softly. "I just don't want you to get the wrong idea."

"Maybe *you're* the one with the wrong idea," he said. "I mean, how do you know what I'm like if you won't even give me a chance?"

He was right. I wouldn't give him a chance. But that was beside the point. What could I say that would both convince him that I wasn't interested while at the same time not hurt his feelings any more than I already had?

It was at that precise moment that the door swung open. Kyle stood there with a startled look on his face.

"Oh, uh, sorry, didn't mean to interrupt." He began to back out.

"You weren't!" I gasped. Talk about people getting the wrong idea! I quickly grabbed The Letch by the arm and led him out of the closet. "We'll talk about it later, okay?"

"Uh . . . sure." The Letch sounded surprised. "I'll call you tonight."

"Yes, do that." *Do anything, I thought, but just go!*

The Letch went. I turned to Kyle and smiled. "Hi."

"Hi. You sure I wasn't interrupting?"

"Karl and I? No, no. We were just discussing the lighting."

Kyle frowned. "In a dark closet?"

"Well, as a matter of fact, we were discussing the lighting in this closet," I ad-libbed. "I can never find anything in here because it's so dark."

"All you have to do is turn on the switch." He

reached toward the wall and the closet filled with light.

"Will you look at that! I never knew it was there!" Rarely have I felt like more of a complete idiot.

"You usually find light switches near the door," he said in a teasing tone.

It was clearly time to change the subject. "So what are you doing back here anyway?"

"Mr. G said you might need some help moving stuff," Kyle said.

"That was thoughtful of him."

Kyle moved things out of the way so I could look for old costumes. There's something wonderful about being near an attractive male who is moving heavy objects. You can almost feel his strength. Kyle was wearing a T-shirt and I watched his arm muscles flex and unflex. I couldn't help thinking how wonderful it would be if someone came along and turned off the light and closed the door . . . and then Kyle took me in his arms.

KYLE

I was watching an international kite-flying competition on the tube when Jackie came into the den.

"Can we talk?"

Uh-oh. Sounded like trouble. I lowered the volume with the remote. Jackie sat down with this little plastic walkie talkie she carries around so she can listen in on IT while he's napping in his crib.

"I've never had a teenaged stepson before," she said, nervously twisting a hair band in her fingers. "But I think it's time we talked, Kyle. I'm very upset about what happened with Jake. I feel that what you did was a hostile act that was really directed at me. . . . Can you see that?"

I'm not big on all this psychology stuff, but for the sake of avoiding an argument I sort of tipped my head up and down to indicate "yes."

"Honestly, Kyle, I've tried very hard to make

this work, but I don't feel that you're trying at all. In fact, all I feel from you is hostility. You constantly avoid me, you won't talk, you've made it clear I'm not to enter your room."

I sort of shrugged "Could be."

"I've talked this over with your father. He's agreed that maybe you and I should go see someone together."

"You mean a shrink?" I asked. "You and me?"

"It's called family counseling."

Who cared what it was called? She may have been married to my father, but I've never spent more than five minutes alone with her.

"Let's wait a day and see what happens," I said.

Jackie's jaw dropped. Then she gave me a knowing smirk. "Couldn't you come up with something a little more original?"

BO

I arrived at the auditorium early for rehearsals today.

Once again I've reached that point in the production where it feels like I spend more time in this approximation of a theater than I do in my own home. I was walking across the stage when I heard someone clear his throat.

"Ahem."

I looked up. Bobby and Alice were sitting on the catwalk.

"Look who's here," Bobby said.

"I remember her," said Alice.

"She probably doesn't remember us," said Bobby.

"What do you expect?" Alice asked. "She's a redhead now."

"Auburn," I said.

"Notice her new attitude?" Alice said.

"Reminds me of Chloe," said Bobby.

"I thought she hated Chloe," said Alice.

"That was before," said Bobby. "Now they're best friends."

"Wrong," I said.

"She says we're wrong," Bobby said.

"I hope so," said Alice. "Because Chloe Frost becomes friends with people so she can use them to get what she wants."

"What could she possibly want from Bo?" Bobby asked with feigned innocence.

"She wants to make *Anne Frank* the best production this school's ever seen," I said.

"How noble!" Alice gasped.

"How selfless!" cried Bobby.

"How amazingly bogus," Alice grumbled.

"It's not," I said. "It's true."

"She says it's true," said Bobby.

My neck was starting to ache from looking up at them.

"How's Kyle?" Alice asked.

"Okay, I guess."

"Notice she acts like she hardly knows him?" Bobby said.

"That's true," I said.

"Didn't you tell me you were in love?" Alice asked.

"All Kyle and I do is talk," I said.

"Think Chloe's noticed?" Bobby asked.

"That girl doesn't miss a trick," said Alice.

"You don't think Chloe's gotten friendly with Bo so that she can keep tabs on what's going on with Kyle, do you?" Bobby asked.

"That's absurd," I said.

"She says it's absurd," Alice said.

"If Chloe thought there was anything between Kyle and me she'd do just the opposite," I said, rubbing my neck. "She'd hate me."

"Not Chloe," said Alice.

"She's too smart," said Bobby.

"All right," I said. "Can I ask *you guys* a question?"

"What do you think?" Bobby asked Alice.

"Let's hear it, then decide," Alice replied.

"What does Chloe Frost see in Kyle Winthrop?" I asked.

"I think the more interesting question is, what do *you* see in him, Bo," answered Bobby.

"No fair," I said. "I asked first."

"She's right." Alice gave in. "Okay, here's what I think. Chloe Frost has to be the best at whatever she does. And that includes having boyfriends. When Kyle Winthrop was captain of the football team, he was the best boyfriend a girl could have, so Chloe had to have him."

"You really think she's that shallow?" I asked.

"Deep down we're all that shallow," Bobby said.

"Ha-ha," I said.

"Maybe not shallow," Alice said. "Driven. I don't think she can help herself."

"And now that Kyle's not captain of the football team?" I asked.

"Chloe's facing a dilemma," Bobby said. "It's been apparent to Chloe watchers lately that she's really not interested in him anymore. But at the same time, she can't face the idea that he was simply a possession. She doesn't want to believe that she's that superficial."

"Deep down we're all that superficial," Alice said.

"Do I hear an echo?" asked Bobby.

"Then what's going to happen?" I asked. Despite the rubbing, my neck continued to throb.

"Bo's asking us to predict," Alice said.

"Sorry, we're not prognosticators," Bobby said.

"Oh, go on." Alice nudged him. "Take a wild guess."

"You sure?" Bobby asked.

"Why not?"

"Okay, here's a possible scenario," Bobby said. "Chloe and Kyle break up; Kyle finds another girlfriend; Chloe starts dating a guy from college; neither talks to Bo again."

"What do you think of that?" Alice asked, looking down at me.

"I think talking to you guys is getting to be a real pain in the neck," I said.

KYLE

I was standing in the kitchen this morning, eating out of a box of strawberry Post Toasties, when IT waddled in clutching a disposable plastic razor with the cover off.

"Wha dis?" he asked, holding it up.

I had this vision of him trying to imitate me or my father shaving, except IT would probably lop off an entire layer of skin and maybe some baby fat, too.

So I bent down, grabbed his pudgy little wrist, and started to twist the razor out of his hand. "It's a razor," I said. "Not for little kids. Very, very dangerous. Understand?"

"Mine!" IT clenched the razor with all his might, like he wasn't going to let go unless I chopped his hand off.

"You have to give it to me," I said.

"Mine, mine!" he shouted again as I slowly pried the razor out of his grip. I couldn't believe how strong the kid was.

"You can't play with it." I finally got the razor out of his hand. I figured he'd go bawling to Jackie and make a real stink. But instead of crying, he just stared up at me with this amazed look on his face, as if he'd never heard my voice before. And I was looking down at this drooling toothless wonder and thinking what a tough, stubborn little guy he was.

And then it struck me. This is my half brother. Maybe it's not so surprising.

BO

Last night the phone rang. My heart leapt into my throat. Was it Kyle? Calling to arrange a secret tryst? I raced to the phone and answered it with a breathless, "Hello?"

"Uh, hi, Bo."

It wasn't Kyle. "Who is this?" I asked.

"Uh, it's Karl."

"Karl?" For a moment the name meant nothing.

"Yeah, Karl, your friendly techie and AV dude."

The memory of that afternoon in the prop closet bounced back like a bad check. He said he'd call.

"Oh, God, Karl," I gasped. "You really caught me at a bad time. I'll have to call you back later."

I hung up, depressed.

KYLE

More news about Jeff Branco. Turns out his girl-friend went to a school across town called Portswell High. About two months ago she was sent to Fairview after she got into a razor fight with another girl and cut her up pretty bad. Sounds like a sweet kid, huh?

According to the paper, the reason Jeff broke into Fairview was to give her a present. The police said they found a jewelry box in his pocket and inside was an expensive solid gold heart-shaped locket with a picture of him.

I bet that's why Jeff was selling pizza in the boys' room. He was saving up money for that gold locket. I kind of wish I'd known Jeff Branco better. I mean, I always thought he was just your average run-of-the-mill headcase. Now it's obvious the kid has depth.

BO

I feel like singing! On Saturday night I went to Kyle's house to baby-sit. Jackie said Jake had taken a long nap that afternoon and would probably stay up late. I wasn't thrilled by the news. I'd rented *A Star Is Born* with Judy Garland, but it appeared that I'd be watching reruns of *Sesame Street* instead.

Just as Jake and I settled in front of the television, I heard footsteps coming down the stairs. For a moment I was terrified that someone had broken in through an upstairs window, but then Kyle appeared.

"Hi," he said.

"Hi," I said, noticing that he was wearing navy blue sweatpants and a white sweatshirt, not exactly the clothes he wore for dates with Chloe.

"Did they leave?" he asked.

"About five minutes ago."

"Jackie didn't say anything about dinner, did she?"

"Not to me."

Just then Jake pointed at the TV and said, "Wha dis?"

Both Kyle and I looked. It was a *Sesame Street* segment on pizza, and we watched the man on the screen toss the dough in the air and catch it, then spread the tomato sauce and cheese on it.

"It's pizza," Kyle said.

"Peet," Jake said.

"Hey, Jake," Kyle said. "How'd you like to see a pizza in real life?"

Jake looked at him with the cutest little confused expression on his face. I suspect I looked somewhat confused, too, since it was probably the first time I'd ever seen Kyle talk to his half brother.

"What do you say we go to the mall and have some real pizza?" Kyle said.

"You're going to take Jake?" I asked, surprised.

"Sure, why not?"

"Should I wait here until you get back?" I asked.

Now it was Kyle's turn to look confused. "Of course not," he said. "We'll all go."

Does that qualify as a date?

◇   ◇   ◇

Please don't laugh. But pushing Jake in the stroller with Kyle by my side was like . . . well, it was like being married.

Sure, sure, I know I have an active fantasy

life, but still, Kyle did take us for pizza and we did cut a slice into tiny pieces to feed to Jake, who managed to smear red sauce over 90 percent of his face. Then Kyle decided to get his car cleaned so we accompanied him to the car wash. I didn't mind. I would've gone anywhere with him.

I kept thinking what a scandal it would be if anyone we knew from school saw us, but no one did. Of course I was dying to ask him where Chloe was. But I didn't. At least not until we got back to his house. By then Jake had fallen asleep so I changed his diaper and put him in the crib. Meanwhile Kyle made a big bowl of popcorn. Then we met in the den.

"Can I show you something?" he asked.

"Uh, sure," I said, a little uncertainly, wondering what he had in mind.

Kyle turned on the TV and slid a cassette into the VCR. The next thing I knew, I was looking at something resembling roast beef on a white bread roll underwater. A tiny worm-like thing was gnawing away at the roast beef, and little flecks of red quickly floated away with the current.

"What is this?" I asked.

"My knee," Kyle said.

"Excuse me?"

"That's the inside of my knee."

"Huh? How?"

"Arthroscopic surgery," Kyle explained.

"They use a little TV camera to look inside the knee. The surgeon watches the whole thing on a monitor while he works with these tiny instruments."

"But the water …"

"That's how he can see. They flush the knee with sterile water."

"What's the ragged red stuff?"

"Torn cartilage," Kyle said, munching on a handful of popcorn. "He's cutting it away. In a second he's gonna get to the ligament."

He offered me some popcorn.

"Uh, no thanks," I said.

"You're not grossed out, are you?"

"Not exactly."

"I can turn it off."

"Has Chloe ever seen this?" I asked.

"She wouldn't watch."

"Leave it on," I said.

◇   ◇   ◇

Around midnight Brian and Jackie came home.

"Okay, Bo, get your coat," Brian said.

Then Kyle said, "I'll drive her."

I couldn't believe it. I kept thinking, *This isn't happening to me. It's happening to someone else.*

Kyle and I went out to his car and got in.

"Can I ask you a question?" I said.

"Okay."

"Do you show that tape to a lot of people?"

"No."

"Was there some reason why you wanted me to see it?"

Kyle gave one of his characteristic shrugs. "I don't know. I just thought you could appreciate it."

A little while later he pulled into my driveway. I wished I lived six hundred miles away instead of six blocks so we could have spent all night in the car just driving and talking. I looked through the windshield and saw the curtain in the living room move slightly.

"I think someone's watching us," Kyle said.

"My mom."

"Guess you better go in."

I felt my heart sink, but he was right.

"Well, thanks. I had fun tonight," I said.

"Me, too."

I waited for a second longer, just in case. But nothing happened. I reached for the door handle.

"Bo?" Kyle said.

"Yes?"

"Do I really suck as an actor?"

I knew it must have taken a lot of courage for him to ask that. "No. And the more you rehearse, the better you'll get."

"We've been rehearsing for nearly two months," he said.

He was right. We sat in the car, in the shadows cast by the street light. Kyle was asking me to be honest. How can you be honest with someone you're madly, passionately in love with?

I decided to take a chance. His right hand was resting on the seat between us and I slid my hand over it. Kyle looked down at our hands and then up at me. He didn't try to pull his hand away.

"You're five times better than you were two months ago," I said. "You're comfortable with the material now. You know what to do. I can't tell you that you'll win an Academy Award someday, Kyle, but you'll do fine in this play."

"Promise?"

"Promise." I squeezed his hand, and couldn't believe what a liar I'd become.

KYLE

Today in Pinhead homeroom Mr. Orillio wrote a
message in big letters on the blackboard:

CHANGE YOUR ATTITUDE
TO GRATITUDE

It reminded me that I'm a seventeen-year-old
has-been. Then I thought about Peter Van Daan,
who probably would have been a never-was if it
hadn't been for Anne Frank. A lot of people in
Europe during World War II never even got to be
has-beens just because they were in the wrong
place at the wrong time.

I guess I'm supposed to feel lucky that I'm
alive, and well fed, and a free person living in the
United States, instead of starving under some dic-
tatorship in Africa or someplace.

But sometimes it's hard to feel that way.
Especially when you're seventeen, and you've
destroyed your knee and you can't do the one
thing you really love.

Sometimes I just feel like life sucks.

Then I catch myself and wonder what good being bummed out does?

Guess I'm trying to change my attitude.

BO

Bobby and I made the rounds with the recycling cart again today.

"If I talk about Kyle, will it make you angry?" I asked.

"Probably."

"Please, Bobby, I have to talk to *someone*."

"Oh, all right."

"I think it's getting serious," I said.

Bobby studied me for a second. "Why?"

"He let me watch the tape of his knee operation."

"What?"

I explained about the tiny camera going inside Kyle's knee.

"So why does that make it serious?" Bobby asked.

"He gave me a glimpse of what's inside."

Bobby stopped the cart. "Bo, are you feeling okay?"

"Giddy."

"I'll say."

"Wait, it gets stranger. I feel like Chloe and I are really becoming friendly."

"I wouldn't count on being friendly with her for too long," Bobby warned.

"I know," I said. "But isn't it fascinating? I mean, who could have imagined Kyle, Chloe, and I, thrown together in a complex triangle of human emotions?"

"You've been watching too many soap operas," Bobby said, and started pulling the cart again.

The funny thing is I don't watch any. Who needs to watch when you're living one?

KYLE

Mr. Orillio was taking attendance when the door opened and Jeff Branco stepped in. I almost didn't recognize him. He was wearing a new pair of jeans and a fresh blue shirt. The bandanna and black leather vest were gone.

We all stood up and applauded.

"All right, Jeff!"

"Way to go, dude!"

"Welcome back, dirtbag."

Mr. Orillio even shook Jeff's hand. "Jeff, I don't usually condone acts of criminality, but I wanted to congratulate you on the sheer originality of your plan. You may be the first person in history to actually break *into* prison just to give your girlfriend her birthday present."

The Rat raised his hand. "Can we ask questions, Mr. O?"

"It's up to Jeff," Mr. Orillio said. Jeff said okay. Next thing we knew, it was show-and-tell.

The Rat went first. "What's your current legal status?"

"I'm out on bail," Jeff explained. "I would've come back sooner, but the lawyer put me in this mental hospital so I could see some shrinks. He said it'll help get me a reduced sentence."

"How come you didn't just wait until visiting hours to see your girlfriend?" Lukowsky asked.

"See, that's where the newspapers really screwed up," Jeff said. "I didn't break into Fairview just because it was Mindy's birthday. It was because it was her birthday and her stupid parents told the 'authorities' I wasn't allowed to see her no more."

"Why not?" Peter asked.

"They said I was a bad influence," Jeff said. "I mean, their daughter slices some other chick into Wonder Bread, and they think *I'm* the bad influence?"

Go figure.

BO

Today was Set Day—the day everyone pitches in and finishes painting and building the set. And that meant I'd be working shoulder to shoulder with The Letch, who was probably wondering why I'd never returned his call. So I went down to the AV room.

A gremlin wearing thick glasses and a Jimi Hendrix T-shirt opened the door. The room was filled with loud Grateful Dead music and body odor. "A lady! Please come in."

"I came to talk to Karl," I said, hesitating before I entered. "Is everyone decent?"

"I think so," said the gremlin. "Hey! Turn down the music, phlegmwads. There's a lady here to see Karl."

A few moments later Karl appeared from behind the gray metal shelves. He didn't look happy to see me.

"What's up, Bo?"

I held out my hand. "Can we just be friends?"

The Letch looked at my hand and then at me. "That's all?"

"Sorry."

The Letch looked disappointed, but he shook my hand anyway.

"Thanks," I said, grateful that he understood. For an instant I considered kissing him on the cheek . . . but then I thought better of it.

◇   ◇   ◇

Later we all got together and finished the set. Chloe always finds a way to avoid getting her hands dirty, and today was no exception. She said she wasn't feeling well and went home.

By 9 P.M. the set was finished and everyone had started to leave. Soon, only Bobby, Alice, Mr. Goodrich, Kyle, and I were left.

"Need a ride?" Bobby asked from the aisle.

I was sitting on the edge of the stage, making some changes in the cue notes. "Go ahead," I said. "I still have some things to do."

"It's late, Bo," Bobby said. "How are you going to—"

He didn't finish the sentence. I turned around and saw that Kyle had just come out from backstage, carrying a paint bucket and some brushes.

Bobby forced a weak smile onto his face. "I get it, Bo. Don't do anything I wouldn't do." Then he turned and left.

I watched him go and then looked back at Kyle. "Almost finished?"

"I just want to wash these brushes out in the sink," he said, and headed toward the janitor's room.

No sooner had he left, then Mr. Goodrich appeared.

"I guess that's it, Bo," he said. "Ready to go?"

"Kyle's in the janitor's room," I said.

Mr. Goodrich looked at his watch and frowned. "I told Dory I'd be home half an hour ago."

"Go ahead," I said. "I'll lock up." As stage manager I was one of the few students in school allowed to have a key.

"Well, all right, don't stay too late."

Mr. Goodrich walked up the aisle and through the auditorium doors. Suddenly, it was very quiet. The only sound was water splashing in the sink of the janitor's room as Kyle washed the brushes.

I took a deep breath and let it out slowly. My heart was drumming. I was about to do something I'd never done before. I was tired of waiting for Kyle to make the first move. Tonight I was going to force the issue.

The sound of splashing water stopped. A door creaked. I could hear the faintest pad of tennis shoes on the floor. My heart was racing even faster than before and my throat felt tight. *Don't chicken out, I told myself. You have a right to know what he's thinking.*

Kyle came through the door and walked along the auditorium floor in front of the stage.

"I left the brushes in the greenroom to dry," he said. He stopped and looked around. "Where is everyone?"

"They've gone."

Kyle stopped a few feet from me and leaned his elbow on the stage. "What a day, huh?"

"It seemed like it would never end," I said.

"Kind of scary," Kyle said.

"Why?"

"The set's done. Rehearsals are almost over. Dress rehearsals start next week. I mean, this whole thing is real. It's really gonna happen."

"You'll be fine, Kyle."

Kyle smiled. "How come you always know what I'm thinking?"

Could you ask for a better opening?

I slid over until I was close to him. "Maybe we're on the same wavelength."

We were barely inches apart now. Kyle looked up into my eyes. Searchingly? I wondered. Was he realizing that I could give him the love and devotion Chloe was too busy to spare?

"Bo, I—" he started to say.

"Don't," I said, leaning toward him.

I closed my eyes and kissed him on the lips. I thought it was the bravest thing I'd ever done.

It wasn't a long kiss. When I opened my eyes, Kyle was staring past me at something. I turned my head and saw the silhouette of someone standing in the doorway at the far end of the auditorium.

She backed away and let the door swing closed.

"Chloe!" Kyle shouted.

The next thing I knew, he ran up the aisle and out the auditorium door.

◇   ◇   ◇

I don't know how long I sat there. I don't know if I really believed Kyle would come back for me. After a while the auditorium door did open. Bobby stuck his head in.

"Bo? You okay?"

I knew if I answered, I'd burst into tears. So I just shook my head.

"I called your house and your mom said you weren't home yet," Bobby said, stepping into the auditorium. "Want a ride?"

I slid off the stage and started to walk up the aisle. Bobby held the door open for me.

"Aren't we supposed to lock it?" he asked as we went out the front door.

I handed him the key and Bobby did the honors.

Then we went to his car and he drove me home.

Neither of us said a word until he stopped in my driveway. I felt tears falling out of my eyes, but I wasn't blubbering.

"How did you know I was there?" I asked with a sniff. "I mean, how did you know I wasn't off parking somewhere with Kyle locked in a passionate embrace?"

"Don't do this to yourself," Bobby said softly.

I glared at him, but the anger melted away. It wasn't his fault.

"Can you take me someplace?" I asked.

"Not Kyle's, I hope."

"No. 7-Eleven."

KYLE

All this time I thought Bo was just being friendly. Like we were teammates on the theater team. I mean, sure we had some nice talks, and we took IT out for pizza that night, but I didn't think I was leading her on in any way. Unless she thought watching my knee operation was a romantic come on.

I felt crummy. I mean, Bo was the one person in the play I could be comfortable and relaxed with. *Whoa!* you're probably thinking, what about Chloe?

You think I could feel comfortable and relaxed with her?

Give me a break.

So here's a question for you philosophers out there: What is love? Is love selling pizza in the boys' room so you can buy a gold locket for your girlfriend? Is it breaking into a girls' house of detention to give it to her? Or is it being with someone just so you know you'll always have a date on Saturday night?

BO

I was sitting on the catwalk, scarfing down a box of Ring Dings, when I heard footsteps.

"Is she back there?" Alice asked.

"No," replied Bobby. "Check out front."

Alice walked directly beneath me and peered out into the empty auditorium. "Not there either."

She was joined by a head full of gorgeous blond dreadlocks. "I know she came to school this morning."

I ripped open a new Ring Ding. Alice and Bobby both looked up.

"Home sweet home," said Bobby.

"I feel like I never left," I said.

"Chloe quit, you know," said Alice.

"What!?" I looked down at them in utter disbelief.

"She walked into Mr. G's room this morning and resigned."

"Why?" I asked.

"We thought you'd know."

"Did something happen last night?" Alice asked.

"She won," I said.

Alice gave me a puzzled look. "Does this have something to do with Kyle?"

My eyes met Bobby's. "I didn't know if you wanted me to tell her," he said.

"Everything," I said.

A door squeaked and I heard heavier footsteps. Mr. Goodrich stepped onto the stage and looked up at me. "I thought you'd given up the catwalk."

"It was only a temporary thing."

"What are we going to do?" he asked.

"Beth Villeta's her understudy," I said.

Mr. Goodrich crossed his arms and tried to look stern. "I want you to talk to Chloe, Bo."

"Why me?"

"Because you've been the closest to her this last month. Try to change her mind."

"This ought to be good," Bobby muttered.

"What?" Mr. Goodrich asked, puzzled.

"Chloe and I have had, er, a personal difference," I said.

"More like a personal similarity, if you ask me," quipped Alice.

"No one asked you," I said.

"This is shaping up to be a disaster," Mr. Goodrich groaned.

"Maybe," I said. "But the show must go on."

KYLE

The girl who played Meip is now playing Anne. Maybe I'm not the worst actor in the group anymore. Actually, I'm probably still the worst, but at least I know my lines. Not being the worst doesn't make me feel any better, though. We all know the play is no good without Chloe.

I tried to talk to her that night after she saw Bo and me in the auditorium, but it was no use. She didn't want to listen.

All she said was, "I wish you still played football."

BO

We had the first run-through today. It was death. I've never seen a more depressed group of people. Beth Villeta was incredibly courageous, stepping into the Anne part just four days before the preview. But it's hopeless. There simply isn't enough time to learn the lead role.

After the run-through, Bobby, Alice, and I sat in the front row of the auditorium, staring at the stage.

"It's a beautiful set," I said sadly.

"Thanks," said Bobby. "Your suggestions really helped. It took a lot of extra work, but it was worth it."

"*Would have been* worth it," Alice corrected him.

"Anyway, they were mostly Chloe's ideas," I said.

"I hate to say this," Bobby said with regret, "but I really do think she made us better than we thought we could be."

"I think back to all those productions where Chloe drove us crazy," I said. "All those times I prayed she'd fall off the stage and break both legs. Now she's quit and it's a nightmare."

Alice slumped down in her seat. "She's just being spiteful."

"I think she feels betrayed," I said. "She tried so hard, and all we did was snake her boyfriend."

"What's this *we* stuff?" Alice asked.

"She's right, Bo," Bobby said.

They were both staring at me. I shrank down in my seat. "Okay, so I made a mistake. What can I do about it now?"

"Make it right," Bobby said.

KYLE

I came out of the lunch line and headed for the team table. Alex Gidden and Jason Rooney were already there.

"Where's Eddie?" I asked as I put down my tray.

Alex pointed over to the window. Eddie was sitting by himself in the corner, hunched over with his head in his hands. "What's goin' on?" I asked.

"The big enchilada went bye-bye," Jason said.

"Nothing?" It was hard to believe no school had offered him a scholarship.

"Zippo. Nada."

I went over and sat down next to him. He glanced at me and stared back down at the floor. Not even a "Hi, bro."

"It sucks, man," I said.

Eddie's head bobbed up and down. "Tell me about it. Not one lousy offer. Not even from one of those cheesy division three schools in the Midwest."

"Are you sure you've heard from everyone?"

"Yeah."

"It doesn't make sense, man. Someone was going to take you. All those scouts who came to watch. They wouldn't have wasted their time."

"A couple called," Eddie said. "They said I came real close and they were sorry."

Eddie and I both stared at the floor.

"It was gonna be you and me, man," he said sadly. "We were the stars. We were gonna bite the big enchilada, get the four-year rides. Now look at us. A couple of losers."

I winced. The word stung. Not me, I thought. I'm not a loser.

"What're you gonna do?" I asked.

"Who knows?" Eddie chewed on his thumb. "Get a job, go to some community college. . . . It doesn't matter. I'm off the pro track. Wherever I go, no one's gonna see me. No one's gonna scout me. It's over. The whole thing was a bust, a total waste."

"Hey, we had some great times." I tried to cheer him up.

Eddie glanced at me angrily. "Who gives a crap?"

"I'm just saying it wasn't a total waste," I said. "We were out there. We were *feared*. Maybe it's over now, but we'll always have that. I mean, we'll always know we once ruled."

Eddie gazed up at me with this look of disbelief on his face. "What are you talking about?"

"I'm talking about what we were. We were it. Better to be a has-been than a never-was."

"Get lost," he mumbled.

"I'm serious."

"I said, get lost!" Eddie gave me a shove.

I got to my feet and almost hit him, but I knew it was dumb. Eddie glanced at me and growled, "Go do your stupid play."

I wanted to tell him that it might have been stupid, but it sure beat wallowing in self pity. Instead I went back to the table.

Alex looked up at me. "Eddie's really bummed."

"It's like his whole life is down the tubes," said Jason.

The other guys nodded in agreement. They were all sitting there with their shoulders sagging and their heads down. Suddenly I felt like I was at a funeral. Did someone die?

"What are you guys talking about?" I asked. "It's only football."

They looked at me with shocked expressions on their faces like I'd broken some religious taboo or something.

Next thing I knew, I picked up my tray and

walked away, not even sure where I was going. I stopped in the middle of the cafeteria, and looked around for a place to sit.

"Yo, Kyle!" Someone waved from the table right in front of me. It was Lukowsky. The Rat, Branco, and some of the other Pinheads were all watching.

"Lookin' for a place to sit?" Lukowsky asked.

"Shut up," The Rat snapped at him. "You know he ain't gonna sit with us."

Lukowsky stared down at his lunch, and the other guys looked away. *The Undesirables . . .*

Think about it . . .

"Make room, you goofballs." I sat down.

BO

It's funny how I knew exactly where to find Chloe between classes. She was hiding in a stall in the girls' room. As I stood staring at her Weejuns under the stall wall, I kept thinking, *Why does Chloe need to hide?*

The bell rang and the girls' room cleared out. I waited by the mirror. Finally the stall door opened. Chloe stepped out and froze. Then she gathered herself together and started to go past me.

"I think we should talk," I said, positioning myself between her and the door.

"There's nothing to talk about."

"There's lots to talk about."

"Please get out of my way."

"No."

Chloe glared at me. "So, in addition to changing our hair and losing weight, we're now taking assertiveness training? I should have guessed. How else would you have gotten up the nerve to try to steal my boyfriend?"

"I didn't try to steal him."

"Oh, please." Chloe rolled her eyes in fine dramatic tradition.

"At least, not consciously," I said. "And anyway, it doesn't really seem like you want him anymore."

Except for the hissing of steam from the radiator, the bathroom became quiet. The bell had rung and in classrooms all around us our fellow students were facing another forty-two minutes of torture. Meanwhile, Chloe and I dawdled in the aromatic netherworld of the girls' room.

"Everything's so complicated." Chloe's shoulders slumped. She checked her Swatch. "Oh, God, I'm late!"

"What's your next class?" I asked.

"Calculus."

"Skip it?"

Chloe's eyes widened. "Bo, I've never . . ."

"Then it's about time."

❖   ❖   ❖

We wound up sitting on the catwalk with our feet hanging in the air and our arms resting on the low railing. Chloe was uncharacteristically quiet.

"Ring Ding?" I offered her one of my chocolate-covered delicacies.

Chloe unwrapped it and took a small bite. "I

hate it," she said with a dainty sigh.

"The Ring Ding?" I asked.

"No, everything else. You'll never believe this, Bo, but I *despise* competition."

"You're right, I'll never believe it."

"The only thing I hate worse is losing."

"*That* I believe."

Chloe took another bite and licked a little piece of chocolate off her glossy lips. "Competing is simply the lesser of two evils. I've never joined a team. All my activities are noncompetitive."

"You always have to be the best," I said.

"Is that really so bad?"

"No. It's . . . just that sometimes, it seems a little . . . compulsive."

Chloe studied her perfectly manicured fingernails. "My father's a plastic surgeon. No one wants a 'just okay' nose job. Everyone wants the perfect nose. There's no room for anything less."

"Why did you quit the play?" I asked.

"I'm not going to compete with you for Kyle," Chloe said.

"But that has nothing to do with the play."

Chloe's eyes widened. "It has everything to do with it."

I knew it was my turn to spill the beans. "All Kyle and I did was talk. I mean, I think he likes to talk to me, and I like to listen because I have a crush on him. He needs encouragement, Chloe.

He wanted someone to watch his knee operation, so I watched it."

"I saw you kiss," Chloe said.

"You saw me kissing Kyle," I said. "It was sort of impulsive. I think he was just as surprised as you. Believe me, Chloe, there's really nothing going on between us. I wish there was, but there isn't."

"That makes two of us," Chloe said with a sigh.

I glanced at her. "Can I ask what the story is?"

Chloe raised her hands and let them fall. "We really liked each other once. Maybe it was even love. Then . . . I don't know."

"He hurt his knee?"

"It started to change before that," she said. "I think we both felt like we were supposed to be together. Like everyone expected it. I think we forgot why we'd gotten together in the first place."

"Do you remember now?" I asked.

Chloe suddenly smiled. "Oh, come on, Bo. He's a hunk, why else?"

"Are you serious?"

"Half-serious. It's not only because he was handsome and on the football team. He was funny and sweet, too."

"And no competition for you academically," I guessed.

"Right. But now . . . it's like a doll you cherish, but don't want to play with anymore." She turned to me quickly. "Promise you won't quote me."

"I won't . . . But you can't keep him on a shelf."

"I know."

"Everyone wants you to come back to the play," I said. "Including me."

"Why?"

"God, Chloe, do you have to ask?"

"I thought I was a big pain. I'm obnoxious and demanding and by opening night everyone hates me."

"True. Is that why you never come to cast parties?"

I took her silence as an affirmation.

"Well, I'll let you in on a secret," I said. "You make us look better than we are, and deep down after we all get finished hating you, we appreciate it."

"And what about Kyle?" she asked.

"Your guess is as good as mine."

KYLE

It gets hot under the lights. You sweat. It's not just the heat. It's nerves. They were all out there: the Pinheads, Mr. Orillio, your dad, your stepmom, even IT, sitting in Jackie's lap chewing on his rag because Bo's the stage manager and Jackie wouldn't trust any other baby-sitter with him.

So you do your best and you mangle a line here and there, but you know the story so well that you can talk your way through each flub and get back on track. It's kind of like holding a one-point lead with five minutes to go. If you can just get through it, if you just don't do anything really stupid, you'll be okay.

Then it's over, and somehow you did it. The curtain goes down and for the first time in an hour and a half, the audience can't see you. You take a deep breath and want to shout or scream or tear off your clothes and run around naked, but you have to do one last thing first.

BO

The curtain had just come down. The actors and actresses were wandering around backstage with dazed expressions, and every time they intersected with another actor they'd hug, even though normally they might have hated each other's guts.

"It wasn't half-bad," Ben McGillis muttered and walked around in circles. "Not half-bad."

Alice trudged toward me with her head bowed. "I was awful."

"You were the best." I hugged her.

"You're just saying that."

"You're the only one among us with even a remote chance of a future in this business."

"You really mean it?" She looked up and actually smiled.

"Cross my heart and hope to die." Over her shoulder I watched Kyle and Chloe exchange awkward little smiles. They didn't say anything to each other. They didn't hug. After a brief, uncomfortable moment, they both turned away.

That was over, too.

"Bows, everyone!" Mr. Goodrich whispered hoarsely.

From my spot in the wings I watched them all line up. For a lot of them, it was the last curtain call of their high school careers, maybe their last curtain call ever.

The curtain went up and the crowd started clapping and cheering. Kyle, Chloe, Alice, and the others stood out there in the spotlights, basking in the adulation. Then Alice and Howie Tardibono ran offstage and dragged Mr. Goodrich out and the cheering surged again. They all deserved it. They'd all worked incredibly hard.

Then Chloe backed out of the line and hurried toward me.

"Get back out there!" I whispered, waving her back. "They're still applauding."

"I know." Chloe grabbed my wrist, then started to pull.

"What are you doing!?" I gasped.

"Getting you what you deserve," she said, pulling me out toward the stage.

I pulled back. "You're crazy! I can't! I'm dressed like a janitor. My hair's not even brushed!"

"Go on, Bo," Bobby said, joining Chloe and

pushing from behind.

Suddenly I was standing in the glare of the lights, facing the crowd. Chloe was still holding my wrist.

"Our stage manager!" she shouted to the audience.

The applause surged. And what was really sweet was that Mr. Goodrich and the actors and actresses all turned and applauded, too.

For that one moment, they were all cheering . . . for me.

Finally.

KYLE

After the show I came out of the greenroom and found Eddie in the hall.

"Pretty good, bro." He held up his hand for a high five.

"You were out there?" I asked, surprised.

"Sure, why not?" He started to chew on his thumb. "Look, Kyle, about what I said the other day—"

"Hey, don't sweat it." I patted him on the shoulder. "I know how you felt. You had a right to be pissed."

Eddie gave me a curious look. "So, you gonna make a career of this?"

"Nah, it was just something to do."

"What're you gonna do next?"

"Go to the cast party. Want to come?"

"That's not what I meant," Eddie said as we started down the hall. "What I meant was—"

"I know what you meant," I cut him off. "I

guess the first thing I'm gonna do is get off Mr. Orillio's most-likely-to-screw-up list. After that, I'm open for suggestions."

"Maybe we could get into something together," Eddie said. "Like plan something for this spring."

"Sounds good."

BO

Kyle brought his friend Eddie to the cast party at Bobby's house and they sat around in the kitchen talking about sports. I waited until Eddie went to the bathroom and then went up to Kyle.

"Can we talk?" I asked.

"Uh, okay."

"Not here," I said. "Let's go outside."

We went out the sliding glass doors to the patio. It was cold and dark and our breaths curled up in white plumes in the moonlight.

"I guess you know how I feel," I said.

He nodded and didn't say anything. I'd been praying it would be different, that he'd sweep me into his arms and tell me he loved me now and forever. But reality set in. I can't say I was surprised.

"I guess I know how you feel," I said.

"It's not you, Bo," he said. "I mean, I've been with Chloe for so long. I'm still trying to figure it all out."

"Maybe once you've had some time . . ." I hated myself for saying it, but hope springs eternal.

"Maybe." Kyle tried to smile, but he knew and I knew it wasn't to be.

For a second I thought I'd burst into tears.

But then I got hold of myself.

Like Alice says, they're just guys.

◇　◇　◇

Chloe didn't come to the cast party, so I got Kyle's friend Eddie to give me a ride to her house. Eddie isn't quite as tall as Kyle and his shoulders aren't as broad. To be honest, he isn't as handsome, but he certainly is good-looking. And he has a nice smile.

"You're the stage manager, right?" he said as he drove.

"I was. Now that the play's over, I'm just Bo. You're the quarterback."

"I was. Now that the season's over, I'm just Eddie."

We smiled at each other.

When you think about it, it's really amazing how many similarities there are between quarter-backing and stage-managing. You both basically run the team.

"Here we are," he said, pulling into her driveway.

"Thanks for the ride," I said and started to get out.

"Uh, Bo?" Eddie said.

"Yes?"

"Think you'll be back at the cast party later?"

"I don't know."

Eddie looked a little disappointed.

"But if I'm not, I'll see you at school," I added.

Eddie smiled. "Great."

I went up the walk and rang the bell. Chloe answered the door holding the portable phone to her ear. She looked surprised.

"Bo, why aren't you at the cast party?"

"I wanted to see you."

"Hold on a second." She turned away and finished her phone conversation. "You'll never guess who that was."

"Who?"

"Morgan Landon. He directs the community theater."

"Really?"

"He was in the audience tonight. He just called to tell me they're doing *Bye-Bye Birdie* this spring. He wants me to try out."

"Serious?" I gasped.

Chloe nodded and her eyes sparkled with excitement.

"Hey, wait a minute," I said. "Lots of people try out for those parts. They get college kids, even semiprofessional actors. You'll be up against some real talent."

"So?"

"Competition, remember?" I said.

"I'll try if you'll try," Chloe said.

"Me, act?"

"No, silly. Assistant stage manager."

"Assistant stage manager for the community theater," I mumbled. "I like the sound of that."

"Got the playbook?"

"Somewhere in my room," I said.

"Let's go get it."

"Now?"

"Sure. Why not? And then we'll go out for no-fat frozen yogurt."

"Fabulous," I said, then hesitated. "Only . . ."

"What's wrong?" Chloe asked.

"Alice. I really think she should try out for the play, too."

"Okay, just as long as she and I agree not to try out for the same part," Chloe said.

"Deal." We headed for her car. The future looked rosy, exciting and unpredictable.

KYLE

Jake was up half the night crying. Around 3 a.m. I think I heard Jackie say something about him cutting molars, but I could've been dreaming. This morning I got up and went into the kitchen. Jake was sitting in his high chair, sucking on a bottle. Jackie was standing at the kitchen counter making a cup of coffee. She was wearing her pink robe with a big white stain of baby cheese on the shoulder. Her hair was snarled and uncombed, her eyes looked puffy and ringed.

"Want some breakfast, Kyle?" she asked.

"I'll get it," I said. I mean, it doesn't take a lot of work to pour a glass of orange juice and a bowl of Cheerios.

I sat down at the table to eat. Jackie leaned against the counter and sipped her coffee. Nobody said anything. The only sound was Jake sucking on his bottle. It was like we were wax figures in a museum, except we were all moving.

Then there was this crash. I turned around, but all I saw was steaming coffee all over the floor, and pieces of the glass coffee pot all over the counter. Jackie looked like she was in shock.

"You okay?" I asked. I didn't see any cuts or anything.

Jackie's eyes filled with tears. The next thing I knew she turned and ran out of the kitchen. I heard the bedroom door slam. Jake was still sucking happily on his bottle like life was normal. I don't know what Jackie expected when she married my father and moved in with us. But I bet it wasn't this.

Jake finished his bottle and chucked it onto the floor. I picked it up and put it on the counter. I had ten minutes left before I had to leave for school so I picked up the broken glass and mopped up the coffee with paper towels. I put the dirty dishes in the dishwasher.

Then I noticed Jake's face was red and he was bearing down pretty hard in the high chair.

Great timing, kid.

Jackie still hadn't come out of the bedroom.

Jake finished his business and gave me a big grin. You're not going to do it, I told myself.

Jake just sat there happy as a clam. What does a one-and-a-half-year-old know?

"Okay, Jake," I said, and lifted him out of the high chair. I carried him into the nursery and got him to lie down on the changing table. I used about a hundred baby wipes.

Then it was time to put on the new diaper.

I know it's one of those things that must be incredibly obvious to anyone who does it often, but I just couldn't quite figure out how it went.

"Kyle! What are you doing?" Next thing I knew, Jackie rushed to the changing table, like maybe she thought I was going to dissect the kid or something. She looked at Jake and saw that I'd cleaned him up. Filled with surprise, she turned to me. Our eyes met for a second and then I looked away.

"Here's what you do," she said, taking the diaper and putting it on Jake. It looked pretty easy once I saw how it was done. I just hoped Jackie wouldn't say anything embarrassing.

"Guess I better get to school," I said.

"Sure, Kyle," Jackie said. But she smiled.

BO

Today I stood before the Honorable Justice Paul Topal in county court.

"Would you please tell the court why you have petitioned to change your name?" he asked.

"How would you like to have a daughter named Bo Vine, Your Honor?" I replied.

The honorable justice frowned and looked down at his papers. "Petition approved," he said.

Back home, I broke the news to my mother. When it comes to things like changing your name, it's always best to do it first and tell your parents about it later. That way they can totally freak, but it's too late to do anything.

"Mom," I said, handing her the petition approved by the Honorable Justice Topal. "I've changed my name. It's legal and everything."

Her eyebrows went up. "You're serious?"

"To Delia, but I want everyone to call me Dee."

My mother read the petition and then looked up at me. "Dee Vine?" she said. Then she actually smiled.

◇　◇　◇

Life is mysterious. Who knows why we fall in love with who we fall in love with, or what we can and can't do if we put our minds to it. If I've learned one thing from all this, it's never to put limits on myself again. You have to try new things. You can hate failure, but you mustn't let the fear of it paralyze you. Like the poet said, "Tis better to have loved and lost than never to have loved at all."

Don't be afraid to try.

Don't be afraid to fail.

Don't be afraid to color your hair.

Try to understand where people are coming from.

Don't forget that most people are really good at heart.

And if you hate your name, change it.

GIRL GIVES BIRTH TO OWN PROM DATE

by Todd Strasser

AVAILABLE AT YOUR FAVORITE BOOKSTORE.

Can Nicole transform next-door neighbor Chase into the prom date of her dreams?

Simon & Schuster Books for Young Readers
An imprint of Simon & Schuster Children's Publishing Division

Don't miss these other coming-of-age tales.

IZZY, WILLY-NILLY
by Cynthia Voigt

LIARS
by P. J. Petersen

RATS SAW GOD
by Rob Thomas

AVAILABLE
AT YOUR FAVORITE BOOKSTORE.

Aladdin Paperbacks
An imprint of Simon & Schuster Children's Publishing Division